ROSE UNDER FIRE

ALSO BY ELIZABETH WEIN

Code Name Verity

ROSE UNDER FIRE

ELIZABETH WEIN

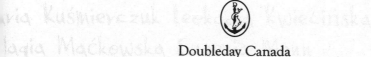

Doubleday Canada

Doubleday Canada and colophon are registered trademarks of Random House of
Canada Limited

"Spring and All, Section I" by William Carlos Williams, from *The Collected
Poems: Volume I, 1909—1939*, copyright © 1938 by New Directions Publishing
Corp. Reprinted by permission of New Directions Publishing Corp.

Edna St. Vincent Millay, "To a Young Poet," "Counting-out Rhyme," and
excerpts from "Scrub" and "Dirge Without Music" from *Collected Poems*.
Copyright 1923, 1928, 1939, 1951, © 1955, 1967 by Edna St. Vincent Millay
and Norma Millay Ellis.

"Canoe Song" (aka "My Paddle's Keen and Bright"), by Margaret Embers McGee.

"Make New Friends" (aka "New Friends and Old"), attributed to Joseph Parry.

"Praise for Bread" ("Morning is Here"), attributed to A.R. Ledoux.

"Rose, Rose," anonymous.

Library and Archives Canada Cataloguing in Publication

Wein, Elizabeth, author
          Rose under fire / Elizabeth Wein.

Issued in print and electronic formats.

ISBN 978-0-385-67953-4 (bound).-- ISBN 978-0-385-67954-1 (epub)

          I. Title.

PZ7.W435Ro 2013   j823'.92   C2013-902637-1
                                                   C2013-903032-8

Jacket photographs: (face) WIN-Initiative/Getty Images; (concentration camp)
photogl/Shutterstock; (airplanes) Ivan Cholakov/Shutterstock
Printed and bound in the USA

Published in Canada by Doubleday Canada,
a division of Random House of Canada Limited,
a Penguin Random House Company

www.randomhouse.ca

10 9 8 7 6 5 4 3 2 1

- For Kate -

TO A YOUNG POET

Time cannot break the bird's wing from the bird.
Bird and wing together
Go down, one feather.

No thing that ever flew,
Not the lark, not you,
Can die as others do.

—Edna St. Vincent Millay

The problem is that it's getting harder

Germans are still hanging on to the po

pain in the neck it is for the Allied fo

supplies, and everything else across to t

corridor between Germany and the Fre

up after the fighting (that is where th

in a hurry). You can't even fly direct

unless a cargo ship. Le Havre is unde

harbor there is taking such a beating

my lunch with Aunt Edie in the Palm

look pretty bush league, which isn't ex

thing else between that would have be

dress up for anything I were the sam

lunch, because the one I were to Mad

flying brakes and bus floors). But you

course, was very elegant. I don't think

everything remade by her own tailor a

greet me and looked sort of slant-eye

survive the dandlebury wedding adventu

will not discuss bloodshed and bombing

front of the Ritz! I told her about my

(I) finished. "So terribly earnest." I la

he proposed to me? He wanted to ge

know everyone is doing it, and I hate

any better protected if you're marrie

and you're being sensible about what

PART 1
SOUTHAMPTON

Notes for an Accident Report

I just got back from Celia Forester's funeral. I'm supposed to be writing up an official report for the Tempest she flew into the ground, since she's obviously not going to write it herself and I saw it happen. And also because I feel responsible. I know it wasn't my fault—I really do know that now. But I briefed her. We both had Tempests to deliver, and I'd flown one a couple of times before. Celia hadn't. She took off ten minutes after me. If she'd taken off first, we might both still be alive.

I've never had to do a report like this, and I don't really know where to begin. Maddie gave me this beautiful leather-bound notebook to draft it in; she thinks it helps to have nice paper and knew I wouldn't buy any for myself, since, like everything else, it's so scarce. She says you need to bribe yourself because it's always *blah* writing up accident reports. She had to write a big report herself last January and also be grilled in person by the Accident Committee. She's right about nice paper, of course, and I have filled up a couple of those pretty clothbound diaries that lock, but all I ever put in them are attempts at poetry. Too bad I can't put the accident report into verse.

There were a few other Air Transport Auxiliary pilots at Celia's funeral, but Maddie was the only ATA girl besides me. Felicyta couldn't come; she had a delivery chit this morning. Along with Celia and Felicyta, Maddie and I were the ones who gave out Mrs. Hatch's strawberries to the soldiers lining up to board the landing craft for the D-Day invasion. It made us into friends. Felicyta was very tearful this morning, banging things around angrily. Probably she shouldn't be flying. I know exactly what Daddy would say—three thousand miles away on Justice Field in Pennsylvania—if it were me: "Rosie, go home. You shouldn't fly while your friends are being buried." But the planes have got to be delivered. *There's a war on.*

Boy, am I sick of hearing that.

It never stops. There are planes to deliver every day straight from the factory or just overhauled, painted in fresh camouflage or invasion stripes, ready to go to France. I got thrown in at the deep end when I stepped off the ship from New York three months ago, and before the end of May I was delivering Spitfires, real fighter planes, from Southampton's factories near the Hamble Aerodrome to just about every air base in southern England. I was supposed to get some training, but they just put me through a few flight tests instead. Being the daughter of someone who runs a flight school has paid off in spades—I've been flying since I was twelve, which means I've been flying longer than some of the older pilots, even though I'm only eighteen. The baby on the team.

There was a lull for a week after D-Day, when the invasion started. Actually, I don't think it should be called an "invasion" when really we are trying to get most of Europe back from the Germans, who invaded it in the first place. Our Allied soldiers left for France in the beginning of June, and for one week only military flights got authorized, so there was no flying for us—the Air Transport Auxiliary in Britain are civilian pilots, like the WASPs at home. That was a quiet week, the second week of June. Then the flying bombs started coming in.

Holy smoke, I can't say how much I hate the flying bombs.

V-1 is what the Germans call them. V stands for "*Vergeltungswaffe*," retaliation weapon. I worked hard at memorizing the real word for it because I always think it means "vengeance": Vengeance Weapon 1. The only thing these bombs are meant to do is terrify people. Everyone puts on a brave face, though—the English are very good at putting on brave faces, I'll give them that! People try to make the bombs less scary by giving them stupid names: *doodlebugs*—sounds like baby talk. *Buzz bombs*—a phrase for older kids to use. The other ferry pilots call them *pilotless planes*, which should seem simple and technical, but it gives me the creeps. An aircraft flying blind, no cockpit, no windows, no way of landing except to self-destruct? How can you win an air war against a plane that doesn't need a pilot? A plane that turns into a bomb? Our planes, the British and American aircraft I fly every day in the ATA, don't even have radios, much less guns. We don't stand a chance. Celia Forester didn't stand a chance.

At the funeral, the local minister—vicar, they say here—had never even met Celia. He called her "a dedicated pilot."

It doesn't mean *anything*. We're *all* dedicated. But to tell the truth, I don't think any of us would have had anything better to say. Celia was so quiet. She was only just posted to Hamble in May, about the same time I was, and for the same reason—to ferry planes for the invasion. She hardly ever talked to *anybody*. I can't blame her—she had a fiancé who was in Bomb Disposal and was killed at Christmas. It's bad enough being a newcomer without being stuck grieving for your sweetheart. Celia wasn't very happy here.

Am I happy here?

I guess I am. I like what I'm doing. I wanted to come *so badly*—I can't believe they gave me that diploma in December, like Laura Ingalls Wilder leaving school at fifteen so she could be a teacher! And now here I am, in England for the first time, not far from where Daddy was born, and I'm actually helping. I'm *useful*. Even without Uncle Roger being so high up in the Royal Engineers, cutting through the red tape for me, I'd have found a way to get here. And I'm a lot luckier than Celia in other ways, not just because I'm still alive—I'm lucky to have met Nick almost as soon as I got here, and lucky to have had so much flying experience before I started.

I've read over that last paragraph, and it sounds so chirpy and stuck-up and—just so dumb. But the truth is I have to keep reminding myself again and again that I want to do this, because I'm so tired now. None of us ever get enough sleep. Not just because we're working so hard; it's those horrible flying bombs, too.

The tiredness is beginning to show. We're all cracking at the seams, I think. Maddie and I ended up being taken out to lunch by Celia's parents after the funeral because Maddie had still been sitting in our pew, sobbing quietly into her handkerchief after everyone else had left, and I'd been sitting with her and sniffling a bit, too. I am sure the Foresters were touched to find anyone showing so much raw emotion at their daughter's short, bleak funeral, when everyone else there hardly knew her.

But neither one of us had actually been crying for Celia. On the train back to Southampton, Maddie confessed to me, "My best friend was killed in action, in 'enemy action,' like it always says in the obituaries, exactly eight months ago. She didn't get a funeral."

"*My gosh*," I said. I can't really imagine what it must feel like to have your best friend killed by a bomb or gunfire. So I added, "Well, it was brave of you to come along today!"

Maddie said, "I felt like a *rat* eating lunch with the Foresters. So cheap and ugly. Them paying for the meal and me trying to think of *anything* to say about Celia apart from 'She was a nice girl, but she never talked to anybody.'"

"I know. I felt that way, too. Look, we're both rats, Maddie—I was being more selfish than you. I couldn't think about anything all day except having to write the darned accident report. Celia had never been up in a Tempest before, and we only had one set of pilot's notes between us, and she'd refused to take them with her. I should have forced her to take them. And I bet now they won't let any other girls near a Tempest till the accident's been investigated, and if we don't get to fly 'em again it'll be MY FAULT as much as Celia's."

"They'll let us fly 'em," Maddie said mournfully. "Desperate times and all that."

She's probably right. The fighter pilots need all the Tempests they can get. They're the best planes we've got for shooting down flying bombs.

When Maddie and I got back to the aerodrome at Hamble, Felicyta was waiting for us. She was sitting in a corner of the Operations room and had made a little funeral feast. She had a plate of toast cut up into one-inch squares with a bit of margarine and the tiniest blob of strawberry jam on each square—simple but pretty.

"We make do with not much, as usual," Felicyta said, and tried to smile. "Here are teacups. Was it terrible?"

I nodded. Maddie grimaced.

"Celia's mother says we should share the things from her locker," I said. "Mrs. Forester doesn't want any of it back."

Now we all grimaced.

"Someone's got to do it," I said. Maddie began pouring tea, and Felicyta touched me lightly on the shoulder, like she wanted to support me but was a little embarrassed to show it. She gave an odd, tight smile and said, "I will take care of Celia's locker. You must report this accident, Rosie?"

"Yes, I'm writing the accident report. Lucky me."

"These papers are for you." Felicyta patted a cardboard file folder on the table's worn oilcloth. "It is a letter from the mechanic who examined Celia's plane after her crash. He gave it to me when I flew there this morning. You need to read this before you write the report."

"Is it secret?"

I had to ask because so many things are confidential.

"No, it is not secret, but"—Felicyta took a deep breath—"you saw Celia crash. You said you thought the ailerons on her wings did not work. This letter tells why. Celia hit a flying bomb."

Now that I'm sitting here with this notebook, I don't know if I should tell the Accident Committee what the mechanic said, because it is exactly the kind of thing they'll use as an excuse to stop girls from flying Tempests—though I bet any guy would do the same thing, given the chance.

Felicyta wasn't kidding. The mechanic thinks Celia ran into a V-1 flying bomb. No, not "ran into" it—not accidentally. He thinks she did it on purpose. He thinks she tried to tip a flying bomb out of the sky.

Oh—it is crazy.

When Felicyta told me, over the sad little squares of memorial toast, it made me angry. ATA deaths are never that heroic. An ATA pilot is killed *every week* flying faulty planes, flying in bad weather, coming down on cracked-up runways—there was that terrible accident where a landing plane skidded and flipped because of the mud, and by the time people got out to the poor pilot, he'd *drowned*—stuck upside down in a cockpit full of standing water. HORRIBLE. But not heroic. I've never heard of an ATA pilot getting hit by enemy fire. We don't dogfight. Our bomb bays are empty; our gun sights aren't connected to anything. Our deaths don't ever earn us posthumous medals. Drowning in mud, lost at sea, engine failure after takeoff.

So I didn't believe Felicyta at first—she was so convinced by the mechanic's letter, but it felt like she was trying to make Celia's death into a hero's death, when it was just another faulty aircraft.

"Antiaircraft guns on the ground are good for shooting down flying bombs," Felicyta said. "But you know the Royal Air Force Tempest squadron takes down as many flying bombs in the air as the gunners do on the ground, and Celia was in a Tempest—"

"She didn't have any guns," I said. "She wasn't armed." Holy smoke, she didn't even have a radio. She couldn't even tell anyone what was wrong as she was coming in to land.

"You do not need guns," Felicyta insisted passionately, her eyes blazing. "The mechanic says if you fly fast enough, you can ram a pilotless plane with your wingtip."

We leaned our heads in together over the tiny decorated squares of toast, talking in low tones like conspirators.

"I've heard the lads talk about that," Maddie said. "Doodlebug tipping."

"In Polish we call it *taran*—aerial ramming. A Polish pilot rammed a German plane over Warsaw on the first day of the war! The Soviet pilots do it, too—same word in Russian. *Taran*. It is the best way to stop a pilotless plane in the air," Felicyta said. "Before it reaches a target, when it is still over sea or open country, not over London or Southampton. That is what the Royal Air Force does with their Tempests."

"But they're armed!" I insisted.

"You do not need to be armed for *taran*," Felicyta said. "You do not need guns to ram another aircraft."

"She's right," Maddie said. "When our lads come up behind a flying bomb and fire at it, they have to fly into the explosion. Absolutely no fun. But if you tip the bomb with your wing before it's over London, it just dives into a field and there's no mess."

I just couldn't believe Celia would try such a trick, her first time in a Tempest. But, as we all kept saying, we didn't really know her.

"Would you do it, Maddie?" I asked.

She shook her head slowly. It was more of an *I don't know* than a *no*. Maddie's a very careful pilot and probably has more hours than the rest of us put together. She is the only one of us who is a First Officer. But I realized, just then, that I didn't really know her, either.

"Felicyta would do it," Maddie said, avoiding an answer. "Wouldn't you, Fliss? You see a flying bomb in the sky ahead of you, and you're flying a Tempest. Would you make a hundred-and-eighty-degree turn and run the other way? Or try to tip it out of the sky?"

"You know what I would do," Felicyta said, her eyes narrowed. "Don't you believe a woman could make a *taran* as well as a man? You know what I would do, Maddie Brodatt. But I have never met a flying bomb in the air. Have you?"

"Yes," Maddie said quietly.

We stared at her with wide eyes. I am sure my mouth hung open.

"It was back in June," she said. "The week after the flying bombs started. I was delivering a Spitfire and I saw it coming toward me, only a couple hundred feet below me. I thought it was another plane. It looked like another plane. But when I waggled my wings, it just stayed on course, and then it passed below me—terribly close—and I realized it was a doodlebug. They aren't very big. Horrible things, eyeless, just a bomb with wings."

Pilotless, I thought. Ugh. "Weren't you scared?"

"Not really—you know how you don't worry about a near miss until later, when you think about it afterward? It was before I'd heard about anybody tipping a doodlebug, and anyway I hadn't a hope of catching it. By the time I'd realized what it was, it was just a speck in the distance, still heading for London. I didn't see it fall."

I haven't seen one fall, either, but I've heard them. You can hear them THIRTY MILES away, rattling along. Southampton doesn't get fired on as relentlessly as London and Kent, but we get the miserable things often enough that the noise terrifies me. Like being in the next field over from a big John Deere corn picker: *clackety clackety clackety*. Then the timer counts down, the engine stops, and for a few seconds you don't hear anything as the bomb falls. And then you hear the explosion.

I hate to admit this, but I am so scared of the flying bombs that if I'd known about them ahead of time I would not have come. Even after Uncle Roger's behind-the-scenes scrambling to get the paperwork done for me.

The mechanic says in his letter that he thinks Celia damaged her wing in a separate incident—separate from the crash, "possibly the result of a deliberate brush with another aircraft." He didn't actually mention flying bombs. But you could tell the idea was in his head.

Now I am upset all over again, remembering the crash. It took me by surprise, watching—I knew something was wrong, of course, but I never expected her to lose control like that, that close to the ground. It happened so suddenly. I'd been waiting for her so we could come back to Hamble together.

I want to talk to Nick about it. He left a message for me—sweet of him, worrying about me having to go to Celia's funeral. It's after nine now, but it's still light out. They have two hours of daylight saving in the summer here—they call it Double Summer Time. So I'll walk down to the phone box in the village and hope Nick's not away on some mission. And that I don't get told off by his landlady for calling so late.

Horrible war. So much more horrible here than back in the States. Every few weeks someone's mother or brother or another friend is killed. And already I am fed up with the shortages, never any butter and never enough sleep. The combination of working so hard, and the constant fear, and just the general *blahness* of everything—I wasn't prepared for it. But how could I possibly, possibly have been prepared for it? They've been living with it for five years. All the time I've been swimming at the Lake, playing girls' varsity basketball and building a tree house for Karl and Kurt like a good big sister, crop dusting with Daddy and helping Mother make applesauce, Maddie's been delivering fighter planes. When her best friend was killed by a bomb, or whatever it was, eight months ago, I was probably sitting in Mr. Wagner's creative writing class working out rhyme schemes.

It's so strange to be here at last, and so different from what I expected.

I have put my accident report into verse after all. (I think I am trying to trick myself into writing this darned thing.) I wish I'd written this poem earlier. It would have been nice to read it at Celia's service. I will send a copy to her parents.

FOR CELIA FORESTER (by Rose Justice)

The storm will swallow
the brave girl there
who fights destruction
with wings and air—

life and chaos
hover in flight
wingtip to wingtip
until the slight

triumphant moment
when their wings caress
and her crippled Tempest
flies pilotless.

Now that I am an ATA pilot at last, I wish I were a fighter
pilot.

And that was the first thing I said to Nick when I got him on the phone. I did get him at last. He wasn't at home, so I rang the airfield, and they said he was on his way but hadn't got there yet, AND he was "busy" tonight, so he might not be able to call back. I was so desperate I waited in the phone box for three-quarters of an hour till he got in, and we talked for exactly as long as my cigarette tin of pennies held out. In three weeks he will be off to France, and I will not.

"Hello, Rose darling."

"I want to fly Tempests," I said through clenched teeth. "I want to be operational. I want to be in the Royal Air Force, blasting flying bombs to smithereens."

There was a good penny's worth of silence down the wire before Nick answered. Maybe that's where the saying comes from, *penny for your thoughts*. Speak up or the operator will cut you off.

Finally Nick said sympathetically, "What's made you so bloodthirsty?"

"I'm not bloodthirsty. There's no blood in a pilotless plane, is there! I'm a good pilot. I've probably been flying five years longer than half the boys in 150 Wing. I flew with Daddy from coast to coast across America when I was fifteen, and I did *all* the navigation. *You've* never flown a Tempest, or a Mustang, or a Mark Fourteen Spitfire—I've flown them all, dozens of times. They're wasting me just because I'm a girl! They won't even let us fly to France—they're prepping men for supply and taxi to the front lines, guys with hundreds' fewer hours than me, but they're just passing over the women pilots. *It isn't fair*."

I stopped to breathe. Nick said evenly, "And there's me,

worrying you'd be upset by your friend's funeral. Instead you're after shooting down doodlebugs. What's going on, Rose?"

"How do you topple a doodlebug?" I asked. "The girls say you can do it with your wingtip."

Nick laughed. Then he paused. I didn't say anything, because I knew he was thinking. "You couldn't," he said at last. "Yes, I've heard that, too, but you need to be flying something fast, not a taxi Anson or a Spitfire with only enough fuel to get you to the maintenance airfield. An ATA pilot couldn't topple a V-1 flying bomb."

"Celia did. She tried to, anyway. We think that's why she crashed. How do they do it? Do you just bash it with your wingtip? The Polish pilots have a word for it. *Taran.* Aerial ramming."

Another longish pause. I had stuffed in the entire contents of the cigarette tin right away—after feeding thirty of those gigantic pennies into the telephone, I felt like I'd just thrown away a pirate's treasure hoard. At any rate it added up to more than ten minutes. I didn't want to be cut off.

And, of course, the operator was probably listening in. Nick's job is very secret. I didn't want to get him into trouble.

"No," he said at last. "No, for God's sake, don't try that, Rose. You'll kill yourself. Is that what Celia did? Good God Almighty. The idea is not to touch them at all. The doodlebug's a bloody brilliant bomb, but it's not a brilliant aircraft. It's unstable, and if you get your wingtip just beneath the bomb's wing, half a foot or so away from it, you can upset the airflow around its wing and make it stall. But you have to fly fast enough to keep up with it, and it'll still go off when it hits the ground. Promise me you won't try?"

My turn to be silent. Because I couldn't make that promise. I guess I'll never get the chance, anyway, but if I did—well, I'm a better pilot than Celia was.

"Rose, darling?" Nick had to prompt me. "I'm not a fighter pilot, either. 'They also serve who only stand and wait.'"

Show-off, quoting Milton. He knows I like poetry.

"That's garbage, Nick, and you know it," I said hotly. "You're not standing and waiting. You're dropping off—" I choked back what I was going to say, thinking of the operator listening in. I'm not supposed to know what he's doing, and I *don't* know much about it, but Maddie's boyfriend is in the same squadron—that's how I met Nick—and you figure a little bit out after a while. They've been flying spies and saboteurs and plastic explosive and machine guns in and out of France for the past two years—secret supplies for the D-Day invasion.

"You're on the front line," I insisted.

There was this long, guilty silence at the other end.

"Oh, you *really are* at the Front," I guessed angrily. "What? They're going to transfer you, aren't they, now that the Front's moved back? Or are they getting the Royal Air Force Special Duties squadron to do ferry work so they can weasel out of sending civilian ATA pilots into Europe?"

"They're moving the squadron," Nick gave me cautiously.

I didn't ask where. He wouldn't have told me anyway.

"Far?"

"Yes."

"Oh."

That means out of the United Kingdom. Maybe the Mediterranean.

"Well . . ." Nick hesitated. "We've got three days' leave before we go. It's not much time, but it matches up with your next two days off. We could get married."

I am sorry to say that I laughed at him.

I mean, it is just so stupid. He is sweet and funny and kind and brave, and we talk so easily when we are together, and he is so proud to have a pilot for a girlfriend—"Looks like Katharine Hepburn and flies like Amelia Earhart" is how he introduced me to his parents (an exaggeration in both cases, but oh, how I burned with joy and embarrassment when he said it!). But we still haven't ever even been on a real date, dancing or to a film or anything like that—it's always lunch in a pub or a quick cup of tea in the coffee shop at the train station just outside Portsmouth, which is halfway for both of us. It is *so hard* to get time together. Apparently, Maddie has supper with her boyfriend, Jamie, at his air base something like once every two months. And the last time Nick and I had the same day off, I had to stand him up because Uncle Roger and Aunt Edie were taking me out. Of course it never occurred to me to stand up Uncle Roger—but I am in debt to Uncle Roger, I mean morally, for pulling the strings that got me here. Nick doesn't get that. I know he was hurt.

And now I hurt him again by laughing at his proposal. I tried to make it up to him and promised we would have a whole day, a real day to remember, all to ourselves before he went away.

It makes me angry. *Why* should it have to be like this, for all of us, all our generation? That the only way for a young couple to be together is to get married? No chance of a honeymoon, no flowers or champagne because the gardens are all full of cabbages and turnips and France is a war zone? No pretty silk dress unless someone manages to steal a parachute for you? No. I know I wouldn't get married suddenly even if it weren't wartime. I'd never do it without Daddy there to walk me down the aisle—with nothing more than a telegram to let him know!

It is the same for every young couple. We are all panicking that one of us will be killed next month, next week, tomorrow. All of us panicking that if we don't do it now, we'll never get a chance. Well, I don't care. I'm not letting the war take over my life.

Maddie laughed, too, when I told her about Nick's proposal.

"I know where he got *that* idea," she said. "Jamie and I are getting married on the twelfth of August. Next week!" She gave another hoot of laughter. "That is Nick all over. He's like a puppy. You said no, didn't you, Rosie? The poor lad! Tell you what—you can give him a good excuse and say you've a previous engagement. Come be my bridesmaid."

"What, *me*? Really?"

I was surprised and very pleased, but what a thoughtless thing to say. Her dead friend wasn't going to do it, was she? And all it did was remind her.

Anyway, of course I will.

I asked her if she knew where Nick and Jamie are going, and she gave me a funny look.

"Careless talk costs lives," she said.

I do know things I shouldn't. I know a lot about what Uncle Roger is doing, because Aunt Edie tells me. She's not supposed to know, either. I am a little uncomfortable about it sometimes, but I think they see it as keeping me Ready for Action—Roger always asks for me when he needs to be taxied anywhere. Felicyta thinks it is very funny that this highly important person wants to be piloted by a lowly Third Officer, and a girl at that! He is building pontoons in France at the moment, as the Allies fight their way inland. The next big push will be to cross the Seine. Then Paris.

It's been a week since Celia's accident. I have submitted my report. I didn't draft it on these pretty, gold-edged pages after all, because I didn't have this notebook with me when I wrote it. The day after her funeral I was stuck at

RAF Maidsend for a whole day due to lousy weather, and I couldn't go home, because there was a top-priority Tempest (of course) that I had to ferry away for repair as soon as the visibility was good enough to fly. It felt a bit ironic, and spooky, to spend the day writing about Celia's accident and then take off strapped into a broken Tempest. The plane had a big hole punched in the windshield. It was perfectly flyable, but WOW, was it ever windy! Even with goggles on, my face felt like I had frostbite by the time I landed—absolutely frozen. It's true I was going 225 miles per hour at 3500 feet, but you'd never know it was August. It's been such a cold summer.

You have to fly that high to get across Kent because you have to be higher than the barrage balloons they've got tethered there to try to catch the flying bombs.

I can't get over how beautiful the barrage balloons are. I can't even talk about it to anyone—they all think I am crazy. But when you're in the air, and the sky above you is a sea of gray mist and the land below you is all green, the silver balloons float in between like a school of shining silver whales, bobbing a little in the wind. They are as big as buses, and I and every other pilot have a healthy fear of them because their tethering cables are loaded with explosives to try to snarl up enemy aircraft. But they are just magical from above, great big silver bubbles filling the sky.

Incredible. It is just *incredible* that you can notice something like that when your face is so cold you can't feel it anymore, and you know perfectly well you are surrounded by death, and the only way to stay alive is to endure the howling wind and hold your course. And still the sky is beautiful.

I am waiting for Uncle Roger to get out of his meeting. I have decided it is a good idea to take this notebook with me in case I get stuck somewhere again, like last week at Maidsend, so I have something to do. We had a heck of a time getting here—we had to fly through a hailstorm that came out of nowhere. It sounded like we had our heads in a bucket that was being pelted with rocks. I don't know when I've ever been so frightened while flying.

Roger seemed to be all unconcerned. He was in the back, in the middle of a cigarette, with his legs up on the second pilot's seat—the aircraft is a Proctor, not very big. Along with the hail came a bit of wind shear bumping us around, which made him accidentally kick me. I snapped angrily, *"Could you please put your feet down."*

It's amazing what a short, sharp command, instantly obeyed, does for your morale. I was absolutely not going to let him know how worried I was! He didn't stretch out his legs again for the rest of the flight.

After we landed and I was taxiing off the runway, I said, "Sorry about the bumpy ride." When I switched off the engine, he reached over my shoulder and shook my hand.

"You're a damned fine pilot, Rosie," he said. "A real credit to your father. For a moment there I thought we were being hit by machine-gun fire!"

I took a deep breath and let myself clench my fists at last, just to get the tension out of them. Daddy never let me hold tight to the control column; he used to make me control it with one finger just to practice the "light touch." I do it automatically now, but it sure does feel good to squeeze your hands shut after a flight like that. "Is that what machine-gun fire sounds like?" I asked.

"Pretty much! Didn't you notice me looking around wildly for the Messerschmitt that was firing on us? I thought we'd had it! Ready to go down fighting, though . . ."

He held up his other hand. He'd got out his *pistol*. Here was me thinking he hadn't been worried.

"Gee whiz, Uncle Roger, it was just bad weather!"

"And that's what kills most ATA pilots, right? You kept your head and got us down safely. I always say there's no other pilot I'd rather have in control of my plane. Except your dad, of course!" He laughed, unstrapped his harness, and put away his pistol. "Ready to take me to France some-day soon?"

I unlatched the door. "Uncle Roger, if you can engi-neer getting me to fly you to France, you really are a Royal Engineer. They haven't let any ATA pilots go to France yet. And when they do, it'll be the men."

Roger gave his characteristic *harrumph* of disgust. "There were American women on the beaches of Normandy four days after D-Day. Army Nurse Corps—plucky girls, carrying all their own gear just like the lads. And our British ladies began to arrive only a few days later. They're at the Front now, or just behind it. I know you're 'civilian pilots,' but at least in a plane you can scarper home when you've dropped me off!"

"You're preaching to the choir, Uncle Roger!" I hauled myself out onto the wing and reached back in so he could pass me our bags. "If you pull the strings, I'm ready to go."

I don't really believe he can pull those strings. But it gives me a warm, excited feeling in the pit of my stomach that he thinks he can, and might actually try.

August 14, 1944
Hamble, Southampton, Hampshire

DOODLEBUG BRIDE / BOMB ALLEY
(Poems by Rose Justice. Not yet written. I just like the titles.)

Maddie had her two days off for her wedding, but I did not, so it was kind of a marathon for me to get to Scotland. I managed to squeeze it in as a series of ferry flights up and took the train back with Maddie. Everyone was as nice as could be, bending over backward to make sure I got the right delivery chits that would take me all the way to Aberdeen and let me stay there overnight. Mostly they were doing it for Maddie. Thank heavens the weather also cooperated. It has been terrible all summer; even the Brits say it's not usually this bad. Great cover for the flying bombs, but no visibility for living pilots, and the ground-to-air gunners can't see what they're shooting at.

It was thick overcast as usual the day after the wedding, when Maddie and I came back on the train together—poor thing, she and Jamie had only one night together. Maddie was in Scotland for two nights, but the night before the wedding doesn't really count, because she and Jamie were still in separate rooms then!

She is marrying into another world. Jamie is the son of an earl and his family lives in an honest-to-goodness Highland castle. Her name has changed from Maddie Brodatt to the Honorable Mrs. Beaufort-Stuart! There are a lot of Beaufort-Stuarts—Jamie is one of six children, though the war is thinning them out. Ugh. His oldest brother was killed in Normandy in June, and his younger sister was killed last year.

She is the one who was Maddie's best friend. It was through her that Maddie met Jamie.

I don't know how Lady Beaufort-Stuart copes—I really don't. She has got *eight* refugee children living with her—all boys, evacuated from Glasgow so they won't be bombed. (For the wedding, they all wore kilts borrowed from the Beaufort-Stuarts.) Before the wedding, this rabble formed a chain across the church door and refused to let anyone in until the bridegroom paid them, which Jamie staunchly refused to do, arguing that if he could kick their soccer ball over the church he was exempt from their entry fee—and he did it, too, amid a huge amount of cheering and yelling. Maddie gave them each a sixpence anyway. Then they tried to carry her into the church, but her grandfather took over at that point and made her walk sedately down the aisle on his arm.

Jamie's family didn't talk much about their dead. They were so happy to have something to celebrate—almost desperate with it. There were flowers and champagne, after all. They have got an amazing rose garden, like the one at the Hotel Hershey, and it hasn't been dug up for vegetables, because they have so much ground that there aren't enough gardeners to take care of it all. So their own garden is where the wedding roses came from. And of course Jamie brought the champagne back with him on one of his clandestine Special Duties trips.

The church they were married in is part of the castle estate, a tiny, crooked building built from local stone. (The boys' ball did not have to go very high to be kicked over the top of it.) Maddie had white heather in her bouquet and pink and yellow damask rosebuds. Jamie was in a kilt, too, the same tartan as the eight kids, and his Royal Air Force tunic; Maddie wore her ATA uniform. (So did I.)

Her grandfather brought a wineglass that had been his mother's in Russia, and Maddie and Jamie used it instead of the traditional Scottish loving cup for the couple's first drink together at the reception afterward. Then they smashed it, on purpose, as per her grandfather's instructions. It was not a Jewish wedding, but Maddie's grandparents are Jewish, and breaking the glass is part of the ceremony.

Lady Beaufort-Stuart was rather shocked that Mr. Brodatt had *wanted* them to break an antique Russian glass that had belonged to his mother, thousands of miles away and a century ago. And he said, "I do not want to wait for Hitler's doodlebugs to get to it first."

Maddie did not throw her bouquet. There would have only been me to catch it, anyway, and we both knew how I felt about *that*. Instead, she left it below the family's memorial plaque in the church, where her friend's name is carved. The older boy's name is not there yet, but the girl died last year. Her dates were carved there, too. And it was her birthday. They got married on her birthday, August Twelfth.

I like that. Because now they will have a reason to celebrate on that day, a new reason and a good one, instead of being miserable every year.

They didn't mention the dead girl on the day, but Maddie said something about her on the train on our way back. It was when we were admiring Maddie's ring. It is French rose-gold from the nineteenth century, a small, square-cut ruby flanked with little triangles of tiny pearls. It belonged to Jamie's great-grandmother and was handed down the generations eventually to his sister, and now Jamie's family has given it to Maddie.

"I love it fiercely," she said. "Because it is a little bit of Julie as well as Jamie, and of their lovely mother, and I will have it with me always. Fifty years from now, if I live that long, it will be part of me. It is all of ours and they are part of me. And I love that it is French, too—their mother's family is French—they are all fighting for France as much as for Britain. Julie, too—"

Maddie shut up suddenly. But I *got it*, suddenly, and I knew that she'd meant me to get it—her friend died in France. She must have been a spy or a saboteur or something. Maddie is very discreet, but she is closer to that clandestine side of warfare than the other ATA pilots. She does a good bit of specialized taxi flying—like me taking Uncle Roger places, only Maddie's passengers are incognito. I don't ask who they are and I know she wouldn't answer if I did.

Her friend Julie's name is on the family's memorial stone in Scotland, but I know Julie's not buried in that church. Maddie said she didn't get a funeral.

"Do you know how she died?" I asked.

"Oh yes," Maddie answered. "I do. 'Killed in action' means we know for sure. But I've often thought it would be worse if I didn't know. If there hadn't been a fight, the Nazis would have shipped her off in the dark to a concentration camp and never told anyone—that would have been worse. It doesn't seem possible, but it would have been worse. We would still not know what had happened to her, eight months later, and the war's not over. How long till we'd have found out? Would anyone have *ever* found out?"

I am making myself miserable thinking about it. I started writing in here because I would like to make Maddie a wedding poem. But it is hard when the wedding is in the middle of a war. Maddie is a Doodlebug Bride. Not for the "usual" reasons, not because she and Jamie couldn't hear their own vows over the rattling of approaching bombs, and not because we had to worry about whether she'd be able to run to a shelter in a wedding dress—we'd have worn our uniform slacks if we had worried about it, but the village of Castle Craig is very quiet! No, Maddie is a Doodlebug Bride because she spent part of the afternoon following her wedding day lying on the floor of a London bus hoping she wouldn't get hit by a flying bomb.

London is covered in broken glass. Glass and dust. You can tell where the bombs have fallen by the piles of glass, which get bigger and bigger until you get to a hole in the ground where a house or a store was. More piles of glass are banked against the buildings that are still standing, and there are little paths cleared on the sidewalks. I thought it was bad around Southampton, but London is just a wasteland of wreckage. The trees have all lost their leaves in bomb blasts so that it looks like winter. Houses with no roofs and no windows have signs on the door that read STILL OCCUPIED to stop people from looting them.

The train line down from Scotland to Southampton had been hit, so we got diverted to a different line and had to get off in London and take a bus to Charing Cross Station, where we got on another train to try to go around the damage. The bus had no glass in the windows; they take the glass out on purpose—people would rather sit in the wind than risk windows exploding in their faces. Two V-1 flying bombs went over while we were on the bus, one of them passing close to the rooftops of the buildings. The driver just sped on. Not much else he could do, I guess! Antiaircraft guns were racketing away, too, from somewhere pretty close by. Every single passenger on the bus, including me and Maddie, dove under the seats and lay there, cowering.

There was a small boy, no more than three years old, just across from me. All the time we were on the floor he was shouting in terror, over and over:

"Not on a bus! Not on a bus! MUMMY MUMMY NOT ON A BUS!"

His mother couldn't do a thing; she just kept kissing him and kissing him—"Shh, shh." But he wouldn't stop and it was more terrible to listen to than the clattering of the bomb as it passed over, terrible to hear such a little kid so frightened and not be able to do anything to make the fear go away. Because the thing he's afraid of is *real*.

Maddie was *just as bad*. It surprised me—she always seems so confident, and so much older than me. She lay there next to me with her arms clamped over her head, absolutely shaking, and sobbing, too.

When the bomb's racket cut out, we didn't know if that was because we couldn't hear it anymore, or if the guns had got it, or if it was falling on us.

"Count . . . count now . . ." the young mother whispered to her kid. "All the way up to thirty and then you'll be safe. . . ."

I had my arm around Maddie's shoulders, but she was still cowering with her arms over her head. I looked up at the little boy, with my hair just brushing the grubby underneath of the bus bench. Now I stopped worrying about the stupid bomb and lay there willing this kid to make it up to thirty.

"Twenty-five . . . twenty-six . . . twenty-seven . . . twenty-eight . . . twenty-nine . . ."

He got there at last, triumphant.

"Thirty!"

Everybody on the bus burst out clapping.

Then we all got up sheepishly and dusted ourselves off, because nothing had happened and we felt a little foolish lying on the floor while the bus sped through the empty Sunday streets.

Maddie still had her corsage of tartan ribbon and white heather and rosebuds from yesterday pinned on her uniform—actually, it had been part of the ceremony, pinning the family tartan on her. The flowers were very crushed and wilted. As we sat down again, she muttered, "No kiddies for me till after we've won the war, I think. Not that it's likely! We were both out like lights the second we fell into bed. Just so tired all the time, you know? Thirteen days on duty and only two off, Spitfires coming and going as fast as the workshops can spit 'em out."

I nodded. I'd been so tired I'd slept in my uniform. Well, I'd taken off my hose and tunic, anyway. American slob!

"And Jamie's away to—well, he's away now, anyway," Maddie finished wistfully.

We made it safely to the train at Charing Cross. It is awful going in and out of Charing Cross when you know perfectly well it's the dead center of London and probably the bull's-eye the Germans are targeting. But for me the most frightening thing happened after we got off the train at Hamble Station. We were walking along the branch line that takes trains down to the airfield except on Sundays (yes, we were walking back to the airfield on Sunday evening, because technically I was working that day and it would still be light for another five hours), and there were a couple of kids leaning over the wall by the tracks and yelling. They straightened up guiltily when they noticed us, but their pal who'd scaled the wall to get to the other side of the tracks didn't realize we were there and gave himself away by shouting to his friends.

"Oi, you lot—I've got another bit, but I need Rob's knife back to cut these wires!"

The kids froze. We probably looked scarily official in our uniforms, especially Maddie with her First Officer's gold stripes. The boys took a couple of steps back. One of them leaned over the wall and tried to shush his pal. And that made me look over the side of the wall to see what the other boy was doing.

He was taking apart a bomb.

Scout's honor, that's what he was doing. It was a flying bomb that hadn't gone off. Sometimes the bombs run out of fuel prematurely and just glide down, and occasionally they just don't go off. It was much smaller than a Tempest or even a Spitfire, really nothing more than a bomb with wings. It had taken a couple of saplings down as it plowed into the strip of waste ground at the edge of the railway, and now it was sitting on its belly by the train tracks, one wing missing and a long strip of the fuselage ripped open where it had connected with the trees. All of its innards were lying exposed to view and ready for small boys to come along and mop up souvenirs.

It must have just happened, or the railway would have already called the unexploded-bomb people out to deal with it. The scavenging boy who wanted Rob's knife back was standing there with a shiny cylindrical metal case in his hand. It looked like a soup tin with the paper label missing. And like he'd said, it was attached by a couple of wires to the inside of the bomb.

"I've got the fuse!" the boy yelled triumphantly, and then he saw me and Maddie staring at him with our mouths open.

The kid glanced around; there was no place to hide. He reached toward the wires inside the plane as if he was about to yank them free.

Maddie dropped her suitcase and tried to scramble over the wall. *"Don't pull! Don't move! Just hold still–"*

I beat her to it. I didn't have a case, just my flight bag over my shoulder.

"Don't drop it–"

Maddie was yelling at me now. "Get him to put it down *gently!* There's an electrical charge in the fuse and some of them are timed to go off *after* they've landed!" She made it over the wall and was three steps behind me as we raced across the tracks. "That fuse could *blow your fingers off on its own*, you daft lad, even without being attached to a ton of explosive!"

Then the boy stood very still. He didn't drop the fuse. He held it out to me across both palms. I remember thinking that this was hugely unfair of God and the universe in general, because now I had to take the fuse. I had got there first and it was mine.

For a moment we were stuck like that, a little boy and a big girl, holding the living heart of a V-1 flying bomb between us.

The silver cylinder had a type number stamped on the cap and a manufacturer's name: RHEINMETALL.

Incredible, to think that someone else's fingers had fit this destructive thing together, inserted the fragile switches and connected the wires and screwed on the cap, and now it was balanced, ready to blow my own fingers off. Or this boy's.

I took it from him very carefully.

"Now scoot," I said sadly, because I really thought I was as good as dead.

As he handed it over, the wires simply fell free. Probably they had been disconnected the whole time. At least if the fuse went off it wasn't going to take the bomb with it.

"*Get out of here!*" I yelled at the boy.

He hurtled back across the tracks. As for me, my body acted on behalf of my frozen brain. I wound up for a pitch and hurled the fuse away from the bomb, away from the railway, into the scrubby, thin woodland along the tracks.

It hit a beech sapling with a small crack and bang. Bits of bark exploded around the tree, and the trunk sagged—it bent right in half as though it had been caught in a tornado. It wasn't a very big explosion. But we all saw it. Maddie crouched next to the wreckage of the bomb with her arms over her head, like she'd done in the bus.

I said to her, "Come on, Maddie. Get away."

I tugged her across the tracks and over the stone wall. Wouldn't you know it, I tore my skirt going back over the wall when everything was safe again and not when I was racing to save a kid from blowing himself up! And unbelievably—or very believably, I guess, as my ten years' experience of being a big sister to those hooligan twins, Karl and Kurt, ought to have taught me by now—the three boys were still standing there rooted to the spot, staring at the destruction with wide, excited eyes.

"Would that have gone off in my hand, miss?"

"How do I know? Maybe! Come on, you've got to let the authorities know what you've found. Come down to the airfield with us and make a real report. Get going!"

Maddie pulled herself together and began to herd the boys along the road. "Go, go, go!"

The kids let themselves be bullied now, eyeing me respectfully. "You don't throw like a girl," one of them commented.

"That's 'cause I played softball at school. Like baseball. Or cricket, sort of—none of us 'throw like girls.'"

"You a Yank?" asked the boy who'd extracted the fuse, pointing to my USA sleeve patch.

"Obviously."

"You proud of it?"

Smart aleck.

I had to think about the answer to this question.

"Yes," I said after a moment. "Yeah, I am."

"That bomb's dead now, right, miss? A dead doodlebug . . ." The boys all snickered. "That's what the UXB teams do—they take out the fuse. . . ."

I hesitated. I don't know a lot about bombs. Maddie said, "Listen, that dead doodlebug's still full of TNT, and if that fuse had gone off *inside* the aircraft, it would have blown you up and probably the rest of us, too. What were you doing, playing UXB team?"

"We saw it come down!" one of them explained eagerly, and they all broke into grins. "We heard it first and came running up to the station bridge to watch—Rob had his dad's field glasses—"

(Crazy kids.)

"—And we realized it was heading *straight for us*, and we lay right down on the road next to the wall till the noise stopped, because we thought we were dead for sure!"

They were all still completely white around the gills, but they were *enjoying* themselves more than anything else. Ten-year-old boys are *crazy*.

We escorted them to the airfield and called out the local Air Raid Precautions warden. He was really nice to the kids and took them along with him to watch from a safe distance as the road and railway were closed off in preparation for the UXB squad to come along and work their magic.

"Does your uncle Roger ever have to deal with unexploded bombs?" Maddie asked as we watched them go. "Isn't he in the Royal Engineers, too, like the bomb squads?"

I never thought about it. I just assumed that all he did was build bridges and dig trenches. Or tell people to do it, anyway. I think of Uncle Roger as having a "safe" job.

I got back to the airfield at Hamble in time to pick up

the last delivery chit for that evening, a new Spitfire to be delivered to Chattis Hill for testing. It's only a twenty-minute flight there, but it took me a couple of hours to get back—no more trains, and of course, since I was the last flight of the day, there weren't any other ferry pilots heading home for me to tag along with. By ten p.m. the best offer I'd had was from a canteen dishwasher who said I could borrow her bicycle if I brought it back before lunchtime the next day, and I had to bribe her with today's chocolate bar (you get a bar of Cadbury's milk chocolate with every completed ferry flight). I'd already handed it over when a fireman who was going off duty took pity on me and offered me a lift on his motorcycle.

By the time I got home, I was absolutely whacked. It was eleven o'clock and I was hungry enough to wolf down one of Mrs. Hatch's awful Spam stews (she assures me the veg in it is cabbage and not nettle). Late as it was, she'd very kindly reheated it for me. I fell into bed and thought briefly of Maddie and Jamie, newlyweds too tired to make love, and then I fell asleep, too.

I dreamed about the Rheinmetall fuse. I dreamed it detonated in the boy's hands and blew his fingers off.

It was so vivid—like seeing a moving picture shot in close-up. All I could see were the boy's hands, palms spread with the silver cylinder lying across them, smooth, round fingertips sticking out just beneath the shining metal, then all of it flying apart. I woke up gasping.

I am spooked by the image. I can't get it out of my head. I was hoping I could forget it by writing about the wedding—I started out to do a poem, didn't I? And all I've done is write about buzz bombs. I just learned that the TNT mix they use in them is called amatol. It is a good word, if a bad thing. Perhaps I should try writing poetry about bombs.

Silver tube of fuse and hollow
Cylinder of detonator
Cap and gyro

Blah. It would be good if my heart were in it—like Edna St.
Vincent Millay's "Counting-out Rhyme." But I don't want to
think about it. Small, smooth fingers blown to bloody bone.
    I am determined to do that wedding poem for Maddie.
I am afraid it will be inevitably bomb-themed, but I have an
idea.

WARTIME WEDDING
(by Rose Justice. I think this poem is too serious to
call it "Doodlebug Bride.")

In a storm of cocktail ice
their silver plane is tossed
from a silver bowl of sky
to a runway rimmed with frost.
The summer evening's long and cold,
the ground crew shovels snow like glass.
Under their feet the crunching hail
breaks frozen blades of grass.

The house without a roof
seventh along the row
has shed its windowpanes like tears
over the street below.
A woman shovels glass like snow
from the sidewalk as they pass,
under their feet a mirrored hell
of bomb-strewn broken glass.

The dead beloved names
march down the gray and cold
walls of the little church.
He gives her the warm gold.
The loving cup is shared,
the crystal goblet smashed.
Their brave, determined, joyful heels
dance in the broken glass.

It is so hard trying to say what you mean. Of course Maddie and Jamie don't fly together—I don't know if they've *ever* flown together—and I'm pretty sure they haven't been for a walk in London together since the buzz bombs started. But it's meant to be metaphoric. It never quite comes out the way you want it to, and you always feel it is a little petty to write such floaty stuff about such serious things.

I am going to slam this notebook shut and see if I can raise Nick again on the telephone to plan our Big Date.

Nick is gone.

We had a wonderful afternoon—he came here and we borrowed the Hatches' canoe and took it down the Hamble, out into Southampton Water. He brought a bottle of champagne along, booty from one of his secret trips to France, and we drank it on the water. We sort of grazed instead of actually stopping for a picnic—it made the Spam sandwiches seem more romantic. We sang camp songs and taught each other rounds. Mine was,

> "My paddle's keen and bright,
> Flashing with silver,
> Follow the wild goose flight,
> Dip, dip, and swing.
>
> "Dip, dip, and swing her back,
> Flashing with silver,
> Swift as the wild goose flies,
> Dip, dip, and swing."

Nick's round was,

> "Rose, Rose, Rose, Rose,
> Will I ever see thee wed?
> I will marry at thy will, sir,
> At thy will."

I refused to sing it until I made him promise it was not a binding contract!

I was in the stern, steering, because he had never been in

a canoe. He was a bit of a pill about me being in control—he would *not* take orders from me at first and kept trying to stand up when he wanted to point things out, or to climb back to get to the hamper. He can't swim. I really didn't want to have to drag him out of Southampton Water before I kissed him good-bye and sent him off to wherever. Why are boys always so sure they're right about everything?

But I'm not complaining. Because it was *so nice*. I don't think I'd have been brave enough to go out into Southampton Water except I knew that Mrs. Hatch's daughter Minna had taken her mother out there a couple of weeks before D-Day, when the harbor was PACKED with battleships and landing craft, and they got away with it. We did, too. Only one person even bothered to ask what we were up to—everyone else just waved and laughed. I guess the picnic hamper and the bottle of champagne were appropriate nonspy accessories. Nick was wearing his RAF blues and I had on a flowery summer top I'd borrowed from Felicyta, and we were clearly on a date.

The one character who did call out to us was a patrolman on a motor launch. It seemed to take about ten minutes for him to putter across to us—exaggeratedly slow once he'd got us in his sights. I had to back-paddle like crazy to stay in the same place. He played Twenty Questions for a while and told us that the Rules of the Road did not apply to hand-powered pleasure craft in wartime (or something like that), and no one on maneuvers would give way to us, so we'd better stay out of the way.

Then he tipped his cap to me and told us to enjoy ourselves. The innocent American broad act is always a sure winner for getting out of trouble!

It was actually hard work paddling in Southampton Water, and I didn't need the Coast Guard's warning to stay out of the way of the shot-up aircraft carrier that came looming toward the maintenance docks behind a pair of tugboats—even without power it made a wake that tossed us around as if we were on the open sea.

On our way back, a trio of Spitfires tore out to sea in formation over our heads—probably just a test flight from Chattis Hill, since most of the squadrons around Southampton have all moved to France by now. But the noise was tremendous, echoing on the water. We were working hard to get back upstream, and we didn't dare stop paddling—breathless, arms aching with effort, necks aching, too, because we couldn't look away from the planes in the sky.

It was such an *adventure* of a date!

Oh, I like Nick—and I'll miss him. He makes me feel so pretty and clever, playing with my hair while he gets me to test him on wind-direction calculations. He is funny and earnest, a bit puppylike, but game, you know? Ready to do nutty things like try canoeing among the battleships. First time in a canoe.

I wanted to write something for him, to send him off with, but it hasn't come out as a true-love sonnet. I am always too ambitious, and also I just can't seem to write about ANY-THING but the darned doodlebugs. I guess I won't show it to him.

SONG OF THE MODERN WARRIOR
(by Rose Justice)

My paddle's keen and bright,
flashing with silver,
swift as the Spitfire's flight—
dip, dip, and swing.

Dip, dip, and swing her back,
flashing with silver,

follow the V-1's track,
dip, dip her wing.

Scour her fuselage,
strip back her paintwork,
pare off her fittings
to keep down her weight,
polish the plane
till she's slicker than silver,
slicing the sky
with her propeller's blade.
Smooth as the water's face,
cannon fire flaming,
follow the V-1's trace,
dip, dip her wing.

My paddle's keen and bright,
flashing with silver—
follow the Spitfire's flight,
dip, dip and swing.

I guess the influence of *Make Bright the Arrows* is pretty obvious. I don't think I'm as warlike as Edna St. Vincent Millay, but she has a lot to answer for as far as Rose Justice, Poet, is concerned—urging me off to Europe! I am a little blue. No more champagne to look forward to now that Nick's squadron is gone—nothing but Spam sandwiches for the foreseeable future. Oh well—back to work tomorrow.

I had that dream about the exploding fuse again—only this time it was Karl who had picked it up and was holding it out to Kurt. GOD.

I bawled so loudly that Mrs. Hatch came in to wake me up and made me come downstairs and have a cup of tea. And I am pretty sure that she telephoned Aunt Edie about it because when I got to the airfield, along with my ferry chit there was a note saying that I'd been invited to have lunch with her in London on my next day off.

Wonderful Aunt Edie! I am looking forward to it.

Wonderful Aunt Edie and wonderful Uncle Roger!

Uncle Roger has sent me a fuse. What a completely goofy family I have. Concerned, but goofy. When I called Edie to arrange our lunch date, she asked me about the exploding-fuse dreams, and I told her about the boys dismantling the bomb by the train tracks, and she must have told Uncle Roger—and his solution to my bad dreams is to send me a fuse from a German bomb. In pieces, with a timing device that attaches to the bottom to delay its going off. It is not a doodlebug fuse but a "Type 17 from a 250 kg UXB" that someone successfully took apart without exploding himself a couple of years ago, and Uncle Roger sent it with a diagram and note explaining how "demystification" stops you from being afraid of something—I guess the idea is that if you know how something works, it becomes less menacing. Like me taking my friends from school flying so they'll stop being scared of it.

It was such a weird thing to have delivered to me at the airfield, and I had to show it off. *Everyone* was interested. Of course nobody had ever seen one, and I very much doubt it is legal for me to have it. Felicyta naturally wanted to know where Roger had got it, which I couldn't answer. Maddie had to take it apart and put it back together about ten times. She is a mechanical nut. Felicyta didn't say anything for a long time; she just sat watching Maddie poking at electrical relays. (I was watching her, too, watching her small, quick fingers with the French gold and wine-red ruby glittering there, and I thought grimly: Now I'm going to dream it's *Maddie's* hands exploding.)

Suddenly Felicyta's face shriveled in a look of hatred and she said viciously, "I wonder if we could reload it." Her heart is in Warsaw, battling for her country with the Polish Resistance.

"And drop it back on the factory where it came from," I improved.

Felicyta and Maddie gave me awkward, pitying looks. *Ignorant American Schoolgirl* is what those looks said.

"My sister is at work in a German munitions factory," Felicyta said coolly. "And my mother. 'Political prisoners.' That is German for 'slave labor.' They are in a concentration camp."

The embarrassing thing is, I already knew this, or sort of. But of course I hadn't really put it together. Anyway, being an Ignorant American Schoolgirl gives me an open ticket to ask brazen, awkward questions, and I'd already put my foot in my mouth, so I just went on.

"What *is* a concentration camp, Fliss?"

She shrugged. "A prison for civilians—for anyone the Germans don't like. Poles because they are Poles, Jews because they are Jews. My mother because she gave a blanket to a Jew. My sister because she told the German police my mother was right to do it. People disappear all the time, and you never hear from them again."

"But how do you know where your family is?"

Felicyta kept her voice steady, her face still wearing an expression of patient tolerance for ignorant foreigners. "Two years ago my father got a postcard from a cousin in the same camp who was allowed to ask him to send her a food package, and she told him she had seen my mother and sister alive."

How utterly impossible it is for me to imagine—Felicyta's mother and sister have been missing for *two years*. That was what Maddie was talking about on the train. She thought it was worse than being told someone was dead—*not ever know-ing* what happened to them.

You can see why Felicyta is so angry at everything.

"Fliss, how did *you* escape?"

She smiled a close-lipped, evil smile, only the corners of her mouth turning up, and said, "I stole a plane. Okay, it was my own plane, but I did have to steal it! I was doing courier work for the Polish Air Force when the Germans invaded. I knew they would take over all communications aircraft, or destroy them, so I took this one myself. I flew to France. It took me three days, mostly flying in twilight, hiding the plane in woodland by day. France was still free then. . . ."

It must have been in 1939. I was thirteen. I was in junior high school. I was *oblivious* to what was going on in Europe. Or anywhere except right where I was—Justice Field, Mount Jericho, PA, the center of the known universe.

Here is what I already knew about Felicyta's sister—what I'd forgotten about hearing before. It happened just after I came to Hamble. I was sitting in the Operations room with a few other girls, waiting for the day's ferry chits to be handed out. I was new enough to be shy and a little bit nervous about sitting down next to people I didn't know, so I was sitting by myself—it was even before Celia had turned up.

The wireless was on, and because I wasn't talking to any-body, I was listening to the radio. And it was this ugly story about a prison camp in Germany where they'd been running medical experiments on Polish prisoners, all women, mostly students—cutting open their legs and infecting them with gangrene, simulating bullet wounds, in the name of "medical science"—to find treatments for German soldiers wounded on the Eastern Front. The BBC announcer read through an endless list of names that a former prisoner had secretly memorized when she knew she was going to be released. I was interested because the woman who'd memorized the names was an American citizen. It was compelling stuff—you couldn't stop listening—but it was so absolutely awful that I couldn't believe it, and I said so.

"That's got to be propaganda!" I burst out. "You English are as bad as the Germans!"

"You should read the *Guardian*," Maddie said. "It's not all propaganda. The reports from the concentration camps are pure evil."

"Poisoning girls with gangrene?" I objected. "It's like trying to get us to believe the Germans eat babies!"

At that point Felicyta slammed her teacup down so hard she broke her saucer right in half and stormed out of the room. The floor shuddered as the door thundered shut behind her.

Maddie thrashed her newspaper into submission and nodded toward Felicyta's slammed door.

"Her sister's in a German concentration camp," Maddie explained in a level voice. She looked back down at the paper without meeting my eyes. "Felicyta thinks the Germans *do* eat babies."

That was three months ago.

I am starting to understand why the Polish pilots are so fanatical about their hatred of the Germans. Thank goodness I haven't got a "good old Pennsylvania Dutch" name like Stolzfuss or Hitz or Zimmerman. Felicyta doesn't know my middle name is Moyer, Mother's maiden name, or that my grandfather still speaks old-fashioned Pennsylvania German sometimes. I will never tell her.

I can't believe I have only been in England for three months—it seems like forever. And yet the war hasn't really touched me. I haven't lost my fiancé or my best friend or my mother or my sister. I'm not in exile. I have a home to go back to and people waiting for me. I have an aunt who is going to take me to lunch at the Ritz and an uncle who sends me fuses!

But I am very glad that Kurt and Karl are only ten years old, far too young to be drafted, and that they are safe at home in Pennsylvania.

Felicyta and Maddie came over to play cards with me at the Hatches' last night, and there was an air raid. The siren doesn't scare me at all when it first goes off—it sounds *exactly* like the hooter at the Volunteer Fire Company in Conewago Grove. I always think, "That'll be a fire somewhere—I'm glad Daddy's not on duty here." Mrs. Hatch shooed us out through the vegetable garden to get to the shelter. The house is on a high slope, and as we stumbled over the cabbages in the dark, we got a frightening glimpse of half a dozen flying bombs traveling across the sky. All you could see were the red exhaust flames of their engines—from far away it looked like a line of glowing balls of fire moving slowly along the horizon.

There is only room for one camp bed in the Hatches' shelter because they built the shelter themselves and it is tiny. The camp bed is ridiculously covered with a candlewick bedspread to make it seem cozy, and we all squeezed together on it to stay out of the mud. Fliss said to me, "Singing will not scare the bombs away!"

I'd been humming nervously without realizing I was doing it. I laughed. "It's a Girl Scout camp song."

"Rosie is *always* singing," Maddie pointed out. I could feel her trembling next to me, and remembered how much she hates the bombs.

"Sing properly if you're going to sing!" commanded Mrs. Hatch. "Then we can all join in."

So we sat in the underground shelter and I taught them camp songs. I sang "Land of the Silver Birch" and "My Paddle's Keen and Bright" (again), and then I got bold and sang my "Modern Warrior" poem to the same tune, and they beat time by clapping. And then I taught them "Make New Friends." It's easy, and we sang it as a round, again and again—

> "Make new friends
> But keep the old,
> One is silver
> And the other gold!"

Kind of corny but it seemed so appropriate.

There we were in the mud, singing so loudly that we didn't hear the "all clear" siren when it went! And Mr. Hatch came home and broke up the party, hustling us all inside and tut-tutting about his wife being so easily corrupted by modern youth.

"You might have *at least* been singing *hymns*," he chided her.

It was the best air raid ever.

Back in bed, I started thinking about how I like to be in a crowd—it's not like being best friends, or even a threesome, where sometimes two of you pair up and leave the other out. There's always someone on your side when you're in a crowd.

> "Make new friends
> But keep the old. . . ."

And then I started thinking about my combination birthday/Halloween party last year at our cottage in Conewago Grove, with Polly and Alice and Sandy and Fran—we all dressed up as the characters from *The Wizard of Oz*, with Polly as Toto, and told ghost stories on the sleeping porch by the light of jack-o'-lanterns. And now we have all graduated or gone to war (me) or married (Polly) or whatever, and we will never again be the team that won the Jericho County Girls' Basketball Championship or even play together, probably.

It was the stupid candlewick bedspread's fault! Mrs. Hatch's bedspreads *feel* the same as the ones Mother has out on the sleeping porch. Anyway, I had the candlewick on my bed pulled up to my chin last night, and after I thought about the house party, I started thinking about the sleeping porch—the thump and patter of squirrels running across the roof, the way the canvas awnings creak and flap, a trapped firefly blinking against the screen, the way the whole room shakes whenever anybody runs water in the bathroom on the other side of the wall—

I got so homesick I began to cry. I just couldn't stop thinking about the sleeping porch!

It's funny what sets you off. You miss people the most—really it is Polly and Alice and Sandy and Fran whom I am lonely for—but it is the candlewick bedspread that makes me ache with longing to be home.

September 1, 1944
Hamble

Paris is free! It's been a nerve-racking couple of weeks, watching the Allied forces inching along. We have a map we stick pins in to track the front lines. During the fighting in Paris, there was no radio communication coming out of the city at ALL—nothing but rumors. The papers said the city was liberated and all the church bells in London were ringing to celebrate, and the next day the papers said, "Whoops, not yet!" It wasn't long before the real news came through, but it was like being on a roller coaster waiting for it. Now the fighting is moving across the Seine and into Belgium.

The problem is that it's getting harder and harder to get supplies to the front lines because the Germans are still hanging on to the ports at Calais, Le Havre, Boulogne, etc. They realize what a pain in the neck it is for the Allied forces to have to ferry fuel, food, spare parts, blood, bandages, and everything else across to Normandy and then truck it two hundred miles north up this corridor between Germany and the French coast—especially with the train lines and bridges all blown up after the fighting (that is where Uncle Roger comes in, getting them to rig up temporary bridges in a hurry).

You can't even fly directly into France without being shot at, and you certainly can't unload a cargo ship. Le Havre is under siege. It is being pounded. We are doing it *ourselves*. The harbor there is taking such a beating that it will have to be rebuilt before it's any use to us.

I had my lunch with Aunt Edie in the Palm Court at the Ritz yesterday. Wow. It makes the Hotel Hershey look pretty bush league, which isn't exactly fair. Thank goodness for my uniform—I don't have anything else to wear that would have been remotely suitable, but in uniform you don't ever have to dress up for anything! I wore the same clothes I wore to Maddie's wedding (in fact I wore my other tunic, because the one I wore to Maddie's wedding is not as sharp-looking as it used to be, due to flying bombs and bus floors). But you never feel out of place or underdressed in uniform.

Edie, of course, was very elegant. I don't think she's had any new clothes for a while, either, but she gets everything remade by her own tailor and she is always so stylish—she kissed me on both cheeks to greet me and looked sort of slant-eyed at my hands because I wasn't wearing gloves (they did *not* survive the doodlebug wedding adventure).

We didn't talk about French cities being liberated—Edie will not discuss bloodshed and bombing while she is presiding over white linen and silver in the Palm Court at the Ritz! I told her about my last date with Nick.

"I like your Nick," she commented when I'd finished. "So terribly earnest."

I laughed. "That's exactly the word I think of, too. Did I tell you he proposed to me? He wanted to get married before he got sent off to wherever he is now. I know everyone is doing it, and I hated to disappoint him, but—"

"But it's not a charm. He won't be any better protected if you're married to him, and if you're really going to choose a boy yourself and you're being sensible about what you do together, there's no good reason to rush into marriage. You did the right thing, Rose darling."

"But I do worry about him," I said. "And if we were married, of course they would tell me right away if anything happened to him. They won't do that for just friends."

"There's something to be said for not being told right away," Aunt Edie mused. "But I prefer simply not to worry. I never worry about Roger. Do you worry about General

Montgomery—or General Eisenhower? They're just as likely to be killed as anybody, but you don't think about it. Imagine Nick a general!"

And we both laughed this time.

"Of course, Roger's just as likely to perish of a heart attack, or flu. Or some nasty disease he picks up in the field. Oh—that reminds me, Rose. He wanted to know if your jabs are up to date."

That drew a blank with me.

"My jabs?"

"Your inoculations. Tetanus and typhoid, principally."

"Oh! We call them shots. Yes, I had boosters this spring, before I came to England. Why?"

"Can't say," Aunt Edie said coyly, folding her napkin in her lap. "Shall we have coffee instead of tea? I hear they have a supply of the real thing from the Americans this week."

"Oh, wonderful Aunt Edie!"

My fingers are crossed because I know they are inoculating other ferry pilots so they will be ready to fly to Europe. But I'm not holding my breath, because so far none of them have been girls. And to tell the truth, I am less enthusiastic about the idea of doing ferry work in Europe than I was. Because it all looks so horribly, horribly *ruined*. The pictures in the papers are unbelievably awful—it looks like earthquake damage. Whole streets are knocked down, and the soldiers have to pick their way over rubble to get through the towns—I think I said before that it's WE who are doing the bombing. Allied planes are dropping thousands of tons of TNT day and night on our own cities. And on German cities, too, of course.

I am going to confess something here that I can't quite bring myself to confess to anyone aloud, and this is what it is. I am scared of the way the Germans are refusing to let go of anything. I am scared of the way they are clinging to the French and Belgian ports, even though they've been pushed out of most of the rest of France. There is something about it that spooks me. They've lost. They must know they've lost—that they're on the run. It's all so pointless. It shouldn't take another year. But I bet it will.

It's not desperation—there is something inhuman in it. That is what I find so creepy. Five years of destruction and mayhem, lives lost everywhere, shortages of food and fuel and clothing—and the insane mind behind it just urges us *all* on and on to more destruction. And we all keep playing.

Now Brussels is free, but more important, Antwerp, too—a port in Allied hands at last! But actually the best news as far as I'm concerned was in the *Manchester Guardian* yesterday, read aloud by our *Guardian* addict, the Honorable Mrs. Maddie Beaufort-Stuart, while we were waiting for our delivery chits. Here's the news: RAF pilots are reporting that they can now fly the whole way across France without running into enemy aircraft!

It has been quieter here, too. As we've been gaining ground in France and Belgium, the launch sites for the V-1 flying bombs are being taken out of action or pushed back—the doodlebugs can't reach as far into England now, and also there aren't as many of them. You really notice it here in Southampton because there just hasn't been *anything* for about ten days. It's quieter in Kent and London, too. THANK GOD.

Operations told us to look out for flying bombs launched from planes—from German bombers. We've had the flash cards out to familiarize ourselves with the silhouette of a Heinkel He-111, just in case. They will probably aim for Paris and Brussels, not London, but they are not licked yet.

I am in France!

I am staying overnight with the American nurses in the Red Cross unit at one of the redeployment camps near Reims, full of GIs on their way to battle. Roger moves on to his own forces near Antwerp tomorrow. They call this place Camp LA, which is short for Camp Los Angeles—all the camps around here are named after some American metropolis, to make the boys feel at home, I guess. No one is fooled. It is an instant city—just add water! (Of which there is plenty, most of it underfoot.) Reims was liberated on August 30, and Camp LA has not been here for much more than a week, but it is huge. There is a grocery store and a cinema as well as the hospital and mess halls, all in tents.

The store is stocked with American loot that seems miraculous to me—Quaker oats and Ivory soap and Hershey bars. Nothing makes me feel at home like Hershey's chocolate! Back at Justice Field, you get the chocolate factory lined up on your starboard wingtip when you're coming in to land, and when the wind's from the northwest, the whole valley smells like roasting cocoa beans.

It doesn't smell like cocoa here. Most of the open space in Camp LA is an ocean of mud, except the freshly surfaced runway. It's been a beautiful clear day for once, and I had no encounters with other aircraft on our way here, although it was sobering to see the utter destruction of Caen as we crossed the coast and the clouds of smoke rising over Le Havre in the north.

When Uncle Roger gets things moving, he moves *fast*. I think that's partly to make sure no one ever has time to say no to him. Here's what happened this morning: I got an "S" chit when I went into Operations at Hamble, which means "Secret"—I'm not supposed to tell anyone who I'm ferrying or where I collected them. I won't write down any of that. Also—this isn't secret—I was supposed to make sure I had my US passport with me as well as my ATA authorization card and pilot's license, and Operations told me to go home and change to full dress uniform with skirt (not slacks)—which usually means you will be taxiing someone important. Only in this case it just meant they didn't know who I'd be taxiing and I ought to be presentable in case I ran into General Patton after I arrived!

Operations *didn't* tell me I was going overnight, so I haven't got anything like a toothbrush or pajamas with me. But it is only for one night and the other girls are having to wash their faces in their helmets, and had to sleep in their ambulances on the way here from Normandy before the tents got set up, so I guess I can spend another night in my clothes. Roger bought me a toothbrush in the grocery store along with a month's supply of chocolate and gum. I am going to be everybody's best friend when I get back to Southampton.

I flew an Oxford to get here, carrying Roger and a handful of other passengers. I felt like the whole sky belonged to me. The Seine was with us all the way through France, great big loops of shining silver out the port side, and I'd already had to shout at my passengers to take turns looking because they were throwing me out of balance by crowding on one side of the plane, and then there it was ahead of me—PARIS, FRANCE.

It was a huge, gorgeous sprawl of wooded parks and broad avenues, and although we flew over some bomb damage in the suburbs, the closer we got to the middle, the more and more beautiful it was, and from the air, it didn't look the least bit damaged. Everybody was glued to the tiny windows, and as we got closer, they stopped trying to crowd at the same side because the city was all around us. I went down to about 700 feet, and it was like flying over a model railway village, with the gleaming white domes of Sacré Coeur presiding over it all and Notre Dame Cathedral like a wedding cake right in the middle. Of course it is the first time I've ever seen Paris, and what a way to see it for the first time, flying low over streets full of flags and red-white-and-blue bunting!

By the time we were over Notre Dame I was singing to myself again. The cabin was so noisy I thought no one would be able to hear me. But Uncle Roger and someone else were crouched right behind me looking over my shoulders because there is a better view from the cockpit than in the back, and they heard me. And then everybody joined in.

> "Allons enfants de la Patrie,
> Le jour de gloire est arrivé!"

I don't know why I know all the words to the French national anthem. I am just like that. I never forget the words to anything! We learned it in eighth grade, when we were just starting to take French.

If Roger and the others hadn't all joined in, I'd have probably ended up in tears—overcome with emotion. As it was, everybody was too noisy and excited for me to get to feeling sentimental. We were *shouting* as I detoured east along the Seine toward the Eiffel Tower, most of my passengers just going "Da Da Da DAH!" since I was the only one who knew all the words.

As we got closer to the Eiffel Tower, one of the wags in the back yelled, "Go under it!"

I did not fly under the Eiffel Tower!

But I bet if I'd been flying a fighter plane, something small and zippy, I'd have been tempted. Maybe tomorrow? No, I won't be that stupid. But the thought that it's even a possibility makes me warm and happy.

So I didn't fly under the Eiffel Tower, but I did fly in big, lazy circles around it while everybody pointed and cheered and somebody snapped a million pictures over my shoulder like a sightseer. At that point I'd stopped singing because I was really too low and I had to concentrate on flying.

I'm BUZZING THE EIFFEL TOWER, I thought. JUST WAIT till I tell Daddy I've buzzed the Eiffel Tower!

It is *the most wonderful thing I have ever done.*

The rest of the day has brought me back to earth with a wallop because after I landed and had my camp tour and went shopping, the nurses I am staying with put me to work in an "outpatient" clinic tent of the field hospital—walking wounded only, thank goodness. I was assisting, holding equipment, and cutting gauze for bandages, not actually changing dressings myself. To tell the truth, I think they just grabbed the opportunity to use me as a morale booster.

"From *Pennsylvania*! A *pilot*! Shouldn't you be in *school*, young lady? Look at those *curls*!"

It reminded me of when Maddie and Celia and Felicyta and I handed out the strawberries to the soldiers on D-Day—except these men weren't as frightened. They'd already been to battle and it's hardened them, or at least made them better at hiding that they're scared. It makes my heart ache, thinking that none of these brave boys are so badly hurt they won't be fighting again in a couple of weeks. I don't want them to be badly hurt, but equally I don't want them to be killed on the front lines. I have got "Battle Hymn of the Republic" stuck in my brain. *Glory, glory Hallelujah!*

It is why I am up so late—I have been working on a poem in my head all day, and I want to write it down in case I forget it.

BATTLE HYMN OF 1944 (by Rose Justice)

O let them struggle wisely, these brave boys
and girls around the watch fires; grant they should
fight with realistic hope, not to destroy
all the world's wrong, but to renew its good.
Make them victors and healers, let them be
unsentimental and compassionate;
spill not their generous blood abundantly
as gifts of stockings and gum and chocolate.
Let them be modest, knowing the irony
of hard-fought peace, our bold united youth
returned in strength across the migrant sea,
rebuilding and restoring law and truth—
then afterward, when the last prayer's been said,
Home for the living, burial for the dead.

And now I am going to go to sleep. I have been scribbling this by flashlight under my borrowed US Army blanket. I'm not flying the Oxford back—they want to keep that here for local taxi runs—so one of the RAF pilots at the Front will come pick up Roger to take him to his next stop, and I am going to swap planes and take a Spitfire back to Southampton for a new paint job (it is being modified for reconnaissance).

Now that I want to go to sleep, I can't put my notebook and flashlight down on the ground, because it's just an ocean of mud, and I don't want to get out of bed and wake everybody up hunting for a place to put them. So I guess I'll shove everything down at my feet and hope I don't kick it out of bed. I'd put the notebook under my pillow except I haven't got one! I hope I don't forget it tomorrow morning.

"Chiltern Edge"
1 Thames View
Medmenham, nr. Marlow
Bucks

4 October 1944

Dear Mrs. Beaufort-Stuart,
    Thank you for all your thoughtful effort over the past three weeks. I wish I had some good news, or even some small shred of hopeful news, to pass to you and your fellow pilots. But there isn't anything—not a single thing. As time moves on and so many others are also lost, it seems selfish to keep badgering for an investigation into one more missing aircraft, especially as it wasn't entirely aboveboard for Rose to be in France in the first place. My husband, Roger, feels keenly that if he makes a fuss about losing Rose, none of the rest of you young ladies will ever be allowed to fly in Europe.
    I do not want to give up hope, but I do not think we are ever going to hear anything now. Roger says her family won't even get a military pension. I suppose you know that, being a civilian pilot yourself. But it does seem dreadfully unfair.
    Perhaps you would like to write to her parents. I think they would appreciate hearing from one of Rose's friends. Sometimes I think I will send them the poem you copied out for me from her notebook,

the "Battle Hymn." *"Home for the living, burial for the dead."* And then I think I won't, as poor Rose will have neither.

I shall leave it up to you.

Thank you again for all your past kindness, to me and to my missing niece.

Yours sincerely,
Edith Justice

Justice Airfield
Mt. Jericho, Pa.

23 November 1944
Thanksgiving Day

Dear First Officer Beaufort-Stuart,

I want to thank you myself for the effort you've
made on our daughter's behalf. You say in your letter
that you don't feel you've done enough, but in every
telegram from Roger and in all of Edie's letters,
they always mention you. I know how many times
you've telephoned Edie to check for news—that you
supplied your husband's squadron in Europe with
Rose's picture so they will know who to look for—that
you took over the sad task of sorting through Rose's
things and packed them up for Edie to send us. She
also sent us the newspaper clipping you gave her
about the shot-down gunner who spent three months
hiding in France. But I think it is better for us to face
the worst than to hold out for good news that will
never come.

Even if there is no way for you to turn back time
or find out what really happened that morning in
September, it means a great deal to all of us to know
that Rose had such a devoted friend so far from
home.

Thank you also for the photograph from your
wedding. It is the last picture we have got of Rose.

You all look so excited and happy, and the ivy-covered church nestled in the heather is an idyllic setting for a wartime marriage—my boys noticed your husband has got a football tucked under his arm! It is hard to believe you were only temporarily "between bombs."

I never imagined—never could have imagined— even flying over the hell of no-man's-land myself in the last war—that less than thirty years later, another war would cost me a daughter.

On behalf of myself and Rose's mother, Grace Mae, and Rose's young brothers, Karl and Kurt, thank you for being Rose's friend.

Yours sincerely,
Jack Justice

Krefeld, Germany

10 March 1945

My bonny Maddie-lass,

   I am flying Hudsons now, transport and
parachutists—dropping madmen deep into Germany
on God knows what missions. I fly only one night
in four. Mostly I sit around all day smoking or go on
schnapps hunts with other idle airmen.

   I look for your Rose everywhere I go. I think I
am really looking for our Julie, who I know is dead.
If I could just win *one damned personal victory*, you
know? We are into Germany but still not across the
Rhine, and all I feel is grief and horror. I cannot
describe to you the horror of this war, Maddie. I do
not want to. I think the biggest surprise is that I don't
have more friends and big brothers and little sisters
who are dead. The destruction we are heaping upon
the German cities is unimaginable—it is *shameful*.
It makes me feel ashamed to be one of the victors.
And then we come across a row of railway wagons
abandoned on a siding under the snow and packed
with hundreds of frozen, emaciated bodies—*hundreds*
of them, unexplained, some of them children—and
I know that we *must* be the victors. Whatever the
shame—whatever the cost.

   I look for your Rose in every face, dead and
living. But there are so many, and all of them are

ravaged by hunger and grief and loss, even the faces of the enemy. I swear, it's sometimes hard to tell which faces do belong to the so-called enemy. Deserters hide as civilians to avoid capture not only by us but also by their own army, and civilians surprise you with hospitality and gratitude. I met a group of four displaced men traveling together—two had escaped from a German prison camp, and the other two were shot-down German airmen trying to get back to their base. All we did was trade cigarettes. Strip men of uniforms and badges and they are just men.

A year and a half ago, when we first lost track of Julie, I remember you described the way people disappear into the Nazi death machine like an unlucky lapwing hitting the propeller of a Lancaster bomber—nothing left but feathers blowing away in the aircraft's wake, as if those warm wings and beating heart had never existed. It has happened to *tens of thousands* of people. Maybe hundreds of thousands or even millions. They are *gone*. They have vanished without leaving even a vapor trail. Everywhere I go I meet people who are hunting for husbands, mothers, children, brothers, sisters, cousins, friends, lovers, and they are *all gone*.

Your friend Rose has evaporated with them. I don't know what else to tell you, Maddie.

What a miserable letter! And your last one to me was so full of encouragement and flying stories. I am afraid you will cry when you read this one. I wish I hadn't mentioned the frozen children. But you know I would never be anything less than wholly honest with you.

Here is better news to end with—surprising, but

positive at least. The Boy Nick has got married. I think it was partly a way for him to cope with losing Rose, but partly, it is true, he has found another lovely girl. His new bride is also American, a Red Cross worker who does counseling and social work for the troops. She is not made of the same strong stuff your Rose was, but to tell the truth, the Boy Nick isn't, either. Maybe it's as well they didn't tie the knot last summer.

I am desperate for it to be over now, and to see you again and to be with you always.

thine ain true
Jamie

This pretty book is all that's left of Rose and her poetry. She's written my name in the front—"A present from Maddie Brodatt." The army nurses she was staying with at Camp Los Angeles found it in her camp bed. I should have sent it to her mother and father, I suppose, but I haven't got the heart. I remember when I gave it to her, to write Celia's accident report in.

Oh Rose, Rose. Bloody, bloody hell.

I've lost you—lost another friend—"as if those warm wings and beating heart had never existed." This war has taken my best friend and my bridesmaid from me in the space of a year. IT ISN'T FAIR.

Oh, Rose—when the US Army Air Force transport pilot from Camp Los Angeles dropped your notebook off at Operations in Hamble last September, for a long time I still hoped you'd turn up and I could give it back to you. I know it's possible to crash-land in occupied Europe and make it out alive. I know.

So I find it impossible to "close the book"—to accept that you're not coming back. And just in case I'm right, I am going to leave your notebook and my letters for you to collect at the American Embassy in Paris. I think you're as likely to end up there as anywhere, if you're still alive. Your uncle Roger is in on my plot and has already filled a safe-deposit box there for you with a little money and a letter from your family. He's told the embassy to put you up at the Ritz Paris until other arrangements are made for you. What it's like to have relatives in high places! Not that it makes much difference to you now.

Writing to you like this makes me feel that you are still alive. It's an illusion I've noticed before—words on a page are like oxygen to a petrol engine, firing up ghosts. It lasts only while the words are in your head. After you put down the paper or the pen, the pistons fall lifeless again.

If this message ever reaches you—I know you have family in England and plenty of loving friends and family back home in America—but my mother-in-law, Esmé Beaufort-Stuart, says that you have got a home-from-home with her as well and please to contact her without hesitation. It is a better address to leave than mine—at the moment I am still being sent all over everywhere with work, and I don't know where I'll be by the time this ever catches up with you. Esmé's address, you probably know, is Craig Castle, Castle Craig, Aberdeenshire. That is pretty much also her telephone number, which I don't actually know—I just ask the operator for Craig Castle when I ring them.

Esmé has always been generous about giving a home to waifs and strays and other exiles. There is a band of Tinkers who stop on their riverbank every year for a month—Julie and Jamie were so familiar with them as children that they picked up their strange dialect! And then there are the evacuee lads from Glasgow, whom you've met—Esmé has actually adopted two of them now, though the others have gone home. She has also got a dozen wounded airmen convalescing there. For Esmé, I think, the war effort will continue for a while after the war has officially ended.

And, of course, there is me. I am one of her waifs and strays, too. She would do anything for me, I think, so on my behalf and by her own invitation, you must consider Craig Castle one of your homes-from-home. Bring your friends.

That's given me hope—a vision of you and a lot of other Rose-like people drinking coffee and singing songs from Girl Guide camp, while Esmé plays the piano, in the morning sunlight of the Little Drawing Room at Craig Castle.

Your fellow pilot and loving friend,
Maddie

P.S. Fliss and I had to go through your things like we did with Celia's, and I kept your fuse—I wanted to keep <u>something</u> of yours. I don't suppose you'll ever want it back, but it seemed a bit horrible to return it to your aunt Edie.

Oh, Rose—what happened to you?

t us. They've executed dozens of us already. But
s all to end up dead anyway, they used us—test
e couldn't find the right words. I don't think she
ords like experiment and trial and medical, and t
at it sounded like she was telling a really bad jo
udents from my transport. My special transport.
ts, Króliki—Kaninchen in German. Actually, what
red on yelled it at one of the doctors and he th
ut us up like rabbits. They'd slice your calf open
r for two weeks. Or they'd cut pieces out of y
your leg and try to stick it in someone else's l
young and healthy, get it? They said they want
eans the Eastern front, which is where most of
ounds on us. Make a hole like a gunshot wound
in a trench and never change the dressing. Gue
edles seemed to waver in front of my face, as
show you what happens—" She barked orders
ey never stopped knitting. They turned around
ere on the table. They stuck their own legs out
ere models at a fashion show. I burst out, t hea
red on the concrete floor and the girl next to
tement, and then suddenly the whole room was b
ou heard? On the radio? On the BBC? What d
"Some of us died of it, some of us have been
hting to get the story to spread outside the Ca

PART 2
RAVENSBRÜCK

Rose Moyer Justice
Handwriting Sample, 17 April 1945
Paris, France

> When in the Course of human events, it
> becomes necessary for one people to dissolve the
> political bands which have connected them with
> another, and to assume among the powers of the
> earth, the separate and equal station to which
> the Laws of Nature and of Nature's God
> entitle them, a decent respect to the opinions of
> mankind requires that they should declare the
> causes which impel them to the separation.
>   We hold these truths to be self-evident,
> that all men are created equal, that they are
> endowed by their Creator with certain unalienable
> Rights, that among these are Life, Liberty and
> the pursuit of Happiness.

They told me to stop after I listed the "unalienable Rights."
By then I had written enough for them to tell it really was my
handwriting, and I was crying so hard I could barely see the
page. *Life. Liberty. Happiness.* Unalienable rights.

I can write again. Oh, God! *I can write again.* All those
months of not being able to write! Of not being *allowed to
write.* More than six months of hiding pencil stubs in the hem
of my dress, hiding chips of charcoal in my cheek, hiding torn
shreds of newsprint in my shoes. Knowing I'd be shot if I was

caught with any of it. And SO MUCH that I wanted to write. It seems like I have been a prisoner for *so long*.

I can write!

It feels dangerous—like stealing a plane. But it is my unalienable Right. And this is my own notebook, which they gave back to me in the American Embassy this morning, along with an enormous pile of cash from Uncle Roger and a temporary passport. The passport is made out in the name of Rose Moyer Justice; date of birth, 22 October 1925; place of issue, Paris; date of issue, 17 April 1945, today. I mean yesterday. And a photograph that Aunt Edie had sent them, a wallet-sized copy of my portrait in ATA uniform from last spring.

I have changed so drastically since then that no one at the embassy could tell this photograph is really me. That's why they made me write out the opening lines of the Declaration of Independence—so they could compare it to my handwriting in the rest of this notebook. My handwriting has not changed. My signature matches, too. Mother had sent them my Pennsylvania driver's license as a sample.

That has convinced even me that I am still Rose—my handwriting has not changed. It is the only physical thing about me that looks exactly the same. I can still write.

In fact, it is the only thing I *can* do. I can't even sleep. The embassy people checked me in here at the Paris Ritz and left me in this gigantic room Aunt Edie has reserved for me, but I sat on the floor for three hours because I didn't dare to touch any of the beautiful furniture. Then I got up and spent another hour pacing, checking the Place Vendôme every time a car or truck went by just in case it was Bob Ernst coming back. But now it is nearly three in the morning and nothing is going by anymore. My brain won't let me go to sleep—my internal clock is tensed for the four a.m. siren. I tried to get dressed again, but I can't *bear* to put those dead women's clothes back on, not if I have to go naked for the rest of my life. It's not that cold here. Anyway I'm used to being cold. And also used to being wide awake when all I want to do is collapse.

What I'm not used to is being by myself.

How could it have happened? I don't know how it happened. I LOST THEM. Irina and Róża, my more-than-sisters, Russian *taran* pilot and Polish Rabbit—I couldn't have escaped without them, I couldn't have survived last winter without them, and I have lost them *both*.

But I'm kidding myself. I do know how it happened. If I hadn't been so set on getting to Paris—if I hadn't rushed off with Bob Ernst in that convoy of American soldiers—if I had double-checked what was going on. We camped overnight with the Swedish Red Cross unit and I was talking with Bob and that Minnesotan chaplain who was interpreting for the Swedes, and I told them *myself* that Róża needed medical treatment. Only it never occurred to me they would leave her with the Red Cross without asking me—without even telling me! Irina was with her and I was in Bob's jeep, and we set off the next morning near the front of the convoy. I never dreamed Róża wasn't following in one of the trucks with Irina. So stupid of me! Of course the Swedish Red Cross unit was going back to *Sweden*.

I've lost Róża and Irina.

I feel like my world has ended.

But it hasn't—not even the war has ended yet. It just keeps going relentlessly on and on and on, like a concentration camp roll call when they can't get the numbers to come out right. And I guess I just go on and on, too.

I wonder what has happened to Nick since last August. Oh, Nick! I have dreamed of seeing him again for so long, made up all those stories about him coming to rescue me— but what will he think when he sees what a walking corpse I've become? How can I tell him what happened to me, all I've seen and had to do?

A lot of it is a blur anyway. I don't remember the first time I thought I was so hungry I was going to die. I don't remember when the chilblains started, or whether it was on my hands or feet first. I don't remember the details of being beaten. I know my sentence was "with force," which means on your bare backside, but I don't remember them pulling up my dress, not either time. I remember trying to count the blows but not what it felt like. I have blocked it out.

I remember standing through a roll call in the dark, at the end of a twelve-hour workday when I'd been so behind that I didn't get to stop to eat, and being so cold it *hurt*, and someone behind me started to cry. And then I started crying, too, and in ten seconds the whole block was crying. And they shut us up by threatening us with the dogs, and then they made us stand there for another hour—just those of us who were crying. Everyone else, thousands of them, went to bed, but Block 32 was still standing there, trying not to cry while we all slowly froze to death.

But I don't remember what it felt like to be that cold. Isn't that crazy? I can't *imagine* what it felt like. And it couldn't have been more than a few months ago.

The strange thing is, nothing about the past winter has taken the edge off the memory of my last ATA ferry delivery, the day I took off from Camp Los Angeles in France and landed somewhere near Mannheim in Germany.

I'm going to write it down. I'm wide awake and I'm sick of thinking over and over about the last twenty-four hours' worth of disaster. Maybe if I think hard about last September I will be able to forget about today for long enough to let me go to sleep.

Roger left Camp LA before I did. The RAF pilot arrived in the Spitfire I was supposed to take back to England, and we swapped planes; I stood next to the mechanic who telephoned Caen to say I might land there to refuel. I wonder if Caen ever looked for me. Maybe everybody thinks I ran out of fuel over the English Channel.

I remember that flight as if I had the map sitting on my lap with the route outlined in china pencil and a great big "X Marks the Spot" over Épernay. That is where I met the flying bomb. Was it aimed at Paris—was it one last attempt to destroy Paris? It must have been air-launched, but I don't know where it was heading. It was too far inland to be aimed at London. I think about this a lot . . . where that bomb was heading. Other than on a collision course with me, I mean.

I thought it was another plane at first. It looked like another plane. I had a perfectly clear view of it as it came slowly closer and closer, seeming to hover in the same spot just ahead of my wingtip, an unbudging speck in the distant sky like a little black star, or a bug. It didn't scare me. I assumed it was an Allied plane because I was over Allied territory. So I did exactly what Maddie said she'd done when she saw a flying bomb in the air—I waggled my wings at it. And of course got no response.

I thought, gee whiz, the pilot must be looking at his map—or blind—or asleep—

—or *there isn't any pilot.*

I should have made a steep turn to get out of its way. This is what I dread telling Daddy. That I went after it *on purpose.*

I was so sure it was headed for Paris, beautiful Paris. Still intact. And if this bomb hit its target, there would be a gigantic crater, broken glass everywhere, dust, summer trees that looked like winter, just like London—I couldn't stand it.

I pushed the Spitfire's nose down and went into a screaming downhill dive to gain speed, and the bomb sped straight on about a hundred feet over me. I glanced up and saw it, huge, in silhouette for a fraction of a second, a black cross of wings and fuselage blotting out the sky. Then I shoved on full power and pulled out of the dive in a climbing turn.

Then I was chasing it.

I wasn't thinking about engine pressure or fuel or anything—I was just hell bent on getting every extra second possible of power and speed out of that Spitfire. And yard by yard, I gained on the bomb.

I must have been going four hundred miles an hour. But it didn't feel fast. It felt like getting your teeth pulled.

"Come on—come *on*—"

I talked to the plane like it was a racehorse. I couldn't hear a thing with full power; I couldn't hear the sound of my own voice.

"Come on—nearly there!"

And then I'd overshot it. Getting the speed right was the hardest thing I have ever done—probably the best flying I have ever done, too. I overtook the bomb *four times* before I found that sweet place on the throttle that let me scream along beside it in the air. And then I got my wing under the bomb's wing on the first try. *I didn't even touch it.* I saw the bomb wobble in the air, and I shoved full power on again to get out of its way. Then I looked back over my shoulder and saw the bomb tip down gently, gently into a spin, just like Celia's Tempest.

I let out a scream of nerve and fury and exhilaration, and cut the power and set up the Spit for a straight and level cruise, and began to battle the first wave of guilt.

Do you have ANY IDEA how much fuel you just wasted?

I didn't even see the stupid bomb hit the ground—I was so busy trying to reestablish myself in real life. It must be what Superman feels like after racing through the sky following a speeding locomotive and then ten seconds later peering at the world through Clark Kent's nearsighted glasses.

How much fuel have I wasted and where the heck am I?

How much fuel have I wasted and where the heck am I and did I damage the engine?

I was starting to panic. I knew I had to calm down, so I began to orbit—long, lazy ovals over rolling French crazy quilt fields and woods. I was too high to see where my bomb hit— or maybe I was already too far away to see it. I knew I had to figure out where I was and how to get to Caen from there. I'd been relay-racing with the bomb for about a quarter of an hour, which meant I was now ironically southwest of Paris, about halfway between Paris and Dijon—that bomb wouldn't have hit Paris anyway. I thought and scribbled on my map for ten minutes while I circled. I knew that all the time I was circling I was wasting still more fuel, but I needed to get it right.

I guess Daddy would say I had my head down in the cockpit for too long. He'd say I didn't keep enough of a lookout. It's true I didn't see them coming. But I don't think I could have done anything about it even if I had.

I didn't know what the intercepting planes were. I knew they were German and I could tell they had jet engines, but I didn't have a clue what the planes *were*. They were in Luftwaffe camouflage, with black crosses on their fuselages and swastikas on their tailplanes. Their engines hung down from their wings like bombs. I'd never seen *anything* fly that fast.

I know now that in German they're called *Schwalben*, Swallows. They were Messerschmitt Me-262s. Those planes did fly just like a couple of swallows, great big enormous swallows with jet engines strapped under their wings. The first one came at me from below and behind, and the other from above and behind, and they corkscrewed around me with their engines roaring, and suddenly they were gone, one of them breaking left and the other right—but I was still in my wide, slow orbit and they came screaming back at me, one passing me on each side. It was exactly like watching swallows flying.

I did two things. I leveled out and headed northwest, straight back toward England as fast as I could go, and I flashed every single light I had—landing lights, nav lights, cockpit floodlights—and I pulled the flares out, something I've never, ever done before, to let them know I wasn't armed. They came at me again and one of them settled on my tail—I could see him over my shoulder as I tried frantically to urge the speed up and flash lights with the same hand. I was so afraid he was going to blast me out of the sky that it took me a while to notice the other one flying calmly ahead of me, deliberately keeping pace with me. He wasn't aggressive. He just flew along and let me set the speed. He was so close I could see the pilot's head in the cockpit. After a moment he rocked his wings at me: *HI.*

I let go of the lights and kept my hand on the throttle. I pushed the control column gently from side to side. Light touch, one finger, trained in me from the age of twelve. *HI* yourself.

God.

He made a wide, level turn to the left, practically a U-turn, and headed off back in the other direction.

I actually sobbed aloud with panicked relief, praying that I would never see him again, that I'd never see another Luftwaffe aircraft in my whole life. But then I glanced back over my shoulder and the other guy was still there, stuck to my tail.

"GO AWAY!" I screamed pointlessly at the sky.

In about a minute the first guy was back in exactly the same deliberate position ahead of me and to my left, and when he knew I was watching, he rocked his wings *again*.

And I figured out what he meant: *FOLLOW ME.*

"No no *no*," I sobbed at the indifferent sky.

I knew what I was supposed to do. I was supposed to rock my wings to answer him and let him know I was ready to follow his instructions. But I didn't. I wasn't ready to follow his instructions. So I just kept flying stubbornly straight in the direction I was heading and ignored him.

And the other guy, the one flying behind me, *fired at me.*

Actually he fired into the empty sky above me. Just one burst, a warning shot of automatic cannon fire. He didn't hit me; I didn't feel it in the airframe like I felt the hailstorm last summer, but the shock of the sky erupting around me had the same effect on me as being punched in the stomach. For a moment I couldn't breathe. My hand forced the throttle automatically, but I couldn't make the Spit go any faster.

The pilot in front of me rocked his wings a third time: last warning.

I was gasping for air now. I didn't have a choice. I couldn't outrun them and I couldn't fight them. So I had to go with them.

I took a shuddering breath and rocked my own wings again: *I'M COMING.*

The pilot ahead of me made another long, lazy U-turn. This time I turned after him. The pilot on my rear end followed me around. I could see them wave casually as they passed each other in the air.

We lined up in formation flying straight and level in the

wrong direction, with me in the middle, one hand shaking on the throttle and one hand shaking on the control column, both feet shaking against the rudder pedals, half blinded by tears and terror. I tried to imagine the report I'd have to file. *Controlled flight into terrain* was all I could think of. That's what they call it when you're flying in a cloud and you crash into a mountain you didn't see—*controlled flight into terrain.*

We avoided overflying cities. We avoided overflying camps and troops. We flew high over the Front and then over the German border, which was marked on my map as the Siegfried Line. We crossed the Rhine north of Mannheim, where my map stopped. But I didn't. I kept flying, with a pair of Luftwaffe jets escorting me deeper and deeper into Germany.

I flew with them for *two hundred miles.* They kept taking turns to zip ahead of me and circle back. There was always one of them with me, behind or ahead of me.

After the first fifteen minutes, once I got used to the whole nightmare weirdness of what was happening, there wasn't really anything for me to do except keep the Spitfire pointing in the direction they chose for me, and try to figure out where the heck we were and where the heck we were going. I realized this was the most important thing I could do—exactly what you'd do if you accidentally flew into a cloud. Pay attention to your heading, the time, and how fast you're going, so you can turn around and *find your way back.*

It looked so much like Pennsylvania! All fields and farms and woods and rivers, and there at the edge of the map was "Mannheim," which is the name of the nearest town to Conewago Grove—Mannheim is where we always go for our groceries in the summer. But it's not the same Mannheim. I can't remember how to convert my indicated airspeed to true airspeed. I'm not being accurate. I am in Germany. I am off the map.

I reached the point where I started to wonder if I was really still alive. I thought maybe I got killed in my attempt to tip the flying bomb or when the Swallow shot at me, and now I was in purgatory, doomed to fly forever and ever over fields that looked like Pennsylvania without ever being able to land. The only way to prove I was still alive was to land in a field, or to turn around and fly in the other direction. But if I *was* still alive, and this *was* really happening, then the Luftwaffe aircraft on my tail would blast me out of the sky if I tried to get away from them. So I couldn't risk turning or landing in case I *was* still alive. I had to keep flying.

I think it's taken me about the same amount of time to write this as it took me to fly it. That's kind of incredible. I am writing at a rate of 170 miles an hour and going nowhere. I'm getting tired now. But my brain is still in the air over Mannheim, so I'd better land before I try to sleep again or I'll be counting the miles and reciting the headings in my dreams.

I don't know the name of the aerodrome where they led me to. The leader pulled out ahead of me over the run-way with his landing gear lowered. He didn't touch down, though; he went screaming away for another circuit. I was so stupid with fear and confusion that I just followed him back up into the sky. The other guy was orbiting above us now, watching the show from 2000 feet.

They wanted me to land ahead of them, leaving them behind in the sky while I came back to earth all by myself IN GERMANY. I refused to play. They were the only friends I had anymore. I was not going to land without them.

We went round and round the aerodrome. Finally the leader landed. I tried to land behind him, but the turbulence of his horrible jet engines knocked my wings around so much I thought I was going to stall, and by the time I straightened out, the runway was behind me and I had to go around AGAIN. I was on my fifth circuit now and I was sick of it.

Show 'em how to land a plane, Rosie.

I wish Daddy had seen it. I floated down with one finger on the control column and I had only a third of the runway behind me when I stopped rolling. I didn't bother to get off the runway. I didn't want to get out. I didn't want to look. I rested my forehead on the control panel and waited.

I can't stay awake another second. It is getting light.

Three hours' sleep. That's about as good as it gets. I did dream about flying—I guess that's no surprise. It wasn't a bad dream. I was over wooded mountains somewhere—it looked like the foothills of the Pa. Alleghenies, but it could just as easily have been southwestern Germany. It was snowing. I wasn't scared.

It is a beautiful, beautiful spring morning out there in Paris—my windows are all wide open, and the air and sky are wonderful. I woke up because I was cold, sleeping in my birthday suit with no covers. I don't even try to pull up the covers in my sleep—I just assume there aren't any covers. My sleeping brain tells me, of course I am cold. I am always cold, right? Curl up in a ball and try to go back to sleep before the next siren.

I am *so lonesome*. I thought I'd want to forget last winter's hell, but now I am in a panic in case I *do* forget. So busy remembering that impossible list of Polish prisoners and the flight times and headings that the faces of my friends, and their kindness and strength and bravery, are fading into a tangled blur of exhaustion and hunger. I am going to write it all down in order, the best I can do. I think writing helped me to sleep this morning—at least it tired me out so much I did sleep. I have really missed being able to write things down. I never thought of writing as a luxury or a privilege. But of course it is. An *unalienable right*.

So there I was, on the ground in Germany at the unknown airfield, clenching my hands shut for the first time in two hours and waiting for the storm to break.

It didn't take long. I didn't see what was happening, because my head was down and my eyes were closed, but after a few seconds the plane started rolling again. I stomped on the brakes but got unexpected resistance, and I jerked my head up wildly to find out what was going on because the engine was off and the brakes were on and the Spitfire was still inching forward.

Twenty men were pushing and pulling at it. One of them saw that I was up and not dead, and he waved at me frantically and pointed overhead. I looked up—the second Swallow still hadn't landed and my plane was in his way. They were trying desperately to clear the runway for him. I think he was out of fuel.

I let go of the brakes and the men around my plane rolled it off the runway at racing speed, just like a bunch of kids getting a go-cart or a sled moving. The other plane came roaring in past me just as I felt the bump as I went over the rough ground at the edge of the concrete.

Someone jumped up on the wing and banged on the canopy with his fist, shouting at me to open up. He pointed a pistol at me with his other hand.

I didn't fight. I really didn't want them to kill me. But also I had no idea, *no idea* what they were going to do to me, so I cooperated very, very slowly. My hands shook so much I couldn't get that stupid, cranky catch on the cockpit door in the right position, and the guy banged on the canopy again and shouted, *"Schnell!"* Hurry up. That was the first time I heard German spoken on the ground in Germany. *"Schnell! Schnell!"*

I knew what it meant because Mother and Grampa say it when they want the kids to hurry. Grampa is very Dutch. We say we are Pennsylvania Dutch, but we are not Dutch. The word is just American for *Deutsch*; it means "German" in German. I am Pennsylvania German. "All men are created equal." *We are all the same.*

I got the sliding hood open, and the man on the wing yanked the canopy back. He gestured with his gun—*get out of the plane.* I still couldn't get the door open and had to climb out the open hood, trying to keep my hands up and my skirt down and not fall off the wing at the same time.

It is a pain in the neck climbing in and out of a Spitfire in a skirt.

In a million years, I bet, those German airmen would not have guessed a girl was going to climb out of that plane. They must have thought all along that they'd captured an RAF reconnaissance pilot taking pictures or on his way to suss out German airfields full of jet-powered Swallows so we could bomb them. Someone doing something secret and interesting. And here I turned out to be a boring old transport pilot—and a *girl.*

I stood on the wing with my hands up. They all backed away respectfully, their mouths open.

Somebody started to clap. Then they all joined in—a brief burst of applause for the perfect landing. The guy with the gun suddenly stuck it back in his holster, jumped to the ground, and held out a hand to help me down. He mimed taking my flying helmet off, so I did, and the curls came tumbling down. I was a mess, with my hair sticking out in all directions and my eyes all red—I'd spent a lot of the last hour sobbing to myself. One of the mechanics respectfully whipped off his cap.

The man who had the gun gave an order, and somebody climbed up to the cockpit to get all my stuff, my parachute and maps and flight bag. They let me take off my life jacket, too, and someone took it from me so I didn't have to carry it. Then we all trudged across the airfield, everybody muttering and whispering to each other, till we got to a crop of concrete buildings and temporary hangars, all draped top to bottom in camouflage. The gunman took me to an office and pulled out a chair for me. Then he dug into the pocket of his tunic and pulled out a *mirror and a tortoiseshell comb*. And he gave them to me and made a little bow and left the room.

For a moment I started giggling hysterically. A mirror and comb!

You know, it was like putting on armor. I combed my hair, and then I realized how awful my face looked, so I dug out a handkerchief—it was one of the ones Aunt Rainy embroidered for me, with a rose in the corner—and I wiped my eyes and then spit on the hanky and scrubbed at my face, and then I dug out a lipstick and did my lips and faked some color in my cheeks, and then I felt better. Less pathetic, more grown-up. On one wall of the office was a huge map of France and Germany and the Low Countries. I sat staring at it, finding the names of cities I'd heard of, and plotting course headings from each of these cities to Paris. It was better than thinking about what was going to happen next.

Someone came in and gave me a cup of fake coffee and something a lot like a bologna sandwich, which I would have eaten if I had realized it was the last bologna sandwich I was ever going to see. But I just couldn't eat. I have had dreams about that sandwich.

After a while people began to file into the office and filled it up. One was a Luftwaffe interrogator, I think, but he didn't talk to me directly. The man who talked to me was just another pilot. They got him to come in because he spoke very good English. There was also a girl in uniform who took notes.

The first thing they did was spread my passport and license and authorization card across the steel desk and then dump out my confiscated Camp LA groceries next to the ID. The translator made a sweeping gesture at the pile of Hershey bars. He said seriously, "You see, you are in a lot of trouble."

I had to clamp a hand over my mouth. It was all I could do not to fall apart with hysteria—it was so funny! Terrible, but *so funny.* What were they accusing me of—chocolate smuggling?

I nodded mutely, because really I did agree with him—I knew I was in trouble. But I had to gulp back squeaks of hilarity. The way he pointed to that candy! He was about Daddy's age—tired-looking, tall and thin, with a wide mouth and a nice smile. He looked like the fire chief in Conewago Grove. He sat across from me, peering earnestly into my face with his hands on his knees, as though he were cross-examining his own daughter over something that had disappointed him.

"You are American?"

I could only nod. I didn't trust myself to try to talk.

"In a British plane?"

"I am—" I got the hysterics under control and sat on my hands to keep them away from my mouth.

"Why is an American flying a British plane?" the translator asked patiently.

"I was—I was only delivering it," I squeaked.

"You are a courier?" the translator asked.

I nodded, because I thought he meant "delivery girl"—then immediately panicked and shook my head violently to take it back. Aren't couriers some kind of intelligence agents?

"No—no! I'm a ferry pilot. Air Transport Auxiliary—I deliver planes for the Royal Air Force."

"What variety is your Spitfire?"

"Mark Fourteen."

The translator looked over his shoulder at the others and told them what I'd said, and they all nodded and muttered to one another. Then the translator asked me, "The plane has a radio device?"

"Yes—"

The stenographer looked up sharply. She stared at me with a face full of awe and suspicion, as though she wanted to see what kind of person would have the gall to fly a plane equipped with a "radio device." I don't know how much English she understood, but she must have understood everything the interrogator and the translator had just said to each other.

What were they after? Maybe they didn't mean a radio. Maybe "radio device" was an attempt to translate something else. I asked, "Do you mean radar?" Radar would make it a surveillance aircraft—a spy plane. And suddenly I was more frightened than I'd been before.

"I mean, no! There's no radar on that plane—"

I stopped abruptly, shaking my head and sucking in a gasp of air. *I didn't know* if there was a radar set on that plane. I didn't think there was—I knew the real thing takes up a lot of space, but I wasn't *sure*. That Spitfire was new this year and was about to be modified for reconnaissance.

"I don't know!"

"You were orbiting when you were intercepted—why? Taking pictures?"

"No! There's no radar and no cameras—I don't think there are—"

I didn't know that, either. I didn't know anything about what that plane might be carrying in its wings, other than fuel—cameras, cannon, spy equipment, plastic explosive—who knows? I don't *think* there was anything like that on board, but who knows?

It just went downhill from there—everybody as polite as possible, and me not knowing the answer to anything they asked me. "But I was in France!" I pointed out miserably. "I wasn't even over your territory!"

"It was ours last week," the translator said calmly.

None of this actually took very long. All the administration was done that day—the telephone calls after they finished questioning me, and the decision from some command center in Berlin, and the paperwork—all magically completed in less than two hours. I don't think the Luftwaffe pilots knew where I'd end up. They just did what they were told to do with me.

The translator was a transport pilot, too. He was delivering a small communications aircraft to its new home base. It wasn't far from a place where they held a lot of women who were political prisoners, and I was supposed to go along with him so he could drop me there.

The little plane looked like a flying lawnmower with awnings. "It is a Storch," the pilot told me. "Fieseler Fi-156. Stork, in English. Bird with long legs!"

I tried to smile at the lame joke.

"Don't be frightened. You will be safe where they send you. The papers we have given you state that you are a transport pilot and that you were intercepted without weapons—you will have to remain in custody here, but you will be fed and clothed and housed—" He hesitated a little. "And given work to do. They will find work for you at a skilled level. Don't lose the written statement our commander gave you—it explains how you came here, and it is important that you show the Luftwaffe stamp and signature, for you won't always be able to find another English speaker as fluent as I to give you assistance!"

We finished the outside aircraft checks, and the pilot opened the door for me to climb into the rear seat.

"I am Oberleutnant Karl Womelsdorff," he said.

"I am Third Officer Rose Justice," I told him. "My little brother is named Karl, too."

"Why this German name for an American boy?"

"My mother's family is from Germany," I said. "Two hundred years ago they came to America from right around here, from Pfaltz. A lot of people in Pennsylvania come from southwest Germany."

Oberleutnant Karl Womelsdorff glanced at me with a tight, sad smile as he climbed into the pilot's seat ahead of me.

"Now you are back," he said.

Holy smoke, that plane. How did I ever fly that plane?

"You will fly the Storch," Oberleutnant Womelsdorff told me. I don't think he meant it to sound so much like a command. It was a present, a wonderful secret between us, one pilot to another, and a very generous present, too, considering I was a prisoner of war or whatever.

Compared with the morning's high-speed chase in the Spitfire it was like being on a bicycle. We didn't go very high, staying out of the way of planes that might be faster than us—or planes that might try to shoot us down. It was a mercy to be flying, to be focused on the unfamiliar aircraft and the heading and being too close for comfort to the treetops and just to be in control.

In the officers' restroom at Köthen, where we stopped to refuel, I sat with my head against my knees and cried for five minutes. It was like digging myself deeper and deeper into a pit that I'd never be able to climb out of. I was halfway across Germany now and I still didn't know where I was going to end up.

When we took off from Köthen, Womelsdorff let me sit in the front.

"What if someone sees me in the pilot's seat when we land? Won't you be in trouble?"

He shrugged and laughed. "Why should I be, if we land in the right place? We'll say you are the American cousin of Hanna Reitsch. You know of Hanna Reitsch? Germany's most daring test pilot is a woman! As long as there are two of us in the plane they will not accuse me of wasting fuel we do not have." I didn't dare to answer. I am pretty sure he wasn't supposed to tell me that the Luftwaffe is low on fuel.

The last stage of the trip was cloudier and bumpier, and Womelsdorff made me stay even lower, to avoid being *bombed*. Once we saw a flight of Allied aircraft crossing the sky ahead of us—high, dozens of them, steady black spots speckling the clouds like a swarm of gnats—heading, no doubt, for Berlin.

We puttered along far below them, slow and out of sight against the ground.

"Daylight raid," commented my guard and guide. "Is this arrogance or desperation?"

I didn't answer. I didn't know. But now I think the answer wasn't either of those—it was really just *persistence. Persistence* is what kept me alive all winter. And persistence will win the war.

Half an hour south of Neubrandenburg we flew almost directly over a pretty town surrounded by serene lakes. We were so low over the biggest lake I could see the reflection of our wings below us in its glassy surface. On the far side of the lake was a gigantic complex of long sheds and wide-open gritted yards, all in the middle of a complicated railway junction—everything surrounded by concrete walls and what looked like miles and miles of wire fences.

"What's that?"

"Fürstenberg industrial area," Womelsdorff answered. "You'll only ever see it from the air—the maps show only the town and the lakes. What they make there is a state secret. Impossible to miss from the air, so it makes an excellent pin-point. That is a pilot's secret."

It was my first sight of Ravensbrück.

I saw it for the first time from the air. I have spent a long time—mostly during roll calls—trying to put together my first view of it from a thousand feet overhead with the view from the parade ground in front of Block 32. I just can't justify in my head that I must have been looking at the same sky in both places. From the air it was forbidding but not menacing. It looked sterile. It was just a place. It didn't even look inhabited—of course, it was the middle of the afternoon and everyone must have been at work, so the grounds were relatively empty.

I wish I'd known—I wish I could remember the detail of what it looked like from the air. Was there smoke coming from the crematorium chimney? Were they loading or unloading transports? Was a train arriving? It was so still, so empty, so impersonal—so distant. It was an ordinary industrial site in the middle of an ordinary day. It didn't mean anything to me, it wasn't significant or ominous, and the detail is gone. A pilot's pinpoint. That's all.

April 18, 1945
Paris

I shocked the chambermaid. Or whatever they are called in France! I forgot to hang the DO NOT DISTURB sign on the door—NE PAS DÉRANGER—and she came in a while ago to make the bed and clean the bathroom. I was sitting at the little vanity table, which I'd pulled over so it is in front of the big window, and I was writing with not a stitch on. I did have that incredible silk bedspread thing wrapped around me, but it slipped right off when I turned around to see who had come in.

Oh, God, we were both SO EMBARRASSED. I look like a corpse. The Red Cross did a good job of delousing me and getting the scabies under control, but you can still see the rashes all over my breasts and arms, and if those scales and Bob Ernst's metric conversion are right, I have lost 45 pounds in the last seven months. (Amazing, because I am still heavier than Irina, who is taller than me. But she was there longer.) I saw myself in the mirror over the dresser when I was taking my clothes off yesterday, and I am so horrible I had to cover the stupid mirror with a sheet so I don't scare myself by accident.

"Come back! Come back!" I mewed pathetically after the chambermaid as she backed out—I got the right word in French but used the familiar form by accident because we did all winter ("*Reviens!*")—trying to pull the bedspread up and to remember how to say "Don't go" politely. She left anyway, shutting the door softly behind her, and I put my head down on the table and cried. I am *so lonely.* I should get dressed and go back to the embassy and see if I can find some way to get back to the Swedish Red Cross people. But I don't even know their unit name or number or where they were headed next. "Sweden" is not very specific.

The chambermaid came back ten minutes later with coffee and rolls for me on a silver tray. Real coffee. She plunked it down on the vanity table and told me her name and rushed away to make the bed.

Her name is Fernande. She doesn't speak English. She is busy with the bed now—she has even brought up a new spread so I can stay wrapped in this one. She hasn't started on the bathroom and *that* will take her some time, because the one thing I did do last night was take a two-hour bath in that gigantic tub. The only reason I didn't make it last longer is because they shut the hot water off at nine p.m. I am going to write as fast as I can while she's here. I've been putting off remembering what that night on the ground was like, and I don't want to think about it when I'm by myself.

They let me use the pilots' restroom at Neubrandenburg also, but they took away all my pilot's gear except my flight bag. Womelsdorff turned me over to a grouchy mechanic, who took me on the back of his motorbike to this so-called women's prison. There *is* a women's prison camp outside Neubrandenburg—it is one of the Ravensbrück satellite camps. But you were supposed to be processed through the main Camp first. I was in the wrong place, I wasn't on their radar, and they didn't know what to do with me when the mechanic turned me over to them.

I remember standing uncomfortably in a drab office somewhere, standing very straight and trying to look more official than I felt—I'd even slapped my uniform cap back on when I handed them my papers. They passed my papers around and argued for half an hour while I just stood there waiting. Then, as it was getting dark, they took me outside at gunpoint and locked me in the back of an empty armored truck. I had no idea I was in the wrong place—I had no idea why they'd put me in the truck (for a few horrible minutes I thought they were just going to shoot me right there). I didn't understand anything anyone said. I know *now* what was going on—I know that the truck was just an empty transport and was returning to Ravensbrück the next day for another load of prisoners, and that they were going to drop me off before loading up again.

But that night—

Oh, God, that truck smelled *so horrible.* If there is a smell that goes with fear and despair, it is like that—sweat and dirty underpants and pee. I was already retching as they slammed the doors shut on me, and for a long time I just stood in the middle of the truck, hugging myself and gagging.

There was no light. I braced myself in the dark because I thought they were going to take me somewhere any minute, and the truck would lurch into action and I'd fall over and have to touch whatever was on the evil floor. But nothing happened. Then I tried to get out, struggling with the doors until all my nails were broken—the sheets of metal interlocked and there wasn't even a crack to feel air through. Near the front of the truck there were slatted air vents high up in the walls, but even if I'd been able to get the slats out, the opening was smaller than my head. Eventually I was so tired that I gritted my teeth and leaned in the corner below one of the air vents, where two walls propped me so I could still stand up. Then later I had to sit down.

Fernande is still here. She's in the bathroom now. I couldn't write about this if I was alone.

I took off my flying jacket and tucked up the edges carefully, so that only the leather of the back was touching the floor, and sat on that. It wasn't very cold yet—still early September.

After a while I opened up my flight bag to count the papers that I'd handed over earlier and then shoved back in without looking—checking to feel that I still had my precious official letter of recommendation from the Luftwaffe, with its stamps and signatures—and beneath the pile of papers I found, mysteriously, two of my confiscated Hershey bars.

I am sure that Womelsdorff put them there.

I was starved enough to eat one, even in the grim stench of the transport truck—I didn't dare eat both, because I didn't know how long I'd be there. Finally I curled in my supportive corner as tightly as I could on the protective island of my flying jacket. I buried my nose in the silver paper that the chocolate had been wrapped in, sucking in the distant smell of Hershey and home to mask the stink, and managed to go to sleep.

I got woken up by the engine starting. Through the air vents high in the walls I could see that it was light. No one looked inside to see if I was even alive—I have always thought the truck driver didn't actually know I was there.

We drove for about an hour and I couldn't even tell what direction we were heading or how fast we were going. After the truck parked and the engine stopped, I sat in the dark for *another* hour. I didn't know it, but the truck had gone through the gate. I was already inside.

I ate the last chocolate bar. We'd both traveled from the same place, me and that Hershey bar—I thought how incredible it was that we both ended up here together. I heard long, slow trains steaming and clunking past a short distance away, a comforting sound, like the freight line that goes past the Lake at Conewago Grove. I heard other trucks coming and going, and orders shouted in German. I heard the siren and nearly jumped out of my skin.

We called it "The Screamer." The first time I heard it I thought there must be an air raid going on. I scrunched myself up in a ball with my arms over my head—of course, nothing happened. The next thing I heard, twenty minutes later, was the sound of hundreds of feet shuffling along at a weary jog and a lot of shouting and dogs barking. I felt my way to the doors to try again to find a crack, to see out.

Then someone opened the doors. I clapped my hands over my eyes and stood teetering on the edge of the truck floor, completely blinded by sunny September brilliance. They didn't give me five seconds. I hadn't even opened my eyes before someone grabbed my skirt and yanked me off balance, and I crashed full length onto the cindered road surface. The fall took the skin right off both my knees and off the heels of both hands, too. I rolled over and sat up, furious and stunned, rubbing my eyes with shaking, bloody hands. Within seconds I was surrounded by half a dozen frantic German shepherds straining at the end of their leashes, all barking their heads off while half a dozen voices behind them barked equally vicious and completely incomprehensible orders over my head.

I just cowered.

Finally, since obviously I wasn't going to obey an order I didn't have a hope of understanding, someone grabbed me by the back of my collar and hauled me to my feet. I ended up being dragged to stand in the back of a long line of women who all looked as bewildered and stunned as I was. They seemed to be civilians, most of them carrying small bags and suitcases. There must have been nearly four hundred of us— all packed five to a row, and I was the last one in the last row.

You know how you look around a new place to see what

it's like? I didn't do that right away, because my hands and knees were so sore. I bent down to look at my knees and cursed, *"Gosh darn it!"* when I saw the humongous bloody holes in my stockings. "Gosh darn it, these are *nylon!"*

You know, it almost makes me laugh to write about it. What was the first thing you worried about when you found yourself a prisoner in a Nazi concentration camp, Rosie? Gosh darn it, holes in my nylon hose!

One of the guards yanked me upright again, by my hair this time, and that is when I lost my cap, because they would not let me pick it up. I never saw it again.

We stood there until after it got dark.

I think it must have been six or seven hours. They weren't punishing us that first day; I think they were just disorganized and there wasn't any other place to put us yet. So we had to stand there, trying not to die of fear or boredom. But it was the first time. That made it harder.

This is what I thought about while I waited:

The walls. Twenty feet high and fenced with electric wire and skull-and-crossbones warning signs. There were a lot of empty trucks parked around us, but you could see the walls behind them. I still hadn't figured out I was *inside* these walls—it was because I'd been locked blindly in the truck when I came through the gate. I kept looking at the walls and thinking, Gosh, I hope I don't end up in *there*, whatever it is. Dreading that I probably would, and blissfully unaware that I already *was.*

The sky. It was the most pure, beautiful blue September sky I think I have ever seen, with frothy clouds floating in it lazily like whipped cream in an ice-cream soda at the Hide-a-way Fountain in Conewago Grove. We stood there so long you could pick out a single cloud and watch it travel right from one side of the sky to the other—and then do it again.

And again. You could see a ridge of pine trees behind one of the walls, too, but the trees just stood there—they were boring to watch. The sky changed.

And then the women who were going to Neubrandenburg came marching past us, five by five by five, to get into the row of waiting trucks.

Those two hundred women had all been turned into drones. They were like rows of plastic dolls. They all wore tattered, grubby dresses that didn't fit (I don't think any one of the forty or fifty thousand people in that whole damn Camp had a dress that fit her)—and there were great big crosses cut out of the fabric across the front and back of their chests and filled in with some contrasting color. They weren't prison uniforms, but they looked like prison uniforms anyway. But the absolutely nightmare thing about these women was that none of them had any hair. We watched and stared as these scruffy, bald zombies were herded into the waiting trucks, packed so close they couldn't even sit down—now I knew why that truck smelled the way it did.

Suddenly, at exactly the same moment, me and the girl next to me turned to stare at each other instead of at the awful robot women. We were looking at each other's hair and thinking the same thing.

After that, we stopped watching the other prisoners climbing into the trucks. We just stared at the long hair of the woman in front of us, thick and brown and uncombed, and full of tangled curls, like mine.

It got hot. By midafternoon, my blouse was sticking to my back, but the guards kept patrolling up and down the lines and whacking people who tried to sit down or talk, and I didn't dare to try to take my tunic off. I hadn't had anything to drink or been to the toilet since I landed in

Neubrandenburg the day before, and I'd eaten only chocolate since then; pretty soon I became consumed by thirst
more than anything else. In my wildest nightmares I'd never
imagined such simple torture—just to have to stand in one
place forever and ever.

I don't remember being scared anymore at that point.
I was just sick of standing there and desperate for a glass of
water.

Late in the afternoon the girl standing next to me whispered something without turning her head.

"*Vous êtes un pilote?*"—You're a pilot?

I didn't answer for a long time, checking around us for
guards and guard dogs without moving my head. Then,
"*Oui*," I answered, also in a whisper. Yes.

I stole a glance at her. She was short and pretty, with
untidy gold bangs that got in her eyes, and a long, shiny scar
down one side of her face. This was the first conversation
I ever had with a French person in real life who wasn't my
French teacher—and also it was the first time I understood
anything since Womelsdorff handed me over to the guy with
the motorbike the day before. I had a pretty good idea what
would happen if anyone noticed us whispering. But it was
such a relief to be able to talk to someone.

She whispered, "*Vous êtes anglaise?*" Are you English?

"*Américaine.*"

"What are you doing here?" she asked in French.

"*Je ne sais pas*," I hissed. "I don't know. You?"

"We all come from different prisons," she told me.
"Arrested for Resistance activity—most of us are *Résistantes*.
I've been in prison for nine months."

I was confused, because if she'd already been in prison
for nearly a year, why was she here now?

"Where are we?"

She shrugged. "Probably Ravensbrück. It's their big women's concentration camp. They move us all the time—away from the Allied armies as they advance. I was in prison in Paris until May, then moved to Frankfurt, then to Berlin. Now here."

Her name was Elodie Fabert.

You know, *concentration camp* translates pretty clearly in French—even in German. *Camp de concentration. Konzentrationslager.* But even though I knew what the words meant, it didn't mean anything then. Not really. The name of the place didn't mean anything to me. Over the heads of the four hundred Frenchwomen ahead of me I stared at the high concrete walls and the miles of electrified barbed wire, and I clung to my flight bag with its official Luftwaffe letter in it. The girl next to me had already been in prison for nine months and she obviously survived it. Our troops were practically over the Siegfried Line. It wouldn't be for long. I wouldn't cause trouble. I would be all right. If they ever let us sit down and have a drink, I would be all right.

The chambermaid has left. It's okay—it was just being alone in the truck I didn't like remembering by myself. Reading it over, I noticed that I didn't actually write down what I kept thinking then: *What if no one ever opens that door?* I'm done with it now—dry words on a page. The reality was much worse.

Also, I didn't write that most of the SS people guarding us were women, too. When I read over the part about being dragged out of the truck and into line, it sounded like it was a man doing it, taking advantage of a poor, dazed female. But it wasn't—it was a girl not much older than me and a couple of inches shorter. She probably wasn't any stronger, either. She was just *meaner.*

I asked Fernande to ask someone to send me some more ink. I know I won't ever catch up with that Red Cross unit. Now that I've glided down, I haven't got enough lift to get airborne again. I don't have any clothes, and I still have this exhausting, rib-cracking cough. If I stand looking out the window for more than ten minutes, I get so tired I have to sit down. Out of an entire hotel menu, I can't keep down anything more exciting than unsweetened rice pudding or boiled macaroni with nothing on it. I *want* to go back out there. But I just can't do anything more energetic than write or sleep, and even sleeping is exhausting. I tried to take a nap and dreamed I was sleeping alone in our barrack, with an icy wind howling through the broken windows, and everybody else had been gassed.

Which is probably a nightmare based on the fact that I *am* alone, and it's my own fault. All I can do is pray Irina takes care of our stubborn little Róża. How how *how* did I lose them *both*, when we were already *out*?

When the six p.m. siren let out its piercing howl, we nearly jumped out of our skin.

We had all fallen into a stupor of exhaustion and misery, and you could see a ripple of attention race through our ranks as the noise shocked us wide awake. Not long after that, they finally fed us. They did it outside, right where we were standing—like CAMP, hah. First they let us help ourselves to water from a row of spigots by the main gate, after about a year of standing in line to get there, and then they brought out two big oil drums of soup. It was absolutely chaotic— seemed chaotic, anyway, the first time, four hundred of us trying to get at two pots all at once. We had about one bowl between four of us to take turns with, which they took away again when we were done, since we hadn't yet been issued *official* bowls of our own. You had to carry your bowl around with you all the time in a little bag or someone would steal it and then you wouldn't get any soup. No bowl, no soup. Of all the unbelievable things about Ravensbrück, I think the Administration and Politics of Bowls must have been the battiest.

Now it just seems incredible that we got something to eat that day. We all got some soup, and we all got a piece of bread, and we ate it standing up. I ate mine, but I don't remember anything about it. I don't remember what the soup was—I mean, you never really knew what it was, but I don't remember it being the worst soup I'd ever eaten. I do remember that I couldn't eat the biggest chunks of whatever mystery root vegetable was in it, because they were completely raw. Inside a month I wouldn't care, but what did I know at that point?

What I remember *most* about that first meal there are the filthy, crawling skeletal beggars who fought over the raw chunks of potato or turnip or whatever it was in the soup that I couldn't make myself eat. There was a Camp word for those beggars, which I never did figure out how to say or spell, because it sounds so much to me like *schmootzich*—Mother's nasty way of describing a girl who doesn't take care of herself. It's Pennsylvania Dutch for "filthy greasy."

They took any food you gave them. The first day, because I was still ignorant enough to be picky about what I ate, I tried to hand over my leftover chunks of raw vegetable to one of these desperate people. In seconds I was being clawed at by ten skeletal hands, grabbing at me anywhere they could to try to get in on the handout—five crawling creatures who had once been women snatching at my skirt, my arms, my hair. One of the guards had to beat them off. It left me shaking with shock. I never dared that kind of charity again.

You could drop a bread crust on the ground and the *schmootzichs* would fight over it. If you dropped a bread crust and stepped on it, or a guard spat on it, they still fought over it. They were like *seagulls*. Like seagulls going after garbage. They were so far from being human that at first it didn't even occur to me they could be fellow prisoners—I thought they must be hoboes who'd crawled in off the train tracks. *God knows what I thought!* Your brain does amazing acrobatics when it doesn't want to believe something.

After we ate, the guards pointed us in the direction of a ditch we could use for a latrine. I kept telling myself, it's like *camp*. It's a camp; I'm at camp.

God knows what I thought I was telling myself.

We got herded into a harshly lit factory shed to be registered and examined and given prison clothes. Elodie and I were somehow always the last in line, and by the time our turn came for *anything* we got the absolute worst of it. But on the other hand, by the time you'd stood in line for an hour or three or four, you knew what was going on. We were able to do a lot more whispering in the administration building than we'd been able to do standing under guard all afternoon, and most information was highly refined by the time it reached me and Elodie. We knew before we got to the line of desks where they processed us that, like all new prisoners, we were in "quarantine"—being "decontaminated" to prevent the spread of typhoid. That sounded plausible, and a good thing, but it was clearly a complete joke—the *schmootzichs* had had their filthy oozing hands all over us.

My ATA pilot's uniform was like a rallying flag. Everybody was ravenously starved for encouraging news from the Front, and only one day ago I'd been a free woman flying over a free Paris. "Caen is ours," I whispered. "And Brussels and Antwerp, and Le Havre just yesterday! I heard before I took off! We're past Reims in France now. We've got most of France and a big part of Belgium. The push is north to Holland and west to the German border. We haven't got all the French ports—we're still fighting for Boulogne, but it'll be any day. And the Luftwaffe—"

Womelsdorff had been cursing his own military for wasting resources.

"They've got spectacular new jets, but no fuel."

People relayed the news to one another in nearly silent whispers. The guards wouldn't let us talk, but they couldn't keep their eyes on all four hundred of us at once. The news flew around the hall.

Other prisoners were already packing everybody's things up and carting them away to be sorted by the time I had to dump out my flight bag on one of the dozens of administrators' desks lined up across the shed. I bit my lip, my stomach churning with worry while the administrator squinted at my papers, because I knew they were going to keep my passport and Luftwaffe letter of reference and leave me without any ID except for whatever they assigned me.

Finally the administrator called someone else over—both of them SS guards, both of them women, maybe five years older than me. They talked to each other in German, studying my American passport. One of them rolled her eyes at the other and made a face. She'd noticed my middle name—Rose Moyer Justice. The other glanced at me, pointed at her friend, and told me drily, *"Das ist Effi Moyer."*

Effi Moyer wasn't happy about it at all. She grabbed hold of the lapel of my tunic and gave it a demanding yank. I took the tunic off and handed it to her. She started to go through my pockets with brisk efficiency and found the wrappers from my chocolate bars.

I'd folded the silver foil and brown paper very carefully, wrapped it in my rose hanky from Aunt Rainy, and pushed it deep into the corner of my tunic pocket. I wanted to keep it because it smelled so overwhelmingly of Pennsylvania, of home, of flying over Hershey and the fields of Jericho County.

When Effi Moyer found the brown-and-silver paper folded up so carefully, she passed it to her friend—they both unfolded the scraps with deep and interested suspicion, as though they expected lumps of gold to drop out. Effi held the silver foil up to her nose exactly the way I'd done in the truck the night before and took a deep breath.

"Schokolade," she said, and passed the empty candy wrapper to her colleague, who also took a deep breath.

They made a fierce, disappointing search through the

rest of my pockets and checked my bag again, and then they divided up the paper between them—each of them got one full wrapper.

I watched the whole performance biting my lip, trying to kill another terrible, *terrible* urge to laugh. And also feeling a new kind of fear taking hold of my stomach and tying it in knots. These were the *prison guards* confiscating my empty candy bar wrappers as if they were hundred-dollar bills. If that's how hard up the *guards* were . . .

Effi tossed my tunic to the woman standing a couple of desks down from her, and it got lost in the pile of hundreds of other abandoned jackets and blouses and skirts. Then I had to take off the rest of my clothes. It wouldn't have been so bad if you didn't have to do it in front of men, too—SS officers and guards who were directing and pushing people and just standing around watching. But everyone else had already had to strip. I was the last.

There was a little office room like a clinic where you had to sit on a table while a couple of people in rubber gloves put you through an unspeakable body search with tongue depressors and a flashlight. When they were done with the search, Effi barked an order at the doctors or whatever they were, and I had to sit backward on a chair (holding on to the back of it) while they sheared my hair off. They really did *shear* it—with scissors up against my scalp, not close enough to my head to count as shaving it off, but so close there was nothing left. If I were going to do that to anyone, I'd time it that way, too—addle her brain with shame and discomfort and then quickly get her hair before she came to her senses. The shock of losing my hair didn't hit me till later. The tongue depressors and flashlights seemed much more terrible at the time—even though that only lasted a couple of minutes, and I was stuck with my hair. Without it, I mean.

Finally I got smacked on my bare backside with someone's clipboard because I hesitated going into the slimy, dark shower room.

Nothing that happened to me that day made me cry. Some of it scared me, but most of it just made me SO MAD.

I'd lost Elodie. The room with the showers was badly lit and murky with mildew—it reminded me of the abandoned bathhouse by the old pool at Conewago Park that they haven't used since before the Great War. Me and the other summer kids used to explore all the old park buildings, but not the bathhouse—it was just too creepy. Here in Ravensbrück, I hesitated in the doorway, smarting but unable to take another step over the slimy red clay tiles toward those black trickling overhead spigots and the dozens of white, skinny, bald women shivering beneath them.

"*La pilote américaine! Mon amie américaine!*"

"*Ici!*" I yelled. "Here!"

Elodie and I got slapped simultaneously on opposite sides of the shower room. But I knew where she was now, and we managed to get back together.

The guards were trying hard to get everybody done with—it was dark, it was late, they were sick of us—and finally they shoved a couple of prison dresses at Elodie and me, and we had to put them on while we were still wet. Her dress came down to her ankles and mine was too tight. Someone threw shoes at us. Between us there was one each that fit—none of them matched. No stockings, no bra, no underwear of any kind.

Back in the long factory room with the prison dresses sticking to our wet backs, we had to pick up patches with our prisoner numbers on them, along with another patch that was supposed to show what kind of prisoner you were—all red triangles for us, which meant we were political prisoners.

Then we had to learn to say our numbers in German. I remembered my number—that wasn't the trouble. After all, when I was two, Grampa taught me how to count to twenty in Dutch, or Low German, or whatever it really is. The trouble was that when Effi Moyer tried to teach me how to say my number, I tried to tell her I wasn't French.

"*Französisch politischer Häftling Einundfünfzigtausendvier-hundertachtundneunzig,*" she prompted me. French Political Prisoner 51498.

Remembering what the Luftwaffe pilots had called me when they were arguing over my papers in Mannheim, I said to Effi, "*Ich bin Amerikanerin.*" I pointed to the others and pointed to myself and shook my head. "I'm not French. *Amerikanerin.*"

Effi looked me in the eye with a face full of disdain and irritation and said, "*Französisch politischer Häftling Einundfünfzig-tausendvierhundertachtundneunzig*"—and honestly my German has not improved very much, but I *know* that is what she said because my name was *Französisch politischer Häftling 51498* for six months.

I repeated the numbers. But not the "French Political Prisoner" part, because I wasn't French. I was *trying* to behave myself. Effi just glared at me and started to put away the ledgers, ignoring me, and I turned away to find Elodie waiting for me with her mouth twisted into a sort of imitation of a grin. She tossed back the golden bangs—she'd managed to keep her hair, presumably because she was such an Aryan blonde—and gestured quickly at our badly fitting dresses with one finger. *Swap you.*

We started to strip the dresses off again, right there. We didn't think anyone would care, because everyone ahead of us was being made to strip again so we could sew the red patches and our prisoner numbers onto our sleeves. But I hadn't counted on Effi Moyer. She'd *noticed* me. I was the embarrassing prisoner who shared her name, the one who'd failed to save her a Hershey bar, the one who'd argued with her about being American.

Effi saw me and Elodie about to swap our dresses, and she came marching over to us and grabbed them away from us. Then she grabbed Elodie by her hair, close to her scalp, and dragged her over to sit down on the floor right next to the desk. Effi jerked one arm fiercely in my direction to tell me to follow Elodie—she wanted to keep an eye on us both as we sewed on our patches.

Elodie suddenly seemed totally cowed. Stark naked, she hunched over the dress, covering her lap with it; her shoulders shook a little as if she were sobbing. She didn't make a sound, though. I sat next to her biting my lip, helpless with feeling so humiliated and *so mad*. We had to wait for someone to pass us a needle, and when we got one Elodie dropped it. Then she couldn't find the patch with her number on it after she'd threaded the needle. We scrambled around hunting for it, and both of us got whacked over the head with one of Effi Moyer's clipboards. Then, when it was my turn to use the needle, I couldn't find *my* number.

Elodie had it. She handed me the patch quietly, and her mouth twisted in a quick little grin. The scar on the side of her face made her pretty smile lopsided.

It wasn't till I was sewing it on my sleeve that I realized she'd swapped our numbers. All the shuffling around had all been a show to distract Effi Moyer from Elodie's sleight of hand. She'd sewn my 51498 onto the sleeve of her pale blue shirtwaisted sailor dress with the too-long skirt that came down to her ankles, its big collar ripped off so that it wouldn't hide the contrasting prison X across the front and back of the bodice. And now I sewed Elodie's 51497 onto my too-tight brown gingham. Effi Moyer had been so busy making sure we put on the dumb dresses we'd been "issued" with, she hadn't paid any attention to the numbers we'd sewn on the dresses.

We put our badly fitting clothes back on, wearing each other's numbers, and lined up in front of the quarantine block to be counted.

The siren for the nine o'clock roll call had come and gone, and thousands of other prisoners had already gone to bed, but for us it was our first real roll call—Zählappell—outside beneath the glaring electric lights, the long shadows of the dogs and the infinite rows of barbed wire making eerie pictures on the high concrete walls. It seemed to take forever. We stood there until after they turned the streetlights out, the SS guards shining flashlights in our faces and making sure we didn't try to sit down.

Elodie and I were still the last two in our group, so by the time they got to us, the guards were utterly fed up with everybody and ready to go to bed, too, and here we were, the last two "French" women with our numbers the wrong way around.

"Fabert, *Einundfünfzigtausendvierhundertsiebenundneunzig!* Justice, *Einundfünfzigtausendvierhundertachtundneunzig!*"—Fabert, 51497! Justice, 51498! Somebody prodded Elodie's sleeve with a club.

"No, I'm Rose Justice!"

Two guards used their clubs to guide us out of line while a third stood hanging on for dear life to one of the awful German shepherds, and a fourth stood glaring down at her clipboard with its endless list of names, flashlight tucked under her arm and pencil in the other hand. Her hair was hanging in her eyes, and she looked incredibly grouchy. She didn't watch us at all. She couldn't have cared less what was going on. She was just waiting to get the stupid numbers to come out right.

They made us strip naked again.

They gave me three cracking truncheon wallops: in the stomach and on the small of my back and over my shoulders—the first blow made me bend over and the second knocked me to my knees, leaving my back wide open for the third. While I crouched there, gasping and reeling, they got out those dreaded shears and cut all of Elodie's golden hair off. I didn't have any hair to cut off, so I got beaten up instead.

When they'd finished battering and defacing us, one of them took Elodie's dress with my number on it and threw it at me, and then took my dress with Elodie's number on it and threw it at her. They made us get dressed again. And then they shoved us back in line and checked our numbers off the list—Fabert, 51497; Justice, 51498.

Elodie whispered, *"La victoire!"* Victory!

I was black and blue for a week, and Elodie had had to stand stark naked in the *Lagerstrasse*, the main Camp street, in the middle of the night and get her hair sheared off. But she was right—we'd beaten Effi Moyer. We were wearing the dresses that fit us, and our own numbers.

You know, if it had just gone on like that for six months, maybe it wouldn't have been so bad.

I hadn't seen *evil.* Or if I had, I didn't recognize it yet. I didn't realize they'd *made* the *schmootzichs.* All I'd seen in the guards were bad tempers and meanness. But not evil. Not horror. Not really. Only . . . you know, they were always so random about dealing out their meanness. I think the randomness should have tipped me off. It was *dark* when they beat me up and cut off Elodie's hair that night. They didn't even have the benefit of much of an audience. It wasn't humiliating; it was just vicious.

The randomness has left its mark. I am scared of anything arbitrary now—of anything that happens suddenly. I am scared of the telephone ringing. It rang this morning, when the embassy called to see if I was okay. I am scared of loud noises in the street. I am scared of dogs, and of talking to people for the first time. It is not a normal kind of being scared—the telephone made me burst into tears. A horse-drawn cart clattering by made me crouch behind the vanity table. It took me about an hour to get the courage to go into the embassy the other day—I just stood there against the wall outside the gate watching everybody else go in and out. I was scared of Fernande the first time she showed up.

I am not scared of this room, but I feel like a flea in a jewelry box. And I am utterly lost in the beautiful double bed, that's for sure.

The bunks in quarantine Block 8 were triple-deckers, bare boards two planks wide, one bug-infested straw mat about half an inch thick with a couple of grubby cotton blankets between four of us. It was a 100 percent improvement over where I'd slept the night before. Elodie and I clung to each other because it was the only way to avoid falling out. We were on a top tier, under the wooden roof and above the windows. I was hungry but not yet starving; my knees, shoulders, ribs, and back were incredibly sore; and I was exhausted but wide awake. I still wasn't really *scared*. I was just seething. So angry! This stupid fight over the dresses. I could have understood if they had a prison uniform they wanted us all to wear. They used to have one, ugly gray sacks with blue stripes—a lot of the women who'd been there awhile still wore them. If we'd all been wearing the same ugly uniform, I'd have understood. But why should we have to swap our own perfectly decent clothes for someone else's that didn't fit? What was the SS going to do with a hand-me-down Air

Transport Auxiliary uniform? I'd have been perfectly happy to let them sew a big X across my uniform if only they'd let me wear it. Or—not happy. But willing.

And our hair. Some of the girls were really upset about it. A couple of them, just after, didn't even try to cover up their privates when the guards grinned at them—they covered up their bald heads, as if this were the most shameful and embarrassing thing that had ever been done to them. I wasn't upset. I was *angry*, as mad as I was about everything else. There was one spiky patch on the side of my head where they didn't really cut it close enough. They cut it too close to Elodie's scalp, in the dark, and she had another nice, long, oozy red scrape to match the scar along her jaw.

What will Nick think when he sees me? I suddenly wondered. Nick *loves* my hair. Maybe it will grow out by the time I see him again. Oh, please let it grow out a *little* bit.

Down at the bottom of the bunk, my toes were still shiny with cherry-red nail varnish, which I'd put on for my last date with Nick. I noticed them in the shower.

Nobody said anything in the dark, but it wasn't silent. People rutched around trying to get comfortable, growling at each other, sighing, coughing, sobbing. I could hear the distant hum of generators or something—of course some of the workshops kept going all night, though I didn't know that then.

Suddenly, on the other side of the thin wooden barracks, an anonymous voice yelled out, "*Vive la France!*"

Instantly there was dead silence.

We were all frozen, holding our breaths, waiting for the lights to snap back on and the dogs to come back.

But nothing happened, and after another tense moment, half a dozen other anonymous voices answered in defiance: "*Vive la France! VIVE LA FRANCE!*"

Then another voice called out fiercely, in English, "*God bless America!*"

It wasn't me. It wasn't Elodie. I don't know who it was. But it was a battle cry. We were still at war and we were *soldiers* and we were *Allies*.

After that, everybody settled down.

It happened every single night I was in quarantine in Block 8. Last thing every night, some unseen voice would yell into the dark, "*Vive la France!*" and someone else would answer, "*God bless America!*"

It was never me. I was never brave enough. My accent would have given me away.

But it was brave of the others to do it for me.

The telephone rang again. I burst into tears again. But it just kept on ringing and ringing. They know I am here, and finally I thought that if I *didn't* answer it, they'd send someone up to make sure I wasn't drowned in the tub or something, and it would be worse having to open the door to a French bellhop—especially since I still haven't got dressed—than it would be talking on the phone to the English-speaking switchboard operator. So I answered and said "Hello" in my best imitation of Before-Ravensbrück-Rose-Justice.

It was Mother.

For a long time after we were connected, she just kept calling, "Rosie? Rosie?" as if she were hunting for me in the Conewago woods, and I was so dumbstruck to hear her voice that I didn't answer at first, which didn't help. Then, believe it or not, I did not burst into tears again. I just said, "Hello, Mother," very calmly, and lied and lied and lied.

I've been in a prison camp in Germany. Yes, a political prisoner. I landed in the wrong place and they wouldn't let me go back over the front lines. Yes, I'm okay. Uncle Roger has me staying in the Paris Ritz!

I talked about the wonderful silk quilt thing and the beautiful, big window and the ridiculous gigantic tub and room service.

"Didn't the Nazis take over the Ritz in Paris?"

"Yes, that's why it's in such beautiful condition! And"—I could talk about this safely, with real enthusiasm—"the Germans didn't bomb Paris at all. The German commander in charge of Paris was supposed to pound the city to pieces before he surrendered, and he refused to do it. Berlin told him to blow up all the monuments—the Eiffel Tower and

Notre Dame Cathedral and the Arc de Triomphe—and he *didn't*. And when I brought Uncle Roger to France last summer, I flew over the whole of the city and it was *just beautiful*."

Mother sighed.

"Oh, *Rosie*. It is *so good* to hear your voice."

She was crying—not me. I had fooled her.

She said, "I thought—we just thought you must have been shot down, of course. It seemed like the only thing that could have happened. Although—have you heard what they're finding now? There are some terrible stories. Have you heard about these concentration camps they say they're liberating? The Red Cross keeps coming up with people who say they've been freed from these awful places. We don't believe any of it for a second—those Jewish women who said they'd been—"

I didn't hear what happened or didn't happen to the Jewish women, because I held the receiver at arm's length until the distant, transatlantic twitter of Mother's voice went anxious and I could tell she was calling my name again.

I put the phone back to my ear.

"Hi, Mom."

"Oh!" she gasped in relief. "I thought I'd lost you."

Every spring, Mother makes us wash the house—actually hose down and scrub the outside of our house. She is probably doing it *now*, getting excited about me coming home. Our house is brick and is about fifty years old. There is a wide front porch with columns, and Daddy always gets up on the porch roof to do the second floor and the bedroom windows. Mother watches critically and directs everything from the front yard. I run back and forth from the kitchen, delivering buckets of warm, soapy water for Daddy; Karl and Kurt play with the hose until it's time to rinse all the soap off.

Afterward, the porch smells of pine soap and the windows are so clean they are just reflective slabs of blue sky.

How can I ever tell Mother about the filth? It wasn't plain old dirt. Dirt's easy to get rid of—you can rinse it away. It doesn't hurt you. The linoleum of our kitchen floor gets scrubbed with Clorox every two weeks. Mother would pick up a ball of pie dough off the kitchen linoleum if she dropped it, and shrug and slap it down on the pastry cloth on the dough tray, and laugh. "We're all going to eat a peck of dirt before we die."

I'm not talking about dirt. I'm not talking about a crumb of dust or a dog hair in the piecrust. I'm talking about more than fifty thousand women locked inside a cinder-and-concrete prison half a mile wide and a quarter of a mile across with no toilets. When I got there, there were three toilets that still worked in Block 8, although they were pretty horrible. There were four hundred of us using them and only one was still working by the time they sent me to the Siemens factory three weeks later or whatever it was. Most of us used the ditch outside.

By the middle of January even the ditches were full. For the last couple of months we went against the wall outside the building we lived in. There wasn't anyplace else to go, and most of us had dysentery or typhoid. You'd have to let it run down your legs if you needed to go during a roll call. How can I ever tell Mother? How can I ever tell her about the filth I have lived in all of last fall and winter and half this spring?

I can't tell her. I'll never tell her.

After one night in quarantine, we had so many fleabites it is a miracle we didn't all end up with bubonic plague. During that first four thirty a.m. roll call, all I wanted to do was scratch until I'd peeled my entire skin off. Why do they go for your ankles, which are the hardest part of your body to reach when you're pretending to stand at attention? Are fleas in league with the SS?

Quarantine was just about bearable. You knew it wouldn't last. Three weeks of Block 8, of overflowing toilets and fleas and eye-crossing boredom during the day, sitting there waiting for the quarantine to finish and not being allowed to talk to anybody, and then we would all get to move on.

If I'd known I'd never see Elodie again when it was done, I might not have been in such a rush to get it over with. I feel like I squandered my three weeks with Elodie by wasting the whole time eagerly looking ahead to some mythic improvement that never actually happened. But you can't blame us for *hoping*, can you? Doesn't hope keep you going? We'd stand in line swapping camp songs in French and English under our breath, and when we discovered we knew some of the same tunes, "Tallis Canon" and "By the Light of the Moon," our delight wasn't desperate—it was *real*. We should have had a chance to be *friends*.

Elodie was a natural organizer. I don't mean that in the normal English-language sense of people who can arrange things. I mean it in the Camp sense of magically being able to get hold of miraculous, hard-to-find, forbidden items like woolen scarves and soap and paper and cigarettes. She pulled stuff out of nowhere like a magician. She bartered with the *schmootzichs*. She bartered with the *guards*, and she had to get someone to translate for her when she did that. I watched her sometimes, trying to figure out how she did it, like it was a knack you could pick up. And it is, of course, but it came naturally to Elodie.

She got us toothbrushes and soap, needle and thread,

a collection of pencil stubs, a razor to sharpen them with. Underpants for me and socks to line her own mismatched shoes and a button to close the gap at the side of the dress she'd swapped with me. She organized *sanitary pads* for me. Most of the other people in our block didn't need them—they'd been in prison so long that malnourishment and fatigue and, I guess, just living with such an intensity of fear and distress had temporarily shut them down. I shut down eventually, too, thank God. But when I first started my period halfway through quarantine, Elodie was the one who scavenged bits of cotton blanket and jute ripped from the edges of the straw mattresses. With half a steel sewing-machine needle and thread unraveled from the ragged edge where the collar was missing on my own dress, we whipped together a small collection of primitive pads, uncomfortable but effective.

Elodie wasn't a leader. She'd been a courier in the French Resistance, delivering messages, doing as she was told. She was just really sneaky. She was the one who figured out that prisoners from other countries had a letter in their triangular ID patch showing what country they were from—Polish prisoners had a black *P* in their patches, Czechs a *T* for "Czech" in German. The French patches were blank—special humiliation for the French. So Elodie embroidered an *F* in her own red triangle. And *USA* in mine.

More dry words on a page. I wish I could capture *Elodie*, make her come alive again—small, scarred, sneaky, singing.

When I think of her—when I *picture* her—I picture her with her gold bangs sticking to her forehead in the September sun on that first afternoon, though I don't know if her hair ever grew back before they gassed her. Of course I didn't see her go—Irina told me. Elodie shouting with Micheline and Karolina from the back of the crammed truck—"TELL

THE WORLD"—and I picture Elodie the way she looked the day I met her. They yelled in French and in Polish, English, and German. "TELL THE WORLD! TELL THE WORLD! *TELL THE WORLD!*"

Micheline Karolina Elodie Zofia Veronica Rozalia Genca Maria Alfreda Apolonia Kazimiera Anna Zosia Aniela—

So many dead. There were probably over thirty thousand living women in Ravensbrück when I got there and nearly sixty thousand or more by the time I left, so who knows how many thousands died in between? And how many died *before* I got there and *after* I left? How many in other camps?

I *will* tell the world.

Mother said she doesn't believe it.

I WILL TELL THE WORLD.

I say that so fiercely. I say it with such conviction, such determined anger. But I couldn't even tell Mother, could I? A few pages ago, I vowed I *wouldn't* tell Mother. How can I possibly tell the world?

I have to. This is a beginning. If I write it all down, later it can turn into a plan.

When my quarantine was finished, they sent me over to the Siemens factory. They just hauled me out of my row in roll call and stuffed me into a smaller group of twenty other women, not from my French transport. They marched us out through the big gates and along the lake. I got a glimpse of the SS staff housing—there were neat, long swaths of red flowers bordering their front yards, and window boxes. A woman in civilian clothes was sweeping up leaves with a couple of tiny tot kids, and the kids were throwing leaves at each other and they were all laughing. They looked so *ordinary*. My heart lifted a little. I was outside those terrible walls again. The last three weeks hadn't been easy, but they were over and I was out.

It is a longish walk from the main Camp to Siemens, about half a mile. You could see Fürstenberg and its church spire across the lake, like a "Scenes from Old Europe" picture on a jigsaw puzzle. On our side of the lake, we passed hundreds of Ravensbrück prisoners busy at something or other—cutting reeds, hauling potatoes and firewood from somewhere, unloading barges full of coal. Finally we came to another complex of long gray buildings behind chain-link and barbed-wire electrified fences that was the Siemens factory itself. Around the buildings here, other prisoners were doing hard, hard labor, unloading iron pigs from railway cars and dragging them away in wagonloads. But this is where my Luftwaffe letter of recommendation suddenly kicked in. *Thank God*, I thought as I realized what was going on—thank you, Luftwaffe commander, thank you, Karl Womelsdorff.

I sat in an office and had to do a couple of aptitude tests (no language aptitude required)—guide a thread around a series of tacks on a board and fold a piece of paper in a particular way, following visual instructions. Finally I had to learn to wind thin copper wire around an iron bobbin. And then I had a "skilled" job, just like they'd told me I would— technically it was even a *paid* job, though nobody ever gave you any money; they just jotted down your wages against your number. I sat at a bench under bright electric lights in a relatively clean and airy factory barracks, wrapping strands of copper wire around iron bobbins. The factory was decent because German civilians from Fürstenberg worked there, too. I was a prisoner, but I was healthy and clean enough that I could work in the same room with normal people, though we weren't allowed to speak to each other (not that I could). The dorms at Siemens were cleaner, too, and less crowded. We were still three to a bed, but the mattresses were better and we had two blankets among the three of us and the toilet worked. We were all issued kerchiefs to cover up how savagely some of us had been scalped.

I missed Elodie like crazy, and most of my ill-gotten belongings (toothbrush, soap, etc.) were still hidden in a crack between the boards of my never-to-be-revisited bunk in Block 8. I didn't meet anyone in my new barracks who spoke either French or English. But see, I'd waited out the dreadful quarantine believing my life would improve, and it did.

I lasted three days.

That's counting the time I stood at my bench doing *nothing* for eighteen hours, waiting for someone to shoot me.

It wasn't that I couldn't do the work. The summer before my senior year in high school I worked at the paper box factory in Mount Jericho. It was the same kind of work—just folding and sticking on an assembly line. Actually, it was *worse* at the paper box factory because the air was so dusty and it was so hot that summer. And it was so boring—the only interesting thing that happened the whole summer was when Polly put that cigarette butt in her pocket and set her apron on fire. The work was worth it—I needed the money for coming to England. But it wasn't a fun job, and I stuck with it and was pleased with myself afterward.

Okay, here I was on another assembly line, doing work that I knew I could handle, and hoping for the war to end at any minute—so why did I go and ruin it all?

I blame it on a couple of civilian workers, although that's not really fair. I'd have figured it out on my own eventually. I heard them talking when we were coming in after the dinner break, and I heard a word I recognized:

Vergeltungswaffe. Vengeance weapon.

I filed meekly back to my place at the long table full of copper wire and iron spools. And in the back of my head, the word was echoing over and over with the clattering rhythm of an approaching doodlebug:

Vergeltungswaffe, Vergeltungswaffe.

I sat down. I picked up a piece of copper wire.

I was making electrical relays for flying bomb fuses.

I put down the piece of wire. Then I just sat there staring at it for twenty minutes. I was so quiet, so utterly unfussy, that it took twenty minutes for anyone to notice I had stopped working. At least, it took the foreman twenty minutes to notice I had stopped working. The prisoners on either side of me didn't say anything—they just quietly beavered away at their own electrical relays.

The foreman eventually came over and gave me a gentle prod in the ribs with the end of a ruler. The civilians didn't like to touch the Ravensbrück prisoners, and no wonder—even when we were clean we were still livid with bug bites. My shins were so bitten they looked sunburned. I knew exactly what the ruler poke meant—he didn't have to say anything in any language. I wanted to be willing—God knows I wanted to cooperate; I didn't want to get in trouble. I picked up the wire thread.

And I just couldn't do it.

Now this, *this* I remember like it was this morning. I watch my hands writing here on the vanity table in the Paris Ritz and I can see it happening. I picked up the wire thread, wrapped it once around the spool, and I saw Maddie's hands instead of mine. Just in a blinking flash. Maddie's pretty, capable hands, with the old French-cut ruby sparkling on her ring finger, taking apart the bomb fuse that Uncle Roger had sent me.

I closed my eyes to make it go away. My own hands were still frozen in place over the new relay. And when I closed my eyes, I saw the little boy's hands from my nightmare—small, dirty fingers blown to bloody splinters.

And I *just couldn't do it.*

It wasn't a conscious decision. It wasn't rebellion. It wasn't sabotage. It wasn't my conscience nagging at me. It wasn't anything noble. God knows I wouldn't have been brave enough to do anything noble! But now that I knew what I was making—I just couldn't do it.

I laid the wire gently on the table. Then I laid my hands in my lap. The foreman called over the SS guard who was in charge of the prison workers.

Gosh, they gave no quarter, those SS guards. They didn't waste any time, *ever.* This one didn't even try to talk to me. She took hold of my skull—just grabbed me by the back of my head—and *slammed* my forehead down on the table. For a moment it felt like my head had exploded, sparkling light everywhere. Then she shifted her grip on my head to force me back upright, and with her free hand she picked up the strand of copper wire and tossed it on the table in front of me.

Beneath her grip I shook my head sadly. NO.

She slammed my face back down on the table, and I have got a scar, just above my left eye, where the copper wire cut me. It's so thin you probably can't see it—I am not brave enough to look. But I can feel it and I know it's there. I count it as a flying bomb scar.

The guard let go of my head.

"*Aufstehen!*"

Get up. You got to know what that meant after a while, because you had to do it so much.

They didn't do anything else—just made me stand up. The copper wire and relay bobbins I was supposed to be working on still lay there on the table in front of me. The prisoners around me were still hunched over their own relays just the way they'd been when I first stopped working, diligently trying not to notice what was going on.

It was like when I took the fuse from the boy on the railway line in Hamble. I was sure I was going to be killed. And it made me sad—not scared, but sad that I had forced myself into this corner where I just couldn't win.

But they didn't kill me. They didn't even hit me again. They just made me stand there.

I stood there for the rest of the day. And all night. And into the next day.

People came and went around me. Production went on during the night, so everybody changed shifts around me and I went on standing there.

They kept an eye on me. There were a couple of extra guards brought in especially for me. They wouldn't let me touch the long table with my hands or lean against the bench. It got harder and harder not to. I started dreaming about my crowded bunk with its thin mattress and shared blanket. The copper wire on the table in front of me danced and gleamed beneath the harsh factory lights. I heard the screaming sirens go and thought smugly, through the daze of exhaustion, *I've missed two roll calls.*

Not that I'd have been doing anything else in a roll call except just standing there!

In the middle of the night, when I'd been on my feet for probably more than twelve hours—and of course I'd been working for six hours before that, and awake since the four a.m. siren the previous day—there was a point when all I wanted to do was lie down under the table and go to sleep. If I couldn't do that, then I might as well be dead. I was pretty sure I didn't care anymore. I'd reached the point when I thought I would do *anything* to be allowed to sit down—so very carefully, I stepped over the bench and sat down and picked up the copper wire that was waiting for me.

It was bliss, sheer bliss, to sit down, even though I was still sitting upright—*bliss* just to be allowed to sit. I didn't think I'd get away with just sitting there, though. I was showing them they'd won, and I was going to have to go back to work. I knew they'd make me finish up the rest of that shift, or make up the time I'd wasted. So I started to wrap the wire around the spool.

And you know what?

I still couldn't do it.

I put the wire down quietly. I put my hands on the table and pushed myself to my feet somehow. And somehow I managed to climb back over the bench so I was standing behind it again.

The other prisoners glanced up at me briefly and then away. Nobody smiled. The guards and the foreman chatted together for a while, and then the foreman took away my copper wire and the spools and gave them to someone else to finish up. They didn't do anything to me—didn't hit me, didn't make me leave the room—just made me go on standing there.

Only, while before it had been a battle of will between us—*stand there until you feel like working*—now I was being punished because I'd refused to work.

This made everything a little different. Also, it woke me up.

I'd sat down because I thought I'd been completely at the end of my strength. Obviously I wasn't. But I was pretty close to it, and now I no longer had a way out. I *knew* this. Also, now I didn't know where the whole thing was going, and that was very frightening. So I had to readjust something in my head to help me focus on not losing my mind with fear and exhaustion.

So I made up a poem.

It sort of started in my head as a chant about wires and fuses. It wasn't anything profound or memorable, just a sort of counting-out rhyme based on something I'd tried to write last summer—rhyming words in a list, like the list of Polish girls' names that we all memorized and that I reported to the American Embassy as well as the Swedish Red Cross, and which I will report again to anyone else who will listen.

It was as though ever since I left Camp Los Angeles I'd been flying a plane so nose-high that I couldn't see anything below me, because if I looked down I'd be looking into hell and I didn't want to see. I knew it was there. But as long as I didn't look, as long as I kept the nose up, I could fool myself into thinking it wasn't. My Luftwaffe recommendation would protect me. There would be better beds and food and toilets when I was out of quarantine. The Allies would be here in a month. I wouldn't make trouble. I would be all right.

So now I'd raised the nose too high, and I was going to lose control of the aircraft and plummet into a spin. And when I did, like Celia's Tempest, I would fall and I would be in hell. Really and truly and for good.

So I stood there until I fell.

I don't remember this part very well. It really is a blur, not because I've forgotten, but because I was already so dazed while it was happening. I ended up soaking wet—I remember being utterly drenched and freezing cold. They must have hosed me down to wake me up so they didn't have to carry me back to the main Camp, and I *did* walk—incredibly, I am sure I walked. I know it was October and early in the morning, and windy, so it would have been chilly anyway even if I hadn't been completely dripping wet. The wind felt like knives of ice, and they wouldn't let me hug my arms around me—I had to walk with my hands at my sides. I don't remember passing the lake or the gates or what the sky looked like or if there were other prisoners around, or even where they were taking me, and when they'd left me locked in a shadowy bare concrete cupboard of a cell, I didn't care, because there was a narrow iron bed with a wooden plank for a mattress and no one in it. I curled in a tight, shaking ball against the dank wall and fell instantly asleep without even looking to see if there was a blanket.

Of course there wasn't.

I was in the cell block, the Bunker, for two weeks. The veterans say you aren't a real Ravensbrück prisoner till you've been in the Bunker. Irina was there for *four months* in solitary confinement while they interrogated her about the Soviet Air Force in 1943, and it is also where they did the last batch of medical experiments on the Rabbits, when they tied the girls down and gagged them before they operated on them. I feel like two weeks isn't really long enough to count as time in the Bunker, especially since they fed me once a day and left me alone in between my two doses of twenty-five lashes—my twice *Fünfundzwanzig*. There was a week in between each round because if you get fifty at once you're likely to die. Twice twenty-five was a mild punishment for failing to make parts for flying bombs. Deliberate sabotage is punishable by *death*, so I was lucky I just stopped working and didn't try to do anything more underhanded. After they finished my second beating, I got put straight back into the main Camp.

They make you count aloud as they thrash you. You are supposed to count, in German, the number of strokes you are given. Thanks to Grampa, of course, I could make it up to twenty, but like a jillion other pathetic creatures, I didn't know how to count beyond that, so they had to prompt me. I managed it the first time but not the second.

I said they left me alone between the beatings and that's true, but the week between them was pretty awful. Because this time I knew what was coming, and I was already in bad shape. There wasn't anything to do but lie in the gloom and wait for next Friday—flat on my face on the bare planks, listening to the Screamer siren counting off the days. My mind skips lightly over that week and that second Friday—even what I *can* remember, I don't want to. I don't remember being tied to the sawhorse or if I saw the stinking Commander, though I know he liked to watch and he was always there on Fridays. The counting, the second time, was the significant thing. The *really* significant thing.

I got to eight, and after that I thought I couldn't speak. They kept going and I was still counting in my head, in English, because I knew that when I got to twenty-five it would be over, and counting was the only thing I could do to move things along. I lost count at fifteen. I must have been unconscious by twenty. At any rate I don't remember how it ended or what happened after.

I woke up lying on my stomach on another bare wood

slab in an acre of endless, empty, stinking plank bunks—there wasn't one above me, but the ceiling was so close I couldn't have sat upright if I'd wanted to, and the closeness made it so dark you couldn't see where the bunks ended. It was gray twilight, and that was because somewhere in the room, below me, there were windows, and it was still light out. I didn't know where I was or how I'd got there, though it was obviously another part of the same god-awful prison complex.

It was quiet and I couldn't move, even though I was awake. I just lay blinking and breathing—not really thinking. Not even feeling sorry for myself.

I'd more or less forgotten who I was.

So then a voice near my head commanded in English, "Say your poem."

The command made no sense, and I didn't even try to answer.

"Say your poem," the voice insisted. "Say the counting-out rhyme."

Counting—that made more sense. The last thing I could remember was being told to count, and the last thing I could remember doing was trying to count aloud, so I kind of assumed we were picking up where we'd left off. I felt certain that whether or not I obeyed I'd eventually wind up unconscious again, if not dead. But maybe if I cooperated we'd get it over with quickly. And so a poem called "Counting-out Rhyme" began to spill abruptly out of me.

> "Silver bark of beech, and sallow
> Bark of yellow birch and yellow
> Twig of willow."

I said it very slowly.

While I was speaking, a strange thing happened. I began

picturing the springtime woods of Pennsylvania, each branch and twig, as I said its name. I had to stop after the first verse— just three lines—because it was exhausting.

"Go on," said the nearby voice.

After a moment of despair, I pulled myself together and went on.

> "Stripe of green in moosewood maple,
> Color seen in leaf of apple,
> Bark of popple."

And you know, it was like I was breathing my own self back into me to say these words, to remember that these things existed—the green trees of the eastern woodland at home in North America, their strong and supple branches, sunlight through the leaves.

Incredible to think these same spring leaves are uncurling there now.

> "Wood of popple pale as moonbeam,
> Wood of oak for yoke and barn-beam,
> Wood of hornbeam."

It was MAGICAL to say their names. It was a blessing. It was holy.

> "Silver bark of beech, and hollow
> Stem of elder, tall and yellow
> Twig of willow."

I was finished. That is the whole poem. There was a pause.

"Is that your poem?"

"No. It's by Edna St. Vincent Millay."

"Do you know more?"

"Dozens," I croaked. "She's my favorite poet."

Oh, what a lot she's got to answer for, Edna St. Vincent Millay, whipping the youth of America into action in Europe. I'm sure she didn't mean for me to end up in the Ravensbrück women's concentration camp in Germany when she signed my copy of *Make Bright the Arrows* in that lecture hall at Jericho Valley College last spring, and shook my hand and wished me good luck ferrying planes in England.

"Is that the poem you said when they were beating you?"

"What?"

"They told you to count and you said it was a counting-out rhyme. They stopped halfway through so they could call in Gitte, our *Blockova*, to watch and to translate, because you knew so much about munitions they decided they would have to put you in high security—here, Block 32. With the Soviet Red Army women soldiers and the Polish experimental Rabbits and the French Night and Fog spies. And when they brought you here, our *Blockova*, Gitte, told me to ask you to tell me your poem, because I am trying to learn poetry in English for my exams."

My interrogator was Polish. Her heavily accented English was just like Felicyta's, though the voice was different—higher, soprano instead of alto. And younger. I could tell.

"*Blockova?*"

"Block leader. You might as well learn *Blockova*, because no one ever calls them anything else. It's a Polish word, not German. The *Blockovas* are prisoners, too. Most of the group leaders are prisoners. The German criminals are the worst. Look out for them; they've got green triangles to show they're criminals and red armbands to show they're forewomen. They'll report you for *smiling* if they don't like your face.

Gitte's all right; she's a political prisoner, a German commu-nist. Handed out one too many anti-Nazi leaflets!"

I can't really write her accent or her idioms without making her sound stupid, and she never did sound stupid. Anyway, I can't remember them. I always understood her. So I am just going to write it the way I understood it, not the way she said it.

"You're learning poetry for your *exams?*" I repeated, com-pletely bewildered.

"Yes, they pulled a lot of us out of school when they arrested us, along with half the professional scholars in Poland—all the ones they didn't just murder right away. So the students are trying to earn our diplomas with the profes-sors. Oh well, it's a good thing to pretend, anyway—that the war will end before we're all shot or starved to death, and that I will need a diploma. Like you reciting poetry while they beat you."

"I don't remember—"

I began to say it, and then suddenly I did remember.

"Oh!"

This is what I'd done: I'd continued my instinctive effort to save my sanity that began when they first took away my relays for the bomb fuses. When I stopped counting during the second beating, I started muttering aloud the poem I'd been making up for the past two weeks—the words I'd had in my head as I stood swaying with exhaustion in the Siemens factory, the words I'd whispered to myself in the dark in the cold, cramped cell in the Bunker.

So now I remembered my sanity-saving poem, but I still didn't move. I was still lying flat on my face.

"Go on," the Polish student prompted me.

I remembered the whole thing.

I wrote a few words of it in England last summer—I think

it is in this notebook, but I haven't got the heart to look back at anything I wrote last summer. This will be the first time I've ever written down the finished poem.

COUNTING-OUT RHYME (by Rose Justice)

Silver tube of fuse and hollow
cylinder of detonator
cap and gyro.

Toppled gyro forcing action,
copper wire to spark ignition,
pulse jet engine.

Amatol before explosion,
Bosch and Siemens, Argus, Fieseler,
in production.

Shining fragile fuse and hollow
warhead fuselage awaiting
detonation.

"Is that by your favorite poet as well?" the Polish girl asked. "Edna Millay?"

"No, that's by me. I made it up."

"What is it about? Not trees this time."

"Flying bombs. It's about making them. Or not making them—that's why they punished me."

"I will give you one slice of bread for every poem you make me. I can do it. I'm one of the Camp Rabbits, the Króliki, and people take care of me. Every time you make me a new poem, I'll get you an *extra* slice of bread."

I didn't know it then. But I know it now and I'm sure of

it. My counting-out rhyme saved me from starving to death this winter.

"What's your name?" I asked.

"I'm Polish Political Prisoner 7705," she reeled off, glib and bitter. "I'm a Rabbit."

"Don't be stupid."

I don't know how I knew I could talk to her like that. I hadn't even looked at her yet.

"My name is Róża Czajkowska," she said.

In my ears it sounded like a meaningless babble of foreign sound. Very humbly, and worried that she would go away if I offended her, I asked her to spell it.

"Oh, I can't do English letters out loud," she answered with deep scorn. "Róża. How difficult is that? It means 'rose' in English."

I turned my head for the first time since I'd woken up. It was exhausting. But I could see her now.

She was—she is—seventeen. She was the tiniest seventeen-year-old I'd ever seen—I thought she was about eleven when I first saw her, the thinnest, most starved-looking kid alive. Being starved-looking was the only thing I noticed about her at first, her only distinguishing feature—it still hadn't dawned on me that this wasn't a distinguishing feature at Ravensbrück, and that Róża had other, more significant peculiarities. She had long hair—a lot of the long-term prisoners did—but it was hidden beneath a headscarf, and her dress was one of the old-style gray-and-blue striped uniforms.

"Rose!" I exclaimed.

"Róża," she corrected. "People call me Różyczka sometimes, little Rose, because I am so little."

"Little Rose—like Rosie? How do you say it?"

"Say 'Ro-shij-ka.' Różyczka!"

"Różyczka!"

"It is my pleasure to meet you, English-speaking French Political Prisoner 51498. What's *your* name?"

"Rose Justice," I said, remembering who I was. "Rose. Or Rosie. Same as yours."

She gave a giggling, maniacal howl of laughter.

At the other end of the narrow aisle that led between the rows of bunks, there came the sound of footsteps. After a moment the footsteps stopped—another turbaned head appeared. (It was Gitte, our extremely wonderful German *Blockova*.) I couldn't have begun to guess Gitte's age when I first saw her face that afternoon—honestly, she could have been anywhere between twenty-five and a hundred. She said something sharply to Róża in German. Róża patted me on the head like a dog. She said to Gitte in English, "Look— Justice has come to Ravensbrück!" and let out another cackling peal of laughter.

Then Róża patted a thin cotton blanket that was folded near my head.

"Listen, English-Speaking French Political Prisoner with the same name as me. I have to go back to work. There's a blanket here if you want it now, but you have to give it back to the others later, and no one will thank you if she has to wash blood out of it, so keep it off your backside. I'll bring your supper here, but you'll have to get up to come to the six thirty roll call." She giggled again before she added, "I'll help you if you can't walk."

Gitte gave a sigh of indulgence. She assured me in English, "Someone else will help."

She reached toward Róża to help her down from the bunk. At first I thought it was just because Róża was so little. She put her arms around Gitte's neck like a monkey, and let herself be lifted to the murky floor. Then I saw the back of her legs and I understood why she needed help climbing down, and why her offer of support to me was such a joke.

Both her legs had been split in half. That's what it looked like—from knee to ankle in the back of her calves were long clefts so deep you could poke your finger in them up to the second knuckle.

I gasped aloud in horror. It shook me physically—I actually flinched backward, away from Róża's awful legs, and then I gasped again in pain because it hurt so much to move.

Róża's injuries weren't new—her legs had healed that way. They were as good as they were going to get. When Gitte put Róża down and she turned around to face me, I could see a trio of sunken, dented scars in the front of her right leg, half an inch deep, *where bone should have been.*

It looked like her legs had been split with a butcher knife and then she'd been shot at close range.

She picked up a makeshift crutch—a Y-shaped stick padded with more of the striped prison cloth—and injected it beneath her right arm.

"Can you knit?" she demanded.

"Sort of."

She pulled a face and mimicked, "*'Sort of.'*"

"You're an 'Available,'" Gitte told me. "*Verfügbar.* That means you're not assigned to any special work."

"You have to line up in the morning and go wherever they send you," Róża elaborated. "Shoveling shit, maybe, or burning corpses. Anything. Usually things nobody else wants to do."

I blinked down at her, still lying flat, too much of a wreck to lift my head. *A skilled job.* Well, I'd had my chance.

"Hey, don't cry. We'll keep you inside the block for a few days—till you can sit down, anyway. Gitte's going to say she needs another knitter to keep the quota up this week, since Zosia and Genca were shot."

Then Róża disappeared into the twilit aisle between the bunks, escorted by the ageless block leader. I was too high up to see them go. But I could hear Róża's progress as her wooden clogs clomped against the dank concrete floor, punctuated by the thump of her crutch.

After about thirty seconds, the clomping and thumping stopped suddenly. She yelled back at me, in English, *"One piece of bread per poem!"*

Until November we had two evening roll calls—that was the way they'd always done it, one at six thirty and one at nine p.m. Eventually they stopped the six thirty one because there were so many of us it was taking up to three hours three times a day to count us all. But the week I came to Block 32 they were still doing both evening roll calls, and I went to both. I have no memory of either one, or of climbing up to and down out of the top bunk. The population of Block 32 was really, really good at propping people up.

In between the roll calls, I am pretty sure I did nothing but lie on my face. I was all burny with a light fever and I didn't want to eat anything, and Róża for whatever reason didn't follow through with her promise to bring me supper—to be fair, there wasn't a notice up saying FEED THE NEW GIRL IN THE TOP BUNK, and I was still nothing more to any of them than just the unknown person who'd be making up the murdered Zosia's and Genca's knitting quota.

Gosh, I was dazed.

What I do remember is that suddenly on this plank where I'd been sprawled flat on my face all afternoon there were three other people trying to make themselves comfortable. We struck a kind of bargain where I got to stay sprawled and the rest of them got the blanket, only they had to sleep sitting up. Or as near upright as you can get when the ceiling is three feet above your head and you are asleep.

We slept that way for five hours, maybe, and then the four a.m. Screamer went, and it was a scramble to the horrible toilet ditches before the four thirty roll call. And that was me back on my feet.

I said my counting-out rhyme saved my life, and it's true, because saying it during my beating is what made Gitte notice me and give me to Lisette to take care of. You were *dead* if you didn't have someone looking out for you. But I never had to worry about finding a teammate. I was *so lucky*. Lisette's bunkmates in Block 32 weren't just a team—we were a proper Camp Family, with Lisette in the role of *Lagermutter*, Camp Mother.

It took me some time to notice Lisette was there, because Róża acted like she ruled the roost and Lisette was so quiet. Lisette was older than *Daddy*, but she didn't really look it, partly because she'd been such a beauty. I like to think she will be again. It was a game I played during roll calls, trying to picture everybody in real life. Lisette Romilly, possibly France's most popular detective novelist, Jazz Age flapper who drank cocktails with F. Scott Fitzgerald in Paris, then surprised everybody by marrying the principal cellist of the Lublin Philharmonic and uprooting herself to move to Poland. She had three boys all as handsome and talented as their parents, she became an archivist at the Catholic University of Lublin, she learned to play the bass violin at the age of thirty-two, and within two years she became so good they let her join the orchestra.

Her husband was Jewish. He and her three boys—the oldest was two years younger than me—were all swept up in 1939 and marched out of the city and shot on the road. They didn't even take them to a camp. Lisette got thrown out of their apartment, and there she was, widowed, her children dead, owning nothing, in a foreign country at war. She had no work, because the Germans had closed down all the Polish universities. She tried to go back to France and got arrested at the train station. When it first happened, she thought it was for carrying a cello without a license or something like that. But actually, they arrested practically anyone who was connected with the Polish universities. I think they shot most of them.

I *loved* Lisette. We *all* loved Lisette.

LISETTE WAITS (by Rose Justice)

Her suitcases are full. But after all
she leaves them standing lifeless in the hall
and takes the cello—for its golden voice
sings back to life her murdered love and boys.

She leaves behind her mother's silver service,
linen and pearls and books. The railway office
demands she buy two tickets; so she does.
The cello's all she has and ever was.

The piercing whistle tells the tracks are clear.
She strains to glimpse the plume of steam draw near
and sees the uniforms, a distant gun
aimed at her breast. The cello cannot run.

She pulls it to her heart, fearing the worst,
still praying for the train to reach them first.

Lisette was in prison in Lublin for a while before they sent her to Ravensbrück, and she was part of Róża's transport. There were about 140 of them to begin with. A lot of them had already been killed one way or another by the time I got thrown in with them, and it doesn't take a genius to see why Lisette adopted me—why she adopted Róża, why she was a natural *Lagermutter*. She *needed* people to mother. It was how she stayed sane.

Lisette didn't care about my head full of poetry in English. She had a reasonable supply in her own head, along with an inexhaustible supply of French and Polish and Russian and German poems, too. I got tucked under Lisette's wing because Zosia and Genca, the girls who had been shot last week, had also been her adopted daughters, along with Róża and Karolina. The *Blockova*, Gitte, hadn't just had Róża's thirst for poetry in mind when she'd boosted me, semiconscious, into that particular bunk under the roof. I was there for Lisette to look after, to distract her from going crazy with grief and fury all over again.

I must have been the slowest knitter of anybody in the block. I hadn't knitted in the round before, and I'd never tried holding the yarn in my left hand like the rest of them; but fortunately all we were making were socks. I didn't *mind* knitting socks for German soldiers. German soldiers need socks. If they were going to force me to do anything for the Axis war effort, keeping conscripted boys' feet warm on the Eastern Front was okay. Making bombs was not okay.

I did my knitting standing up. I ate standing up. The back of my dress had dark brown stripes of dried blood across it that I never managed to wash out in the whole time I wore it.

The knitting went on in the block itself. There was a big main room on either side of the so-called washroom in the middle. We ate in the big rooms, and that was also where the knitters worked in the day. Older women knitted, or people who couldn't walk. There was a guard who watched over everything as we got to work, but mostly they left things up to Gitte, the *Blockova*. As long as we got the required number of socks knitted, they didn't waste time keeping an eye on us. And as soon as the SS guards were gone in the morning, everybody relaxed a little bit. We still had to work like fury— if we didn't meet the quotas, everyone got punished with an extra hour or two of *"Strafstehen"*—punishment standing— waiting outside the barrack in the dark after the last roll call of the day. But the knitters could talk to one another, a huge advantage and privilege.

Róża sat on the table facing me, resting her feet on the bench. She'd stowed her wooden clogs and her crutch underneath the table. She didn't say anything to me for about an hour—just eyed me up and down critically, while another woman carried on a quiz session in Polish. They played school, mathematicians and geologists and historians taking turns at tutoring the younger girls. I didn't understand any of it, and after a while I began to hate the sound of their meaningless foreign voices. It was a nightmare I could never really define, to have so many people packed around me and not be able to communicate with any of them unless they felt like it.

They took a break in the lecture after a while, though we all kept on furiously producing limitless amounts of gray wool tubing (which of course we were never allowed to use ourselves, even when it was snowing). By the time they got to their recess, I was swaying on my feet. I couldn't sit, but I couldn't really stand yet, either—not for the whole day. It was about ten o'clock in the morning and I'd been up since four.

"So how come you're French, if you don't speak anything but English?" Róża asked. "Are you another parachutist?"

I shook my head. "I don't know what you mean."

"There are a few English ladies here who were dropped into France by parachute, as spies. Are you a spy?"

"Gosh—would I tell you if I *was*?"

She laughed. It was a real laugh this time, a bubbly giggle of a laugh, not the other bitter, ironic cackle. "You look French—bald. When Paris was liberated, they shaved all the French prisoners' heads again as punishment. What are you, then? And how did you end up here?"

"Are your English ladies here now?" I asked.

"No, they're not in this block. And even if they were, they're not cripples. They have to do real work," Róża said offhandedly.

"Are you *all* crippled?" I asked, looking around the room. I wondered, Am I here because I've been crippled? No, I'd been given six hours to recover and now I was already on my feet. Apart from the Polish girls who'd come back inside to knit after the morning roll call, all the rest of the Block 32 prisoners were fine—none of the French or Russian women had anything wrong with them apart from being filthy dirty and covered with scabies and starving, and they'd all marched off on work details that morning. "What *happened* to you?" I asked.

"Why don't you tell me what happened to *you*, since I asked first," Róża said seriously. "Because if we start talking about me, you won't believe me, and we'll argue. Tell me about 51498, the French political prisoner with no French."

"*Pardonez-moi, mais je parle un peu de français,*" I said. Excuse me, but I do speak a little French. More now than I did then, of course.

"*Moi aussi, plus bien que toi,*" she answered. "Me too, better than you. And I learned most of it here, in Lisette's French class. You should never use *vous*, the formal 'you,' to another prisoner—we're comrades. Not even to Lisette, who's older than my mother was. Are you sure you're not a spy? How did you get to Ravensbrück speaking only English?"

"I'm American. I'm a pilot in the Air Transport Auxiliary

in England—we ferry aircraft for the Royal Air Force. I landed in the wrong place, and they sent me here. I got registered with a transport of French prisoners and they counted me as French, too."

"Hah! Too bad you can't speak German or you could report the stupid bitch who signed you up as French. She'd get in trouble for sloppy record-keeping."

"Boy, I wish she would," I said with feeling.

Róża gleefully repeated my story in Polish so that it could be passed around the rest of the room, and once again everyone shot questions at me about the invasion and the Allied advance and how soon the war was likely to end. (The Polish prisoners were pretty good at English, it turned out; later I realized they carried out some of their lessons totally in English.) I told them about D-Day and how we handed out the strawberries to the soldiers, and my gosh that was a hit.

"How many did each soldier get?"

"Did you eat any yourself?"

"How big were they?"

"What variety?"

We switched topics from politics to food and I described the way Felicyta had made the little squares of toast with jam on them after Celia's funeral.

Someone burst out with an exclamation in an excited voice, and everybody laughed.

"They think we could do that, too," Róża explained drily. "The next time somebody gets jam. Sometimes a food package makes it through without the goddamned SS stealing everything in it except the paper it was wrapped in."

"They took *my* paper," I said. "I had chocolate."

"*Chocolate!*"

They were off again.

"Hey, why don't you lie across the table here?" Róża said

suddenly. "Here by me. You can lean on your arms with your wrists over the edge so you can go on working. Pile the wool on the bench. Yeah, like that. Better?"

It was better. The women on the other side of the table had to squeeze up a little to make room for my legs, but they compromised by using them as a backrest.

"Just be ready to get down in a hurry if one of the guards comes in. Code word this week is *muffins*." (I don't really remember what the code word was that week. It was always food-based: "Oh, how I wish I had ten muffins for lunch!" I know a lot of Polish words for food now.) "Listen to Maria— she can see the window."

Lying flat on my stomach across the table with my not-very-advanced sock dangling over the edge next to Róża's knee, I had a close-up view of her thin right leg with the row of holes gouged in her shin. I couldn't see anybody else's legs, because they were all sitting the right way around with their feet under the table, and everybody was packed very close together. The absolutely awful thing about the damage to Róża's leg was that it was so obviously permanent—it had *healed* that way.

"Have you made me a poem yet?" she demanded.

"No."

"No extra bread for you today."

I said to Róża, "I'm not giving you a poem till you tell me what happened to everybody's legs."

She tapped her shin with one of her knitting needles. I didn't dare to look, but I couldn't help seeing out of my peripheral vision. She was poking the tip of the steel needle into one of the holes—*just awful*. Macabre and awful. Then she made a loud announcement in Polish. People turned interested heads in our direction. Nobody stopped working.

"Everyone in my transport is condemned to death," she

explained in English. "*Special Transport.* Condemned, all of us. They've executed dozens of us already. But some of us they didn't kill right away, and since they plan for us all to end up dead anyway, they used us—tested us. . . ."

She hesitated, not with emotion, but just because she couldn't find the right words. I don't think she could find the right words in English *or* Polish. She used words like *experiment* and *trial* and *medical,* and they came out of her mouth so laden with sarcasm and hatred that it sounded like she was telling a really bad joke.

"They *'operated'* on seventy-four of us, all Polish, mostly students from my transport. My *special* transport. Like experimental rabbits. That's why we still get called Rabbits, *Króliki—Kaninchen* in German. Actually, what we said was that we're *not* rabbits; one of the first girls operated on yelled it at one of the doctors and he thought it was funny. And it stuck. So that's what they did; they cut us up like rabbits. They'd slice your calf open and fill the wound with gangrene and then seal it up in plaster for two weeks. Or they'd cut pieces out of your muscles or your nerves. Or they'd cut a chunk of bone out of your leg and try to stick it in someone else's leg. I am special—I got operated on five times! Because I am so young and healthy, get it? They said they wanted to learn how to treat 'wounds in the field'—'the field' means the Eastern Front, which is where most of Germany's wounded soldiers are—so they'd 'simulate' war wounds on us. Make a hole like a gunshot wound and then see what happens to it if you put a dirty bandage on it in a trench and never change the dressing. Guess what happens."

I swallowed but couldn't answer. The iron needles seemed to waver in front of my face, as if I were looking at them through a sheet of old glass.

"Look, I'll show you what happens—" She barked orders in Polish at the girls sitting on her left and on my right.

They never stopped knitting. They turned around on the bench—they had room to do it because Róża and I were on the table. They stuck their own legs out in front of me, turning and showing off their scars as if they were models at a fashion show.

I burst out, *"I heard about you on the radio."*

Róża dropped a needle.

It clattered on the concrete floor, and the girl next to her dived to pick it up. They chattered together in rapid excitement, and then suddenly the whole room was buzzing again—really *buzzing*—and they were all focused on me.

"You *heard?* On the *radio?* On the BBC? What did they say? Does everyone know?"

Róża explained very quickly, "Some of us died of it, some of us have been executed, but most of us are still alive, and we have been *fighting* to get the story to spread outside the Camp. We smuggled out letters addressed to the BBC and the Vatican and the Red Cross headquarters in Geneva. Now we are such an embarrassment to the Camp administration that they don't know what to do with us—we're all still condemned to be killed, but they're scared to do it. They know we've been telling people, they know it's leaking out—we got a blessing sent to us by the *Pope!* A civilian worker in Siemens will hear, or someone from the men's camp, or a prisoner who knows about us will get released or transferred to another camp. It's getting out. *Someday*, the bastards will have to *account* for what they did to us. What did you hear?"

"I don't know who it was. The report was about an American woman who'd been in a prison camp in Germany—she had a list of names."

"It was *Aka!* She *does* have American citizenship! It was *us!* See, *it's working!* What did you do when you heard? What did you think? What did people say?"

I hesitated. They were so excited, and my answer was going to be so disappointing.

"We didn't do anything," I said. "We just thought it was anti-German propaganda. No one believed it."

"No goddamn extra bread for you *ever*," Róża snarled with venomous resentment.

Instead of snapping back at her, I sang softly,

"Rose, Rose, Rose, Rose,
Will I ever see thee wed?"

"You bitch," she murmured, just as soft.
"It's a round. It's easy. I'll teach you."

"Rose, Rose, Rose, Rose,
Will I ever see thee wed—"

Suddenly the girl on my right sang the first line back to me—*"Rose, Rose, Rose, Rose."* She even picked up the unfamiliar English words of the second line, *"Will I ever see thee wed?"*

"I will marry at thy will, sir,
At thy will."

When I started to sing it a third time, a voice across the table joined in, too.

It didn't take them long. It is an easy round. They were practiced and fast at learning things by heart, and starved for beauty.

And, of course, they knew we were singing to Róża.

"MUFFINS!" yelled the girl at the window.

Instant silence. A dozen hands dragged me off the table. In five seconds we were all bent with our heads over our knitting and a guard stomped in to yell at Gitte for reasons I never figured out.

I got my fair share of bread that night. I didn't recognize the girl who handed it to me as we crowded around the drums of soup. "Thank you!"

"You've got Zosia and Genca to thank, because they're dead," Róża informed me brutally.

"Shut up, Różyczka." The girl who'd given me the bread made a face and told me in a mixture of French and English, "Lisette is your *Lagermutter* now, your Camp Mother, and she's mine and Róża's also. So we'll treat you like a sister."

"I'm Rose," I said.

"I know you're Rose. Rose Justice, American poet. Well, I'm Karolina Salska, Polish filmmaker. Not famous yet. I worked as a projectionist before the war, but what I really want to do is animation, like Disney, you know? You'll pay for the bread by telling me all about *Fantasia*." She added as a breathless afterthought, "You *have* seen *Fantasia*, right?"

"Well, yes, but . . ." What had happened in *Fantasia*? Mickey Mouse in a wizard's hat and flying horses and . . . dinosaurs? "It was about four years ago and I don't remember the music."

"Don't worry, I haven't seen it, but I know what they play in every sequence, and Lisette is like a walking music library. We'll get her to hum and you can describe what happens, okay? Gitte sometimes lets us sing after lights-out."

"But—"

"Look, I said don't worry. If you can't remember the whole thing, you can teach me some new American dance tunes as compensation." Karolina herded me toward one of the long tables where the knitters worked—Róża curled up under the end of the table on the concrete floor with Lisette and squeezed over to make room for me and Karolina. It was their little family place for a quarter of an hour twice a day, a private nook under the table and out of the chaos of the hundreds of people trying to get to the soup and bread. Karolina tried to let me creep in first, but I couldn't sit. I had to stay on my knees at the table's edge. As Karolina shuffled in past me I noticed that she was wearing a Camp Police armband. Then I glanced down at her bare legs and saw the scar splitting her shin.

"You're a Rabbit!"

She glanced up at me. She'd gone red. "And I like to dance to American music."

I probably went red, too. "Oh! I didn't mean you couldn't dance! I was just surprised about your armband!"

"A few of us are Camp Police. Rabbits are *privileged*. I patrol the antiaircraft ditches and don't have to go around with SS guards breathing down my neck all the time."

She tossed her head defiantly, smoothing her kerchief with the back of her hand as if it were her hair. "I don't limp," she said. "One operation only, a bacterial infection, very neat. They didn't peel off the muscle or cut out pieces of my shinbone like they did to Róża—"

"You were sick for longer," Róża interrupted. "You couldn't walk for eight months."

"But you wouldn't notice now if I was wearing stockings." Listening to the Rabbits talk about their operations was like watching a horror movie in a foreign language. You sort of hoped you'd misunderstood what was going on. And then when you figured out what was really going on, it was worse than you'd thought.

"I can walk without limping," Karolina said again. "My legs weren't even worth a picture, remember?" She turned to me again. "Róża got two snapshots all to herself, front and back."

"What kind of pictures?" I asked in an agony of confusion. I didn't think she meant *art*. Did the SS make them *pose*?

"We stole a camera a couple of weeks ago. There's a soldiers' prison camp not far from here, and sometimes the Ravensbrück work units have to deliver things there, and people get to talk to the boys. They got us a camera. We took an entire roll of film of the worst damaged legs."

Róża said savagely, "They'll kill us all eventually, but at least we've got evidence." She let out one of her bitter cackles of laughter. "If somebody ever gets the pictures developed. One of the French prisoners is hiding the film—"

At that point Lisette raised one finger to her lips, and both Róża and Karolina gave her their full attention, waiting expectantly.

Lisette said something in Polish. The second she'd finished, they all took a tiny bite of the stale bread, and a moment later I realized that Lisette had just said grace. They were crouching on a dirty concrete floor under a table and they said *grace*.

I was astonished at the time. Now, I understand. It was one of the ways Lisette held herself together.

Then Lisette turned to me and said in casual English, just carrying on the conversation where she'd interrupted it, "Karolina helped take the snapshots, but we can't risk letting her guard the film. That's what you were arrested for in the first place, isn't it, darling? Illegal filming!"

"I didn't film *anything*. I made a short cartoon showing a bunch of wolves herding rabbits into prison trucks," Karolina corrected with satisfaction. "And I still can't believe I got the rabbits right! Anyway, I was arrested for *showing* the film, not for making it." She gave her empty tin bowl a swipe with the hem of her dress and tried to tilt it so she could see her reflection, then sighed at the hopelessness of this project. She stowed the bowl in a little bag on a string tied around her waist. "Believe me, I can't wait to get out of here and do an updated sequel, involving wolf bites. What were you arrested for, Rose?"

"I landed my plane in the wrong place," I said.

Róża snickered and leaped into the conversation. "I was arrested for being a Girl Scout. They arrested my whole Girl Scout troop in the summer of 1941. I was fourteen."

I gaped at her.

"We were delivering plastic explosive for bombs," she said. "You know, little homemade bombs to sabotage officials' cars and throw in office windows. Most of us got released, but they kept the oldest—and I didn't stand a chance, because I'd actually been stopped at a checkpoint and, well, it was pretty obvious I was smuggling explosive. You know how it is when you're fourteen—you think you're so much smarter than everybody else and nothing will ever hurt you. . . ." She trailed off, wiping her own bowl with her last crumb of bread, and then said in her offhand way, "They didn't beat me, but they made me watch while they beat my mother, trying to get me to tell them who I was working for. Lucky for me I didn't know. Someone always dropped off the stuff in our baskets with a note that said where to take it. They beat the crap out of our Girl Scout leader and then they shot her. So, 51498, what were you doing when you were fourteen?"

"I'm older than you," I said faintly. "The war hadn't started yet."

154

It had, though. It had already been going on for a year, but the USA wasn't in it yet. MY GOD, it's been going on SUCH A LONG TIME.

"Well, what *were* you doing? Do they have Girl Scouts in America?"

"Yes—we—"

Oh—we hung May baskets on people's doors. Daddy got a brand-new Piper Cub for the flying school, and he took me along to pick it up from Lock Haven, and I flew it all the way home, and Hemlock Council gave me a special "Young Pilot" badge. I went on my second Juniata River canoe trip that summer. We took the Brownies on a picnic to the Conewago Grove Lake. We were not smuggling explosives and we were not being arrested by the Nazis. Nobody executed my troop leader. I did not have to watch my mother being beaten.

That is one of the very simple horrors I can't shake—I can strip the clothes from a pile of dead bodies without retching, but thinking about this ninth-grade Girl Scout having to watch her mother being tortured still makes me feel sick. Though I am not sure Róża would have grassed on anyone even to save her mother. *Lucky for me I didn't know.* Why lucky for *her*? Not lucky for the people she was protecting, but lucky for *Róża*. She didn't have to choose.

"Do they still—these experiments on people's legs, do they still . . . ?" I couldn't finish the question.

Karolina glanced down at my own bloodstained dress. I'd been kneeling for a quarter of an hour and my knees were aching, but I couldn't sit. I hung on to the edge of the table to hold myself up.

"Don't worry, you're safe," she said. "I mean, your legs are safe. They stopped the experiments last year."

"They might shoot you, of course, but they might do that to anybody," Róża offered.

"Hey, *hey!*" Karolina said, and Lisette suddenly crawled out next to me and grabbed me around the shoulders.

"Don't be scared, darling. Don't let Róża scare you! She makes fun of *everything*. It's how she is."

"She laughs when she's in pain," Karolina assured me. "She doesn't cry, just laughs like a mechanical fortune-teller in a glass box. Don't cry!"

"The war's nearly over," Lisette said soothingly.

"Look, I'll let you in on a secret—" Karolina peeled back the edge of her kerchief. She was hiding a new crop of soft brown curls. "I want to look nice when the American soldiers get here. I've got to make sure no one sees that I'm growing my hair out, though. The guards really hate curly hair."

It had been drizzling all afternoon and was pouring with rain by the nine p.m. roll call, and it was the coldest it had been since I'd got to Germany. I was burning with fever by lights-out—it nearly killed me to have to climb up to the top bunk.

"Why do you sleep so high up?" I gasped. "With your legs the way they are?"

"When people get the shits, it rains down on the lower bunks," Róża explained. "We had to fight the Red Army bitches for the high ones. Mother in heaven, you've never had to fight for anything, have you?"

I was still only capable of lying flat on my face in the crowded bunk, and they all used me for a furnace. Róża and Karolina snuggled up on either side of me, Karolina behind me with her arms right around me, and Róża in a sodden, shivering ball of misery between me and Lisette.

"Okay," Karolina demanded. "*Fantasia!* Start with 'The Sorcerer's Apprentice'—that's an easy one. Sing, Lisette!"

"Shh," Lisette said. "Tomorrow."

Lisette's word was law, and she'd been watching me

closely; she knew I couldn't perform any more that night. But I had to give them something, payment for the bread, for being adopted into their family, even if I wasn't going to give a movie commentary.

"'If I grow bitterly,'" I whispered, and managed shreds of Edna St. Vincent Millay's "Scrub."

> "If I grow bitterly,
> Like a gnarled and stunted tree,
> Bearing harshly of my youth
> Puckered fruit that sears the mouth . . .
>
> "It is that a wind too strong
> Bent my back when I was young,
> It is that I fear the rain
> Lest it blister me again."

"Perfect," Róża whispered in astonishment. "Beautiful and twisted and exactly like us! Did you think it up today? When did you ever get a chance? You are better than I thought you would be."

"It's just more Millay," I confessed. "My poems aren't that good."

The rain on the thin barrack roof sounded exactly like the rain on the roof of the sleeping porch. I ached with such desperate longing for Pennsylvania that I couldn't tell where the homesickness ended and the dull throb of the bloody slashes on my back began.

I will never be as good a writer as Edna St. Vincent Millay, I thought miserably; my poems will *never* be that good, because I will die here before I get the chance to write anything worth reading.

AIR RAID AT RAVENSBRÜCK (by Rose Justice)

"*Runter!*" they screamed. "Get down!" As if we'd all
leap up like mongrel dogs with our teeth bared.
But being obedient curs, down we all went,
not knowing why yet, flat on our faces, prone,
wet cinders in our mouths. The lights in the street
went out. The guards took cover, their well-bred
Alsatians with them. Open siren throats
shrilled an empty threat to swallow us whole.
We lay like forty thousand corpses in rows ten deep
by ourselves, and one thought hit us all hard in the
    head:

*Run NOW. In the dark—get up and run now. Dare
the charged barbed wire NOW. No one sees or cares.*

But when our brothers-in-arms in the bombers
    swarmed
over the blackened street, the howling night
leaped up in fury wielding searchlight whips
to flay the planes and skin the moon; the beams
broke harsh across our backs and froze us where
we lay revealed—wild does, not fanged or clawed
but weaponless rabbits and deer, blinking and
    blind.
No one ran or tried to run, lashed down
by the bright perimeter straps of light, bonds lighter
than moonlit air, heavier than iron chains.

My first air raid was during a roll call. It was about a week after I got to Block 32, the day before I was deemed well enough to be booted out of the knitting brigade. As the sirens went off, they made us lie on our faces. We were like a great big living, breathing target with nowhere to run and nowhere to hide. They turned out the spotlights, but they had searchlights in the antiaircraft ditches sweeping the sky for the planes.

When I heard the planes, I rolled over onto my back—no one cared. I lay with my dress bunched up under my backside and my hands beneath my thighs, cushioning my legs a little because they were still sore, with the back of my bare skull and most of my legs cradled by the cold, damp grit of the ground. I counted thirty-one US Army Air Force Flying Fortresses in the first echelon blacking out the silver moonlit sky, with an escort of fighter planes too far away and tiny to identify in the dark. Barely a mile away from me, 6000 feet above my head, were American boys not much older than me, carrying Pennsylvania Hershey bars in their emergency rations, one hand on the control column and one hand on the throttle. They were looking down at the same scene I'd looked down at a month ago. Beneath the searchlights they'd see the dim outlines of a factory complex and the black rows of barracks roofs, the long black threads of the railway junctions, and the cool lakes shining silver in the light of the glorious full moon.

They'd be too high and it was too dark for them to see any of the forty thousand women lying facedown on the damp gravel, trapped in our wire-and-concrete cage.

A pilot's pinpoint. That's all.

Five rows away from me, someone stood up suddenly. From where I lay she was silhouetted against the sky in the moonlight, six feet tall and skeletal, with a shock of spiky short white hair like an old man with a crew cut. She didn't say anything, just stood with her head thrown back, staring up at the passing planes. The moon lit her bristling hair like frost.

The woman next to her pulled at her skirt, trying to get her to lie down. She completely ignored this, and after a minute she raised one arm to the sky with her fist clenched—not raging, but saluting the airmen above her. Then suddenly she started to shake with sobs. I couldn't hear her—the noise of the next wave of planes overhead and the sirens on the ground drowned out everything else—but I could see her shoulders heaving, and after a moment she stuffed her clenched fist against her mouth to shut herself up.

The other woman was still pulling at her skirt fearfully, and the tall one snapped at her angrily and reached toward the sky again. This time her hand was open, grasping—as if she were trying to snatch the planes out of the sky like King Kong, or trying to catch hold of them to pull her away with them.

I burst out unthinkingly, "Don't cry!"

She turned to look for me. She didn't lower her arm.

"Ne pleure pas!" I repeated in French, because it was the only other language I had a chance in.

She answered me in French that was worse than mine, heavily accented and without any real grammatical connections.

"It hurts me that I do not know the planes. These are new since I became a prisoner. The big ones are maybe American? I do not know. They could be my own; I would not know. It always makes me cry."

"They're American," I agreed.

She lowered her arm.

"You know this?"

"I'm a pilot."

She burst out in joyful laughter and swore incomprehensibly in her own language. Then she took five long strides over the huddled bodies between us and came to lie down next to me—on her back beside me, squeezed in between me and Lisette, so that the two of us were lying side by side looking up at the sky like stargazers on a beach.

"American planes," she said. "What kind of planes?"

"The big ones—" I didn't know the French for "bomber," either, so I just said it in English. "The big ones, the bombers, are B-17s, Flying Fortresses."

"Four engines," she added. You could see them.

"Wright Cyclone engines," I told her. "Crew of ten. The little planes, what-do-you-call-them, I don't know the French for 'fighters,' I think Mustangs."

She hugged me passionately, and I gave a surprised yell of agony as my hands got knocked out from beneath my thighs and my backside hit the rough ground.

"Oh! What?"

"*Fünfundzwanzig,*" I gasped. "Last week."

"Sorry!"

She inched away respectfully. She knew it was pointless to try to help (she did know how it felt). She said, "I am Irina Korsakova."

Róża, flat on her face beside me, hissed, "Don't talk to her—Russian scum!"

The timing was bad for Róża and Irina. Usually the Poles and the Russians in Block 32 got along pretty well—they were united in their disdain of the French, who were shy about undressing and rouged their faces with carefully saved slivers of beetroot. Block 32 was split down the middle with the French all on one side and the Russians and Poles on the other. But when Irina first threw herself into our row, the

Warsaw Uprising had just come to a disastrous conclusion, and all summer the Soviets had done a lousy job of giving the Poles any useful support. When the Germans finally beat the rebellion down, they practically destroyed the city—Block 32 knew perfectly well what was happening because imprisoned Polish women and children from Warsaw had been pouring into Ravensbrück for the past two weeks. So when I met Róża, she was holding a grudge against the whole of the USSR. Also, she was just by nature a jealous little thing.

On the other side of me, Irina asked in a bored voice, "What did the fucking Rabbit say about me?"

"She told me not to talk to you."

They had a brief argument in Russian (I think), spitting and hissing like a pair of cats.

"Fucking Poles," Irina said to me in French.

"What?" I asked. "What did you say? What did she say?"

"Fucking Russians," Róża half translated. (Róża taught me to swear like a sailor in about half a dozen European languages. The Polish students from Lublin spoke *everything*. It made me feel so stupid sometimes, this uneducated American who could only speak English and barely scrape by in French.)

"Go ahead and talk to her," Róża sneered permission. "Witch. That's what the Germans call those Soviet girl pilots—*Nacht Hexen*. 'Night Witches.' Go ahead and listen to her propaganda."

I couldn't imagine what kind of propaganda I was going to get from a girl who'd been in prison so long it had turned her hair white. In all the time I knew Irina, I never heard her say the words *communist* or *party* without turning away from me and spitting. But most of the Russian women at Ravensbrück were Red Army soldiers. Irina was a little different.

Her lanky height and hollowed face and white crew cut gave her the look of a grim, battle-worn king—Macbeth, maybe—someone competent and ruthless and experienced.

"I'm not a Night Witch," Irina murmured low in my ear. "I never flew those tired old sewing machines except when I was training students. I am in Soviet Air Force 296 Regiment, based at Stalingrad. Men and a few women, flying Yaks, chasing together."

"Chasing together?" I pictured a school dance, everyone running around after other people's partners. "Chasing what?"

"Chasing the Fascists." She always said "the Fascists" when she was talking about the Germans. "Chasing Fascist aircraft."

The French word doesn't mean *chasing*—it means *hunting*. Irina was a hunter pilot. In English we say *fighter*, not hunter. *She was a combat pilot.*

I was so thrilled it took my breath away. It was like meeting Amelia Earhart. Irina was a woman, and a *fighter pilot*.

"What's your score?" I asked breathlessly.

She hesitated, trying to think of the right word. "Eleven?"

"*Eleven?*"

That couldn't be right. Shooting down five enemy aircraft makes you an official ace. She'd said eleven—a *double ace*.

She held her hands up so they were silhouetted black against the bright moonlit sky—ten fingers. Then one more, shaken for emphasis. "Eleven kills. Decorated Hero of the Soviet Union. Have you many kills?" she added casually, as if we were comparing notes. She called them *kills*—a hunter bringing down prey.

"No, I'm a transport pilot."

"Why are you here?"

"I was—" I didn't know the French for "intercepted."
"I was caught—caught in the air by Luftwaffe jets. Jets? Fast planes. I had no guns."

"When my guns were empty, I made a *taran*. Straight into a Fascist bomber, a fast dive from above. They did not know what hit them. Lost my—" She didn't know the French for "propeller"—she sketched a tight, fast spinning circle in the air above our faces. "Forced to land in Poland, and Fascist soldiers picked me up with a face full of glass and half my ribs broken."

"You made a *taran*!"

She must have thought I didn't know what she meant. She smacked the palm of one hand with the fist of the other. "In the air. Like this—"

Róża's high voice pitched in suddenly at my other ear in fluent French. "*Taran* is a Polish word."

"I know! My friend Felicyta told me about it! Aerial ramming!" And in an agony of excitement, I punched a fist at the sky.

Taran. It is the same word in Polish and Russian. There is a technique to it, which Irina showed me—her hands became planes, wings spread and rigid, above our faces in the sky.

Irina had the most beautiful hands!

TRIOLET FOR IRINA (by Rose Justice)

Rigidly spread, like taut wings, fly
her open hands. Above her head
mute ruthless fingers slice the sky
rigidly spread like taut wings, fly
while forty thousand women lie
in frozen cinders, blind with dread,
rigidly spread. Like taut wings fly
her open hands above her head.

(I am amazed I remembered the rhyme scheme for a triolet. Mr. Wagner would be proud of me.)

These are your weapons, Irina's hands told me—pointing with the left, demonstrating with the right. Propeller, fuselage, wing. Go for the enemy wing or rudder, clip it with your own wing or prop.

All around us people were weeping in fear, facedown in the dirt, while Irina's hands flew over our heads. She showed me how she rammed her last kill. Then I showed her how I tipped my V-1 flying bomb.

When the air raid began, anyone who was Camp Police like Karolina had been hustled off to the perimeter ditches to haul sandbags and drag the antiaircraft guns into position; but Róża and Lisette were both watching and helping along the conversation, which was now going on in four languages. I made my hands chase each other in slow motion. My left hand crept up on the right, passed it, slowed down again as the right caught up, four times. Finally, thumb to thumb, wingtip to wingtip, a sliver of space between them, until the slight triumphant moment when the wings caress—

And I dropped my right hand like a falling bomb.

"Again," Irina said. "There was no touch—no contact?"

I showed her how I'd made the other aircraft stall, filling in English words when I didn't know the French. Lisette helped in Russian.

Róża suddenly interrupted in a hiss of a whisper, "51498! You told us they arrested you because you landed in the wrong place! Now you're saying it was because *you knocked down a Luftwaffe plane in a* taran *attack?*"

"Well—I got caught because I was lost. And I got lost because I went chasing after a flying bomb."

"*You knocked down a flying bomb and you landed in one piece on a runway afterward?*"

"Well—" I held my hands up against the sky. "It was the wrong runway."

"Think she's a liar?" Róża asked of no one in particular.

"A good one, if she is," Irina said mildly. "The hands know what they are talking about."

"Maybe you're a liar, too, Russian bat girl."

"Maybe I am, Polish Rabbit. What do you care? I think I have met another *taran* pilot."

Two things happened—another wave of American bombers began to whine past overhead, and one of the watchtowers on the concrete walls exploded with machine-gun fire, followed by distant screams.

The guns were aimed at *us*. Or not at us personally—at some of the other prisoners. "*Karolina!*" Lisette gasped in horror.

Instinctively I snatched my hands out of the air and held them tight against my chest. Instinctively Róża grabbed me. Instinctively, on the other side of me, Irina gripped my other hand.

"It's not Karolina," Róża insisted, fiercely reassuring. "They're screaming on the *Appelplatz*, not in the ditches." The *Appelplatz* was the big open square where the Camp gathered for work details. I don't know what the prisoners there had done to deserve getting fired at with machine guns. We clung to one another, cowering beneath the invading aircraft and the guns and the sounds of agony on the *Appelplatz*.

Then Irina let go of my hand and held her spread fingers a little bit over our faces, the silhouette of a plane in the dark, and rocked her hand as though she were rocking the wings of an aircraft at me. "*Taran*," she whispered.

Like Elodie whispering, "*La victoire!*" A secret sign of hope, of the slow, inevitable end to this NEVERENDING WAR.

I rocked my own hand above our faces in the dark for a silent reply.

"*Taran*," I whispered back.

Irina invaded our bunk. There wasn't even much of a fight. Some of the Russian prisoners had been put on night work, and it was less crowded in the bunks than it had been—at least, in ours there were only me and Lisette and Róża before Irina turned up.

"What's the ugly Russian bat girl doing here?" Karolina asked, crawling back in exhausted ten minutes after the rest of us. (She asked it in Polish, but I *know* that's more or less what she was asking.)

"She's Rose's friend," said Róża. "They're both aerial combat aces. And I am the prima ballerina of the Warsaw Ballet. Let her stay—she'll protect you from the other Russian pigs."

Do you know what I ended up with stuck in my head?

> "*Make new friends*
> *But keep the old,*
> *One is silver*
> *And the other gold!*"

Six hours later the clear sky was gone, and I stood for roll call in the pouring rain, eaten up with anxiety over the thought of all those young American bomber pilots having to fly home through such spectacularly horrible weather. I wasn't paying any attention to the SS guard screaming incomprehensible numbers in German.

"*Französisch politischer Häftling Einundfünfzigtausendvierhundertachtundneunzig! Die Verfügbar!*" she yelled. She advanced on our row like a turkey buzzard, red in the face with rain streaming from her black cape. Her awful dog tried unsuccessfully to shake itself dry all over our entire row.

"That's you, my dear," Lisette whispered from the other side of Irina. "She wants an 'Available.' *Verfügbar*."

No one else looked up. No one else even said anything, not daring to risk the narrowest chance of punishment with the dog standing there, grinning savagely at us.

"*Die Verfügbar!*" the buzzard-woman screeched again. "*Häftling Einundfünfzigtausendvierhundertachtundneunzig!*"

Róża gave me a little push. "*Available 51498.*" I stepped out of line feeling like I was going to my doom. Róża's words from my first day in Block 32 rattled in my head: *You have to line up in the morning and go wherever they send you. Shoveling shit, maybe, or burning corpses. Anything. Usually things nobody else wants to do.*

The guard looked me over, then glanced at Irina standing there next to my empty place in line, her gaunt six-foot frame towering over tiny Róża. The guard beckoned to Irina with a royal shake of her head. Irina tried to protest—she wasn't an Available. She was supposed to work in the power plant with a bunch of other Russian girls.

The guard couldn't have cared less what Irina was supposed to be doing. She slapped Irina in the face for protesting and herded her out of line to join me. Then she drove us both ahead of her through the gate in the chain-link fence that separated our block from the rest of the Camp. Standing woefully soaked and miserable out there was a group of a dozen other Availables, waiting for me and Irina to join them in some unknown backbreaking and nasty work assignment.

The guard turned us over to our group leader, a German *Kolonka* (*Kolonka* is a Ravensbrück word, short for something I can't remember, but basically means "forewoman")—the *Kolonka* wasn't an SS guard, but a German prisoner. She wore a green triangle and a red armband. The red armband showed she was a forewoman and let her go anywhere she wanted. The green triangle showed she was a criminal. One of the very first things Róża had told me was how a German criminal with a red armband was exactly the worst combination of work leader, and to my utter terror, this one homed in on me right away.

She was nearly as tall as Irina. She had the stub of an unlit cigarette clamped in the corner of her mouth, and she barked orders around it like a gangster. I stood quivering as she pinpointed me to question on the first day I turned up in her work crew. Right there in the pouring rain she pointed to the letters Elodie had embroidered in my sleeve patch. "USA?" she asked curiously.

"Ich bin Amerikanerin," I explained.

In perfect, almost unaccented English, she asked, "Why are you here?" She had intense pale green eyes the exact color of a Coca-Cola bottle. I didn't answer, and she shrugged a little. "Just wondering. I don't give a shit why you're here. I went to college in America. But you're the first American I've seen in Ravensbrück." Then she began firing these weird, casual, ordinary questions at me. "Have you ever been to Chicago?"

I swallowed, at sea as to where this was going. I gave her terse, suspicious answers.

"I stayed overnight once."

"Who's your favorite bandleader?"

"Um—Tommy Dorsey?"

"Do you know a recipe for Boston cream pie?"

I shook my head.

"Too bad!" She twisted her mouth in disappointment. "I'd give a lot to get a recipe for Boston cream pie. Don't worry, I'm not going to report you for being American. If you don't understand anything I say in German, just ask. Now I'm going to shout at you all to straighten up and get moving, okay? French morons."

And she did, just launched into a long tirade of orders in German.

French morons? I wondered.

Irina, who was Russian, was in line next to me. I stole a glance at the girl walking ahead of her, whose left sleeve I could see pretty well. Her red triangle had a defiant black *F* embroidered in it the way Elodie had embroidered hers, and I could just make out the number above her political prisoner patch—51444. She was from my original French transport.

Then I tried to check the other women around me. I could see the numbers of the two ahead of me—we were all from the same transport. None of them was Elodie, but they were from Elodie's transport.

Elodie! I thought, my heart lifting in the ridiculous way it did at any faint promise of hope—a tattered kite soaring and going nowhere. Elodie, my comrade-in-arms from the first three weeks in quarantine! Maybe I could get a message to Elodie!

Our German *Kolonka* barked another incomprehensible order at us, then unexpectedly followed up with a quiet translation first in French and then in English. "Stay over this side. Don't go near the tent. *Don't look.*"

We tried not to look. But the tent was between us and wherever we were going, and we couldn't help *seeing*.

It was as big as a circus tent and had been put up while I was still in quarantine, in an open place too marshy to build on, as a temporary shelter for the new prisoners who were pouring into Ravensbrück every day—thousands of civilians from beaten Warsaw, from Auschwitz as they started to evacuate it before the Red Army got there, and from a ton of other camps and prisons closer to the Front as they moved people around. You could see the tent from inside the fence around Block 32, but I hadn't paid much attention to it while I'd been working with the knitters. Today there were more guards and dogs than usual all around the tent perimeter, keeping people inside, and the reason everyone in there was trying to get out in the rain was because they were dying of thirst.

Really dying of it, I think.

Hands and arms and heads stuck out anywhere there was a gap—cupped hands collecting rainwater, some holding bowls or even just a piece of cloth to collect moisture—I saw one woman lying on her back with her hair in the black cinder mud at the tent's edge, her mouth open, letting a rivulet of water stream down the canvas and into her mouth.

You know, it set you at war with yourself.

A back-of-my-mind part of me wanted to help—the Lutheran-church-bred Girl Scout in me wanted to race back and forth with buckets of water for everybody.

But another back-of-my-mind part of me, cowed and self-centered, was going, *Thank GOD I am in Block 32. Thank GOD I am not in that tent.*

And the front of my mind—the biggest part of me—was just screaming over and over in denial and disbelief, *WHAT AM I DOING HERE?*

"*Don't look,*" the German *Kolonka* advised again, and then her voice suddenly went hard and flat. "Oh, what the hell, go ahead and look. If they throw any bodies out of the tent, we'll probably have to pick them up. But stay on this side just now!"

There were twelve of us, all with numbers in the 51000s except for Irina and the *Kolonka*, and when we got to work I realized that what we had in common was our height—all of us were tall. That's why the guard had pulled Irina out of line on a whim when she'd come to get me that morning.

The *Kolonka* wasn't kidding about picking up bodies. We got marched down the main street of the Camp, the *Lagerstrasse*, to a depot. There we collected half a dozen hand-carts, and then our very first job was clearing the top bunks in the *Revier*, the sick bay, which shorter women couldn't see or reach as easily as we could. We left the carts standing at the back door of the *Revier* and lined up to go in. The *Kolonka* pulled the neck of her dress up over her nose like a gas mask and yelled another order at us through the blue-and-gray striped cloth, and we marched inside like we were going to war. The stench was unbelievable. Within seconds we all had our dresses pulled up over our noses.

And I do not remember what we did.

I *know* what we did, of course, and I remember doing the same thing later—we moved hundreds of corpses this win-ter. We lifted them out of the bunks and undressed them. We stacked them in rows on the floor of the mortuary. We carried them out to our handcarts and hauled them to the crematorium and unloaded them again. But I don't remem-ber the first time I did it. It was worse doing it for the first time. And I have blocked it out.

This is what I do remember about that first day of work as an Available: just before we marched back to our blocks for the six o'clock roll call, our *Kolonka* assembled us in the washroom of the *Revier* and gave us each a vitamin C tablet out of a green triangular package.

"These are from the Swiss Red Cross, and yes, they're stolen. Take them *now*—nothing leaves this room. Any of you breathe a word and I'll get you transferred to the Punishment

Block. Not the Bunker—don't expect a cozy private cell with nothing to do all day. You'll be digging toilet pits and hauling road rollers."

She didn't have to threaten us again. Even I knew already what the Punishment Block was, and it wasn't the extra hard and filthy work people dreaded about being sent there. The women in the Punishment Block were known for being the nastiest people in the Camp. Probably with good reason, but you didn't want to have to fight for sleeping space or food with someone who'd kick you under the bunks and steal your bowl and make you buy it back with your bread ration for the entire week.

The *Kolonka* watched us all closely while we swallowed the vitamins, her pale green eyes narrow with suspicion. Suddenly she advanced on Irina. She seized hold of Irina's jaw and rammed her head back against the tiled wall, pinching her nostrils closed and holding a hand over her mouth.

"*Häftling Einundfünfzigtausendvierhundertachtundneunzig!*" the *Kolonka* rapped out over her shoulder. Prisoner 51498! Me. I stepped forward fearfully.

"Does this bitch understand anything but Russian?"

I gulped. "A little French."

"*Swallow!*" the *Kolonka* ordered Irina in French, punctuating her command by bashing the back of Irina's skull against the wall. Irina choked and spluttered and finally swallowed.

The German girl turned around and told us, "No hiding stolen vitamin pills under your tongue to take to your friends back in your block. I'm not being nice or doing you a favor. I'm taking care of myself. No one on my team gets scurvy. Line up!"

We lined up meekly.

"My name's Anna," she growled at us. It seemed like an

odd thing to finish up with. I think it was the closest she could come to an apology.

"So what did they make you do?" Róża asked cheerfully as we scrambled to get our tepid soup that evening.

My hands were shaking. Karolina put her own hand under my bowl so I didn't spill anything.

"We were working in the *Revier*. Irina tried to organize vitamins for you," I told Róża. "She got bashed in the head for it."

"For *me*? *Really*, Russian Bat Girl?"

Irina shrugged. "No, not for you, Rabbit. If I got away with it, I would have sold them."

"Can you get calcium tablets?" Lisette asked.

Irina shot me a warning glance that said clearly, *Shut up or Anna will get you transferred to the Punishment Block.* But Lisette wouldn't let it go, and after we'd all squeezed into our spot under the end of the table and she'd said her grace in Polish, she said to me again, "Calcium tablets."

"Why calcium?" I asked.

"For the Rabbits who have had bone operations. For Róża, so she doesn't break her leg walking on the damaged bone. It can happen. Calcium helps make bones stronger."

I thought about it for a minute. Anna was like a guard dog—trained to be vicious, but maybe if you handled her the right way . . . *I'd give a lot to get a recipe for Boston cream pie,* she'd said.

Irina caught my eye and raised two fingers to her lips, miming smoking.

She was right—I was ready to bet Anna could be bribed with cigarettes. Except for Irina, the other girls on my work team were all from my original transport. If they were still sharing bunks with Elodie, if they were still in the same block with her and she was still alive, maybe one of them could carry a message to her—I felt sure Elodie was capable of organizing cigarettes for me to give to Anna.

"We'll work on it," I said.

The next morning Irina and I joined the tall French girls again and marched through the mud past the tent, with Anna marching next to our column, where she could keep an eye on us. Irina stood between me and Anna to hide the fact that I had a whole day's bread ration hidden in the blouse of my dress, about a quarter of a loaf. That was the standard unit of Camp currency, a day's bread ration, and we'd scraped it together in anticipation of our great calcium caper.

Hope—you think of hope as a bright thing, a strong thing, sustaining. But it's not. It's the opposite. It's simply this: lumps of stale bread stuck down your shirt. Stale gray bread eked out with ground fish bones, which you won't eat because you're going to give it away, and maybe you'll get a message through to your friend. *That's all you need.*

God, I was hungry.

I don't mean I was more hungry that day than I'd been the day before. I mean I was constantly, hopelessly, stupefyingly hungry. I said earlier I can't remember when I first felt that way—though I know I wasn't able to eat much right after I got out of the Bunker, I don't remember ever *not* being hungry. The thing is, when you're that hungry it's almost impossible to think about anything else. You know you ought to, and you want to, and sometimes you're forced to. Calcium and cigarettes. Air raids. Feeling sorry for the people who are dying of thirst and the half-human *schmootzich* beggars licking spilled soup off the kitchen steps. But it takes an effort.

We got marched past the tent, past the Bunker and the sick bay and kitchens and out through the main gate, but without our handcarts this time. Then we went around the walls toward the crematorium, the path we'd taken with the corpses yesterday, and I had a bad moment thinking they'd make us work at the incinerator ovens today. But we passed the crematorium and ended up in the building next to it, a long shed with a sort of huge garage door entrance. It was being used as a storage area for building and maintenance equipment. Our team of Tall, Strong Amazons was supposed to clear it out.

The shed was full of tools, shovels, long lengths of rail, stuff like that. I don't think I could ever in a million years describe what it was like for me and three other underfed girls to pick up a steel rail—two of us on each end—and carry it on our shoulders to a pile by the train tracks. If any one of us had dropped her end, or stumbled, our feet would have all been crushed.

Irina and I worked together, but on our third rail we somehow got swapped around with a couple of the French girls, and I ended up next to Prisoner 51444.

"I have some of your things," she muttered suddenly. "Your friend Elodie sent them."

We were at the unloading point and let our end of rail come thundering down into the muddy ground. We had to shift the rail over to line it up, and the girl hissed in my ear as we worked, "Wait till we're back in the shed. I'll hand them over."

Hope is the most treacherous thing in the *world*. It lifts you and lets you plummet. But as long as you're being lifted, you don't worry about plummeting.

"I have bread for you to give Elodie," I whispered back. "Can she get me some cigarettes?"

51444 gave a panicked, explosive laugh. "What if I eat the bread myself?"

I hissed in her ear, "You won't. You just said you're Elodie's messenger." I hazarded wildly, "You can have half."

"I'm Micheline," she said.

Later on, she stumbled against me and grabbed at my arm for support, and suddenly I was holding something soft and silky balled up in the palm of my hand.

I stuffed the silky wad into the neck of my dress and gave her the bread.

I didn't know what she'd pressed into my hand until I got back to Block 32 that night and had a chance to look. It turned out to be my hose. Elodie had sent me my stockings! They were actually little socks that she'd made out of my hose. She'd been put to work in one of the workshops where they repurposed everybody's clothes, and she'd got hold of my torn nylons and cut them into pieces and made me three little pairs of socks—they just slipped over your feet so they'd be hidden by your shoes. I hope she kept a few pairs back for herself.

And—this is so Elodie—she'd embroidered a tiny rosebud on the instep of each one. The thread was from my own dress, the one I was still wearing, from the same ball of thread we'd unraveled from the torn collar when we were together in quarantine. A little blue rose on each foot.

Oh, wonderful Elodie!

Three pairs of nylon socks. If I'd worn all three on top of each other, my feet would have still been cold—but of course I gave a pair to Róża. And another to Lisette. I passed them around under the table when we'd finished eating. Lisette tried to give hers to Karolina—Karolina wouldn't take them. They had a fight over them. Or rather, Karolina refused heatedly. Lisette just kept calmly insisting, "I won't wear this newfangled nylon, my dear, so you may as well have them."

"*Idiots,*" Róża blazed. "Give them all to me if you're going to be stupid!"

"Take turns," Irina suggested as though she couldn't care less.

I am almost ashamed to write this down, but it never occurred to me I could have given away all three pairs. Not till this minute. I gave a pair to Róża because she couldn't walk. I gave a pair to Lisette because she was the mother of our Camp Family, and I'd been told to treat her like my mother. And I kept one for myself because they were *mine* and my feet were cold. Irina, I figured, was perfectly capable of organizing socks for herself, and Karolina—well, Karolina kept insisting she wasn't a cripple, and I didn't want to offend her.

And anyway, she was just so delighted by my fire-engine-red toenails when I put on the little nylon slipper socks for the first time that she didn't care about her own feet.

"*Nail varnish!*" Karolina hissed in delight. "You are a *painted woman*! No wonder they slapped you with a French prisoner's triangle!"

It is true. The nail polish for my date with Nick still hadn't come off. My toenails had grown out a bit, so there was a bare gap between the nail bed and the enamel, but if you didn't look too close and you didn't look at the skin of my blistered feet, my toenails were still pretty.

Róża rolled her eyes. "Karolina is the vainest creature in the world. Last time she tried to grow her hair out they made her wear a sign that said 'I have violated Camp rules by curling my hair.'"

"*Shut up,* Różyczka. What's the color called? The color of the varnish?"

"Cherry Soda," I said. "It was a little bottle I brought with me from America."

Karolina and Róża both sighed in ecstasy.

"*Cherry Soda!* No wonder your toes look like balls of candy."

"My mother never let me wear makeup—*ever*," Róża vowed with vivid envy.

"You were fourteen when you were arrested!" I protested. "My mother didn't let me wear makeup, either, when I was fourteen!"

"Did you paint them yourself or was it done by a beauty specialist? How long does it last? What shoes did you wear with it? Were they open-toed—could you see your toenails with your shoes on?"

"Sandals. It was for a date with my boyfriend, Nick."

"Did he like them?"

I shrugged and looked away. I don't think he'd noticed them. It wasn't the first time I'd thought of Nick, and the thought of him always made me ache. What would he *think* if he could see me now? There wasn't any way I could ever be mistaken for anything but a concentration camp prisoner, hairless, in my torn dress with its missing collar and big mismatched fabric X's and the brown striped bloodstains across my backside. Early on I used to dream about him, though I stopped dreaming about anything but food after a while—I dreamed he was touching my head and asking, "Where is your hair?"

Karolina stifled a giggle. "Let's name your toes. That'd be a hilarious little cartoon, a row of dancing toes like the Rockettes! Each a different flavor. Cherry! Peppermint!"

"Red currant!" said Lisette.

"Beetroot," said Irina.

"Beetroot!" Róża sneered.

"It is sweet. And red."

They coaxed me into putting the rhymes together.

"Strawberry, cranberry—"

"—grenadine, raspberry!"

And I made a rhyme about painted toes. It is a sort of insanely starved person's version of "This Little Piggy."

No penny candy
so stubbornly sweet
as plops of red sugar
adorning my feet—
strawberry, cinnamon,
red currant, cranberry,
peppermint, sugar beet,
grenadine, raspberry,
cherry, and mulberry—
come look at Rose
and join in the feast
of my lollipop toes!

Of course it was not just the illicit beauty of my toes that everyone admired—it was also, and in a big way, the fact that they looked so edible.

I wasn't the only one who'd been scavenging that day. Irina turned out to have an entire newspaper hidden in her shirt. She must have picked it up in the maintenance shed we'd been working in, though I hadn't noticed a thing at the time (she was fantastic at organizing paper, it turned out). As we were climbing into the bunks, just before the lights went out, she pressed most of the paper thin and hid it wedged between the bunk slats and frame. But one last piece she twitched in front of Róża's nose, and when she'd got Róża's attention, folded the scrap of paper while we watched.

It was only about as wide as her palm. Her hands moved so quickly you couldn't follow what she was doing. Oh, Irina's hands were pretty! And suddenly she'd transformed a yellowed corner of a stolen Nazi newspaper into a little paper airplane with short, broad wings. She held it out to Róża.

"Fly this," Irina said. She mimed the action of throwing a dart.

Róża lifted the paper plane toward the ceiling and pitched it across the bunks. She didn't even throw it very hard, but it glided away into the gloom, and after a moment someone threw it back with a sharp cautionary warning in Polish. It flew better than any paper airplane I had ever seen.

"I like to fly them over the walls," Irina said. "When no one is looking."

You know how I stood in roll calls making up poems to keep from going crazy with fear and boredom? Irina made up aircraft.

That was a good day, nylon socks and painted toes and Irina's first paper airplane. Some of the ones she made later Karolina decorated—she'd put Nick as the pilot, though of course she didn't know what he looked like. He was our hero—I whispered stories about Nick to Karolina and Róża after lights-out, where he'd come to rescue us, sneaking into the power plant with wire cutters and disabling the electric fences, carrying a knapsack full of chocolate bars. Karolina made him look like Clark Gable. Or she'd draw caricatures of us on Irina's planes, with Irina and me in the cockpit and Karolina and Róża and Lisette as our passengers. They were very funny and she could do them *so fast*—sometimes when we were standing in a roll call she'd make doodles of the turkey buzzard guards with her toes in the cinders at our feet. Just a couple of broad swipes and you'd see it and you'd have to pretend to sneeze so you didn't burst out laughing. And then she'd kick it into dust before she got caught.

Oh, God, dry words on a page. How can you grow to love a handful of strangers so fiercely just because you have to sleep on the same couple of wooden planks with them, when half the time you were there you wanted to strangle them, and all you ever talked about is death and imaginary strawberries?

"Rose, let's make a book," Róża whispered to me as we lay sleepless and shivering and scratching in the restless dark. "I want to do something like your poems. Karolina makes moving pictures, Irina makes planes—I want to *make* something. So you could write the poems in English and I could translate them into Polish—a kind of memory book—"

"We could get everybody to do her own memory!"

"A page for each of us, for each of the Rabbits—"

"Your whole transport. The whole Lublin Transport."

"Yes, the ones who have been murdered, too. We'll have photos of them as civilians—you'll have to track those down after you get out, okay?"

"We'll need paper."

"And recipes! We can get a recipe from everybody!"

"*Paper.*"

"Irina can organize some paper for us. It will be better than just a list of names—it will be about *people.*"

Our *Blockova*, Gitte, came crashing through the evening soup squabble, like a speedboat plowing up waves in the Arctic, tagging people. Karolina Salska was one of them.

"*You're on tomorrow's list.*" Half a dozen of us heard the icy whisper. There was no reason I should know what she meant, but I knew. I knew intuitively, along with everybody else who had experience of what it meant, and the hair stood up all down my spine.

"No!" Lisette gasped fiercely. "They're not going to execute any more Rabbits."

"That's why I'm telling you now," Gitte said. "There are

seven from my block on the list. We'll hide you all in the tent with the transfer prisoners."

Block 32 was tucked away in a southern spur of the Camp, in a corner, which gave us a sort of "back to the wall" advantage sometimes—we always knew when anyone was coming for us because they could only approach from one direction. And it was right next to the tent. I hadn't ever thought about that being an advantage.

When Gitte said about hiding in the tent, Lisette went white. And then her face closed down. "They'll miss us at roll call. They pull you out of the morning roll call. They'll pull someone else out instead."

"They'll know we're hiding people, but what else can we do? We've got to show them we're not going to give you up without another fight. They don't like it when we fight back. Too many people find out."

Karolina, also white, asked, "How will we get in the tent?"

"The fence gate's still open. I'll let you out now."

The Block 32 numbers didn't come out right in that night's roll call—no surprise. They shouted and hustled the dogs around us and checked our numbers about a hundred times. We had to stand there with our arms at our sides, looking straight ahead.

They made us stand there for a solid day.

When they made you stand there for hours and hours like that as punishment, they called it *Strafstehen*. Punishment standing. But this time it was *different*. It was the worst *Strafstehen* of the whole time I was there, the longest and the hungriest; but it didn't feel like punishment. It felt like a battle.

All night, all the next day, and past lights-out the next night—with nothing to eat and nothing to drink. It wasn't the coldest day we ever had to stand out there for hours and hours, but it was November now and it was darned cold. It snowed for most of the afternoon, squally blowing flurries that didn't stick. They let us march in place because the one thing they couldn't stop us from doing was shuffling our feet to keep warm. I held my breath and let it out slowly, watching how it made a little cloud in front of my face, amazed there was enough warmth somewhere deep inside my body that the air in me could condense into cloud on its way out.

People started to collapse. Róża collapsed. Irina and I pulled her to her feet. Róża tried to fall over again on purpose, throwing her full weight into it, but she weighed *nothing.* We linked our arms through hers to keep her up. Lisette gave a sob and Irina risked hissing a command in Russian at Róża to get her to behave—none of us wanted an SS guard to notice us.

But it was *different.* We had a purpose—we had a mission. We were standing there because we were *fighting.* Maybe if we'd given up the seven hiding in the tent they'd have let us go earlier. But none of us gave up *anybody.*

At midday, in the snow flurries, we heard the gunshots over the walls—they always took people outside the Camp to shoot them. Three. There were supposed to be ten. Our seven didn't get shot.

They let us go, I think, because they'd grown sick of guarding us. We staggered in a wild rush for the faucets in the washroom and handed out water to each other in bowls and buckets and tin cups, all of us crazed with thirst. Lisette stripped off her messed-up underpants and ran water through them and put them back on wet. We piled into the bunks, hundreds of us climbing over one another in the dark, and collapsed in gasping, clinging bundles of misery. The snow turned into rain again, pattering on the wooden roof. It sounded just like the rain on the sleeping porch.

"Don't cry, don't cry, don't cry," Róża chanted in my ear, under her breath. "We won, we won, we won. Don't cry."

"We won?" I echoed, stupefied.

"*We won.* Not like last time, when they shut us all in the block for three days in August with the windows closed, and we nearly suffocated, and then they threw us into the Bunker and operated on us there instead of in the *Revier.* Oh—Lisette—which was worse, standing in the snow till you turned into a block of ice or being slowly roasted alive? Remember that day we had one cup of water between the five of us till it got dark and you made us share it out by dipping our fingers in it?"

"Holy Mary, you stupid Rabbit, shut up and go to sleep." Irina yawned. "They will get us up again in three hours."

"*We won,*" Róża rasped in my ear, and it was the last thing I heard, and then I was unconscious.

"No coffee this morning."

Róża collapsed in mirth. "*No coffee!* That's one hell of a punishment. Wow, what did we get yesterday? I don't remember any *coffee.* What did we get the day before? Was that *coffee?*"

Our daily dose of "coffee" at six a.m. was brown and lukewarm and tasted of nothing. It was the idea of coffee, though, brown and lukewarm. We'd stood in the snow for over twenty-four hours, we'd slept for three hours, we'd stood in the drizzling, freezing dark for another two hours, and then we had no coffee. And then they sent us all back to work, even though that morning's roll call hadn't come out right, either.

The real miracle is that we didn't all kill one another that morning and save them the trouble of their executions.

The whole week that Karolina and the six other con-demned Rabbits were hiding, Irina and I had to go back each day to our weird work crew of tall girls, doing jobs that shorter people couldn't do as easily as we could—dismantling shelves, boarding up broken windows, carrying stacks of boxes—clearing top bunks of people who'd died in the night, especially in the *Revier*, where people were too sick to do it themselves.

Anna, the *Kolonka* with the green badge and green eyes, was contemptuously familiar with the *Revier* because she'd worked in it before. She took over the back washroom to use as a temporary morgue because the real one was always too full. She'd stand guard at the door by the sinks to make sure we had the place to ourselves and get a conversation going with me in English so she could pretend not to see if some of us sneaked a dead woman's wooden comb or a pair of socks down our blouses. I never took anybody's clothes. I couldn't bear the thought of wearing some dead girl's socks fresh off her dead feet. I had other things to think about, anyway: Elodie had managed to smuggle me five tiny cigarettes via Micheline, something that looked like tobacco rolled in thin airmail paper, and I was waiting for my moment to try to bargain with Anna for the calcium.

The only thing Anna ever wanted to talk about with me was American food. Popcorn and root beer and hot dogs with mustard and relish and sauerkraut. (She'd been to a ball game once.) Gosh knows what I will eat when I get home— anything I talked about in the shower room with Anna will taste like sawdust and fill me with nausea.

"Do you have pork barbecue in Pennsylvania?" she asked breathlessly. "When I was in Chicago, there was a diner we used to go to after the lab shut, and they had these fluffy white bread rolls that they baked themselves, and they'd pile the meat in with an ice-cream scoop—"

She broke off with a sob, and suddenly we were *both crying over pork barbecue*. Abruptly we turned our backs on each other at exactly the same moment. I stopped crying first. I spun around and said, "Calcium. I'll write you out a pork barbecue recipe if you can get me calcium tablets."

"Calcium!"

"Isn't that good for bones? My friend had her bones broken here."

"Oh."

The German *Kolonka* went tight-lipped. She thought about it for a moment.

"Not tablets. She'll need injections—calcium gluconate. You're friends with the Rabbits, huh?"

Anna had a guilty secret—before she'd been sent to Ravensbrück as a prisoner, she'd worked at Ravensbrück as an employee.

After a lot of wheeling and dealing, I got the dirty story and the calcium out of her in exchange for the cigarettes, the promise of two bread rations, and Mother's *fasnacht* recipe. I tempted her into that one by mentioning how Mother and I had spent two days making deep-fried doughnuts for the church sale for Fasnacht Day, the last day before Lent. Anna let me sit on one of the filthy sinks in the converted washroom-turned-mortuary for a couple of minutes before I started to take the clothes off that day's corpses so the rest of my crew could cart them off to the incinerator. For a few seconds she watched me writing my recipe against the tiled wall with a stolen pencil stub, and then she just suddenly began talking.

"You might as well know because if your Rabbits *ever* find out who I am, they'll never trust you again," she said, leaning against the other sink and smoking furiously. "I'm a pharmacist. I got a job here in 1941, requisitioning drugs and bandages—antiseptic, aspirin, glucose, things for the sick bay. Just stocktaking, really, because I'm not a nurse. I was here in 1942 when they did the first operations on the Polish girls. I *saw* what they did. I wasn't involved at first; I just tiptoed around behind the scenes making sure there was fresh plaster for the casts and that the knives were sharp. It was my *job*."

My hand stuck in the middle of a sentence that began, *The day before you're going to cook, wash and peel a bushel of potatoes, then—*

I couldn't write the word *cut*. I think I left it out. Actually, the writing had now become an excuse so I didn't have to look at her.

"So, I did my job," she went on. "At first I didn't have to go near the—um, the patients. I got my backside pinched by the doctors now and then because I was a pretty German patriot and not a Polish Special Transport Ravensbrück scarecrow condemned to death and good for nothing but scientific experimentation, but I didn't *enjoy* knowing what was going on, you know? I didn't feel proud to be advancing medical research, and I didn't believe we *were*, anyway. They were sloppy about monitoring the experiments, and sometimes they never followed up on them. And I didn't *like* my work enough to want to do it well myself." She let out a gasp of smoke. "You wouldn't believe the shitty jobs I've had to do in the last three years. This"—she waved her cigarette at the bony corpses stacked against the wall in the unused shower stalls—"this is harmless. Stripping dead bodies—not much fun but harmless. Sharpening knives that you know are going to be used to carve up some kid's tibia and fibula so they can swap pieces of them around—that's hard to justify."

She asked suddenly, "Are you listening?"

The scrap of paper slid out from beneath my pencil stub

and fluttered into the sink. "Of course I'm listening."

"They'd give the girls ether before they operated on them and inject them with Evipan to knock them out. One day, the usual nurse assistant wasn't there for some reason, and they got me to step in for her. Those poor kids knew by then what was going to happen to them, but they really *were* like rabbits—just so glad to get a bath and clean sheets to sleep in, so it *must* be okay, right? Afterward, after they woke up and the anesthetic wore off and the fever and infection set in and they couldn't even see what had happened, because they were up to their hips in plaster, they'd lie there screaming or sobbing or begging for lemonade—*lemonade!*" She gave a hoarse bark of laughter. "I stole morphine for them. I'd go around injecting them when no one was looking. They called me the Angel of Sleep. I didn't try to talk to them—they all hated me like poison because they knew I'd helped put some of them under for the operations. But they took the morphine when I could get it."

Anna took another drag on her cigarette. It was nearly done. We could risk only another minute or two—maybe less, if someone brought another body in.

"So, well, then I got transferred to an office job for the Occupation army in France for a while because they needed a pharmacist and a driver and a translator, and they got all three for the price of one by hiring me. I thought that job would be better, but it turned out worse, so then I got transferred back to Berlin, and my new boss got mad at me because I wouldn't fuck him. So he gave me a choice—strip for him or go back to Ravensbrück, as a prisoner this time. He thought he had a sure winner with that one, seeing as I'd *been* to Ravensbrück and knew what I was getting into, but actually I was fed up with playing their game by then. I'd seen a lot of . . . things I didn't like. And I didn't want to spread my legs for him *at all, ever*, and I knew that I'd be a *Kolonka* or a *Blockova* here—and also, when I'd been here before, it was run like a soldiers' camp, much cleaner and more orderly—we used to show it off to the Red Cross—none of these *schmootzichs* grabbing at your bread, no shithole tent full of evacuees from other camps, only two to a bunk and enough blankets and toilets that worked. So, yeah, that was my choice."

There wasn't a thing left of her cigarette but a damp shred of stolen onionskin typing paper, which she spat into the sink.

"The bastard raped me anyway before he arrested me. The fucking *bastard*. He had to get help from a bunch of his pals because I fought back. I got convicted of assaulting my boss." She pointed to her green triangle. "German criminal, right? So I'm back in the *Revier* at Ravensbrück, where I started. Okay, I'll get you some calcium injections. But don't you ever tell anybody who you get them from. Much better they don't know I'm a fellow prisoner now."

I nodded. I held up the crumpled scrap of paper with the half-finished *fasnacht* recipe.

"I'm not done."

"Do it next time."

We hid the recipe in the quarter-inch gap between the wall and the sink.

Karolina and the other condemned Rabbits were still hiding, and Gitte bargained for them with the Camp authorities. "Take these seven off the list and the whole Lublin Special Transport will cooperate with you—they'll line up for you in perfect order—they'll testify that they've been treated well— they'll *sign their names* as testimony."

The Lublin Special Transport had refused to do that in

the past, and no one really believed they were going to do it now.

In desperation Gitte threatened, "The whole Camp knows. The *whole Camp* knows what happened to the Rabbits. Their names got out before and they'll get out again. If you kill any more of them, *someone* is going to tell the world."

It doesn't sound like much of a threat, does it? *Someone is going to tell the world.* But when the war is over, that stinking Commander and those soulless doctors will all have to get real jobs again, and who will want Doctors Fischer and Gebhardt cutting up their legs after what they did to Róża's? They *knew* what the reaction would be when people found out, when the Allied soldiers found the camps. When people started to ask them to explain, to account for what they'd done. They knew. And they were scared.

"You need to learn our names," Róża whispered as we all struggled to get comfortable in our crowded bunk.

"I know your names."

"*All* our names. You need to learn the list, the list of Rabbits' names. Then, if you get out, you can tell everyone about us. You might be released back to your Air Force, or the Red Cross might come for you. But that won't happen to any of us, because we're all condemned. *Special Transport.* So if you survive the war, you have to tell everyone our names, our full names. All seventy-four of us, the living and dead."

"There were more than that, darling," Lisette reminded her. "Also the German Bible Student and the Ukrainian girl. And the others whose legs they amputated."

"Never mind the amputees," Róża said heartlessly. "They're all dead and no one remembers their names anyway. There are no witnesses and there's no *evidence.*"

"*God!*" I exclaimed. "They *amputated* people's legs?"

"Those girls were mentally ill to start with—no one will *ever* know who they were. Anyway, you've seen *us*. You know what happened. You know it was real."

"Oh, Róża, how can I remember all your names?" I wailed. "I can't even spell *your* name!"

"In a poem," said Lisette. "Make a poem for a mnemonic. Make yourself another counting-out rhyme."

I know the list by heart now, too, their real names. But I started just the way Lisette suggested, by making myself a counting-out rhyme of all their given names. Some of them had the same first name, so I only used each name once in the rhyme to keep it simple. I whispered it to myself in roll call and recited it in my head as I shivered between Róża and Irina in the bunks, my head and stomach aching with hunger, my frozen feet too numb to feel my painted toes.

> Izabela, Aniela, Alicia, Eugenia,
> Stefania, Rozalia, Pelagia, Irena,
> Alfreda, Apolonia, Janina, Leonarda,
> Czeslava, Stanislava, Vladyslava, Barbara,
> Veronika, Vaclava, Bogumila, Anna,
> Genovefa, Helena, Jadviga, Joanna,
> Kazimiera, Ursula, Vojcziecha, Maria,
> Wanda, Leokadia, Krystyna, Zofia.

The seven Rabbits' names came off the list of people they were going to execute. We were pretty sure it was just a postponement so they could catch us off guard later.

Karolina staggered back to us after nearly a week in the tent, more ravenous than we were and full of news. She'd been talking to the Jewish women in the tent who'd been transferred from Auschwitz.

"They were killing tens of—*tens of thousands* of people there every day this summer," Karolina stuttered. "TENS OF THOUSANDS. Gassing them and burning the bodies, or just—just burying them in piles when the incinerators got behind—if Fischer hadn't infected me with gangrene on purpose for no reason at all, I wouldn't believe the numbers, either. TENS OF THOUSANDS EVERY—EVERY DAY—"

What a meaningless number. It would have wiped out Ravensbrück in a couple of days, and Ravensbrück was enormous. No wonder Karolina was stuttering.

"Ten thousand a day in your dreams," Róża challenged bitterly. "Who was doing the counting? How *big* is Auschwitz?"

"Bigger than Ravensbrück." Karolina took a deep breath and crossed her arms over her chest, hugging herself. "Listen, 7705, your number has not come up on the death list yet and you haven't spent a week in that hellhole under the tent. Oh, I want a *bath*—I want to wash my hair! They pile the corpses at one end if no one comes to take them out. They dig gravel and mud out of the ground with their hands to try to cover them up. They have no toilets and they can't go outside. They catch rainwater and snow in the tent flaps or they'd all be dead of thirst. And that is only the ones who are still capable of doing more than rocking back and forth and wailing and trying to eat their own hands—"

Lisette put a gentle arm around Karolina's waist.

"I saw a woman doing that," Karolina said, shuddering. She shook Lisette off and lowered her voice. "Listen, just before they started evacuating Auschwitz so the Soviets won't be able to liberate it, there was a prisoner rebellion there. In October. The prisoners destroyed one of the crematoriums— they tried to blow up the gas chambers. They killed guards with *hammers*."

"Where did they get explosive?" Irina asked quietly.

"The women in the munitions factories smuggled gun-powder out to them. It took them months. Hundreds of them escaped—they escaped—" Karolina made a funny noise, a cross between a sob and a laugh. "Of course everybody got caught and they were all shot, two hundred of them in a day. Except the ones who'd planned it, and the women. They were all slammed into the Auschwitz Bunker. You can imagine what's going on there *now*." She gave that gulping laugh again. "They say the men gave out the women's names. But—but the women aren't giving them *anything*."

Lisette was listening with twenty kinds of horror—horror at what had happened, at what was still happening back in Poland, at what was happening under the tent, and mainly at what had happened to Karolina and at the half-crazed way she was telling her stuttering story. But Irina and Róża were listening with ambition and admiration. I could tell. They'd stopped thinking about food for a minute and were thinking about rebellion.

A couple of mornings later, the Camp authorities distributed coats, and that made everyone's hopes soar, too, because we were sure they wouldn't waste winter coats on people they were about to execute. The coats got dumped in big piles outside the chain-link fence around our block, arranged by nationality, with numbers and prisoner patches already sewn on. You were out of luck if your coat didn't fit. Lisette, who was used to dropping her status as honorary Pole whenever they made us line up in national groups, grabbed me by the arm and pulled me to the French pile of coats along with the spies and Resistance couriers in their beetroot rouge.

Not surprisingly, these garments had all seen better days; their linings had all been ripped out, and every coat had had one sleeve ripped off and another sleeve of a wildly contrasting color sewn back in its place, to make them obviously prison coats. We tossed them back and forth, trying to find our own numbers, and suddenly Lisette burst out laughing. She shoved a lightweight pale green wool at me—it had a velvet collar so moth-eaten that no one had bothered to salvage it.

"Come on!" Lisette pulled at my arm again. "Back in line!"

I started to pull on the coat she'd given me and suddenly recognized the navy contrasting sleeve.

It was from my ATA tunic. My USA patch was still in place on the shoulder. That was what had made Lisette laugh.

Wonderful Elodie!

Later, when I had a chance to check out the coat more closely, I discovered that Elodie had tucked my rose hanky from Aunt Rainy into a pocket hidden on the inside. With the blue thread from the collar of my dress she'd embroidered another rose on the hanky in the corner opposite Aunt Rainy's, and on either side of it she'd put our initials, with a little French flag under the *EF* and a little American flag under the *RJ*.

And she'd hidden cigarettes in the hem of the coat, and a couple of threaded needles, and three sugar cubes wrapped in paper (worth more than their weight in gold in terms of bribing the insatiable Anna). Hope, hope, soaring like a kite! We were clinging to anything we could. A coat without a lining, full of hidden pencil stubs! What treasure! It was already so *cold* in November.

We had a regular supply of calcium for Róża by then, too. She screamed and carried on the first time we tried to inject her, until Irina threatened to tie her down and gag her like the SS did when they operated on her in the Bunker. Who do you think Róża finally let give her the jabs? NO

ONE. She did it herself. She'd rather do it *herself* than let anyone else poke a needle into her.

Thorny little Różyczka.

THANKSGIVING (by Rose Justice)

From the steaming kitchen it's a quarter mile
across the crowded wasteland to the patchwork
   barrack,
and we two get to haul the drum of soup
heavier than we are. The challenge is
not to let go. It's a race against time (it will be cold,
already it's cooled down), a race against
the several thousand grasping hands and gulping
   mouths
we have to pass before we eat.

(Thank you for the gold November sky,
the warm steel kissing my cold hands, no mud today.)

But first we have to get it down the steps.
We stop to rest outside the kitchen door—
the barrel still is gently hot between us,
steaming like a bath. One second's pause
to take a breath, gather the strength to lift
and then to drag ourselves and the drum of soup
the endless quarter mile over the cinders.

One second too long on the steps.
Behind us blows and screams (we are too slow),
and in the square a hundred hungry scarecrows
race toward us ready to lighten our load.
Trapped between buzzards and gaping beaks

we fight like the mutts we are—I *won't* let go—
I'll fight with teeth and feet, I'll bite the girl
who tries to scoop a bowlful under my clinging fist—
but when we kick it's our mistake.
The careful balance goes. The whole thing tips.

(Thank you for the hands that caught the heavy drum
and those who saved what spilled in bowls of soup
and cups of dirt and their cupped palms,
and those who sponged it up with bread
and those who licked the thirsty earth—
Thank you for the chagrin that let us go
with no one begging more, thank you
that now our load was lighter for the long walk back.)

April 28, 1945
Paris

Guess what—I am dressed.

I have been sitting here writing or pacing around this room stark naked for over a week, and now Fernande has taken me quietly in hand. It started with the extra quilt and now she has moved on to clothing. She brought me a pile of panties and camisoles and a couple of skirts and blouses. She's built a lot like me, tall and bony. Not as bony as I am now, of course, but she's built like I ought to be. I don't think the clothes are hers, though—I think they are her daughter's. She wouldn't say they were, but she did tell me her daughter had been put in prison and she doesn't know what happened to her. I am probably wearing another dead woman's clothes. But it is easier to wear these than the clothes Elodie organized for us because these have been lovingly looked after in the hope that their owner might come back for them someday.

And maybe Fernande's daughter will come back. But I doubt it.

This is what's so heartbreaking: the fact that I am here, alive, has no doubt given Fernande some grain of hope for her daughter. But the fact that I was *there* makes me sure there isn't any.

My hair is not too bad now—softer, the curl coming back. It's very short. I have been taking ridiculous long baths and stuffing myself with French cream—I eat it in spoonfuls, like soup, separately from the coffee. It is wonderful just on its own, mixed up with a little sugar (I mix margarine and sugar and eat that, too). Fat mixed with sugar is the richest thing I have eaten since forever and I just *crave* it. My hair likes it, too.

And I have been able to sleep a little longer each night. I don't jerk awake at four a.m. expecting the Screamer anymore. But I still have the dream about the cold wind in the empty bunks. Funny how my Ravensbrück nightmare is about the bunks being empty, because by the end they were *never* empty. The whole Camp was so overcrowded we had to sleep in shifts, even during the day.

I have got to keep writing. I can't talk about it at all, not to Mother or Aunt Edie over the telephone, not to Fernande in broken French. It would break her heart, I think, if I told her about it. I keep wishing I could talk to Nick, but how could I explain any of it to Nick? How could I *possibly* make Nick understand?

I wrote him a poem for a Christmas present, though of course I knew I couldn't give it to him then. I still feel the way I do in the poem. Apart from the clean clothes, I am still a walking ghost. I don't know how I can possibly explain to him what's happened to me. *There won't be anything to say.*

LOVE SONG & SELF-PORTRAIT (by Rose Justice)

At first I dreamed that you
offered warm arms of comfort and strength,
pulling me close,
your soft lips brushing and kissing my bare head,
all of you loving me,
the nightmare over and the dream come true—
Now I only dream that you
offer me bread.

My dreams still produce you
out of habit, but the sweet
longing for your touch is gone.

I long for nothing from you anymore
but something to eat.

And if I did come back,
what in return could I offer to you,
who used to make so free
with my softness and kisses and verse
as if it were your due?
Imagine me
on your doorstep—would you laugh in the old way
and greet me lovingly:
Hello, it's been a long time,
how are you today?

I would offer you myself
in mismatched shoes and blood-soaked rags,
shaved scalp all scabs
and face gone gray,
no old woman but a walking ghost
on a skeleton's frame—
And you would be forced to look away.

There won't be anything to say.

If it was a clear night during a roll call, we'd get a whispered astronomy lesson from one of the imprisoned university professors. The astronomy lessons drove me crazy because they were in Polish.

"What did she say?" I whispered, getting frustrated, because I really *loved* learning the names of the stars—except for languages, astronomy was the one class we could do *practically*, and I couldn't understand the Polish astronomy teacher.

Karolina whispered, "She said it is December, and we won't see Arcturus in the evening until spring. When we see Arcturus again, the war will be over!"

I gasped. "It's *December*! My gosh—I'm nineteen! I forgot my birthday!"

"Forgot your birthday!" Róża snickered with scorn. "You've missed your name day, too. Yours is the same as mine, Rose, September Fourth, and I *never* forget. We have a party *every year*, and my sixteenth, last year, was so special. Zosia and Genca were on firewood-gathering duty in the pine forest, and they made me a flower wreath. And Gitte brought me a *cake*. A cake, honestly, a centimeter thick and as big around as the palm of my hand, with jam and margarine— they stole it from the infirmary—I'd just been operated on for the fifth time and I was too sick to eat the cake, but I wore the wreath." Róża knew perfectly well how utterly pathetic this sounded and poked me slyly. "Tell us about *your* sixteenth. Did you have a cake with roses made out of pink frosting?"

"I *did*!" I exclaimed in astonishment. "How did you guess?"

"Your name is Rose."

Irina shook with silent laughter.

"Was there champagne?" Lisette asked.

"No, Mother wouldn't let us. We had Shirley Temple cocktails—ginger ale and grenadine. And Daddy hired a dance band. The party was in the hangar at Justice Field, and we spent the whole day before it moving planes out onto the field to get the hangar ready, and then we decorated it with dozens of colored paper lanterns shaped like owls—"

Crushing, black embarrassment kicked me in the head at this point and I clammed up.

"It's not a crime you weren't in prison on your sixteenth birthday, darling," Lisette said gently.

Róża let out one of her insane giggles. "Have you *ever* committed a crime, Rosie?"

"Shut up, 7705!" Karolina hissed. "I don't want to hear about her criminal activities. I want to hear about her pink cake and Shirley Temple cocktails."

I know why I forgot my birthday. It was sometime while I was in the Bunker. I had entirely forgotten who I was by the end of that two weeks. I lost count long before nineteen.

The Camp authorities shot our *Blockova*, Gitte, next. We didn't see that coming, but we should have, shouldn't we? Since they didn't shoot the Rabbits? We should have known we weren't going to get away with our desperate war of passive defiance. But we thought they'd take it out on us, not on Gitte. Although, of course, murdering Gitte and replacing her with the demon *Blockova*, Nadine Lutz, *was* taking it out on us.

After Nadine arrived there was no talking while we ate, no talking while the knitters worked, no talking in the bunks—we were allowed to talk outside on Sunday afternoons only. Most of our communication happened while we were going to the toilet because Nadine wouldn't come near the waste ditches when everyone else was going. But she'd dole out soup herself for the sheer pleasure of smacking you on the head with the empty ladle afterward. She brought reinforcement guards with their dogs inside the barrack, even at night. It didn't stop us from trying to whisper, but it made every word we said to each other weighted with terror. One night she set a couple of dogs loose in the *bunks*. Gosh, we hated those dogs. The most common injury people turned up with in the sick bay, according to Anna, was dog bites.

I can't describe how *desperate* we were to fly below the demon Nadine's radar—to fool her, to go behind her back.

We did *crazy* things. We'd be standing in a never-ending roll call and I'd inch one foot out of the mismatched shoe that was a little too big, so slowly you couldn't see me moving, and then I'd nudge Róża in the rib cage and she'd turn her head and glance down at my toes and stifle a giggle. You could still see the nail polish, disappearing into a thin ruby crescent as my toenails grew out, like the waning moon. Róża would poke Karolina in *her* ribs and hiss, "Candy store's open." And Karolina would poke Irina, and we'd all stand there poking each other and snorting with stifled mirth until Lisette exclaimed, "*Shhh!*" as Nadine looked in our direction, and I'd ram my foot back into the muddy shoe and stare vacantly at the back of the woman in front of me.

PLAYING STATUES (by Rose Justice)

If I sigh my shoulders rise and fall.
It counts as movement. I won't sigh. I'll blink.
I'll count how many blinks it takes before
the shadow of the smokestack hits the wall.
But if I blink I'll fall asleep. I've closed my eyes before
standing in line; it's dangerous to blink.
I'll watch the sky.
I'll count how many crows
touch the long cloud behind the trees.

Oh, God, but then I'll cry.
Wings in the pine boughs always make me think
of freedom. I won't count or blink or sigh.

I'll think of food. I'll think of bread and meat,
pretend that when we're told to go
there will be pepper pot

thick with tripe chunks, spicy and faintly sweet,
like Mrs. Kessler sells on Union Street.

God no, and no, and no! Of all things, not
Union Street: Don't think of Union Street!
Don't think of home.
Anything else but that. I'll throw
myself on the electric wire. I'll wiggle my toes.
I'll sprint to the end of the row
and sock that pretty dog handler in the nose.

That makes me smile and clench my fist.

I'm out. She sees me move. Now I
can blink and sigh and sob.
She'll make me count the blows.

My work team of Tall Girls got sent back to the maintenance shed we'd cleared out earlier.

Since we'd been there some prisoners from the men's camp had boarded up the windows and the big garage doors of the shed and replaced them with just a normal-sized set of wooden doors. Now we had to paint the interior walls black as high as we could reach. Once the guards made us understand what they wanted, they locked us in—Anna was allowed to make herself a little camp outside the new door of the building, with a crate for a chair and a coffee can or something for a stove with a fire in it like a hobo. Where she got the coal and how she got away with burning it right out there in the open, I will never know. But she was a red armband. She could get away with a lot.

And because we had Anna for a guard, we could get away

with little acts of rebellion while she wasn't looking. Inside the shed, Irina scavenged in the corners—nails, scraps of thin copper wire like they used in Siemens, wood splinters. French Political Prisoner 51444, otherwise known as Micheline, got busy painting Allied defiance all over the walls in letters three feet tall: *VIVE LA FRANCE! VIVENT LES ALLIÉS! MORT AUX NAZIS!* and a token GOD BLESS AMERICA! Her friend 51350 followed behind frantically covering everything up so they wouldn't get caught.

"You'll get us into so much trouble!"

"You should have seen what I got up to when I worked in the post office," Micheline said. "We'd put big black censor stamps all over instructions being sent to German officers, or we'd steam open envelopes and swap letters around so they went to the wrong people, or steam off stamps so there was postage due—and anything that came from Paris with a German name on it we'd return to sender. Every now and then we'd send off a mailbag with a burning cigarette butt tied up inside it. My God, I miss the thrill of being a civil servant!"

We all laughed. Everything I know about passive resistance I learned from Micheline. She always appeared to be doing exactly as she was told, but everything she did took twice as long as it should have.

We sure did drag out that paint job as long as we could. It was wonderful to be able to talk to each other for a little while without having to whisper or worry that someone would hit us.

I also painted words on the walls. It was such a relief to be able to write down what I was thinking instead of having to memorize it. It is true that I had to obliterate everything I'd written, but I think it is much easier to write a poem when you can write it down. I couldn't have written "The Subtle Briar" without that paint job. I spent three days slapping black paint on the walls of a disused warehouse and refining the most complex and ambitious poem I've ever written.

When we'd caked the entire interior of the building in black about three-quarters of the way to the ceiling, they turned out all the lights and shut us in so we could paint over the places where cracks of light came in through the boarded windows and around the newly built front wall.

Try standing on a ladder in pitch darkness with a bucket of black paint and not get any on yourself or the girl who's on the ladder beneath you. When they let us out as it was getting dark, in time to eat, all of us were covered head to foot in black paint. I had paint *in my ears*. We stood blinking blindly in the harsh streetlights, but of course we didn't get any time to readjust to reality—just got shoved back into our fives and marched back to Camp.

"What the hell are they making you do?" Róża demanded.

Our shed-clearing-and-painting job was a fierce discussion topic whenever we were allowed, or able, to talk. Lined up along the ditches in the dark at four a.m., usually.

"They're repurposing a maintenance shed."

"By boarding up and blacking out the windows? Why does it have to be so *dark*? What are they going to put inside it?"

"Maybe it's a new quarantine block—someplace to process new prisoners," Lisette said.

"You know what it's for," Karolina accused quietly. "You know it. You won't say it, but you know it. They have all these prisoners evacuated from Auschwitz and nothing to feed them. They are building a gas chamber."

"They are building two," said Irina. "A new building is going up outside the north wall. The men's camp is building it."

Lisette insisted, "That is a laundry, my dear. Ravensbrück is a work camp, not a death camp—an ordinary camp!"

"They don't dare shoot us in handfuls," said Karolina. "They're going to kill us all at once."

THE SUBTLE BRIAR (by Rose Justice)

When you cut down the hybrid rose,
its blackened stump below the graft
spreads furtive fingers in the dirt.
It claws at life, weaving a raft
of suckering roots to pierce the earth.
The first thin shoot is fierce and green,
a pliant whip of furious briar
splitting the soil, gulping the light.
You hack it down. It skulks between
the flagstones of the garden path
to nurse a hungry spur in shade
against the porch. With iron spade
you dig and drag it from the gravel
and toss it living on the fire.

It claws up toward the light again
hidden from view, avoiding battle
beyond the fence. Unnoticed, then,
unloved, unfed, it clings and grows
in the wild hedge. The subtle briar
armors itself with desperate thorns
and stubborn leaves—and struggling higher,
unquenchable, it now adorns
itself with blossom, till the stalk
is crowned with beauty, papery white

fine petals thin as chips of chalk
or shaven bone, drinking the light.

When you cut down the hybrid rose
to cull and plough its tender bed,
trust there is life beneath your blade:
the suckering briar below the graft,
the wildflower stock of strength and thorn
whose subtle roots are never dead.

It took me a long time to write "The Subtle Briar," but it was translated into three languages in a day. Every time it got passed on I got another bread ration. Oh, God, we needed *something* to cling to. We were scared.

They shot half a dozen Red Army women from our block, and six more from the Lublin Transport, though not Rabbits. No one knew anything about it ahead of time. It was a week before Christmas, and I'm sure of the timing because Karolina wasn't there with us for roll call that day. Nadine had caught Karolina showing off a little paper tree with tiny pop-out birds that she'd made for Lisette for a Christmas present and had sent her to the Bunker for *Fünfundzwanzig*. We were standing in the early-morning roll call—before breakfast, hearts aching for Karolina—when they just pulled the girls right out of line and made them take their coats off and hand them over to someone. That's how we knew they wouldn't be coming back.

That one girl's face, looking back at us in defiance as they led her away, bleak and desperate, biting her lip. She went shivering to her death in the dark, in the flowered summer dress she'd been wearing when I got here. One of the other girls tried to take her hand, and the guards wouldn't let her—they had to walk alone to their execution. We stood in silence for another half an hour while they counted us, but all I could think of was when I'd hear the shots and I'd know they were dead.

No one would ever know what happened to them.

The distant claps of sound made me jump half out of my skin when they finally came.

Lisette gave a single, angry sob. But the executed Polish and Russian girls hadn't cried as they'd walked away, so I bit my lip like the one in the flowered dress, bit my lip until it was bruised and bleeding, and I didn't cry, either.

They booted Karolina back into Block 32 as soon as they'd finished with her. She was at work later that day, knitting socks until she was well enough to go back to her patrol.

Being lashed in the Bunker turned her into a spluttering wreck. We had to let her lie on the edge of the bunk so she could have her back to the narrow aisle. She clung to me like a monkey, and I held her hands so she wouldn't fall off. Her mouth was so close to my ear that she could speak to me in almost less than a whisper. "Do you think the scars will be as bad as yours? I don't want scars like yours! It's not fair, it's not *fair*. They ruined my leg and now they've destroyed my back! I want to go to the Venice Film Festival awards wearing a Chanel evening gown. I want to wear a red bathing suit and sunbathe on the beach at Lido. . . ."

Róża didn't tease her. Actually, I don't think Róża could hear her. But even if she could, you didn't make fun of someone who got *Fünfundzwanzig*.

"You had twice five and twenty," Karolina whispered to me in wonder. "*Twice* in a week. I only had one round, and

I can't stand up and I can't sit down, and I have to go back into the antiaircraft ditches tomorrow. How did you bear it when they beat you the second time?"

"I don't know." I really don't. "I can't remember."

"I don't want people to see the scars!"

"Who cares about the scars! I'll wear a red bathing suit anyway. I don't care who sees my scars! Not me—I can't see them! I'll wear a two-piece!"

"Your Nick will like you in a red two-piece," Karolina whispered. "Tell me a Nick Story."

The Nick Stories were evolving from fabulous rescue fantasies into rhapsodies about food that often had nothing to do with Nick—I couldn't stop myself. But it was dreamily distracting to make them up.

This one was just for Karolina. I didn't dare whisper loudly enough for the others to hear, but Karolina needed distracting. My lips barely moved against her ear.

"Okay. It's just after supper and there was meat in the soup, chunks of sausage, so you're feeling strong. You and me are carrying the empty barrel back to the kitchens. And there's a full moon, everything is light, all silver, and the *Appelplatz* and the *Lagerstrasse* are empty—they haven't started the evening roll call yet. And then you hear this clattering, old-fashioned airplane engine. It's a German plane, with ugly long wheel struts like a stork—actually it *is* a Stork. Nick's stolen a German Storch so the antiaircraft guns won't shoot at him, because it's a German plane. And Nick lands right in the middle of the empty *Appelplatz*. You and I drop our empty soup pot and run, and Nick opens the door, and we jam ourselves into the backseat—you can sit on my lap. And he flies us back to—"

Here I stalled, brutal reality kicking in. Where would we go?

"—Lido," Karolina whispered back. "Let's go to the beach on the beautiful Adriatic Sea. Red bathing suits for both of us in the backseat."

I wonder where Nick is now, what he's doing. If he's still alive. Oh, I hope so—I hope so.

April 30, 1945
Paris

I had a phone call today from Aunt Edie, but the line was very bad and she was in a hurry—I didn't ask about Nick. Edie is coming to get me this weekend. I am panicking about that now—having to see Aunt Edie and be polite. I can hardly bear to think of the shock on her face when she sees me. It's one thing to fool Mother on a transatlantic phone call, but I won't be able to fool Aunt Edie face-to-face.

I don't understand why I don't want to go home. How can it be possible for me to feel more desolate than I did on Christmas Day?

Christmas presents—poems and feathers and bracelets made of string or paper. Elodie sent me a minuscule tea set made out of tinfoil. I tore my rose hanky in half diagonally to make two little triangular ones, and gave Elodie the side with Aunt Rainy's pretty embroidery. Karolina made me the most wonderful tiny flipbook that played a two-second cartoon she'd drawn, of me in my Spitfire ramming the flying bomb. The bomb exploded into stars in the last frame.

There was a Christmas tree set up in the *Lagerstrasse*—with *lights*—cross my heart. They played German carols over the loudspeakers, "Oh Christmas Tree" and "Silent Night." And gave us jam and margarine with our bread. The SS guards got blotto, staggering drunk. In Block 32 we were allowed to sing carols, mostly in French and Polish and Russian, so I couldn't join in—but I told a ton of fantastic stories. Nick performed a series of daring rescues, and we all ended up skating on the Conewago Grove Lake, and then there was a rambling Hotel Hershey story involving sleds and a sumptuous Pennsylvania Dutch smorgasbord buffet.

I mostly gave everybody poems for Christmas, but I made

another for Lisette, after our Christmas Day disaster. Actually, it was for thorny little Różyczka. But neither one of us ever told her about this one.

It had been my idea to do the Christmas bread, and Karolina who did the artwork—we were so excited about surprising the others. We cut our entire ration into squares an inch wide, like Fliss did back in Hamble, and we decorated them with *stars*, a scraping of margarine and a tiny star-shaped blob of red jam on each square.

HOLIDAY GRACE (FOR LISETTE) (by Rose Justice)

"Now we'll give thanks," you said, "and bless this
    food."
Smiling, you passed around the Christmas feast—
a loaf sliced small in diamond panes and spread
with stars of glittering jam, bright tinsel treats
to put us in a festive mood.
We took the pretty stars and you, devout and pleased,
wished us *"Joyeux Noel!"* and gratefully blessed the
    food.

Irony turned your frail adopted daughter
into a sneering brute.
"Bless *what?*" she snarled, wild with angry laughter.
"Why, are these holy wafers? Call this *food?*
Tasteless stale bread, a smear of sour fruit!
Call it Christ's body and his blood!
The Host can double as our Christmas treat—
now we can take communion as we eat!"

The tinsel turned to dust. All of us looked away
in shock and shame, stunned not so much

by her coarse, bitter blasphemy as that she'd say
something so cruel to you on Christmas Day—
you, who so love us all without condition.

You told her quietly,
"Sit by yourself. Give thanks alone. We'll wait
for you before we start." No indication
of how she'd speared your childless, pious heart.

We didn't eat. She sulked for half an hour
on the dark boards alone. After another
of us began to cry she crept back to your side,
and you were full of love and joy, because you
      always are.
She whispered quietly, "I'm sorry, Mother."

—Though you are not her mother, only she
who once, some time ago and in a different hell,
covered her tearful face and sang to her
while others dragged her mother's body from your
      overcrowded cell
so that she would not see.

Sandwiched in between Róża and Irina that night, I
thought about Christmas in Pennsylvania. Not about past
Christmases—I was thinking about *this* Christmas. I thought
about *my* mother and Daddy and Karl and Kurt and Mawmaw
and Grampa, and how they'd be sitting around the table for
Christmas dinner—maybe they were doing it *now*, this very
moment—sitting at the cherry table with Mother's Limoges
china from out of the corner cupboard, and the poinsettia
tablecloth and the brass-and-china candelabra with the tall
red candles on it, and Daddy starting to carve the turkey.

Mawmaw would be trying to say funny things to make the boys laugh, and Grampa would be starting on his third bourbon. Suddenly Mother would leap up from the table and run into the dark living room, lit only by the low fire and the red and blue and green lights on the Christmas tree, and she'd curl on the sofa and sob.

She'd be doing it *right now*. I could see it so clearly, as though I were looking in the living room window from the front porch.

She'd know I was missing—she'd have known that for months. And she hoped and hoped I was still alive, but she didn't really believe it.

And the worst thing was that even though I *was* alive, I would never be able to tell her—and even if I could tell her, if I could have come through the feathers of frost on the windowpane and whispered in her ear, "Your Rosie is still alive," what hope could I have given her when I told her where I was? That I was starving and freezing and covered with lice and scabies and would probably be dead of typhoid or shot for stealing a turnip before the war ended?

Well, anyway, I started to cry again.

After a while Róża wiped my face with her sleeve.

"You are thinking about Pennsylvania now, aren't you?"

"I am thinking about my mother."

"You idiot. I never think about my mother. I'd rather pinch the holes in my leg until they're black and blue than think about my mother."

I could understand that—it was probably less painful for *her* never to think about her mother. But it didn't help *me*.

"My mother will *never know* what happened to me," I said. "At least your name is out there on the BBC. Your legs are in those photographs. I'm just French Political Prisoner 51498. They don't even have my nationality right. No one will *ever know*. And I bet they'll incinerate all their precious prisoner records anyway, when the Allies come. They won't want anyone to find out what's going on here, just like they don't want anyone to find out what happened at Auschwitz last summer."

"Don't think about your mother. Think about the food she's eating," Róża advised cheerfully. "You have a special meal on Christmas Day, like the Germans, right? What do you have for Christmas dinner in Pennsylvania?"

How she could be cheerful about food after what she did to Lisette I do not know. But we had the Christmas dinner discussion anyway. I won't bother to write the rest of the conversation, because it was boring.

But now I am longing again for Cope's Dried Corn, boiled for two hours in milk and butter and sugar and salt. I am daydreaming about a tablespoon heaped with golden milky corn—just one spoonful.

On New Year's Day, they made us line up for a special roll call, and the stinking Commander gave a speech over the loudspeakers.

It is one of the things I have nightmares about—that tinny voice droning on and on all around me, in words I can't make heads or tails of, on and on and on. In my dreams I don't understand the words, but at the same time I know exactly what the voice is saying.

That's because while we were standing there, in real life, Lisette was translating like sixty on one side of me and Karolina on the other, a sort of madwoman's stereo speaker setup. So I had to listen to it all twice, Karolina a little behind Lisette.

"He says, *You'll never get out alive—*"

"He'll never let us out alive."

"They won't let the Allies get near us—"

"He'll kill us all before the Allies get here."

"They'll dismantle the Camp—"

"He'll mine the Camp, rig it with bombs, blow up the whole thing with us in it—"

"—And one of the gas chambers is working now—"

"And the first selections for gassing will be tomorrow."

This was the same stinking Commander who liked to come and watch people get their backsides beaten raw every Friday. It could have been his idea of a joke: see if I can make all fifty thousand of them cry on New Year's Day. It was hard to know whether to take him seriously.

Róża didn't. I could see her shoulders shaking as she tried desperately not to laugh.

"Oh, God," she cackled. "He must have really hit the New Year with a bang last night!"

He might have been kidding about the mines. He wasn't kidding about the gas chambers, though.

They started with the old and the injured and the sick, and they'd just pick you out of roll call. They tricked people into *volunteering* for it by telling them they'd be taken to a "rest camp." It didn't take us long to figure out what was going on. The Lublin Special Transport reckoned they were doomed: most of them limping, all of them condemned to death more than three years ago.

When it rained, when hail rattled on the roof, when the wind howled, when a train came clattering by, when the planes roared overhead or the air raid sirens wailed, when the antiaircraft guns thumped and the demon *Blockova*, Nadine Lutz, couldn't hear us, we all burst into a frenzy of whispered plots and panic.

Irina hadn't let Nadine stop her from scavenging. She carried the copper wire from the shed wrapped around her waist like a belt. It was thin and flexible and she'd get it out under the table or over the ditches, sometimes even working at it lying blindly in the dark bunks with her hands held up over her head. Then she'd twist what she'd built carefully around her waist again and get it out later. Eventually she had to hide it in the roof behind the ceiling panels.

"Are you making a bomb?" Róża whispered in an agony of delight and curiosity, as we all balanced ourselves outside in the dark over the stinking sewer. "Like they did at Auschwitz?"

"Kite!" Karolina guessed, more sensibly.

"It's a plane," I said.

I'd been watching Irina shape the wings, the long and narrow wings of a glider. I could see where she was planning to reinforce the fuselage with her stolen strips of wood. It would be too heavy for a kite. But it might glide like a model plane, if she got a chance to cover it with her stolen paper. In the right wind it might soar for miles.

Róża choked back one of her insane giggles. "That's not going to be big enough for all the Rabbits."

"Big enough for all your names, though. Another escape for the Rabbits' names!"

"You have to write in piss so it's invisible," Róża said knowingly. "That's how we got the letter to the Pope."

It was getting harder and harder for the guards to keep track of what we did—we couldn't get out of the camp, but the whole place was so crowded and filthy that it was easier to hide sabotage and thievery, if you weren't too sick to move.

"It will need a hell of a wind," Irina said. "If we could be ready to launch—find a place to hide it—"

"I can launch it!" Karolina said. "I can launch it from the air raid ditches. I can hide it in the sandbags till we get the right wind. You can sneak it out to us in one of your Corpse Crew carts!"

"Corpse Crew"—more and more, that's what they were using my team for. During the winter, as everyone started collapsing with cold and starvation and a million diseases, that's *all* we did—they stopped giving us other jobs and we were just one of a dozen Corpse Crews. They gave up on us boarding up broken windows and concentrated on clearing the bunks in the *Revier* and the other sick bay blocks (they kept adding extra ones, trying to keep the typhoid and tuberculosis cases separated from everyone else). There were always dead bodies piled outside the tent in the morning, and there were usually a few from our own block, with so many new people coming in—the incinerator in the crematorium was always working, greasy black soot splattering the daylight sky and red cinders spattering the sky at night.

I carried so many dead women this winter that I am—I don't know how to put this. I want to say it's like typhoid—I have been inoculated. I am immune. After the first couple of weeks, it stopped being appalling and became ordinary. It was better than if I'd been put to work in the crematorium. Wasn't it?

It was better. I didn't do anything I'm ashamed of. Some of it was too fearsomely gruesome to write about, even to think about anymore, and my mind skips lightly over it, the same way I can't remember the week between my beatings. There was that time we had to pick up one of the *schmootzichs* and it turned out she wasn't dead—this pathetic bundle of bones and rags lying in the *Lagerstrasse*, still breathing. The guard who'd found her made us load her up anyway, but we managed to sneak her into the washroom in the *Revier* on our way out to the crematorium. She was dead when we got back.

I made the place a little cleaner, a little less of a hellhole. Not much less, but what can one living girl do when there are two dozen dead women she has to move in a day? What can one starving girl on her feet do to help out a couple of hundred others who can't get up? Especially if you don't want to catch typhoid yourself.

I kept telling myself: *I've been inoculated. I've had the "jabs."*

I am sure that Anna's stolen vitamin C tablets helped, too, but even so I was the *only* one of my work team who didn't get sick this winter. None of us ever got admitted to the *Revier* ourselves. We lived in horror of it, partly because of what we saw there several times a week—for me it was also because I knew in much too much detail what had happened to the Rabbits there. For a while, Micheline had a fever high enough that she could have begged off work and got herself into the sick bay—you had to have a fever of 102 before they'd let you in—but instead she hid for three days in one of the blocked-up toilet cubicles in her barrack. None of the guards *ever* went in the broken toilets. Micheline was such a genius at pretending to follow rules that the whole time she was sick she didn't miss a single roll call.

We never launched Irina's glider. We did get it hidden in the sandbags, but we never got the right wind or a moment when we wouldn't be spotted trying to hurl a model airplane an open-arm-span wide over the twenty-foot-high walls. Who knows what happened to it, whether anyone found it, whether the names scribbled all over the fuselage were still legible? But dreaming about the potential success of our airmail service, doing it all in secret, kept us *alive*.

Hope is treacherous, but how can you live without it? When you lost hope, you turned into a *schmootzich*, nothing more than a starved mouth and snatching hands that even the guards ignored except when they were counting everybody—or you *died*.

KITE-FLYING (by Rose Justice)

> Hope has no feathers.
> Hope takes flight
> Tethered with twine
> like a tattered kite,
> slave to the wind's
> capricious drift,
> eager to soar
> but needing lift.
>
> Hope waits stubbornly,
> watching the sky
> for turmoil, feeding on
> things that fly:
> crows, ashes, newspapers,
> dry leaves in flight
> all suggest wind
> that could lift a kite.
>
> Hope sails and plunges,
> firmly caught
> at the end of her string—
> fallen slack, pulling taut,
> ragged and featherless.

Hope never flies
but doggedly watches
for windy skies.

Lisette had bigger plans than paper airplanes.

"There are transports leaving every day for Ravensbrück's satellite camps," she directed. "We need to get the Rabbits out of here. We need to be *organized*. We'll start with the youngest—all the Rabbits under twenty-one, the schoolgirls. Smuggle one or two at a time into the evacuation transports as they leave. Now listen, my darlings, the next time they try to pull any more Rabbits out of a roll call, we're going to have to be brave. We're going to have to disrupt things so violently they can't count us. *Everyone* switch numbers—something like that. And every one of the girls who gets out will take the list with her—the names from the Lublin Transport, everybody who was operated on. We are going to *tell the world*."

Lisette got dragged out of line the next morning without warning, and we thought she was dead. I marched off to my hideous work sniveling like a two-year-old. I sobbed quietly to myself all day—Micheline worked beside me and Irina without asking what was going on. It wasn't the first time one of us had sobbed quietly to herself all day. But Anna got so fed up with me that she smacked me with someone's empty shoe.

And it turned out Lisette wasn't dead anyway. Because she was an archivist she'd been handpicked to do some secretarial work in the record office. She came back unbelievably excited. She whispered her news to us in the evening roll call.

"There's a radio in the record office—a radio! It's always on! We've pushed the German army back!"

"Really?" Karolina gasped. "*Really?*"

"Well, back to where they were in December—everyone is fighting up to their hips in snow."

We groaned. It was the end of January, and the best we could do was beat the Germans back to their December starting point?

"What about France?" Róża and Karolina clamored together. "What about Belgium? Have the Allies crossed the Rhine yet?"

"No, no. Look, darlings, forget about the Western Allies! The Soviets are going to get here first. *Yesterday they liberated Auschwitz!*"

It was all I could do not to yell. We stamped our feet wildly in the black slush, a little defiant dance of triumph.

"Shit," Irina said. "I will go straight from a Fascist prison camp to a Soviet one."

"Why? You're a double ace! A decorated Hero of the Soviet Union! You spent four months being interrogated by the enemy and didn't tell them anything!"

"When a person spends four months being interrogated by the enemy and is still alive at the end, the Soviet Union calls her a traitor, not a hero. No, thank you. I would rather hang myself than go home."

She sounded like she meant it, too, which kind of put a damper on our excitement about being rescued by the Soviets.

Anna caught me in the horrible converted washroom and handed me a list of numbers written on a strip of gray paper a quarter of an inch wide.

"What is this?"

"Tomorrow's list."

"Tomorrow's *death* list? But—"

There were dozens and dozens of numbers there. I started

to read them and realized that I knew almost every one of them. I associated *faces* with most of them. 7705 especially—Róża. Karolina, too. Every single one of the Rabbits was on that list, and a few others, including Lisette.

"They're going to shoot *eighty people* in a day?" I gasped.

"Just tell everyone you see. That's what I'm going to do. Maybe . . ."

I was reeling. Except Irina, my whole family was on that list.

"They can't execute *all* of them!" I burst out, and the German girl laughed at me.

"Of course they can. They can do whatever they fucking want. And what they're doing now is burning the evidence."

She pointed to the last number on the list—32131—a lot higher in sequence than the others. Also a familiar number.

"*You, too!*"

"I'm a witness," she said with bitter irony. "*My God.* I never thought I'd end up shoveled into the Ravensbrück incinerator with that pathetic bunch of Poles." She suddenly took the unlit cigarette butt out of her mouth and tucked it down the front of her dress. She looked away. "I'm sorry."

"Tell me how to tell people in German!" I gasped. "Tell me how to say, '*They're killing the Rabbits.*' If I tell people in German, everyone will pass it on!"

She wasn't even listening.

"They'll gas us," she said, gripping the sides of the dry sink and staring at the stained tiles. "That many at once—they won't waste the ammunition. They'll do it all at once, now that they've got that gas chamber operational. It *hurts.* If you stand by the wall near the crematorium you can hear them screaming. *Ach*—"

She swore in German and let out a sob.

"Listen, Anna," I said fiercely. "It won't happen! Okay?

No one in this whole Camp will let it happen. Last time they tried to execute any of the Rabbits, we hid them. They killed our block leader because she wouldn't give them up. But that was just us, fighting back on our own. You've got to tell *everybody* this time."

She looked up at me with wild, wet eyes and gave a croak of a laugh. "You really believe we can do something, don't you, kid?"

"*We can try!*"

Anna stared at the wall, avoiding looking at any of the bodies piled at our feet. Two more of my team came in, carrying another. I hadn't started undressing any of them yet.

"Anna's on the list!" I cried, holding it up.

Anna, gray-faced, added indifferently, "So are all the *Kaninchen.*"

"*Les Lapins!*" the French girls exploded in outrage. "The Rabbits? The *KRÓLIKI? All* of them? *No. Never!*"

"Hide them!" Micheline exclaimed. "Hide every one of them tonight! All of Ravensbrück will fight for the Rabbits. People are *waiting* for a chance to fight for the Rabbits."

"Karolina?" Irina asked me. "Róża?"

"*All of them.* The whole Lublin Transport. Lisette, too."

Unlike me, Irina didn't panic.

"Let me have your armband," she said to Anna. "And one hour. I can do something."

"Where will you go?" Anna asked sharply.

"To talk to my friend in the power plant—we were electricians in the Moscow Metro together, before I flew. I think she can switch off the lights. She will do it in roll call tomorrow morning. They will find no one."

Anna moved slowly and cautiously, like a person with a migraine. She peeled off her red *Kolonka* armband and held it out to Irina. Irina slid it over her own sleeve and stalked out, her shock of white hair catching the gleam of the bare electric bulb overhead as she turned to go.

"You'd better hide, too, Anna," I said in English.

"Who'll hide me?" she scoffed with bleak fatalism, her pale eyes bright and wild. "You could break my leg, maybe, make me look like a Rabbit. See if the disguise fools anyone."

We all looked at her in pity and looked away. I sure couldn't invite her to hide with my Block 32 Camp Family— and even for twenty loaves of bread the Auschwitz evacuees in the tent wouldn't hide a German criminal. I thought about offering to swap coats with her, to swap our numbers. I really did. It is the Girl Scout in me, always wanting to help. She was an okay group leader, and now she just seemed so grim and crazed—so *afraid*. But I couldn't come up with a good reason to sacrifice my *life* for her.

Micheline saw me thinking about it. She shook her head at me to stop me from opening my mouth.

"No one will notice another body here tomorrow morning," Micheline suggested to Anna brutally. "No one counts the corpses more than once. If we get the chaos the Soviet electricians promise, hide in here."

FOR ANNA (by Rose Justice)

Your sullen sneer,
thin lips and
unlit cigarette
have disappeared
without a trace
and no one cares
and we'll forget.

I don't care, either,
but I saw
desperate and raw
fear in your face—
you said you'd hide.
I wonder now
how hard you tried—
and if you lived
or if you died,
I wonder how.

Block 32 that night was a prison all on its own, swarming with guards and dogs, the wire gate locked, the door to the barracks barred. It was almost surprising they let the rest of us back in, but they did, and we got our soup ration as usual. We even fought over it sort of as usual:

"Here, take mine, you need all the energy you can get tonight."

Or more realistically, "Look, just give me yours, 'cause you won't need it if they kill you tomorrow morning anyway."

Karolina had the same fierce, dazed gleam of insanity in her eyes as our German *Kolonka* Anna—the look of crazed disbelief at the UNFAIRNESS of it.

Lisette just looked like Lisette. Róża was a pain in the neck.

"What do you think I'll look like when I go up in smoke from the crematorium chimney, Rosie? As sexy as Karolina, slinking across the sky?"

"*Will you shut up!*"

She wasn't trying to be funny. She was trying to be brave, Różyczka-wise. But it was making Karolina cry.

Irina took hold of my hand and pressed it against her waist. Tied inside her dress was a pair of wire cutters. The hard line of her mouth was set in the ghost of a grin. She spread her palm and rocked her hand at me. Still a combat pilot.

The thing was, so many people were sobbing and crying and praying that night that neither the guards nor Nadine could hear us as the Rabbits made their escape. I crawled with Róża and Karolina over the infested bare boards that counted as our bunks—people moved out of our way. *Everybody* helped. When one of the guards shouted or the dogs started growling, we lay flat and sobbed loud and genuine sobs of fear and frustration. It was easy.

Irina and a couple of the other Russians got out first, and they did the dirty and dangerous work of cutting a hole in the wire that fenced off Block 32 from the rest of the Camp. Then we spent most of the night hoisting all the Lublin Special Transport girls out a couple of the broken windows. I had an easy job—I had to keep stuffing wads of newspaper over the jagged glass around the edges of the window frame.

The tricky part was crossing the yard between the barrack and the fence without being seen, and getting through the fence. I didn't have to do it myself, but it still makes me shiver to think about it. Nobody got caught, but, my gosh, we worked *slowly*—though after the first dozen Rabbits had made it through the fence, we got good at it.

It took two of us on one side of the window and two on the other to lift one person out efficiently. Then, one by one in the dark, Irina and her Red Army friends escorted all the Lublin Transport Rabbits through the fence into the main Camp. After that they were on their own—on crutches or limping or clinging to each other.

Irina caught Róża herself when it was her turn.

"The tent is the nearest place to hide," Irina whispered.

"*I'm not going back there,*" Karolina fired down at her, next in line to sneak out.

But Róża couldn't walk—not really, not in the dark—and Karolina was stuck with her.

"If we don't come back, Rose knows all our names," Róża said in ringing tones of menace, a little too loud.

"*Shut up*, you stupid little girl!" Karolina gasped hysterically. "Or they'll kill Rose, too, and there will be NO ONE who gets out of here alive to tell anyone!"

"The whole Camp knows. Everybody knows. Rose will tell the world." Róża growled orders at me. "You are to tell the world, Rose, you hear me?"

"I will! I promise!"

Irina took her under her arm to help her scuttle, limping, toward the hole in the fence.

Sometime before the four a.m. Screamer, Irina and I crept back to our own bunk in the pitch black, and that hellhole was so darn overcrowded that when we got to our spots, there were new prisoners sleeping soundly in place of Lisette and Karolina and Róża—I don't know who they were.

We lined up for roll call at four thirty a.m. in what felt like a crowd of strangers, Irina and I at sea without our Camp Family. The whole Lublin Transport was missing.

"Think they'll kill us instead?" Irina whispered.

"Maybe." I gulped, thinking of Anna's relentless description of poison gas, and my impossible promise to make sure that everybody knew everything when it was all over.

Irina tilted her hand at me. "*Taran.* We go down fighting."

They read the list of numbers in German. It was like listening to a swarm of droning hornets.

"*Siebentausendsiebenhundertzwei, Siebentausendsiebenhundertdrei, Siebentausendsiebenhundertvier . . .*"

I looked down at the cinders, scuffling my feet nervously, trying to keep warm. A small black pool of slush and dirt formed beneath me.

Siebentausendsiebenhundertfünf. That was Róża, 7705. They called Karolina's number, and Lisette's. I glanced at Irina, but she was staring straight ahead.

The messenger doing the announcement was an SS woman, in one of their grim black rain capes over her uniform. She came to the end of her long list of numbers and paused. Then she barked an order in German. She paced from one end of our first row to the other, her cape flapping shadows in the dark as she peered at the numbers on people's sleeves. It was pretty quiet, except for the usual coughing and sniffling. The turkey-buzzard messenger yelled at us again. No one moved. She hadn't called *our* numbers.

She barked an order at the guards. They'd sent extras, expecting a fight. She took hold of a dog's leash and started prowling among the first rows of silent, stubborn language professors and music teachers and widowed mothers and orphaned daughters, and projectionists and spies and bartenders and cleaning ladies and Resistance agents and Red Army soldiers and Girl Scout saboteurs. And *taran* pilots.

And, in our first real moment of glory, the lights went out.

I think, if there could be anything I am glad I was there for, it is that moment.

We let out a ragged roar of sheer excitement, all fifty or sixty thousand of us at once. I swear, it was all of us at once, and this time they couldn't control *anything*. We had nowhere to go, of course—we still couldn't get out—we were all too starved to overpower anyone, and we couldn't see who we were fighting anyway, but BY GOD *we weren't going to let them count us.* They weren't going to count *anybody* that morning.

"Line up for work! Work details!" we all shouted ridiculously—like we were trying to get organized, when in fact we were hurling handfuls of gravel.

I felt the flat of Irina's hand against my shoulder. She rocked her palm. *Taran.* She did it against my shoulder because we couldn't see each other in the dark.

Maybe it wasn't really fighting back—maybe it was just pathetic passive resistance. The lights go out and everybody runs around in the dark, throwing dirt and screaming. But it *felt* like we were fighting back. There's only so much fighting you can do in one day on a slice of bread made mostly of bonemeal and two bowls of lukewarm turnip broth.

I *wish* I would stop sidetracking onto food. Even now, when I am not hungry, I can't stop thinking about what it was like to be starving.

It is true, though—we got tired. Some of the women actually just went back to bed, climbing back through the broken windows of the block to snatch another hour of sleep. That also made it hard to count us! By the time it was light, we were so disorganized that they gave up on the roll call—they also halfheartedly tried to stop Block 32 from getting our morning "coffee" (there I go again), but a group of Polish prisoners from another block came running over with a couple of the big saucepans from the kitchen and passed us a desperate breakfast through the chain-link fence.

And there weren't even any Rabbits in there with us at that point. That's how determined everyone was.

The lights went out again at the evening roll call. Irina and I stood pressed close to each other, our shoulders touching, standing still amid the chaos.

"How many times will she get away with it?" I whispered. I was worried about Irina's friend from the Moscow Metro, the Russian technician responsible for the lights going out. Irina didn't answer; I hadn't really expected an answer anyway.

The lights went out at every roll call for a week.

"Rose! Rose Justice! *Rosie!*"

Through the never-ending background of coughs and groans and creaking bunk slats I heard my name, low and tuneful, coaxing me in my sleep. The demon Nadine, asleep on her mat by the small stove in the knitters' workroom, would never have been able to hear it. I sat bolt upright and banged my head against the ceiling. Irina grabbed me by the arm to steady me, instantly awake like a soldier.

"Outside the window," Irina said.

We climbed down to the level below us and crawled over people to the broken window. There was a sort of human-shaped bundle of rags standing there in the black slush, tapping for attention on the window frame with a stick while simultaneously trying to hang on to the side of the building and avoid the filth that was smeared all over the wooden wall from the ground to about three feet up—that was where we all went to the bathroom now.

"It's one of those *schmootzichs* begging to get in," I whispered. "Oh, God, they're so creepy. How do they get away with wandering around the Camp like this? How did she figure out how to get through the Block 32 fence? Nadine will kill us if we let a *schmootzich* into the bunks."

I do not like to admit how much the *schmootzichs* scared me. Ever since that first day, when they swarmed over me with their starved claws, I had been scared of them. I was scared of them touching me and I was scared of becoming one of them.

"Rosie, that is not like you! She would sleep *under* the bunks if we let her in," Irina suggested. "The *schmootzichs* do not care about the mess."

"*You fucking morons!*" the *schmootzich* hissed. "I'm Róża!"

The stick she'd been tapping on the window frame was her crutch. Irina climbed out the window and hoisted Róża up to me, and I hauled her in, using my coat to pad the frame this time (we all slept in our coats by then, and they let us because there were so few blankets left).

"What are you *doing* here, Róża? You've got to hide!" We scolded her in several languages.

"I don't care," Róża snarled. "I'm sick of hiding."

"But Block 32 is the first place they'll look for you! Are you hungry?" They'd cut Block 32's food back by ten loaves and a barrel of soup to try to coerce us into turning over the Rabbits. A bunch of us kept trying to save bread to sneak out to the people hiding, but it was just impossible with the rations down—people would snatch it out of your *mouth* if you weren't fast enough.

Róża shook with bottled laughter at my question and hissed, "Do you think we get five-course meals in the tent? Of course I'm hungry. You're hungry, Irina's hungry, everybody's hungry. We're all fucking starving. I didn't leave because I'm hungry! I'm *bored*. You thought I was a *schmootzich*! That's a fabulous disguise. I can go around pretending to be a Camp beggar. I can carry messages!"

"You can't WALK."

"I'll ride in your wheelbarrow."

She'd ripped off her Ravensbrück sleeve patches. She'd managed to get some dead woman's number inked on her wrist like an Auschwitz prisoner's tattoo. Carefully darned woolen hose from Elodie covered up her maimed legs. And in fact Róża *could* walk without her crutch, but it was this

233

impossible crablike, lurching, gimpy series of dives and landings—she wouldn't put weight on the leg that was missing pieces of bone, because one of the girls who'd had the same operation had snapped her tibia in half trying to walk on it and died of the infection that came raging in afterward. And without Anna, our calcium supply had dried up.

"What messages will you take?" Irina said. "Translation for the dead?"

"I've got a message for *you*, smart aleck. Lisette and Karolina are coming out tomorrow, in broad daylight, because they're not going to hide anymore, either. They're going to be our delegation to the Commander."

"Are they *crazy*?" I whispered back.

"No, we've done it before. We really did! We took a petition to the Commander before this one, saying we refused to be operated on again. He didn't pay any attention, but this one is such a weasel he always pretends to be polite—he makes a show of negotiating with us so he'll look good to the Red Cross. And yesterday Lisette got six of us out! There were three trucks transferring people to other camps, and she got six other Rabbits to sneak on board—we cut all their numbers apart so that only the symmetrical ones were left, and then we mixed them up and sewed them on upside down and backward. They'll get more of us out today—they take hundreds of people to the satellite camps every day because there's no damn room here. Lisette wanted me to go, too, but Karolina wouldn't let me because of my legs—it has to be people who can walk without looking like they're dancing." She giggled. "Karolina wants me to go, but she wants to go with me—I need taking care of, right?"

"Like fun!"

But of course, little Różyczka *did* need taking care of. She couldn't go without help. I lay awake with my emotions whirling like the beaters on an electric mixer, feeling stupidly envious of Karolina's bravery, elated that we'd got people out, fearful that they might have climbed into the wrong truck—the transfer trucks were usually closed in and the gas chamber trucks were usually open-topped, but you never, never really knew.

"Elodie," Micheline uttered under her breath to me as we got dragged off to work as usual.

"Elodie?"

She clamped her lips together, because a caped turkey buzzard with a dog was keeping an eye on us.

They'd closed the Camp streets and put guards and road-blocks at all the intersections as they tried to catch the women who were hiding. By now, the second week of February, there were nearly twice as many women in the Camp as when I got there. Hundreds of people came in and hundreds of others got taken away again every day. We had extra roll calls so they could try to count us—daylight roll calls, six in a day once. In my head every single one of them takes place in a snowstorm, but that wasn't true, because I can also remember watching planes going over against a sky as blue as a summer day at the Lake, and I remember just *longing* to be up there with my hand lightly on the control column, just *longing* to be back in my other, half-remembered existence.

Every day, me and Irina and our Corpse Crew of a dozen tall French girls still had to go around making our collection with carts and wheelbarrows up and down the *Lagerstrasse*. It still had to be done—it couldn't go more than a couple of days without being done. We had a new *Kolonka* who didn't speak English and didn't like to come too close to us—she did a lot of screaming at us, but as long as we did our job she didn't smack us. We never saw Anna again. I didn't have any idea if she'd managed to save her own skin. I still don't know.

And now Micheline was mumbling Elodie's name without telling me anything else, and I was frantic with worry.

"Elodie gives," Micheline muttered as we loaded the dead into the incinerator-bound trucks waiting by the main gate. We weren't allowed outside the gate anymore—prisoners from the men's camp had to do the unloading on the other side.

That's all she said. *Elodie gives.* Then Micheline went white-faced and tight-lipped *again* as we got herded aside and slapped and kicked until we took our clothes off. The guards weren't supposed to let us through the various blockades unless they searched the carts first. But that was such a repugnant job that a lot of the time they'd just search us instead—make us strip and stand quivering with cold and embarrassment, stark naked with our arms at our sides, while they paced around us looking suspicious. The less cooperative we were the longer they made us stand there. So we got in the habit of being almost unbelievably meek and mild when we were working, and this included hardly daring to breathe a word to each other.

And really, sometimes you didn't feel like talking. That day the guards didn't even bother to tell us we could get dressed again—they just walked off to pester someone else and left us standing there at attention in our stunningly unattractive birthday suits until after a quarter of an hour Irina got mad and risked dragging her clothes back on without getting anyone's permission.

"Clothes," Micheline muttered as we pulled our ragged dresses over our heads.

I sighed. "Clothes," I agreed.

Later, as we carried a body together through a narrow aisle

between befouled bunks, she grunted, "For the Rabbits." She gave me a *look* as we lowered the poor thing onto the pile, like she wanted me to answer her somehow.

I frowned at her, not daring to say anything. Micheline held my eyes with hers—she had gorgeous eyes, a clear yellow-brown hazel with dark brown flecks.

I thought back over the handful of words she'd sprinkled me with that day, like a puzzle or a radio serial, and came up with:

Elodie gives clothes for the Rabbits.

"Yes," I hissed. *"Oui."* Just to let her know I understood.

This is what she meant: the women who sorted the clothes taken from the new prisoners were organizing civilian outfits for all the remaining Rabbits. Civilian clothes were the first thing you needed if you were going to escape. Not that anyone *really* escaped—there was that Gypsy girl they caught in the woods, and her own block beat her to death because they'd had three days' *Strafstehen* while the guards hunted for her. Everyone knew about her. But it didn't stop you from thinking about escaping.

Just getting people out of Ravensbrück, even on a truck bound for another camp, counted. Hundreds of the newest prisoners were transferred in or out without being put in quarantine or even getting issued with prison clothes, and civilian clothes would help the Rabbits blend in with them. We had the clothes now, and my team was good at organizing false numbers from the bodies we picked up. Even if the Rabbits couldn't get out, they could hide in the other blocks, replacing the dead.

Lisette and Karolina had diplomatic immunity—that's the right term. They were the only contact the Camp officials had with the Rabbits. That incredibly slippery character, the Camp Commander, *wanted* to negotiate with them. This is the same stinker who on New Year's Day told us over the loudspeakers that he was going to blow us all up. Here's what he tried to get the Rabbits to do for him now:

"Please sign a form saying you hurt your leg in an industrial accident."

"Please, when the Soviets get here and turn this place inside out, could you tell them how well you've all been treated, since it was the previous Camp administration who authorized the first operations and the current administration who kept you alive?"

"Please, all of you come forward and we will send you together to another, more comfortable camp."

That was the best one. We knew the camp they named had already been shut down, so . . . did he really think people were all going to climb meekly into a lot of empty trucks specially designated for the doomed Lublin Transport and let them drive everybody out the gates toward—where? Around and around the outside walls of Ravensbrück till they got back to the gas chamber? As if we had *no idea* what happened to the people they loaded into trucks and drove around the walls every day? You could *hear* them going around. You could *hear* them stopping at the warehouse we had to paint black on the inside. You could hear the sobbing and yelling when they made people get out of the trucks on the other side of the wall. And then their worn and lice-ridden clothes would come back inside, and Elodie had to sort them.

We knew what would happen when they loaded two hundred of us into open trucks before breakfast.

"The Commander's a stinking weasel," Karolina said. "He's scared and he's desperate. The Nazis are beaten and they know it, but they *just won't stop*. It's like—it's like Róża when she's angry at something—she just gets nastier and nastier, even though she *knows* everyone will end up crying. The Commander wants signed statements from us all, so he can prove to General Eisenhower how generous and humanitarian he is when the Americans get here, but when he's got his signed statements, *then* he can safely kill us and pretend it was an administrative error."

"The Rabbits are safe, my dear," Lisette vowed, "because no one will sign anything. We will agree to nothing."

"No one is safe. You and I could be sentenced to execution *anytime*—they're only letting us come and go because we're still wearing our numbers and can be counted. The others are only safe till someone finds them," Karolina retorted grimly.

Kaninchen Króliki Lapins Králíci

Králíci is Czech. I don't know how to write *rabbits* in Russian, but it sounds the same as in Polish. By the end of February, everybody in the Camp knew all the words for *rabbits* in every language of every nationality at Ravensbrück, because the Rabbit Hunt was the one thing that united us.

The Rabbits sometimes called themselves something else. They used the word *król*. I would not have figured this out except that Karolina made a lot of caricature portraits for people showing them as rabbits wearing little crowns, and Lisette explained it to me, because she knew I love the subtleties of words as much as she does. *Król* is a rare Polish word for "rabbit." But also it means "king."

There is a rare English word for "rabbit," *coney*, which also sounds a little like the German word for king—*könig*. It's also like the Dutch word for "rabbit," *konijn*. I'd turn all this into a poem if only I could find a connection that wasn't a coincidence, or if it worked better in English. *The Kings of Ravensbrück.*

Because in a crazy way, they ruled the place.

I want so desperately to remember it. Hiding the Rabbits gave us back our lives. But so many of the things we did to save them were *unspeakable*, and I don't think I can write about it. Róża hitching rides with me and Irina as we worked—as though we were hauling turnips? Filling in the missing people at roll call with bodies stolen from the *Revier*, so that our numbers always came out right when they counted us, no matter who wasn't there? Only in Block 32. I said before that we were really good at propping people up.

It's not unreal to me yet, though it might get that way soon. It still feels very real. And not even horrible—the dead are just the dead. I am convinced that the living people they once were would have been proud of their protective bodies hoodwinking their murderers to save someone else.

But it's not *civilized*. There is something indecent about it—really foully indecent. The civilized Rose-person in me, who still seems to exist beneath the layers of filth, *knows* this. And I can't write about it.

I did make up a poem about it, "Service of the Dead," but I just can't write it down.

I think it is the most terrible thing that was done to me—that I have become so indifferent about the dead. I would be able to do a human anatomy course without ever feeling faint, do surgery with steady hands, clean up *anything* and not be sick and never mind the blood.

Maybe I could be a doctor.

A real one—go to medical school—

Maybe I could! I could be a poet *and* a doctor—like William Carlos Williams! A new direction—a new *world*—I could help *fix* things now. How does his poem go, "Spring and All"—

> THEY ENTER THE NEW WORLD NAKED,
> COLD, UNCERTAIN OF ALL
> SAVE THAT THEY ENTER. ALL ABOUT THEM
> THE COLD, FAMILIAR WIND—

A poet *and* a doctor. Maybe I could.
This is the first I have thought of it. *Maybe I could.*

There were five dozen people from the Lublin Special Transport in hiding. That's a lot of people to hide. Worse than that, it's a lot of people to feed when there isn't any food.

We had to keep moving people around, and sometimes they spotted us doing it. They'd corner people, and we were just so desperate we'd do *anything* to get away—a couple of girls picked up another prisoner and *threw* her at the guards who were after them. Standoffs with dogs. Climbing in and out of broken windows, hiding in the bunks in the tuberculosis block with dying women so horribly contagious that the guards wouldn't come in. Irina's wire cutters got passed around because you never knew who'd need a weapon. Most of the girls weren't strong enough to do anything with them anyway, but it made you feel brave just to carry a pair of stolen wire cutters. They always came back.

They saved a dozen lives when Irina and Róża and I got caught by SS guards with guns, cornered against the fence around the *Revier*.

It was a Sunday. On Sunday, theoretically, you were allowed to walk up and down the *Lagerstrasse* for a couple of hours chatting with a friend and drying your underpants, if you had any—you could wash them under a spigot, but you couldn't hang them anywhere or someone would steal them, so you just paced up and down holding them out in front of you and flapping them around. That Sunday we weren't drying underwear. We were shifting a bunch of Rabbits from one hiding place to another. You weren't supposed to walk with more than one or two other people on a Sunday afternoon, and we'd followed that rule. But we were more or less together just because the street was so crowded, and the guards were on the lookout for people who limped. That day there were too many Rabbits together in the same place.

It happened fast. They rounded us up and backed us against the fence. I think it was partly our own fault, because we were so used to being herded that it took us a moment to realize the guards had spotted our Rabbits, and weren't just trying to clear a path for some high-ranking official or a transport truck.

"A selection!" Irina guessed, and a couple of people heard her and started to cry, because now we all thought we were going to be gassed.

"Shut up! Stand up straight!" Róża barked at the other Rabbits in German, like an SS turkey buzzard herself. Selections weren't usually random—they went for the older women, or the sick ones, or people who looked sick. Having a face full of cold sores or impetigo put you at high risk for being gassed. So you stood up straight and tried to look healthy during selections. Or pinched each other's cheeks to make them glow, like we used to do in the bathroom before a school dance, when we were too young to wear makeup.

In the back of our huddle, Irina struggled to hack a hole in the fence around the *Revier* behind us. The rest of us tried to hide what she was doing. The guards surrounding us weren't the usual SS women—these were men, armed soldiers. For a moment we stood facing each other like opposing dodgeball teams.

I wonder what we looked like. Fifteen filthy, haggard, ragged, wild-eyed girls—half of us crippled—facing off against two dozen tall, strong, well-fed boys with rifles. *What did it look like* as the troop leader slowly raised his gun? I wish I had a picture of us all. I wish there was a picture of it on the front page of the *New York Times*. No one will ever believe me.

Except—the picture wouldn't tell you the whole story, would it? It wouldn't show you how Irina was frantically trying to cut us an escape route in the fence behind us, or tell you that the front row of us was defensive—me and the three brave Red Army girls from Block 32 who liked to pretend they were heavies had all moved to stand in front of Róża and the other Rabbits. The man who'd raised his gun swept the barrel up and down our pathetic front line, looking for an easy gap.

Róża screamed in Polish at the top of her voice, "*Bread! Bread! The SS are giving out bread!*"

A mob swarmed over us, first right off the street, and then a horde of starving women came piling toward us from the tent.

"*BREAD! BREAD HERE!*" we all screamed, because nobody cared if there *was* any or not—just the *idea* of bread was enough to cause glorious chaos. Irina and I and the Russian girls pushed Róża and everybody on their stomachs through a plate-sized hole between the fence and the ground, and they hid in the *Revier*. The rest of us were safe in the crowd.

Safe. What a completely loony use of the word *safe.* Exactly the way I have been using *hope.*

We pried up the filthy red clay tiles in the Block 32 washroom and dug a pit under the floor of the barrack, stinking of sewage and cold as the Arctic, and lined the hole with straw and a couple of the last rotting cotton blankets, and we hid Róża and five of the worst-damaged girls there for a week.

The SS didn't kill any Rabbits. It didn't stop them from gassing two hundred other prisoners every day. You always think you're immortal, don't you? I mean, it hasn't happened yet. *I am still alive.*

When they read off my number over the loudspeakers, I didn't even hear it. I was so busy listening out for Róża's number, or Karolina's, it never occurred to me to listen for mine. But of course I was still wearing it, and I was still being counted every morning and night as Available Prisoner 51498. They called out lists of doomed prisoner numbers all the time. Not everyone could hide. One of the French girls in our block had escaped a selection only because her mother had swapped numbers with her and been gassed in her place.

It was still dark and no one had had breakfast yet. Karolina grabbed me around the waist.

"*Einundfünfzigtausendvierhundertachtundneunzig,*" she hissed in my ear. 51498.

Then I heard her, but I still didn't take it in for a moment or two. And then my heart turned into a block of ice.

"What? *Why?*"

You face it with a total lack of comprehension, even though less than two weeks ago when we got caught in front of the *Revier* fence I'd thought they were going to shoot me.

"It is your transport," Lisette gasped. "The French girls you came with. All of them."

I stood frozen and staring, completely unable to believe it or react. A deer in headlights.

Irina peeled away Karolina's arm and took me by the wrist. She stepped out of line with me, and led me quietly out of our row and through the gate toward the *Lagerstrasse*. No one else from our block had been called, so there wasn't anyone to go with me to the trucks, and they let Irina lead me out.

I went with her meekly.

We walked hand in hand past the tent. But instead of heading toward the gates where they parked the terrible open trucks, Irina guided me to double back around the far side of the tent. When we got close to the fence around Block 32, she put a hand on my shoulder and gently pushed me to the ground, and got down beside me, and we crawled back into the parade ground around our block through the hole in the fence. People saw us, but no guards did. No one said anything as Irina and I climbed in the back window of our barrack, the one we'd used as an escape route when we first hid the Rabbits.

Inside the barrack, Irina made me take off my damp coat and sit on the floor close to the cranky little stove that was supposed to heat the whole place. There wasn't a fire in it now, but it was still warm to touch because the demon Nadine slept next to it and sometimes managed to stoke it up with scraps of coal or wood before she went to sleep. Irina got me a drink of water. Neither of us said anything; she just stood there, waiting patiently while I drank the water, and then finally she reached down to help me back to my feet.

"Come, Rosie," she insisted. "Hide with Różyczka."

I shook my head because I didn't see the point—I wasn't a Rabbit.

But I was too numb to rebel or take control of myself. So I let Irina lead me into the washroom, to the place under the sinks where the boards and filthy matting covered up our six hidden Rabbits in the pit under the floor. Irina pulled up a board and made me crawl in with them.

Invisible hands pulled me down beside the others. Irina laid the false floor back in place above us, and the six girls already hiding there found an impossible space for me along-side them—like playing sardines. For the first ten minutes, I couldn't do anything but retch. I thought I'd suffocate.

"Worse than being gassed," came Róża's infuriatingly cheerful whisper. "Is that who I think it is?"

When I figured out how to breathe, I started to cry.

Someone hissed angrily, *"Shut up, you idiot!"* because I was making too much noise. And wasting air.

"What are you doing here, 51498?" Róża whispered in my ear.

"They are gassing *my whole transport*," I sobbed.

"Bad luck. There isn't anything special about your transport!"

I wanted to kill her.

"Micheline is special. Elodie is special," I hissed through clenched teeth. "Kiss your wool hose good-bye, you miserable Rabbit."

We curled against each other in the dank, stinking underground in silence after that, trying to breathe and not kick anybody and waiting to be found and shot. I knew I had to stop crying, and the only way to do it was to recite poetry to myself, moving my lips without speaking, clinging to words, to sense and beauty—

"Silver bark of beech, and sallow
Bark of yellow birch and yellow
Twig of willow."

Róża knew what I was doing, even in the silent dark. I felt her familiar thin arms wind around my waist and hold me tight.

I don't know how she held out there for a week—I don't know how any of them did. I think I was there for two days. You could hear the Screamer, muffled, telling us when the roll calls and meals and work details came. That was the only way to count the time passing. We ate stolen bread—no soup—and nothing hot, ever—we had to eat lying down.

"Tell us something warm and sunny. Tell us a Lake Story," Róża whispered.

"We are all wearing red bathing suits. But all different, with flowers on yours and stripes on mine. Big white polka dots on Karolina's, like Minnie Mouse, and Irina's is silver with red stars, like a Soviet aircraft. You are all staying in our summer cottage with me, and we are going to lie on the beach in the sun and drink Coca-Colas, in frosty green bottles right out of the icebox—one by one, boys will come and ask us to go for a canoe ride with them. And when we are each in a different canoe with a different boy, we will line up at the rental dock and have a race across the Lake."

"Lisette, too."

"Gosh, yes, Lisette, too. There is a very handsome famous actor from the Summer Rep Theater at the Chautauqua Playhouse who's come to the Lake for the afternoon, and he spots Lisette right away. So we race the canoes, and your team will win. And we'll all be annoyed, so we'll gang up on you and tip your canoe. Then everybody will tip each other's canoes and we'll all fall in the water, and it'll feel wonderful because we'll be hot and sweaty from racing, and while we're splashing around there will be belted kingfishers scooting overhead and scolding each other—"

The only thing that makes this a fairy story is the idea that we could ever all be there together.

The Nick Stories were all these ridiculous rescue dramas, Hollywood hero antics that could never happen in a million years. But the Lake Stories—I didn't even bother to pretend the staff at the refreshment stand would bring us our drinks in a Lake Story. We'd help ourselves and pay, just the way anyone would. Even the boys asking us for a canoe race really happened last summer—I mean the summer before last, 1943, on that wonderful weekend before Labor Day when I'd nearly finished at the boring old paper box factory and I spent the day at the Lake with Polly and Fran.

And that is what makes it *so unfair*. It is such a *simple* fairy story.

Lisette dragged me and Róża out of the pit during breakfast on the third morning and helped us change into clothes I knew had been organized by Elodie—plain, respectable stuff—navy skirt and stockings, and incredibly good coats, with wool cuffs and collars and lining still attached, though the elbows were threadbare. Numbers stolen from dead women were attached to the right sleeves, and there was no evidence of yellow star patches on the fronts. Warsaw coats, not Auschwitz coats. Lisette's hands were cold and her face was drained and grim. I knew something terrible had happened, something that had changed her world.

"What's wrong?"

"Irina came back to that roll call wearing your coat," Lisette said. "And Karolina fought her for it."

"They fought over my *coat*?" I repeated dumbly, astonished. They wouldn't do that, either one of them.

Róża understood instantly. "They didn't fight over your coat, you turnip head," she said coldly. "They fought over your *number*."

Lisette looked away from me, her cold hands still helping me into the warmest clothes I'd worn for months and months.

"Did Irina win?" I whispered.

"Karolina won."

I feel like it is the worst thing I have ever done—lie weeping in a hole in the ground while Karolina—

I can't write it.

Karolina on the beach at the Lake in a red bathing suit, sunbathing under a blue sky.

"Now pay attention, my dear," Lisette said, holding me fiercely by the shoulders. "You are going with Róża." I know that's why Karolina did it—for Róża, not for me. Everyone Róża's age was already gone, but she was so crippled she couldn't go by herself. Karolina and Lisette were counting on me to get her out, to get her scrawny, mutilated legs out where someone might see them—because Róża was a better piece of evidence than Karolina, who could walk to her death without limping.

"You have *one task only* this morning, and that is to keep anyone from noticing Róża's legs. Hide her, hold her up—if she falls over, make it look like you have knocked her down. Irina is going to be on the same transport, so look for her and she will help you. There can be one of you on each side of Róża when you get to the other end, but you will be on your own until you find Irina."

"Where's Irina?" we asked together.

"She's in the Punishment Block—"

"Because . . . ?" Róża interrupted, and then guessed, "For fighting with another prisoner during roll call, right? For trying to steal another prisoner's coat?"

Lisette pressed her thin lips together, and I caught the crazed wet gleam in her eyes that had been there when I'd first met her, right after Zosia and Genca had been shot. Not for the first time, I wanted to punch Róża in the teeth.

"For trying to steal another prisoner's coat," Lisette

agreed. "They are shipping out the whole Punishment Block this morning; I don't know why, but you are going with them."

"In *these* clothes?"

"There will be some Warsaw evacuees as well; they're still wearing civilian clothes. You know where the transport trucks line up? You'll have to wait till they bring Irina's block out and then get into line with them. Oh, darling *Różyczka*—"

"Rose will take care of me," Róża said with composure. Because I couldn't say it myself. I wasn't sure.

"What if they take you straight to—"

"What if they take us straight to Monte Carlo? We'll be rich!" Róża laughed hilariously.

Lisette kissed Róża on both cheeks. She gave me six slices of bread, wealth beyond imagining—two slices each, two days' worth, to last us who knew how long. And who knew where she got it. Then she kissed me, too.

"*Get her out,*" Lisette said. She didn't say good-bye to us. But of course she hadn't said good-bye to any of her other children. And this time she had a slender hope we weren't going to be killed.

And this time she was right, as it happens, though she never knew, and may be dead. I can't believe Lisette is dead, but she probably is, and I'll never know that, either.

It was about six weeks ago—I have been in Paris for just over two weeks, writing and writing, and we left Ravensbrück late in March. It hadn't stopped snowing when we left—at that point I thought it was *never* going to stop snowing.

Irina was easy to find because she is so tall, and because of her white hair. She looked as dazed and crazed as Lisette, standing in line, waiting to climb into the transport truck. She was staring at nothing. We couldn't get near her, but we got into the same truck.

You know, I think we could have climbed into any truck we wanted to. Who'd have ever dreamed that any prisoner would *willingly* climb into one of those stinking, overcrowded hell-bound crates? Who'd have dreamed that *I* would?

It was bomb fuses all over again—like taking the fuse away from the boy on the railway tracks, or refusing to make the relay. *I didn't have a choice.* I really didn't. I *had* to climb into that truck with Róża. For Karolina—for Lisette. For Micheline and Elodie. For *Izabela, Aniela, Alicia, Eugenia*—

Controlled flight into terrain.

We were expecting something like a three-day trip with maybe a bucket of water to share among us, nothing to use for a toilet, and having to sleep standing up because there wasn't any room to sit down. We were expecting that, prepared for it. Resigned to it, anyway. But the journey didn't take much more than an hour. And we knew we'd really been driving somewhere, not going in the slow and terrible final circle around the outside of the Camp.

They didn't let us out right away. The hours crawled by. When they finally opened the trucks, for the first few minutes, while everybody was untangling themselves from one another and gulping in fresh air, there were only two things I thought about: hiding Róża's legs, and getting to Irina. I dragged Róża under one arm and shoved my way toward Irina's white head. Irina caught Róża under her other arm, and then I'd done both my jobs.

"Where is this place?" Irina asked pointlessly. Who had any idea? It was a rhetorical question and I looked around rhetorically—

And I knew where we were. *I knew where we were.*

We were in the exact same parking lot I'd pulled up in on the back of the mechanic's motorcycle when Karl

Womelsdorff and I flew to Neubrandenburg last September. It could have been anywhere, the loading area for any factory complex. There wasn't really anything distinctive about it. But it is emblazoned on my brain and I recognized it.

"We're in Neubrandenburg," I said. "It's one of the Ravensbrück satellite camps. They make aircraft parts here— there's an airfield. And a town."

Róża acted *so fast*. "Give me the bread," she demanded in a whisper, and I stupidly gave it to her.

"*BREAD!*" she screamed, just the way she'd done in front of the fence by the *Revier*. "*Das Brot! Chleb! Le pain! The SS are giving out bread!*"

There was another instant riot. Only this time there really was bread.

She threw it with calculated cunning and accuracy into the middle of the crowd of hundreds of starving women climbing out of the trucks. They didn't mob us—they mobbed the bread. All the available guards piled in after them to sort out the havoc. There were big chain-link fences topped with barbed wire around the yard, but the vehicle gates were still open wide.

Róża ran. Or didn't run, exactly, just hurled herself in her ridiculous lopsided gimpy lurch away from the crowd and around the truck we'd just climbed out of. Irina and I sprinted after her, but she was in the open before we were, and before we could catch up she was out of the gates and into the road.

That was our escape. It took thirty seconds and six slices of bread.

We didn't know it then, though. We were just in a frenzy of panic and fury that Róża could have done anything so utterly, desperately, monstrously *stupid*. We were out of Ravensbrück, out of the danger of being gassed, we'd got her scrawny Exhibit A legs safely into an ordinary work camp, and now she'd killed us all by trying to escape.

But they hadn't counted us getting into the truck back in Ravensbrück. Well, maybe they'd counted Irina, but they hadn't counted Róża and me, and they didn't count us getting out. So that was lucky—they didn't know we were there, and thanks to Róża's staged food fight, no one noticed us leaving. We caught up with Róża easily as soon as we broke free of the bread ruckus. The road outside the gates was also full of trucks. In a couple more seconds, the dogs would come after us, we'd be dragged back into the factory yard, and they'd beat us all to a pulp and shoot us. We didn't turn back. How could we turn back? They'd have beaten us to a pulp and shot us if we'd turned ourselves in.

Irina threw Róża under the nearest truck and dived in after her. So did I.

For another minute or two we lay there panting. Running fifty feet had just about killed us. We were still so close to the fence that we could *see* the riot in the parking lot.

"Come on—" Irina gasped, and we crawled beneath the trucks, moving slowly from one to another, until we were a little farther away and we felt safe enough to rest again.

We were also lucky the ground was frozen. We didn't get coated head to foot in mud or slush. I shrugged off my coat and gave it to Irina. She pushed it away and I threw it back at her insistently, too fearful to talk. I wasn't being noble—I was being sneaky.

"*Put on the coat*, you stupid bat girl," Róża snarled. "You look like a *schmootzich*. We don't have a hope in hell out here with you in stripes. Cover up! As soon as we stand up we have to look like normal people—"

I'd caught what was usually Róża's disease: inappropriate

hysterical laughter. I lay on my face on a sheet of oily ice under a German munitions truck, smothering myself and shaking with mirth.

"Holy Mother of God!" Róża swore, "I'm surrounded by lunatics!" She began to giggle, too. Irina did not, but she quietly put my coat on and then lay next to me with her arm over my back.

"You threw away *all our bread*," I pointed out to Róża. "Talk about lunatics!"

And we both broke into muffled hysterics again.

Irina took hold of my ear and twisted it hard. I shut up.

"We have no papers," she said. "We speak no German. What is our story when someone stops us?"

Róża improvised wildly, "We are French—"

"*French!*"

"French servants. We have to be French—it's our only common language. You and Rose are *cooks*! And I am your sister. Only I speak German. We are servants for a German officer—I do all his sewing and cleaning—"

"I bet you do," Irina snickered.

We lay quietly for a few minutes, feeling falsely secure. It was cold, but no colder than standing in a roll call in the dark.

"We better move," said Róża. "If they notice the bat girl's gone, they'll look for her."

We crawled for half an hour. We crawled underneath the entire row of trucks. When there weren't anymore, we had to stand up and walk, vulnerable and obvious, along a barren stretch of road outside the camp and factory complex. We could see the town in the distance, church spire and silhouettes of buildings, and there wasn't the faintest question that we could go that way.

"Maybe we should try to get into the woods," I said. A lot of the landscape around us was the same sandy tracts of pine and birch that surrounded Ravensbrück.

"We'd just freeze to death. We should go into town and walk down the middle of the street," Róża countered. "Right down the middle, like we belong there. Slowly." She turned and gave me a witchy grin. "Smiling at everyone."

"Gee whiz, not smiling like *that*."

"You look almost human in that skirt and sweater, Rosie," she said critically. "Like an SS secretary, almost human. The kerchief is the best part."

"Shut up, Rabbit." The kerchief was ridiculous. But I was more ridiculous without it. I'd had my head shaved again very recently, as punishment for annoying the demon Nadine with nervous humming.

"Dark in a few hours," Irina said to me.

"We can't stop here. But—I know! There were farms on the other side of the airfield—I saw them as we were landing. This is the road they brought me in on. We'll go back past the airfield. Maybe hide in a barn—find some turnips or potatoes—"

"A cow!" Róża improved wildly.

"Maybe a cow! Maybe send you into someone's kitchen to organize a loaf of bread. Maybe—" Now I was thinking about what I'd find in the summer kitchen of the Mennonite farm just on the other side of Justice Field—succotash and applesauce and smoked sausage and shoofly pie. Talking like this was just going to lead to fantasies about *fasnachts* and bologna. "Anyway, we'll be safer on the other side of the airfield. Come on, girls!"

And we walked down that road in broad daylight, Róża lurching between us tucked beneath our arms. There was no one else walking there, and we were careful to cower in the weed-filled ditch at the road's edge, gritting our teeth among last year's dead stinging nettles, whenever traffic passed. We kept chattering to one another, insulting one another, discussing the weather—*anything*, like walking through a den of lazy lions and praying they won't get up. If they raise their heads and keep an eye on you as you pass, that's a little disconcerting. But as long as they don't come after you, you're safe. You know you better not run. Well, we couldn't run. We had to stop and rest about every quarter of a mile. It was probably a four-mile walk to the airfield.

"How is Lisette?" Irina asked.

"Brave," I said.

Róża asked conversationally, "What is the officer's name?"

"Which officer?"

"The one we all work for. In case someone asks."

"Oberleutnant Karl Womelsdorff," I answered.

"Wow, that was fast! Oberleutnant Karl Womelsdorff! I thought you didn't speak any German, French Political Prisoner *Einundfünfzigtausendvierhundertachtundneunzig*. You must have a devious streak after all."

Except that I feel like I have never lived anywhere else but this big room and its gorgeous bathroom, this could have happened yesterday. I think it is partly the reason I haven't even ventured out to find a dining room. The *terror* of that first day in the open, with the treacherous future yawning in front of us like the Grand Canyon—on foot with no food and no money and no papers in the middle of Germany, eternally at war, probably with people hunting for us—although I'm pretty sure now that if they had been, they'd have already found us for sure. But you don't think everything through logically when you have no real future except to plummet over the edge of the Grand Canyon.

We didn't make it past the airfield. I guess it is a miracle we made it that far. The ground crew who caught us were very kind. They were all airmen and mechanics, not SS guards. Maybe this isn't fair of me, but I actually think they were *smarter* than the SS guards—I mean, they were doing skilled jobs, not siccing dogs on starving women. Seems like that must automatically make you a nicer kind of person. Not necessarily, I guess, but it's a good start.

These guys knew perfectly well what we were and where we'd come from. Irina was still in her prison uniform beneath the threadbare coat; Róża couldn't walk; I had no hair beneath my bandanna. And only Róża spoke any German.

We got stopped along the barbed-wire fence by the airfield perimeter. There wasn't anyplace to hide. It was an unarmed man on a bicycle who caught us—he pulled up alongside Irina and laid a hand on her arm. I saw her assess him, recognize that she couldn't take him on, and her shoulders sagged. She didn't try to shake him off. I didn't run. Róża couldn't, and Irina was caught. There was nowhere to go anyway.

Róża tried to feed him a line. I don't know what she said, but I swear I have never seen her be so charming. When was the last time she sweet-talked anyone—maybe the Gestapo officer who made her watch while they beat her mother to a pulp? Anyway, she was like Snow White persuading the huntsman not to kill her—heart-melting. As well as being the only one of us who could speak German, Róża was the only one of us who was actually dressed inconspicuously, since I'd given my coat to Irina. Lisette had combed and braided Róża's hair and twisted it up before we left. If you could look past Róża being filthy and skeletal and crawling with bugs, she was lovely, really, in a waiflike Orphan Annie kind of way.

I remember worrying about how close we were standing to the wire fence, thinking it was probably electrified.

The mechanic on the bicycle didn't threaten us. He got off his bike so he could walk alongside us, and escorted us back to the main gate and onto the airfield. Over Róża's head, Irina shot me an agonized glance. I spread my hand into a plane and rocked the wings at her. Irina's mouth cracked into a small, sad ironic grin, and she briefly rocked her own hand back at me.

All right, they are really going to shoot me this time, I thought. And I have completely *failed* to get Róża out safely. *Idiot!* What was she THINKING? But at least if they kill me with Irina, as a prisoner on a Luftwaffe airfield, I will have died as a combat pilot. My father was a combat pilot and so is Irina and so am I. We are soldiers and *I am not going to make a fool of myself.*

At the big vehicle gate, the guard in the sentry box made a telephone call, and after a minute, a couple of other people came out to meet us. One of them took my arm the way the mechanic had Irina's. They still let us support Róża between us.

They frog-marched us to a bleak, cold maintenance room in the hangar. One side of the room was crowded with a million paint cans and tubs of dope for lacquering fabric aircraft wings, and the rest of the room was stacked with empty buckets and brooms and mops. They took the brooms and mops away in case we might try to use them as weapons, then locked us in and went away. The mechanic whom Róża had been charming earlier left her a small canvas bag, like a gas mask bag, that turned out to contain two margarine sandwiches and a thermos of watery beef broth.

We fell on this unexpected feast like turkey buzzards. My gosh, food—or lack of it—makes you stupid. We couldn't do a thing until we finished eating, and it never occurred to us to save any of it.

Afterward, Róża stood staring out the window across the acres of Luftwaffe concrete and wire that surrounded us again. After a moment she said matter-of-factly, "We're fucked."

Irina and I glanced at each other. Irina nodded once in grim agreement.

"I'm sorry," Róża said.

We went and stood next to her at the window. Róża licked a smear of leftover margarine from the back of her hand and repeated sadly, "We've had it. I really thought we might win. I'm sorry."

I thought so, too. I think we all did.

We stood quietly, staring across the airfield with her.

Standing on the apron, only about thirty yards away and gathering a crown of snow like icing sugar, stood a familiar ungainly Luftwaffe plane with a black iron cross painted on its side and a black swastika painted on its tail.

"That is a Storch," Irina murmured.

"A stork!" Róża translated, and let out one of her mirth-less giggles. "A sign of spring, right? Of new life! Good luck in the coming year! We had one nesting on our chimney the year I was arrested."

"It's a German liaison aircraft," I said. "Um, for communications. And they use it for ambulance work."

"*Pffff.*" Róża gave a dismissive snort and turned away.

"Controls for two pilots? Room for three?" Irina asked quietly.

We were both forming the same desperate, insane idea.

We knew Róża was right. We knew we'd had it. We were locked inside a building inside an electrified perimeter fence with dogs patrolling it—a more comfortable prison than the one we'd just come from, but nearly as secure, and in maybe less than an hour they'd send someone to collect us. And if they didn't shoot us on the spot, they'd haul us back where we'd come from like they did with the Gypsy girl who tried to escape, and after they were done with the dogs and the beating, we'd probably be too dead to execute.

So Irina and I had a quiet little discussion about the plane, without speaking our crazy idea out loud, because we didn't want to get Róża excited. She'd already decided we didn't stand a chance and was dealing with it in her own way. She wasn't listening to us anymore; she was making her own last desperate statement. She'd begun ransacking the shelves and paint tins and was leaving behind her a good-sized trail of destruction.

"Flight controls front and back," I told Irina. "But you can only control the flaps and throttle from the front seat."

She gave me a funny look. "Have you *flown* a Stork?"

"I've flown *that Stork,*" I whispered.

Her white eyebrows soared into her hairline. She grinned. "Rosie, you are full of surprises."

"That's the plane I came in on. But of course I haven't flown for six months."

"Who gives a damn?"

I shrugged. I didn't think I could do it—I didn't think I was *strong* enough to do it, but I didn't like to say so. We'd no other chance. Irina hadn't flown for two years.

"I haven't flown in the dark. Or in snow, much."

"Controls for two—I can help you. You have flown this plane, and I have flown at night in snow. We can do it together. If we go down burning, we will take another Fascist aircraft with us, yes, Rose Justice? *Taran!*"

"*Taran!*"

We didn't need to say another word. We both began to assess the window. There was iron mesh pressed between the glass, not prison bars but like chicken wire, and even if we smashed the glass we'd still have to cut the wire somehow—Irina's wire cutters had not gone with her to the Punishment Block. The main window was just a sheet of plate glass like a shop window, but there was a narrow transom at the top that slotted open with a lever to let in air.

"Little Różyczka will fit," Irina said.

"And then?"

Irina shrugged. "She can take the hinges off the door."

"Break it down," I improved.

It was just as likely. Róża's starved hands would never be strong enough to unscrew the steel door that shut us in, even if she had the right tools.

"Give her a hammer and she will break the lock—"

"She'll find a blowtorch!"

We laughed together mirthlessly and turned away from the window to look at our pet Rabbit.

This is what Róża was doing: she'd found an open bucket of black paint, and she was covering the walls with graffiti, just like me and my doomed French work team had done last November. Róża hadn't wasted any time. In letters six inches high, she was writing out the list of the Rabbits' names, as high as she could reach, all seventy-four of them, dead and alive. She was covering the walls with names in black paint beneath a thick black heading in German that said something complicated and accusing like, "Polish women used illegally as medical specimens in the Ravensbrück women's concentration camp at Fürstenberg"—a great big shout of defiant witness that they'd have to scrape off the walls with a razor blade if they wanted to hide it—or paint over it, of course.

We wasted a few minutes helping her complete the list.

"Różyczka, we want you to climb out the transom window."

"Oh, yes, I'll run to Berlin and get a job as a showgirl," she said. We'd finished the list, but she'd started again, slapping paint on the shelves and counters, which would be a darn sight harder for anyone to scrape clean than the walls.

"Be sensible. We want you to find a way to get us out. Find some wire cutters, a screwdriver, a crowbar—hand us in some tools and maybe we can break out of here."

"I'll get eaten by dogs!"

"If we see them coming, we'll throw paint pots at them. Come on, Rabbit, earn your keep! Get up there and get out of here."

We hoisted her up to the transom. She stood on Irina's

shoulders and clung to the window frame, and then somehow the three of us managed to push her feetfirst through the narrow opening. She giggled maniacally, leaning over the transom back into the room, looking down at us from above.

"Oh, *hell*, it's cold out here, this is SO UNFAIR—" Róża wriggled her way out and lowered herself down. We watched her collapse in a heap of bones and threadbare wool on the concrete wasteland just outside the window. At least the snow wasn't sticking, except on the plane.

Róża pulled herself to her feet and banged on the glass.

"Keep painting!"

Then she scuttled off in her lopsided lurching bunny hop, supporting herself against the side of the building.

There wasn't anything else useful for us to do while we waited, so we obeyed Róża's last order. We covered the windows with names. And the steel door. And the floor. We'd begun on the ceiling when the bolts in the lock on the door started to click.

I froze. Irina leaped down from the counter and positioned herself beside the door, armed with a paintbrush.

But it was only Róża coming back. Irina let out a soft whistle.

"They left the key in the door!" Róża said. "To make it easy for whoever they send for us. We're dead anyway. We'll never get through the fence—it's all patrolled and they've shut the gate. The only thing we can do is hide, and that'll just make them madder when they find us. Actually, it'll make them use the dogs to find us." Suddenly she sounded defeated. "I'm not going to hide."

"Neither are we," I said. "Come on."

"*Dogs!*" Róża protested.

"Just *come on.*"

We locked the door behind us, to confuse things and maybe buy us a minute or two extra time. The Stork wasn't guarded. There wasn't any reason for it to be guarded. It never occurred to anyone we might try to *steal a plane*. It wouldn't have occurred to anyone on that airfield, in a million years, that two of us were pilots. Probably when I got out of that Stork six months ago it didn't occur to anyone on that air-field that I was a pilot.

In the back of my mind, I began thinking about Karl Womelsdorff—I wondered if he was still alive, or shot down by enemy aircraft—*our* aircraft. Or if, like me, he'd been taken prisoner.

"No no no no no no I *won't*—"

Róża fought like a little kid as we scuttled across the apron in the gloom, dragging her with us and trying to stay low. She tried to scratch and bite, and we had to hold her arms behind her back.

"I won't I won't I won't—"

"Darn it, Róża, keep it down!" I growled.

"I won't get in that thing!"

"Then we will leave you for the dogs and the gas cham-bers!" Irina said brutally. "I will drop you *right here* if you don't stop fighting!"

Róża stopped fighting, but she began to weep.

"What the hell is wrong with her?" Irina demanded, because Róża *never* cried. We were both gasping with the effort of manhandling her. The ground was slippery with hidden patches of ice, and the snow flurries were beginning to stick. The longer we were there in the open, the more likely we'd be noticed. Although I don't think it looked like we were protecting Róża—more like we were hauling her away to be punished somewhere. Maybe I *did* look like an SS secretary—a skinny, miserable, worn-out drudge, somebody who'd had to drop everything and run out after this little creep who'd stolen a pen or something, and I'd left my office so fast I hadn't even bothered to put on a coat.

"I think she's afraid of flying," I said.

Actually, I was *sure* she was afraid of flying, because that is exactly how Polly acted last year before I left for England, when I tried to bully her into flying with me. But Róża wasn't going to get a choice.

We dragged her beneath the Stork's wings. We crouched by the fuselage, hiding between the ridiculous long front wheels, lying on the ground just the way we'd lain beneath the military trucks earlier. Irina gave Róża a quick, harsh lecture in Russian, I think, which I know that Róża understood. Róża spat venom back at her in Russian the way she'd done on the night last October when Irina invaded our row for the first time.

"Enough of this."

Irina stood up close to the plane, under the high wing. She tried the door. Róża and I heard the latch click.

"Get up," I told her. "I'm going to get in first, in the front. You get in the back after me and wait for Irina. When she jumps in, get out of her way as fast as you can. You'll have to sit on her lap."

"Why can't *you* sit in the back?" Róża wailed. "I want *you* to sit with me!"

"Irina's stronger than me. She has to start the plane. She's got to swing the propeller."

"Start the plane! Who's going to fly it?"

"Well, I am, Różyczka," I said apologetically. And then, in self-defense, "I've flown this plane before."

Irina climbed up to the wings to sweep off the snow and check the fuel tanks.

"Hard to see," she called down. Then a second later, as she dipped her finger in, she exclaimed in astonishment, "Full! But why—"

"It's got an auxiliary fuel tank, too. Did you see that? That's new."

Irina checked. It was also full.

"The pilot of this plane maybe knows something we do not," she suggested drily.

She was right, of course; the Allies crossed the Rhine *the next day*. I don't know if the Neubrandenburg Stork was all set that night for an escape mission or a rescue mission or a spy mission, but it sure was loaded up and ready for someone to fly it. We were *so lucky*. Without the auxiliary tank, without full fuel, we'd have never made it over the Front.

"How will you go? Due west?"

"Gosh, no, we'll end up in Holland. It's still under German control! Southwest," I said firmly. The headings of that flight across Germany are imprinted on my brain forever. "Toward Paris."

Irina gave a wild laugh at last. "*To Paris!*" She jumped to the ground. "Are you tied in? If I start it, and you cannot hold the brakes, leave me."

"I'll hold the brakes," I said. "There are straps on the pedals for your feet."

It was so gloomy now, and the snow so fitful, that I couldn't see Irina standing in front of the plane. I could hear her, though—the grunt of effort as she hung her not-very-substantial weight on the edge of the propeller, and the dull *thunk* as the engine turned over without firing.

I have always really hated swinging the prop, or waiting for someone else to do it. Daddy never let me do it myself until I was eighteen anyway—he finally showed me how just before I left for England, in case I had to do it when I got there. I don't know how Irina did it—or how I held the brakes so she didn't get chopped in half when the engine finally fired. It helped to have my feet strapped to the pedals so they had no chance of slipping.

Irina came bounding in and slammed the door.

"Go, go!"

Where would we go?—Lido. To the beach on the beautiful Adriatic Sea.

It didn't matter. I was going to get Róża out of here after all, anywhere. For Karolina and Lisette. For all of them. A living witness, living evidence. I opened the throttle and cranked down the awnings. Irina and I pulled back the control columns in front and back together—neither one of us would have been strong enough to get that tail up on our own. But the Stork leaped into the sky, straight off the apron. There was a faintly lit compass in the control panel, and I made a long, steady turn toward the south.

"How is Róża?" I asked. I could still hear her sobbing.

"No help," Irina grunted. "Stay low. We will be harder to see from above."

The dusting of snow highlighted the fields around the German airfield in the darkness.

"Good," Irina yelled from the back. "Good visibility! The snow will help if it is not too heavy. Light clouds, high moon. Full, too, or almost full!" She was right—it was easier to see than I'd expected.

"No chasers," she added briefly. Then the plane lurched as she leaned over my seat again to see out the front, and hauled the sobbing Róża up beside her. *"Look—there! Look!"*

Ravensbrück at 800 feet was like a beacon, a glaring, self-contained bonfire of harsh white light in the blacked-out landscape—the lights of the *Lagerstrasse*, the column of red sparks from the crematorium chimney, the blue-white beams of the antiaircraft searchlights.

"That's it?" Róża said. "That's *us*? That's what the American bombers see!"

She clambered forward, hanging perilously over my shoulder and staring.

"It doesn't look very big from up here!"

"I know," I said. "I know. But—"

I couldn't let myself cry. I was *flying*. I clenched my teeth and muttered in the back of my throat.

"Are you doing the counting-out rhyme?"

"*No.*"

"Is it you, or Millay?"

"Millay."

"Say it so we can hear."

I choked out the last lines of "Dirge Without Music."

"Down, down, down into the darkness of the grave
Gently they go, the beautiful, the tender, the kind;
Quietly they go, the intelligent, the witty, the brave.
I know. But I do not approve. *And I am not resigned.*"

I turned. I didn't want to fly into the searchlights. I told Irina the new heading.

It was a pilot's pinpoint. That's all.

I knew we didn't have enough fuel to get to France, even with an extra tank. I knew this because of having to refuel last September, halfway to Neubrandenburg, when Womelsdorff brought me there. And when we were flying back, I didn't have any accurate way of measuring *time*. Irina made Róża count, just to keep her occupied, but we were basically faking it. Róża fell asleep eventually anyway, which was a good thing because it meant Irina was able to do some of the flying. We took turns. It wasn't hard work, once we were in the air, but I couldn't have done it all myself. I really couldn't.

I tried to fly parallel, but farther north, to my original course. I did a pretty good job because we ended up somewhere in Belgium before we ran out of fuel. You could see every single place they were bombing—all of Germany on fire, the sky stained red in the distance. And we *knew* when we came to the Front because we could *see it*. Fire and tracer and searchlights in one long line that just stretched on and on and on like a wall of shifting, glittering light in front of us.

It was beautiful, really, fireworks and bonfires, but terrifying. And we'd been flying for what, three or four hours through the burning night before we got there? If my flight *into* Germany made me wonder if I was in purgatory, the flight out of Germany was pure hell. We'd left one of the prisons in hell, we'd flown all night through hell, and now there on the horizon ahead of us was the boundary—the gates of hell.

Irina said so, looking at it as we approached the Front.

"*L'enfer.*"

She said it in French, so she wasn't even cursing, just stating the facts. We're in hell.

I must have pulled back the control column instinctively, trying to go higher, to get away from the guns. Irina pushed the plane nose forward again from her controls in the rear seat, keeping us level.

"I will fly," she told me. Because even if she counted my flying bomb as a *taran*, she knew I wasn't a combat pilot. And she knew we were about to get guns fired at us.

We didn't get hit, and I'm not sure they shot at us on purpose, or even which side was doing the shooting. Irina just kept smoothly on course, steady as—well, steady as a fighter pilot, I guess; as steady as *Daddy*—straight across one of the darkest stretches of the line of fire, until the noise was behind us, though we never really lost the orange light on the horizon.

We didn't even wake the sleeping Rabbit.

"Now you can land in one piece!" Irina said cheerfully.

Oh well. I did my best. I didn't break any of *us*, anyway. We landed in a field in the dark. It was not my best landing ever, for many reasons—exhaustion and inexperience being the main reasons, I guess—but the plane came down the right way up, if not entirely in one piece (I smashed the wheel struts and the prop). We all got violently bounced around— none of us were strapped in (only my feet were strapped in!)—and when everything had become quiet and still in the dark, Róża untangled herself from Irina and hurled herself at me like a rabid squirrel.

"*I hate you*, Rose Justice, *I hate you*, and I am never getting in another airplane as long—"

Irina grabbed hold of her by the back of her neck, hauled her away from me, and gave her a wallop across the face that was as brutal as anything she'd ever got from an SS guard.

"*You Russian BITCH!*" Róża screeched.

Irina slapped her again, not quite as hard. Irina said in fury, "*You are alive. You are over the Front. You and your skinny Rabbit legs are safe with the Allies.*"

She switched to Russian for the rest of the lecture, and Róża screeched back at her in Russian, and then *I* began to cry. Irina heaved an impossible sigh, probably remembering her last crash landing, when she'd been captured. Róża scrambled around, trying to open the door of the plane, and discovered a thick woolen Luftwaffe overcoat that had been jammed behind the backseat until the heavy landing.

"You want to get out?" Irina said neutrally. "Or we could just sleep here, where it is warm—"

Róża laughed until she broke off choking. "Oh, so now that I've got a decent coat I'm supposed to stay in the plane with the crazy *taran* pilots!"

"Oh, *Różyczka*." I sighed, too. I didn't know how to explain to her that she could *stop fighting* now. Or stop fighting *us*, anyway. "This plane isn't going anywhere else tonight."

So all three of us jammed into the back in a pile, sharing the luxury of the Luftwaffe overcoat. I was asleep in about thirty seconds, and didn't wake up until the local truants found us there after it got light the next morning. Not their fault they were truants, I guess. Their school gym was full of refugees.

Trust small boys to be the first people to turn up at a crash site!

That was near the end of March. I think it was a little more than two weeks between when we left and when I got to Paris in the middle of April, and it is early May now. I have been here for three weeks—as utterly out of touch with the world as when I was in prison—maybe *more* out of touch. I know that President Roosevelt just died, because Fernande told me so. But I knew more about the Allied advance when Lisette was tuning in to clandestine radio broadcasts.

You know how sometimes you just keep going and going, and then, when you get a chance to rest, you collapse with the flu or something like that? That's what happened to me after we landed. I woke up in the back of the Stork with the scratchy beginnings of a sore throat, and by midmorning I had a streaming cold, after waiting absolutely forever for the kids to go away and come back with someone's big sister who could tell us for sure that we were in Belgium. *We'd made it.* The whole place was supposedly crawling with Americans because they kept sending weapons and soldiers to the Front through the town, and bringing wounded soldiers back the same way.

When did it really sink in? Not that day—not that week. On our first day of freedom, we spent a couple of hours sitting on someone's doorstep drinking fake coffee and eating minuscule slices of bread with nothing on it—the people whose house it was wouldn't let us farther inside, and I don't blame them. Later that day we had to walk a mile or so to the school that the Americans had set up as a refugee center. But there weren't any Americans there that day. The middle of the town was nothing but one big, dusty crater. The nearest working telephone was said to be twenty miles away. Everyone looked like ghosts, and already we were letting ourselves be herded again.

We waited in the school for not quite two weeks, and then an American convoy came through and Bob Ernst picked us up—he was with the convoy that took us to the Swedish Red Cross unit, the night before Bob brought me to Paris. I don't remember much about the first two weeks in the school. It was like after being let out of the Bunker—a lot like that. For about five days I had a fever so high it would have got me admitted to the *Revier*, and I coughed so hard that two weeks later, when the Red Cross nurse checked me, she bandaged up my ribs because she thought I'd given myself stress fractures. She guessed I had bronchitis. My ribs still hurt now when I cough, but I got rid of the bandages when I took that first long bath.

Róża caught my cold, too, but she had something else wrong with her, and I still don't know what it was.

I mean, I do, sort of—she'd picked up an infection in her leg. Her right leg, the fragile one.

I *think* I can remember her announcing cheerfully, "Well, it's broken now! I'm not getting up again." She said this as she sat down next to me in the school gym holding two chipped, grubby mugs of cabbage soup, but I thought she was talking about the dishes. I *think* that she didn't get up after that—not without help. Irina quietly fed us and took turns dragging each of us to the ditch in the schoolyard a couple of times a day.

When I write it—and I know this is partly due to the gaps in my memory—it doesn't sound a lot different from what we'd escaped. It was the same kind of food, doled out sparingly, the same desperate toilet arrangements, the same incomprehensible babble of people shouting at you in a language you didn't understand. But there were two blankets between the three of us now, thick, scratchy US Army blankets—and the soup was salted sometimes—it wasn't full of dirt, because whoever made it actually cleaned the earth off the potatoes or turnips—and no one cared if we didn't get up all day. That was the real difference.

I should never have stuck to Bob Ernst like that. It was because I knew he was a reporter, and I wanted so badly to give him our story, even though I was never brave enough to begin. We got going talking about my poems. He *sang* with me. I'm pretty sure, thinking back (and I don't remember it as clearly as I should), that what he meant about interviewing Róża was that it was the *Red Cross* who wanted to talk to her, not Bob himself. And of course they didn't want to tell her story in an international newspaper; they wanted to know how they could help her.

And somehow I ended up going with him in the front of the convoy, and twelve hours later when we stopped—

I can't believe I lost them.

Before the Red Cross camp, during that wonderful spring day when we were all together driving through the forest, riding in the back of Bob's jeep and singing the "Battle Hymn of the Republic," I asked Irina, "Why are *you* going to Paris?"

She shrugged. "It takes me away from the Red Army. I have no place to go. Why is *Róża* going to Paris?"

"I'm just sticking with my family," Róża said.

Because we were all she had.

This notebook—I can't believe I am the same person who wrote in this same notebook less than a year ago. I can hardly stand to think of my earnest last-summer-self sermonizing about heroism and how much fun it is to be part of a crowd. "Home for the living, burial for the dead." Irina will never go home. Elodie and Karolina will never be buried.

I thought I'd finished writing, and Edie is coming for me tomorrow, so I finally dared to skip back to the beginning of this notebook so I could read what I wrote about my Big Date with Nick—the one when I painted my delectable toenails with Cherry Soda nail enamel. And when I opened this book to the front, I found the letters from Maddie. They were tucked in a little cardboard pocket inside the cover of this beautiful fat notebook, which is why I hadn't found them before. I've been so obsessed with what I'm writing and so scared to look back that I just didn't notice they were there.

Nick is married. He is *married*. Married to some other girl—he didn't even wait till the war was over.

All that time I was alive, all that time I was—all I've seen, all I've had to do—cartloads of skeletal dead women, gas chamber paint in my ears, Karolina and Irina fighting over my coat, the list of mutilated girls stuck in my head, crumbs of stale bread for Christmas dinner, that day of *Strafstehen* in the snow, twice *Fünfundzwanzig*—telling fairy stories about him rescuing us! We'd never even split up—he *proposed* to me on our last date! And he went and *married someone else*.

> And if I did come back,
> what in return could I offer to you,
> who used to make so free
> with my softness and kisses and verse
> as if it were your due?
> Imagine me
> on your doorstep—would you laugh in the old way
> and greet me lovingly:
> Hello, it's been a long time,
> how are you today?

There won't be anything to say.
I did stop dreaming he was touching my hair, and all I dreamed about was bread. But he could have *waited*. He could have waited till the war was over.

My gosh, how Różyczka would laugh.

Fernande took away my Camp clothes about a week ago. This morning she returned what she found in my pockets, all the pointless things I'd stuffed there in a panic before I left Ravensbrück: a couple of poems I'd managed to write down, a paper airplane decorated with a silly drawing of Lisette nitpicking my scalp in the pilot's seat, a pencil stub. Irina's airplane, Karolina's drawing of Lisette. Nothing of Róża.

And the half of Aunt Rainy's hanky that Elodie embroidered for me with the blue rose and our flags and our initials.

I can't believe that this is all I get—a torn handkerchief and a drawing on half a piece of folded paper. That these scraps of garbage are all I have left of *any* of them. And there isn't a thing I can do about it—maybe not ever.

I'm not going to go home, either.

...hurts the earth, so to get something
...mean is the same, but it isn't. When
...at the beach—there's an m...
...system in the air, you have to in...
...a nice place to fly your kite...
...who introduced me to the editor...
...me her daughter's clothes an...
...d the US Air Force pilot w...
...around the Eiffel Tower over...
...to sext a plane from time...
...are so many of us coming...
...experience. How he got turn...
...he went interested in women...
...get ready? I can't work as a...
...effort, too. And I like Caliu...
...have space now, and now I have more. I c...
...war and already the weight doe...
...over two years and a half to keep my li...
...to get reauthorized again. The...
...but on for just a front of th...
...from Kardashians? She hadn...
...people I'd loved and fought bec...
...to kill any of those I'd last see...
...but the sightless signal—the one w...
...much more successful and talente...

PART 3
NUREMBERG

I am thinking about that line from the first paragraph of the Declaration of Independence—the words they made me write at the Amercian Embassy last year to prove that I am really Rose: *A decent respect to the opinions of mankind requires that they should declare the causes which impel them to the separation.*

DARN IT. *Declare the causes.* That is another way of saying, TELL THE WORLD.

It is a year and a half since I got back from Germany, and I haven't really told the world. I have been fooling myself about it for a while. I gave the Rabbits' names to the US Embassy. *Olympia Review* published most of my Ravensbrück poems—but not "Service of the Dead," "Gas Leak," or "The Ditch," which the poetry editor, Sue Parker, thought were all just too *nasty* to print. It says in her letter: *We feel these are so grotesque that they detract from the lyrical sensitivity of your other poems.* And I didn't argue.

To be fair to Parky, she called the other poems "magnificent" and had the inspired idea of combining "The Subtle Briar" with the counting-out rhyme of the Rabbits' names. But it was easy going along with her editorial suggestions. I didn't have to do anything except type them up for her. She forwarded all the nice letters that came in to the magazine afterward, and she didn't let me read the ones accusing me of "sensationalism" and "false reporting."

When the Mount Jericho Rotary Club asked me to come and talk to them, I was able to say no because I live in Scotland now and it was too far for me to travel. But when the English Department of the University of Edinburgh got hold of a copy of the *Olympia Review* and wanted me to come read the poems aloud in one of their classes, I couldn't do it. *I couldn't do it.* I said I would, and I went, but I *couldn't do it.* I couldn't even stay in the classroom while someone else read them. The professor took me into his office and made me drink a glass of sherry while it was going on, and I went back in afterward when it was over, and they all applauded very soberly. I said thank you and then ran away while they were getting out of their seats, before anyone could talk to me about the poems.

So much for telling the world.

But I just couldn't escape the ripples spread by the *Olympia Review.* The officials organizing the trials against the Ravensbrück administration managed to track me down as well. They asked me to come be a witness at the first Ravensbrück tribunal in Hamburg, in Germany, which has just started. Of course all this summer I was wolfing down the news of the international tribunal in Nuremberg, as the Allied governments tried and sentenced the high-ranking Nazi officials. If the invitation to the Ravensbrück trial had come a week earlier I'd have been nervous about it but I'd probably still have said, yes, of course I'll come. Unfortunately, I got the letter right after that Edinburgh University poetry-reading fiasco. I said no. When I got Lisette's letter a week later, I'd already weaseled out of it.

I have been feeling *miserable* about it ever since—I *am* a witness. I am a victim and a witness. And the Ravensbrück tribunals are being run by the British; so being an English-speaking witness, of English heritage, imprisoned while working for a civilian British organization, makes me a *valuable* witness. I *want* to be a witness. I want to be *responsible.* I want to keep my promises to the people I loved whose lives were violated and ruined. But I have never spoken aloud to *anyone* in detail about what happened to me at Ravensbrück.

I made a life-and-death promise that I would, and I am scared to do it.

Also, at the Nuremberg tribunal they handed out a lot of death sentences. I want retribution for my friends, and for the millions like them whom I don't know about. But I am fearful of having a hand in anyone's death sentence. It may be just punishment for what they did—it may be the *only* just punishment. And the sentencing won't be my decision. But it seems like an empty victory to me, killing all the perpetrators. I want retribution, but so much more than that, I just wish everything could be put *right*.

I have *always* felt this way. Even before Ravensbrück. I put it in my "Battle Hymn of 1944" poem:

"Fight with realistic hope, not to destroy
all the world's wrong, but to renew its good."

Then I had the idea of doing a new story for *Olympia*. I wrote to Parky, telling her about the poetry-reading fiasco, and my cowardice about the trial, and Lisette's suggestion that even if I didn't go to Hamburg, I should go along to watch the Nazi Doctors' Trial in Nuremberg—and I offered to go as a journalist for *Olympia*. I wouldn't have to talk to anyone; I could just sit in the gallery with the other reporters and listen and take notes. It would be relevant to my studies as a medical student—I could write a report for my university tutor as well as for *Olympia*. I could help to "tell the world" from behind the mostly anonymous shields of my notebook and typewriter. Parky sent me the world's most enthusiastic yes—she wired me money for a train ticket. So I went.

Now I'm back, and everything's changed. Everything!

I'm not much of a journalist. But I didn't get a chance to feel like an imposter at the Doctors' Trial last week, because Dr. Alexander, the American medical expert, kept me so busy. The medical report for my tutor will be straightforward and mostly a matter of typing up my notes. The sizzling human-interest story is harder to write, especially since I ended up sitting in court for one day only. I've got an idea for how to tell it, though—how going to the Doctors' Trial changed my mind about going to the Ravensbrück trial. I still don't *want* to go and even if I *am* going now, I feel kind of ashamed and embarrassed for being such a scaredy-cat about it in the first place, but I'll use this story for *Olympia* as a chance to defend myself.

I'm going to try writing a draft of it right here in my Ravensbrück notebook. It seems like the right place to do it. And that's why Maddie gave it to me in the first place, after all, to bribe me with nice paper. There's enough room left because the Ravensbrück bit is all written from top to bottom and edge to edge of every page in absolutely *minuscule* writing. I don't remember doing that on purpose—in the back of my mind, I probably thought someone was going to take the paper away from me.

I like the idea that if I draft this article here, then the story will be complete and in one place, even if the last part—the part I am about to write—gets typed up later and published somewhere else.

KITE-FLYING: FOUR PRINCIPLES OF FLIGHT
(by Rose Justice)

A pilot's greatest challenge is not bad weather or low fuel or getting lost. It's not even getting shot at. My greatest challenge is a friend who is afraid of flying.

I got my high school diploma six months early because I had a job in the British Air Transport Auxiliary, ferrying aircraft for the Royal Air Force in the spring of 1944 just before the Allied invasion of Normandy. Before I went to Europe, I decided I was going to take every one of my best friends from the girls' varsity basketball team for a joyride in one of my dad's Piper Cubs. It only has two seats, so this was a fun project, just me and my friends without my dad. We'd fly over their houses or over the Lake where we swam in the summer, or west to see the state Capitol building, and they'd take pictures, and then we'd get my dad to take a picture of us standing together by the plane afterward—laughing and windblown, arms around each other's shoulders, looking very pleased with ourselves.

It never occurred to me Polly would be any different from anybody else on the team. She didn't *say* anything. She was probably trying hard to be brave. After all, everybody else had gone flying with me, and they'd all come back safely, bubbling over with enthusiasm and snapshots.

So when Polly walked out to the plane with me, I didn't even know anything was wrong until she sat down on the brown winter grass of the airfield and burst into tears.

I thought she'd twisted her ankle!

"Hey, what's wrong?"

"*I won't I won't I won't I won't I won't*—"

"Won't what?"

"I won't get in that kite! I don't want to go anywhere *near* it! I *told* you I didn't want to come—"

She had, sort of, but she'd made it sound like her *mother* didn't want her to come.

I knelt down next to her and put my hand on her shoulder. "Don't worry! It's not scary getting in, and there are shoulder straps. The cockpit shuts up tight just like a little car. It's so beautiful in the air! If you close your eyes while we're taking off—"

Polly, my best friend, socked me in the eye.

That might have been the biggest shock of my entire life up to that point. In a million years I wouldn't have guessed that my best friend could possibly be *so scared* of something that she'd *punch me in the face* for trying to talk her into doing it.

I burst into tears. Polly was already crying. After a moment she clapped her hands over her mouth and gasped, "Rosie—I'm *so sorry*! Gosh, we're like second graders pulling each other's hair! I just—"

She didn't actually pack much of a punch. It had just been such a surprise. I laughed shakily and said, "No, *I'm* sorry, and you should have told me you were scared! I wouldn't bully you into doing something you're that scared to do—it's supposed to be a treat! It's not important enough to *make* you do it!"

I really believed that when I said it to Polly. It was true for Polly. I guess it's still true for Polly, but under other circumstances—sometimes it *is* important enough.

1. LIFT

My sense of who I am is partly based on the fact that I learned to fly when I was twelve. But there are a lot of other things that define me. I am a Pennsylvania Dutch Lutheran. I am a student at the University of Edinburgh in Scotland, halfway through my second year of a bachelor of medicine degree. I am a published poet, in this magazine and one other, with two poems soon to be printed in the *New Yorker*. And according to the findings of the International Military Tribunal completed in Nuremberg three months ago, I am one of the millions of victims of Counts 3 and 4, War Crimes and Crimes against Humanity, brought against the Nazi leaders convicted there. I am one of the lucky ones, because I am still alive.

Marie Claude Vaillant-Couturier, whose testimony about the gassings at Auschwitz was so shocking that people listening in the courtroom took their headphones off so they couldn't hear the translation anymore, was my fellow prisoner at the Ravensbrück concentration camp for women. I was also there in the Ravensbrück infirmary, the *Revier*, counting bodies. I, too, am a witness. But I am not as brave as she is. I start to sweat when I think about standing up in front of a room full of newspaper reporters and helmeted soldiers and robed judges from four different countries, not to mention the twenty-some high-ranking Nazi leaders on trial there. When I was asked to appear as a witness at the Ravensbrück trial currently going on in Hamburg, I said no. And the shame of it is that I didn't see or suffer anywhere near as much as Mme. Vaillant-Couturier, because she was imprisoned at Auschwitz for over a year before being transported to Ravensbrück, and I was imprisoned at Ravensbrück for only six months. And Ravensbrück was an ordinary camp. Mostly.

After I got out of Ravensbrück, I locked myself in a hotel room for three weeks and wouldn't come out. I was scared of freedom. I was scared of *space*—of being in the open and of having to decide for myself where to go—and of having to talk to people, and of being stared at. I was also afraid to face my aunt, my elegant, gracious English aunt, who was supposed to come collect me and fatten me up and put me on an ocean liner back to Pennsylvania, where I would, presumably, resume normal life.

My English aunt Edie is elegant and gracious, but she is also very, very smart. When she discovered that a friend of mine, fellow transport pilot Maddie Brodatt, was making a delivery flight to Paris only a couple of days after Edie had been planning to come get me, she asked my friend to meet me in her place. It was the second week of May in 1945.

Aunt Edie had taken the hotel room next to mine, so she gave it to Maddie instead. The rooms were connected by a pair of private communicating doors, so we could lock each other out if we wanted to. Maddie called from reception to let me know she'd arrived. I knew I didn't have a choice, and I was clean and respectably dressed by then, so I let her come up.

I'd been her bridesmaid the year before.

When I opened the door, she stood for a moment staring at me as if she didn't recognize me—or as if she thought I'd disappear in a puff of smoke.

I stepped aside to let her in. We didn't hug each other. She said, "Oh, *Rose!*" in a pained voice, and I tried to smile at her.

"I'm okay. They didn't feed us very well." (I was still less than two-thirds my normal weight.) "And I just had bronchitis, and—well—my hair's growing back."

I touched my own head with both hands. "They shave your hair off—" I stopped. I couldn't explain.

"Because of nits?"

"No, just to make you miserable. The last time they did it to me was because I was humming during roll call. It's okay—really, it's—"

"*Stow it*, Rosie," she said very gently and persuasively, and took me by the elbow and made me sit down at the vanity table by the open window, where I'd been pouring out the story of my imprisonment in pen and ink for the past three weeks.

"What's the view like?" Maddie asked. The drapes and shutters were closed because everything was still under blackout restrictions; we were still at war.

"Fantastic. Turn out the lights and we can open the curtains. Not much to see in the dark, though." Maddie followed my orders and then stood behind me with her hands on my shoulders. There was no light in the Place Vendôme, but it was so open and so dark that it seemed like the whole sky was on fire with starlight.

"You know we are staying in the former Luftwaffe headquarters!" Maddie exclaimed suddenly.

"Oh!" It hadn't occurred to me. "I never thought about it being the Luftwaffe."

"How could you not!"

We both laughed a little. "I haven't been out since I got here," I confessed.

"What, not even in that smashing bar in the courtyard? This place is swarming with Americans! Journalists and war correspondents, lots of writers! You should be talking to people, sharing your poems!"

I shook my head. "All those strangers staring. I couldn't."

"Golly, Rose, I'll go with you tonight. We need to celebrate. Germany surrendered this morning. Everyone at the airfield was over the moon! General De Gaulle is going to make an official announcement here in Paris tomorrow afternoon—it'll be a holiday *everywhere*."

And there was Arcturus, rising over the other side of the square, just like Karolina had told me we would see it in the spring when the war was over.

Karolina was dead. I started to cry.

We didn't go to the bar. Maddie stayed with me in my room, and I let her read what I'd written over the past three weeks.

It was so easy just to hand over the notebook. I didn't have to talk about what had happened to me, I didn't have to burst into tears or go red or stammer or choke up and not be able to get any further. I just gave her my notebook, and she read it and she knew.

I went to sleep before she finished, and when I woke up in the middle of the night, she was sitting next to me on the bed, with the bedside light on and my notebook propped against her knees, still reading. She didn't know I was awake—I was curled up because I always sleep curled up now, a habit of trying to keep warm when there's no mattress and no blanket, no glass in the window below you and no fuel in the coal stove on the other side of the barrack. I was turned away from Maddie, but I could feel her there next to me, warm against my back, and hear the flutter of paper every now and then; she turned pages with one hand, because her left hand was on my shoulder, just resting there firmly, and I could see the light in the ruby on her old French wedding ring.

I thought, Thank goodness I won't have to explain anything. She'll understand. And I went back to sleep, *so glad* to have someone next to me. Because even though the six months at Ravensbrück had been nothing but a battle for sleeping space on the bare bunk slats, those people crowded next to you were the only warmth and the only comfort you could get. And I missed them like crazy.

I wish it could always be that easy. I wish I never had to tell anyone and they would just *know*. I wish I could always have someone next to me.

The church bells didn't wake me, but the sound was in my ears and head when I woke up again—all the bells in Paris. The official announcement wasn't supposed to come till three o'clock in the afternoon. Nobody cared. The war was over and all the bells were already ringing.

Maddie had gone back to her own room and shut the communicating door behind her, so I got dressed in the worn, neat skirt and blouse the pitying chambermaid had given me—her missing daughter's clothes—and knocked on Maddie's door. She opened it almost immediately, and this time we threw our arms around each other. And this time both of us began to cry.

"Come on!" Maddie said. "Come on, we're going out."

I shook my head, but she had me by the arm and took advantage of me being easy to bully. It was stupidly easy to bully me then—I would follow directions meekly, without tears, cowering. That is how the chambermaid finally forced me to get dressed after my first two weeks of hermitlike so-called freedom.

Hanging on to my arm, Maddie stuffed her flight bag with chunks of French bread off the breakfast tray they'd grown used to sending me (she'd taken it in earlier), then grabbed her Air Transport Auxiliary uniform tunic and forced me into it.

"No no no, I'm not a First Officer—"

"No one will know or care. You are an ATA pilot and you are going to look like one."

She gave me her side cap.

"*Wizard.* You look *perfect.*"

Then she pulled on her leather flight jacket over her blouse and straightened her tie. "One uniform between the pair of us—that'll do! We both look the part, right?"

I nodded, trying to smile. Her tunic was a little too short and a little too broad for me, but she belted it tight around my middle, and it probably looked okay. Actually, it probably disguised how thin I was. We both wiped our eyes at the same time.

"Let's go. I'm taking you flying."

Maddie tucked her arm in mine. I didn't need propping up, but I needed someone hanging on to me, as though I were blind and couldn't see where I was going and had to be led. Out through the sumptuous lobby, which I took in as though I were seeing it for the first time, and into the May sunlight in the Place Vendôme. It was already full of people—kids sitting on shoulders, waving paper flags and wearing paper hats that people were selling out of buckets and boxes like they'd been saving them up for weeks, everybody so dressed up.

Maddie was shameless. I think she started out heading for the Metro, but we didn't make it across the square before she'd hitched a ride on a truck crowded with American pilots all waving and holding up two fingers in a V for "Victory."

"Le Bourget!" Maddie cried. "We want to get to Le Bourget!"

The ATA uniform worked its magic—even though we were sharing it.

"Come on up, sister!" They pulled us in with them.

For one long moment the world seemed hideous. The

smell of engine exhaust and sweat, the bodies so close together—

Maddie, who'd been up most of the night reading about the prison where I'd spent the winter, held tight to my arm and cried out, "Let's ride on the roof!" And they boosted us up on top of the cab like a couple of figureheads. It was precarious, but it was nothing like being in a prison transport truck, and I could breathe again.

It took us hours to get through the crowded main thoroughfares. But it was fun and like nothing I'd ever done before, sitting on the roof of a slow-moving military truck, clinging to my borrowed ATA cap—with my friend's arm secure around my shoulders and an enormous bundle of lilacs in my lap (where did *those* come from?), and our brave boys blowing kisses at everyone and trying to learn the words to the French national anthem.

At Le Bourget there was a line of Dakotas taking off and landing. They were giving people rides. For the past month they'd been shuttling all over Europe—hospital supplies, social workers, bringing home prisoners of war and "civilian hostages"—thousands of people like me who'd been sent to concentration camps in the far corners of the continent and were trying to come home now. Maddie and I lined up with the other joyriders, and our shared uniform got us boosted up front with the flight crew. And off we went—low over the teeming streets of Paris, so low you could see the flags flying—so much red, white, and blue! The French Tricolor, the Union Jack, and the good old Star-Spangled Banner. There were Soviet flags in there, too. We sailed in stately flight up the Champs-Elysées, so low we could see the crowd waving as we passed overhead.

"Ever buzzed the Eiffel Tower?" the pilot shouted lazily over the whine of the engine.

"Rose did last year," Maddie yelled. "Flying an Oxford. Two weeks after Paris was liberated!"

"Flying it *herself*?"

"Of course!"

The pilot glanced at me.

It's hard to describe what I looked like. I'm not even sure what I looked like; I covered up the mirror in my room when I got there, and that had been three weeks earlier. No doubt starved; no doubt exhausted, because I still had a lot of trouble sleeping. Probably haunted. My hair was only a little longer than the pilot's crew cut.

"I wanted to fly under it, but the plane wasn't really small enough," I said.

The pilot laughed and asked me in his casual drawl, "Ever flown a C-47?"

"Gosh, no, just light twin engines!"

"Well, you better give it a try, then," he said. "I reckon if you're smart enough not to fly under the Eiffel Tower in an Oxford, you won't risk it in this baby, either."

That is how I got to buzz the Eiffel Tower for the second time in the biggest plane I've ever flown.

We had to take the Metro back. I slept on my feet, lulled by the rhythm of the train and clinging to a strap hanging from the ceiling. I was used to dozing standing up, a skill acquired during interminable Ravensbrück roll calls.

It was dark by the time we got back to the Place Vendôme, Arcturus blazing above us. But now Paris, too, was blazing, lights everywhere, yellow light gleaming in open windows and strings of Christmas lights in balconies and in the trees. It was spring and the war was officially *over*. Maddie pulled me, half awake, into the glittering leafy night of the Ritz's private inner courtyard and found a single chair for us to share.

We held hands. I knew she was thinking about her best friend, who was killed in France a little over a year ago. But it was nice to be there with Maddie—this half stranger who knew me so well, who didn't have to be told anything about me.

She said suddenly, "Julie would have died there. I read what you wrote. She'd never have made it. She'd have died there."

She squeezed my hand. "But you didn't."

Within five minutes, a young American civilian presented us with a bottle of champagne. I nearly fell off the chair with shock. It was Bob Ernst, the man who'd driven me to Paris last month.

"Nice to see you again, Rose Justice," Bob said, grinning from ear to ear and holding out his hand. He shook hands with me warmly. "Who's your friend?"

I gulped and remembered how to be polite. "This is Maddie Beaufort-Stuart. She flew with me in the ATA."

"You're a pilot, too, Maddie!" he exclaimed. "Never met a flygirl in my whole life, and Rosie knows 'em all." He poured and handed out glasses.

"Victory!"

"*Victory!*"

I took a sip—the first sip was *awful*. The contrast with the months of turnip soup was so extreme, and the last time I had champagne was on a date with the boy who'd got married to someone else while I was in prison—I'd only found this out a couple of days ago. With the first sip my anger at that thoughtless betrayal hit me again like a kick in the ribs, and I made a face like I'd never drunk champagne in my life.

Bob laughed. "It's the idea of the thing." He didn't have a chair. The place was packed. He squatted down next to us.

"What are you doing here?" I asked. Bob had picked me up at a refugee center in Belgium, with Irina Korsakova and Róża Czajkowska, the prisoners who had escaped with me.

"Looking for you, Rose," he said seriously. "I've been looking for you ever since I waved good-bye to you at the embassy. I thought I'd never forgive myself for not making sure you were safe."

I put my glass down on the crowded table we were sharing with about a dozen other people. I stared at Bob.

"Looking for me?"

"I knew you were here at the Ritz, and you hadn't checked out," he said. "They wouldn't tell me what room you were in—fair enough—and I would have felt pretty underhanded watching the lobby to catch you going in and out. So I thought I'd sit in the bar in the evening, and maybe you'd come down one night. As long as you were still checked in, you might come down. So I waited. And you did."

I didn't say anything at first. Finally I asked the only thing that mattered. "Did you look for my friends?"

Because that was what I was most upset about: losing Irina and Róża. It was mostly my own fault. But a little part of me blamed it on Bob, for taking me away from them without my realizing that they weren't traveling with us in the back of our convoy.

"I did look for your friends," he said. "I managed to get the unit details of the Red Cross folks we camped with. One of the wounded GIs remembered it. But I don't know where they are now. Probably still on their way back to Sweden—I think it'll take them a while because they were stopping along the way to set up field clinics, like the one we camped with. They're off the US Army's beat, that's for sure. I tried contacting their HQ in Stockholm, but I always get blind-sided by the girl on the switchboard. And I don't know your friends' last names, or how to spell their first names—how are they going to find Russian Irene and Polish Rosie among tens of thousands of refugees they're relocating? When things settle down, we might have better luck. It's been making me crazy. They can't just *disappear*."

We had their unit details.

It was a start.

Maybe Bob thought I was upset with him, because he added quickly, "The real reason I'm in Paris is that I'm on an assignment for my paper—I think I told you that. But I've got a sort of more creative personal project I'm working on now, too—it's a story for a literary journal out of Olympia University in Ohio, about people coming home. I got the idea after I dropped you off. I couldn't stop thinking about you and your team. So since then I've started talking to others like you."

"Like me?"

"You said you'd been in prison in Germany, but you were in a camp, right? You weren't a prisoner of war. You're a civilian. So I guessed you must have been in a concentration camp. There are plenty of camp survivors in Paris, on their way home, men and women both. You get an eye for spotting them."

"We're all skeletons," I said, and looked away, my face burning.

"No," Maddie suddenly interjected. "It's somewhat in the eyes. You look like you're in shock."

Bob slapped the table and everyone's glasses tinkled. "That's it exactly. The POWs from the military prison camps are skinny, too, but anyone who's been in the concentration

camps—they all look a little crazy." He bit his lip and red-
dened. "Sorry. Not you."

"It's okay. I bet I do. I bet that's how you figured it out."
I *felt* a little crazy.

"Well," Bob said, leaning back on his heels, "I'm telling
you this because you said you wrote poetry, and I thought
you might want to send something to the poetry editor at
my magazine. It's quarterly, and they're doing a special issue
focused on the war—social issues, how the war's affected education, things like that. There's a story about the massacre of
university staff in Poland and a story about the past five years
of Hollywood films, so you get some idea how flexible they're
being. If you wrote anything this year—"

Maddie leaned across me and coolly accepted the offer
on my behalf, as though she were my literary agent. "She'll
take your card."

He had it ready and waiting in his breast pocket. I felt a
little bit like a starlet being discovered by a director. I nodded.
I didn't smile, but I let him know I'd consider it. Maybe this
was the way I could tell people about it—without having to
say anything, just the way I'd given my notebook to Maddie.

"I've got a few new poems," I said cautiously. I wasn't
convinced any of them were good enough to be published
in a literary magazine. I wasn't convinced any of them would
even make *sense*, outside Ravensbrück.

"That's my girl," Bob said, and refilled our glasses.

I picked mine up again and took a tentative sip of victory champagne. I remembered now I'd drunk champagne
at Maddie's wedding, too, and it tasted better when I was
prepared for it. It wasn't sweet but *exciting*—new and exotic
and sparkling, but dry and cold, too—like everything that day,
joy mixed with *agony*.

"Thank you!" I said, and held my glass to Bob and Maddie and the light. "Thank you for waiting."

There are four forces that work together if you want to put something into the sky and have it stay there. One of these is *lift*.

Lift is made when the air pressure under a wing is greater than the air pressure over the wing. Then the wing gets pushed upward. That's how birds fly. That's how kites fly—a kite is basically just a solitary wing. That's how airplanes fly.

But people need lift, too. People don't get moving, they don't soar, they don't achieve great heights, without something buoying them up.

There's nowhere else in the world I'd have rather been to celebrate victory in Europe than in Paris on VE Day, but I don't know if I'd feel the same if it hadn't been for my friends Maddie and Bob generating *lift* for me—buoying me up at the heavy ebb of my life.

2. WEIGHT

Each force in flight is balanced by an opposing force. The opposite of lift is *weight*. Weight is always trying to pull an object back to earth, so to get something to stay *up*, lift has to be greater than weight.

You'd think your weight would always be the same, but it isn't. When you do aerobatics or go into a dive—like a kite that's plunging into the sand at the beach—there's an increase in gravity, and that makes you weigh *more*. If you want your heavy kite to stay in the air, you have to increase the lift, as well. Maybe by waiting for a stronger wind. Maybe by finding a windier place to fly your kite.

Maddie brought lift back into my life by forcing me outside. So did Bob, who introduced me to the editors of this magazine. So did Fernande, the chambermaid at the Paris Ritz, who gave me her daughter's clothes and made me get dressed and brought me coffee every morning for three weeks. So did the American Air Force pilot who let me take over the controls of his C-47 so I could fly it in long, lazy circles around the Eiffel Tower over the cheering crowds on VE Day.

My dad sends me an allowance and pays for me to rent a plane from time to time at a civilian flying club outside Edinburgh. I can't find work as a pilot—there are so many of us cooling our heels with nothing to do now that the war is over. Plenty of women with more experience than me get turned down for the few instructor and air taxi jobs available. The new commercial airlines aren't interested in women except as hostesses. But my dad, who taught me to fly, wants to make sure I don't get rusty.

I can't work as a pilot anyway, because the university is taking most of my time and a huge amount of effort, too. And I like Edinburgh, except for the weather. I already had friends in Scotland when I moved here, and now I have more. I am healing. I have scars that show and scars that don't. Even when you're flying high and steady, the weight doesn't go away—it's just balanced by lift. I have worked pretty hard over the past year and a half to keep my life in balance. But the weight's still there, waiting for an increase in gravity to pull me earthward again.

There was one factor of weight last year that was sometimes so heavy it made me curl on the floor in front of the tiny coal fire in my tiny student bed-sitting-room and sob. A year after escaping from Ravensbrück I still hadn't found my friend Róża. Or *anybody* I'd known at Ravensbrück. Half of the people I'd loved and fought beside in the concentration camp were dead, and I knew that, but I hadn't managed to find any of those I'd last seen alive, either.

In the end, they found me. I was, after all, the one who broadcast the distress signal—the one who fired the flares.

Lisette Romilly tracked me down. Lisette is also a writer, a much more successful and talented writer than me. About two months ago Lisette's editor at *Les Éditions de Minuit* in Paris handed her the Spring 1946 edition of the *Olympia Review*. He thought Bob's concentration camp survivor story, "Half-Remembered Faces," would interest her—and also the young American poet Rose Justice's "Ravensbrück Poems."

Here is her letter to me:

22 October 1946

Happy birthday, my dear Rose!

How astonished I was to see on the printed page your poems, which I only know by heart! The biographical note at the end suggests you are well. You will understand both my delight and my anguish at finding you.

You may know that Róża is now working at the Polish Research Institute in Lund, Sweden, helping to translate and catalogue witness testimony as evidence in trials like the International Military Tribunal recently held at Nuremberg, where the high-ranking Nazi leaders were indicted, and the trials held elsewhere to convict those responsible for individual concentration camps. Trials for Ravensbrück staff are currently being organized by the British in Hamburg, and you may also be aware that three of the Ravensbrück doctors responsible for the medical experiments forced on the Lublin Special Transport will be tried with other Nazi doctors by an American court in Nuremberg in December.

I have suggested Róża go as a witness to Nuremberg with a number of other girls who were experimental "Rabbits" and who will be appearing at this American tribunal indicting the Nazi doctors. I myself am going to appear as a witness at the first of the Ravensbrück trials in Hamburg, so will miss the Doctors' Trial in Nuremberg. Perhaps you will be able to go to Nuremberg yourself and see Róża there. I have also suggested that the organizers of the Hamburg trials contact you as a potential reliable and articulate witness to the atrocities committed at Ravensbrück.

I visited Róża in Sweden in the beginning of the summer. She is in good health and so appears much changed from the desperately crippled Rabbit we knew at Ravensbrück. She does not seem to enjoy her work, but she is wholly obsessed with it. She still has not taken her high school diploma, which makes me a little sad as a teacher and her "camp mother"— however Róża is Róża.

She says that Irina is an air hostess with Sabena! She married a Danish pilot just after the war ended. I think it was a marriage of convenience—it conveniently prevented her from being sent back to the Soviet Union. I cannot imagine Irina content for long to run up and down the aisle of an aircraft, fetching pillows and mineral water for bankers and screen stars, when she really ought to be designing aircraft, but at least she is traveling the world and is back in the air.

I hope you are back in the air, too, my dear Rose.

Your loving friend,
Lisette

So it was Lisette who suggested me as a witness—Lisette, who knew better than anyone our duty to the living and the dead. But it was also Lisette who gave me the idea of going to Nuremberg to see Róża instead.

I squeezed all my end-of-term exams into one week so that I could be in Nuremberg for the second week of the Doctors' Trial, the week that the Rabbits would be there. The *Olympia Review* advanced me a small stipend for my hotel stay, the train from Edinburgh to London, and the amazing boat train from London to Paris (it is called the Golden Arrow). My uncle Roger arranged an onward flight for me from Paris to Nuremberg with the US Army Air Force—not with Sabena, so I didn't see Irina on board.

Maybe you've seen the Air Force moving pictures. Europe is in ruins. It is as visible from the air as it is from the ground. The only difference is that from the air you don't see the grubby kids playing in the rubble and the old women gathering pieces of furniture to use as firewood and the piles of broken German planes stacked along the roadside waiting to be cleared. But from the air you really get the *extent* of it. Imagine if you took the train from Philadelphia to Boston, and the whole way, all through New Jersey and through New York City and on up through coastal Connecticut and Rhode Island, all the way to Boston, just imagine if the *whole way* every city that you went through was smashed to smithereens. That's what it looks like. The entire East Coast turned into a demolition site.

We have heaped more destruction on the German cities than they have heaped on us, and that is the truth. Weight. Rubble to clear.

Nuremberg—it is correctly *Nürnberg* in German—is one of the cities that we hit hard. But it got chosen for the International Military Tribunal for war crimes because the

Palace of Justice is still standing, with a good, secure prison still attached to it. And of course it is the symbolic center for the birth of Nazism, so it seems like a good place to restore things. The IMT earlier this year was run by the Allied powers. The Doctors' Trial is being run by the Americans—it's actually called "*United States of America v. Karl Brandt et al.*" The city of Nuremberg is still a wreck, and I was pretty much forbidden to go out of the hotel alone after I got there. I didn't see anything of the medieval city the whole time I was there, although I think it would have made me sad if I did—90 percent of it is destroyed.

I got driven to the train station to meet Róża. The GI who did the driving had a gun with him, so I felt pretty safe, but the medical expert from the tribunal, Dr. Leo Alexander, came along, too.

"I don't mind going by myself," I said.

"Neither do I," he said, smiling through his mustache. "We'll be braver together."

He'd been very kind to me ever since I arrived—warm but serious, an intense, earnest man *impassioned* with his job of interviewing and examining the Ravensbrück Rabbits and preparing their statements. That's the right word for it—*impassioned*. He was born in Austria and emigrated to the US in 1934, I think because he was Jewish; you could still hear the German accent (or Austrian or whatever it is). He was eager to meet Róża, the first of the Rabbits to arrive. She'd taken the train all the way from Sweden—it crosses the Baltic Sea on a ferry, like the Golden Arrow. As far as I knew, Róża hadn't been in another airplane since the snowy night in March 1945 when I flew her out of Germany.

It took us a moment to recognize each other—even though Róża still had to walk with a supporting stick and she still had the crazed gleam in her eyes that Maddie and

Bob had agreed on in the Ritz on VE Day. It was over a year and a half later, and she still had it.

She had to switch sides with her cane so she could shake hands.

"I am pleased to meet you, Dr. Alexander," she said in English.

"The pleasure is mine, Miss Czajkowska," he answered.

Róża held her cane hooked over her left arm, swinging it a little. She turned to me and held out her hand. She didn't smile or rush to swallow me in a bear hug, but I felt *everything* in our clasped hands, even through our gloves.

"Hello, Rose Justice," she said coolly.

It's no wonder I didn't recognize her. When I'd first met her she'd been so emaciated I'd thought she was about eleven. She wasn't any taller now, still petite, but so *curvy*—she wasn't carrying any extra weight, but there was nothing angular or pointy about her anywhere—all curves. She was incredibly lovely. I'd once seen a glimpse of that, but had never imagined I'd see her in her full glory. Her hair was exactly the color of caramel, coppery gold and gleaming, not long but stylishly permed and framing a face like a china doll's. She had on a camel-hair coat and a gray wool suit, dull but smart—and showing off all the amazing curves.

"Hello, Różyczka," I said—*little Rosie*.

We were subdued in the car going back to the hotel. The bomb damage isn't as obvious at night as it is in the daytime, but when you do notice it at night, it's eerier. A dark row of empty windows with stars shining through them. A big pale heap you think is a snowbank until you get close enough to see it's a pile of broken marble. A gray shadow like a naked torso crawling through the rubble in a vacant lot. By day you'd just see a scrap of newspaper fluttering aimlessly.

"I didn't think Germany would look like this," Róża said.

"All of Europe looks like this!" I exclaimed. "Haven't you *seen?*"

"Sweden doesn't."

Sweden was neutral during the war, of course—no bombs dropped on it.

Dr. Alexander leaned back from the front seat. "You won't mind spending time tomorrow going over your story in my office in the Palace of Justice, will you?" he asked Róża. "I have the daunting task of interviewing all the young ladies appearing as witnesses. I must also make an examination of your injuries. But it would be appropriate to conduct the exam after the other four 'Rabbits' arrive tomorrow, when you are all together. In the meantime we have only four days to prepare your statements, so I'd like to begin with yours tomorrow morning."

"All right," she answered softly.

As we climbed out of the car in front of the hotel, she whispered to me, "Are you going to be a witness also, Rose?"

"No, I'm going to be a reporter. I have to write a story for the magazine that published my Ravensbrück poems."

It was absolutely freezing—you felt like your breath was turning to ice when you talked. Róża didn't say anything. And suddenly I felt cold not because of the winter night, but cold inside.

The Róża I'd known at Ravensbrück had been a live wire of defiance and daring and desperate hope, the girl who'd taught me to curse like a sailor in five languages, who'd wise-cracked instead of sobbed when she was told she was going to be executed the next day. Something was different. She seemed like a person who has been on a tear for a week and now has sobered up again.

The Grand Hotel in Nuremberg was crawling with reporters and soldiers but *not* with young, curvy, porcelain-complexioned girls, or even tall, angular ones. In fact, there weren't very many women there at all, because the US military had a halfhearted rule about not letting spouses come along, though some of the judges' wives were there helping out. It wasn't exactly like having French strangers grabbing kisses from any pretty girl on VE Day, but Róża and I caused heads to turn. People smiled and nodded politely and held open doors and grabbed Róża's bag. People ushered us into the dining room and though my meals were included in my board, I'd have never had to pay for them even if they weren't, because people kept offering to buy us drinks and coffee and cigarettes.

There was a buffet. I carried both our plates so Róża could walk, one hand gripping her cane and the other pointing to what she wanted. We'd hardly said anything to each other since we got out of the car, though we'd smiled and thanked our entourage of helpful suited and uniformed men. But when we sat down across from each other at the little table over steaming plates of bratwurst sausages and potatoes, and another plate piled with a mountain of gingerbread *Lebkuchen*, which Róża had collected without my noticing, we both suddenly started to laugh.

"I eat by myself most nights, and everything is *still rationed* in Britain," I said. "I have one room and no kitchen, just the coal fire and a gas burner. Cheese on toast and bouillon cubes."

"I live in a boardinghouse. I have meals cooked for me!" Róża said. "As good as this, most of the time, but still—here we are! You and me in Germany, eating like kings!" She paused, and challenged in a low voice, "Bless this food, Rose."

This was more like the Róża I knew—everything she said

heavy with hidden meaning. Lisette had *always* said a brief grace over our thin prison soup.

I sat up straight and sang a grace from Girl Scout camp. Not loud, but I sang.

> *"Evening is come, the board is spread—*
> *Thanks be to God, who gives us bread.*
> *Praise God for bread!"*

There was delighted laughter and a scattering of applause from the nearest tables around us. Róża ducked her head demurely, one hand shielding her face beneath the short, shining caramel waves of her permed hair, as though I'd embarrassed her.

"You never taught us that one!" she accused.

"I forgot about it," I admitted. "I don't think I ever felt thankful enough to sing that one. I never really felt *thankful* to get food there—just relieved."

"We are both ungrateful wretches," Róża said. "But praise God for bread anyway. Praise God for *gingerbread!*"

It felt so strange to eat with her—to eat a real meal together. We had slept pressed against each other like sardines for six months. We had stood naked in the snow side by side for two hours because one of the female guards had lost a watch or something and they made our entire barrack line up outside and take all our clothes off so they could hunt for it. But we'd never sat at a table together and eaten a decent meal, not even after we got out. It made us both self-conscious.

"You're making me think I have to stuff it in before you take it away from me," Róża accused.

"*I know.*" And of course we'd never stolen food from each other, ever, which made the sensation of covetous greed very weird. We'd both been reasonably well fed for the past year and a half, and now we were in a restaurant in a fancy hotel. It had never occurred to me that simply being with a fellow prisoner would make me feel like I was still in prison.

We asked the hotel reception to fix it so we could share a room, which they were happy to do, because it freed up another room for the overflowing reporters and trial observers. When we got undressed for bed, Róża proudly showed off to me her Exhibit A legs.

"I broke my right leg in the refugee center in Belgium. This is the leg they took the bone samples from. It held for two and a half years in their Camp and then it broke, just like that, a week after I got out. I wasn't even doing anything—just carrying your soup across the gym hall for you."

I realized, suddenly, the notable difference about her— she'd stopped swearing.

She peeled her thick wool hose down to her ankles. "See? Here, in my shin. The new scar is where they operated on it in Sweden. I have a steel rod in there now, holding everything together. I couldn't stand up for four months!"

I took a deep breath. "I don't know how I lost you, Róża."

"Oh, well, I do." She flung her hose on a chair. "You were crazy about that reporter. You forgot us the second you laid eyes on him."

"I wanted to tell him all your names! I wanted to tell him about the Rabbits, about the experiments! You spent six months drilling everybody's names into my head—Karolina and Elodie got dragged off to be gassed yelling that we should tell the world about it, that's what Irina told me—and Bob was the first reporter I ran into! It was like he'd dropped out of the sky. And then I wasn't brave enough to tell him anything."

Róża laughed, not the old raucous cackle but a soft, regretful sigh of a laugh. The ghost of a laugh. "That was us dropping out of the sky, not him. Remember? We're the ones who crash-landed."

"I told the American Embassy your names," I said defensively.

We turned out the lights. It was a little room with twin beds. We lay in the dark wide awake with the weight of where we were and what lay ahead of us pressing on us.

"Rose?" she said softly.

"Yeah?" I answered.

"It is just as strange to know you are there, and to be warm and comfortable, as it is to eat with you."

"It really is."

"Tell me 'The Subtle Briar' again," she asked.

She knew I would still know it by heart.

I whispered to her in the dark.

"When you cut down the hybrid rose,
its blackened stump below the graft
spreads furtive fingers in the dirt.
It claws at life, weaving a raft
of suckering roots to pierce the earth.
The first thin shoot is fierce and green,
a pliant whip of furious briar
splitting the soil, gulping the light.
You hack it down. It skulks between
the flagstones of the garden path
to nurse a hungry spur in shade
against the porch. With iron spade
you dig and drag it from the gravel
and toss it living on the fire.

"It claws up toward the light again
hidden from view, avoiding battle

beyond the fence. Unnoticed, then,
unloved, unfed, it clings and grows
in the wild hedge. The subtle briar
armors itself with desperate thorns
and stubborn leaves—and struggling higher,
unquenchable, it now adorns
itself with blossom, till the stalk
is crowned with beauty, papery white
fine petals thin as chips of chalk
or shaven bone, drinking the light.

> "Izabela, Aniela, Alicia, Eugenia,
> Stefania, Rozalia, Pelagia, Irena,
> Alfreda, Apolonia, Janina, Leonarda,
> Czeslava, Stanislava, Vladyslava, Barbara,
> Veronika, Vaclava, Bogumila, Anna,
> Genovefa, Helena, Jadviga, Joanna,
> Kazimiera, Ursula, Vojcziecha, Maria,
> Wanda, Leokadia, Krystyna, Zofia.

"When you cut down the hybrid rose
to cull and plough its tender bed,
trust there is life beneath your blade:
the suckering briar below the graft,
the wildflower stock of strength and thorn
whose subtle roots are never dead."

Róża gave a long sigh. Then she whispered, "Rose, I really miss you."

Róża spent most of Sunday telling her story to Dr. Leo Alexander—we had supper with him that night afterward, before the other Ravensbrück witnesses arrived. Everyone I met who was involved in the trial was friendly and straightforward, as though we were at a conference. This was not quite what I was expecting, but I think it is a result of everything being pulled together at the last minute. And although I wasn't one of Dr. Alexander's witnesses, he was interested in me, because I am a writer and a medical student, which is a less advanced version of what *he* is.

Róża told him at supper, "Rose could be a witness here. She has scars, too."

He looked at me with sudden intense interest. "You *do?* An American witness?"

I shook my head violently. "I wasn't operated on. I was just thrashed because I wouldn't work. So was everybody who didn't work, or who did anything else they didn't like. We're a dime a dozen and nothing to do with a trial for medical staff."

"I hate to say it, but you're right," Alexander agreed. "I'll admit I've already rejected several so-called witnesses exactly like you." He turned his mild, smart gaze back to Róża. "You will likely have heard of the concept of *genocide*, a term coined by your countryman Raphael Lemkin, which the IMT used as a basis for their charges against the Nazi leaders? We are using a parallel concept in this trial: *thanatology*, the science of producing death. These men are being charged with *murder*. The charge is that their experimentation was designed to discover not how to heal, but ways to kill. Simply put, you're a survivor of attempted murder. A punitive lashing, however ugly the scars may be, is, unfortunately, irrelevant."

"I couldn't show off my scars anyway!" I protested, taking refuge in being ridiculous to hide my cowardice. "What would I do, step onto the witness stand in a bathing suit? A two-piece!"

"It would be *sensational*," Róża exclaimed.

"No one would notice any scars!" Dr. Alexander teased. What a very weird dinner conversation.

The other Rabbits arrived. They were *all* as unrecognizable as Róża—well-fed, well-dressed, wearing their hair fashionably styled beneath new hats, smiling for the flashing press cameras at the train station. We hugged and kissed as if we were all long-lost family: Vladyslava, tall Maria, Jadviga, and little Maria, who'd had to stay in the *Revier* for a year and a half. I hadn't known any of them very well at Ravensbrück, but I knew their names. I'd hidden with Vladyslava and Jadviga in a pit dug beneath our washroom for two days. They'd hidden there with Róża for a week.

We were all on the bus to the Palace of Justice at eight thirty the next morning and stayed there till six p.m., and I didn't see much of anybody that day. I got asked "Can you type?" and I said yes, and suddenly I was part of the team landed with the tortuous job of organizing Dr. Alexander's notes as fast as he could hand us paper. I was set up in an office with the chief prosecutor's wife, who was also working there, because I wasn't allowed in the interview room with the Ravensbrück witnesses. Róża ran piles of paper back and forth between me and the rest of them, since she'd already been interviewed. I spent the first three days of that week in unwaged labor, gaining a little understanding of the trial and a lot more understanding than I'd ever wanted to know about the hideous things that had actually been *done* to Róża and the women I'd been imprisoned with.

The whole week was a race against time—the medical examinations, the interviews, translating everything from Polish to English to German, working out the order for the Rabbits' performance and practicing what they'd say, and then we had *one day* to present everything before the whole court shut down for its Christmas break. We were in the Palace of Justice every day, but we never went into the courtroom. We knew where it was; we got our ID checked and got ushered in and out of the building with the reporters and observers every morning, and ate with them in the canteen in the basement; we gaped wide-eyed at the armfuls of headphones and the miles and miles of telephone wire that trailed everywhere as the IBM technicians struggled to keep the translations going around the clock.

Róża and I were standing outside the entrance in the forecourt on Thursday evening with a few other people, on the side with the trees, waiting for the shuttle bus to take us back to the hotel. Suddenly, Róża grabbed my arm and hissed in my ear, "Look, that's Fischer. And that's Gebhardt. *They did it.*"

She let go for one second to point. Soldiers were leading a group of the defendants somewhere—well-dressed, sober civilians under armed guard.

"Did what?" I asked.

"Tied me down in a prison cell and cut chunks out of my bones."

I stared.

Being on the winning team gave us no strength. Róża clutched my arm, and there we were, standing in the dark in a flurry of German snow, and we might as well have been standing in the roll call square back in Ravensbrück.

"*That's Oberheuser,*" Róża choked.

"*Shhh!*"

There wasn't any reason to hush her. There wasn't any reason except I felt instinctively that we'd be walloped for talking and pointing.

"Oberheuser's the woman?" I whispered.

"Yes—she helped." They were being led to a different

entrance. I knew that Oberheuser was the only woman of the two dozen accused doctors. Right in front of us were all three of the Ravensbrück doctors, Gebhardt, Fischer, and Oberheuser—maybe going to a separate interview before the Ravensbrück witnesses gave their testimony the next day.

There was another woman who had come out with the others but was now left guarded on her own. She stood hopping from foot to foot to keep warm, a little to the side of the tall, imposing entryway, chatting with one of the helmeted American guards. She wore a halo of cigarette smoke.

Róża and I recognized her at exactly the same time, for different reasons.

"There's Engel," Róża said. "She was one of the lab technicians, the creepiest thing on legs. She was always sneaking around injecting people with morphine. We called her the 'Angel of Sleep.' Hah! She wasn't working in the *Revier* anymore when they did the Bunker operations. Bet she never dreamed the Americans would catch up with her."

Our bus pulled up. I stared back over my shoulder as I climbed on, in shock. Róża had recognized another Nazi on her personal vendetta list—but I'd seen a ghost. Anna Engel had been the leader of my work crew at Ravensbrück, scheduled to be gassed at the same time as the Rabbits. I'd thought she was dead.

And I admit to *joy* when I realized she was still alive.

People on the bus gave up seats for us. I leaned over Róża to rub a clear patch in the fogged-up window and stared at the girl standing there in her plume of smoke and condensed breath, hugging a thin raincoat around her and listening with a cynical expression to something the GI in the helmet was saying. She handed him her cigarette and it glowed as he put it to his lips, and then they both laughed. And then the bus pulled away.

Anna had been a prisoner herself by the time I knew her—a German prisoner. We'd got along all right. She'd told me she'd been an actual employee at Ravensbrück in 1942, quit her job, and got sent back as a criminal in 1944.

"That was *Anna*!" I exclaimed. "My *Kolonka*! I thought they gassed her!"

"I wish they had," Róża snarled. "That was the bitch who put me under for the first operation."

We didn't say anything to each other on the short bus ride back to the hotel, because I didn't trust Róża with what I knew.

I knew that Herta Oberheuser was the only woman on trial. I'd done a lot of boning up on what was going on, and I'd talked with Dr. Alexander. Róża, on the other hand, focused on vengeance, was not paying much attention to the mechanics of the trial.

If Oberheuser was the only woman on trial, any other women involved must be here as witnesses—possibly even as witnesses for the defense. So Anna must be a witness, like Róża herself.

I didn't dare tell her. I'd liked Anna.

Róża sat on the edge of her bed and slowly rolled down her hose the way she had on our first night in Nuremberg. I started to get undressed, too. Róża said suddenly, "Your scars are nasty, Rose. Do they hurt?"

I craned my neck. I'd never actually seen much of my scars, which start on my lower back and go halfway down my thighs.

"They don't hurt, but I got a stupid infection last winter that had to be operated on. I couldn't sit down again for a week. *So* embarrassing. I'm fine now." I pulled my night-gown on.

"You never make a fuss about anything. You don't even want *revenge.*"

I turned around to look at her. She was still sitting there with her stockings around her ankles.

"For my beating? Gosh, I don't even know who did it!" I exclaimed. "I don't want it to happen to anyone *else,* ever again. But how would I get revenge for *that?* They used to bribe other prisoners to do the beatings sometimes, by giving them extra bread! What if they'd held back your rations for two weeks, then given you extra bread to beat me? I wouldn't have blamed you!"

"Holy Mary, you sound just like *Lisette,*" she sneered, and I could tell she didn't mean it as a compliment. " '*Faith, hope, and love. But the greatest of these is love.*' Forget about revenge! These trials aren't about revenge. They're about *justice.* Don't you want *justice,* Rose Justice?"

For a moment I thought she was going to burst out in her evil cackling laugh at her own stupid pun.

Instead, she started to cry.

I'd only ever seen her cry once before, and that had been a full-fledged tantrum. She always made such a big production out of laughing like a witch that I was unprepared for the simplicity of her despair now. She hardly made a sound or moved, but big, silent crystal tears like Cape May diamonds slid quietly down her cheeks.

"*Of course I want justice,*" I said through my teeth, aching with guilt and loss and the colossal *unfairness* of it all. I buried my face in my hands for a moment.

"Rose, I can't do it," I heard her gasp.

I looked up. "What?" I said. "You can't do what?"

"I can't do the trial. I can't be a witness. I just *can't.*"

"Oh, *Różyczka!*"

I sat down beside her and pulled her into my arms because I knew, *I knew* exactly how she felt.

She buried her face in my shoulder and sobbed. I'd never seen her cry like this—not ever.

"I don't want to do it," she sobbed. "I don't want to stand up in front of all those men, all those strangers, barefoot with my skirt pulled up so they can stare at me, and have that dry little man point with his stick and explain it all in words I'll *never* make sense of. I don't want to have to turn around and tell everyone how they did it. It made me cry in the interview, telling about how they stuffed the rags in my mouth in the Bunker so I couldn't scream, and twisted my arms back and held me down while they injected me—how I fought and fought and just woke up to my hips in plaster again with chunks of bone missing *anyway*, only in *prison* this time. They hadn't even washed the mud off my feet—they did the same thing to Vladyslava, but she's so much more sensible than me. I told Dr. Alexander in his office, but I just *can't* tell that hall full of strangers. With that sickening Fischer *listening.* Men *scare* me."

Since she'd been fourteen, all the men in her life had done nothing but hurt her.

"But you're Róża! You're so strong!"

"Yes. That's the other thing. I'm brave and strong and young—and little and pretty. Dr. Alexander wants to show off all that. It'll make people feel sorry for us, wring their hearts, shock them—"

"As it should!"

"But Rose, I'm not *smart.*"

"*What?*"

Róża, as far as I knew, was pretty fluent in six languages, not counting Ravensbrück Camp patois. She'd memorized every song and poem I'd ever recited after hearing it three times. She knew more about Polish politics than I'd know about anybody's politics in a lifetime.

"Holy Virgin Mother, I felt so *stupid* watching the others get interviewed. Vladyslava is a teacher and the rest of them are all scientists. They always understand what Dr. Alexander's talking about, what was done to them. Their brains are crammed with mysterious expertise in bacteria or chemicals—or medicine, like you."

"Well, you've got a translation job!"

"Who told you that? Oh, Lisette." Róża heaved another desperate sob. "I lied to her about that. You have to have a degree to do that kind of work for the Polish Research Institute. I'm just the girl who makes them coffee and puts the stamps on envelopes. They pay me mostly because they feel sorry for me. It doesn't matter now anyway, because they've run out of funding and I won't be able to work there when I get back. But I don't even have a high school diploma—"

"So get one!"

"I can't, Rose, I *can't*." She burst into fresh tears. "I *tried*. I tried to take an exam and I *can't do it*, and that's how I *know* I can't do the trial tomorrow. I *dread* it all happening again. I was going to start with mathematics, because I'm good at it and it's neutral and I could do it in Swedish, and all I did was sit there for an hour *cringing* while the proctor walked up and down between the candidates, making sure they weren't cheating. Every time she passed me, I ducked. I kept expecting her to hit me. And finally, just to prove to myself that I could do anything I wanted and she *wouldn't* hit me, I crunched up the test paper and threw my pencils on the floor and walked out. Then I sat in the toilets and cried until the exam was over."

It was almost exactly what had happened to me, when I'd tried to read my poems aloud to an audience. I knew *exactly* how she felt.

Róża sniffed, wiping her eyes on her sleeves.

"I *know* I'll do the same thing tomorrow. It'll be *worse* tomorrow. Vladyslava and Maria were operated on in the Bunker just like I was, but they can talk about it and I can't. They'll answer the questions so calmly and precisely, and I'll just burst into tears or start screaming at Fischer again—"

"Well, that could be impressive, too, you know."

"I'm not going to do it, Rose. They've got four smart, educated grown-ups to show off, and they don't need my testimony and I'm not going to do it."

I held on to her tightly while she calmed down a little.

"Will you tell Dr. Alexander for me?" she begged.

I could see why she didn't want to do *that* herself.

The wily Ravensbrück prisoner in me rose to the surface.

"I'll tell him for you," I agreed. "But only if you sit with me and watch the trial."

"You bitch," she snapped automatically, and I was *so relieved* to hear her being nasty. But she didn't act like she was mad at me. She hugged me tightly around the waist, snuggling all her weight against me.

She was so much heavier than I expected. No lift balancing her life at *all*.

3. DRAG

Dr. Alexander took it very well, considering how early it was and that I had to interrupt him in his office right before the session started so I could catch him privately, and this was the last day before the Christmas recess. He is such a kind man.

"I'm not surprised," he admitted. "I thought *someone* might back out, and I'm glad it's Róża. She's a volatile witness. She's different from the others."

"Different how?"

"She isn't *finished*. She has no sense of who she is. The others knew that before the war started—but how old was Róża when she went to prison, fourteen? Fifteen when she underwent the first experiment? She grew up in Ravensbrück. In a way, she's still there."

I knew exactly what he meant. There wasn't any part of Róża that wasn't connected to Ravensbrück, even her work, even the parts of her body that had escaped experimentation— she hadn't started her period until she was eighteen, after the war was over.

It is true that Ravensbrück shaped me—whatever I would have been without it interfering, I am someone else now. On the simplest level, I don't think I would be in Scotland or in medicine. But Ravensbrück doesn't *define* me. I had a lot of being Rose to cling to when I landed there—I was a pilot, I was a poet, I was a Girl Scout, I was part of a family, I was the captain of the Mount Jericho High School County Champion Girls' Varsity Basketball Team, and I still bore traces of all these things even in the concentration camp. I wore my Air Transport Auxiliary USA patch on my shoulder and identified the aircraft that flew overhead, so we could guess at how the Americans or the Soviets were advancing. I was given jobs only tall girls could do; I taught my companions Scout songs and learned theirs; I produced more poetry in six months than I'd ever produced in my life, most of it in my head. And I was part of a family—Lisette, Irina, Karolina, Róża.

Róża was part of my family. But her own real family had all been killed before she'd even arrived at Ravensbrück. I'd known mine was safe. That made a difference, too. Róża's Camp Family was her *only* family.

When I told anyone at the Camp who I was, I'd say, "I'm Rose Justice. I'm a pilot."

When Róża first told me who she was, she'd said, "I'm Polish Political Prisoner 7705. I'm a Rabbit."

When you're flying, the changing balance of lift and weight pulls you up or down. But another pair of forces pulls you forward or backward through the air: thrust and drag. *Thrust* is the power that pulls the kite forward—you run with it to get it up in the air. You have to have thrust to create lift. *Drag* is there because your kite's surfaces push against the air and slow the kite down. Drag doesn't pull you out of the sky; it makes you fly more slowly.

For the most part, Room 600 in the Palace of Justice, the Doctors' Trial courtroom, looked just like you'd imagine any courtroom—actually, it looked spanking new, with its wood panels gleaming with varnish and modern lighting installed in the ceiling. That was all done last year just before the IMT, the International Military Tribunal. The four American judges were all wearing new robes flown there specially from Washington, DC. But the outstanding feature of the courtroom was that it was entirely snarled in telephone and electronic cables for the simultaneous translations, everybody caught in a huge black spiderweb. *Everyone* was connected by this web—defendants, witnesses, lawyers, judges, observers, reporters, and of course, the panel of translators themselves—*everybody* had his or her head plugged into this amazing machine. You could tell right away who'd been here before and who was here for the first time by their nonchalant or inept use of the headphones.

Talk about drag! You were so *dependent*. Also, it was easy to see why people just stopped listening when Madame Vaillant-Couturier was telling them about the gas chambers at Auschwitz. It was like turning off the radio. You can't bear to listen? Just pull the headphones off.

Róża, who understands English and Polish and German, didn't need headphones.

We sat in the gallery to watch, just in front of one of the film crews. We were surrounded by an intense crowd of German medical students my age who were frantically taking notes. Róża perched ramrod straight on the edge of her seat. She gripped the sides of her chair. I don't know what she was thinking, but she looked like a Fury. Her face was set in a sneer and her eyes were burning. She didn't watch her friends giving evidence; her gaze was locked on the defendants, the twenty-two Nazi men and one woman.

Dr. Alexander's evidence and his questioning of the Rabbits took the entire day, and no one else dared question them. The presiding judge, Walter B. Beals, would ask if the defense wanted to cross-examine a witness, and there would be flat silence. One of Jadviga's scars had been inflamed that whole week and she stood there anyway, *still* in pain, telling about how they tied her down in the Bunker.

How you *knew* they were going to operate on you because the first thing they did was shave your legs.

Telling how Fischer had smoked cigarettes between operations without bothering to change his gloves.

How Oberheuser would make the girls stand in line, hopping on one uninjured leg, to get the filthy bandages changed on the other leg, and then instead of changing them, she'd tell them to come back the next day.

How sometimes, if you fought, they'd blindfold you for the operation, or wrap your head in a blanket.

About the woman guard who'd said, "They must be made to *suffer* before they're executed."

Fischer wouldn't look at Jadviga. He couldn't look at any of them. He'd done most of the operations himself, under Gebhardt's instruction.

By the time little Maria finished her testimony at the end of the day, it sounded like there wasn't anyone breathing anywhere in the crowded, wire-webbed room. Maria is only a couple of years older than me. She'd had muscle peeled away from her leg right down to the bone—half her leg was gone. She looked very vulnerable up on the raised platform with her back to the court, in a stylish new dress but holding her skirt bunched up around her thighs, barefoot, barelegged. Dr. Alexander did a juggling act with his notes and his microphone while he pointed out how they'd torn apart her leg, but all I could do was stare at the tendrils of hair curling at the nape of Maria's bare neck, escaping from where her hair was elegantly pinned up.

No wonder Róża's backed out of this, was all I could think. Next to me, Róża didn't stop gripping the sides of her chair.

I followed her gaze to the defendants, tied up in their telephone wires. Only Fischer looked remotely unhappy, his forehead resting against his fist. The others just sat staring straight ahead as though they were made of stone.

Then I looked around the room below us. There really weren't very many women at all, and when I found one in the crowd I'd stare at her for a moment, wondering who she was—someone's secretary? A German doctor's wife? A reporter or photographer?

In front of us, a girl with straight dark hair clipped back in a flat ponytail with a metal barrette was looking back at me—waiting for me to meet her cool green gaze. Hers was the only face turned toward the gallery and not toward the witness stand. It was Anna.

She'd seen me and remembered me. She didn't smile—it would have been weird for anyone to be smiling at that point, even in greeting. She gave me a brief, curt nod.

I nodded back.

She hesitated a moment. Then she rubbed her hands together deliberately, turning her palms over each other and rubbing the backs of her knuckles, briefly miming washing her hands. Just for a second. I knew exactly what she meant.

Meet me in the washroom.

When the day's session was over, the last session before the Christmas recess, we gathered in one of the vast ornate lobbies shaking hands with people and congratulating Dr. Alexander on his moving presentation. Vladyslava and Jadviga and Maria and the other Maria got their photographs taken. Some of the photographers wanted to include me and Róża, too. I refused because I wasn't a Rabbit. When Vladyslava insisted Róża join them, it was the perfect time for me to disappear for a few minutes.

"Powder room," I told Róża. "Back in a minute! You all look beautiful—I hope they slap you on the front page of the *New York Times!*"

Anna was waiting for me, leaning against the sink and smoking—exactly the way I'd left her in the *Revier* in Ravensbrück not quite two years ago.

"*Häftling Einundfünfzigtausendvierhundertachtundneunzig!*"
she rapped out—"Prisoner 51498!"

I don't think I've ever been hit so hard by a handful of
words.

It was probably the first thing that came into her head
when she saw me—an exclamation of surprise, not a command. She usually did call me by my number because she was
supposed to. But to hear my number barked at me in German
like that was more than my brain could react to sensibly. I
snapped to attention, head up and staring straight ahead,
arms straight at my sides.

There was another woman in the room, an old woman
sitting in the corner with a bundle of knitting, who stood up
in alarm when I made my dramatic entrance. I realized she
was the attendant for the ladies' restroom, and I relaxed and
kind of melted against the doorframe, hanging on to it with
one shaking hand as though I had missed my footing. The
way a cat washes itself when you catch it doing something
clumsy, pretending you never saw that.

I recovered myself and startled Anna back by throwing
my arms around her. She held the cigarette away and stiffly
returned my ridiculously enthusiastic embrace with her
other arm.

"Calm down, kid. Sorry! It slipped out—like being slapped
in the face, isn't it? Gives you power."

She was still fluent enough in American slang to sound like
a gangster. I guess she'd been chatting a lot with the soldiers.
The attendant sat down and picked up her knitting again with
a *hmph*, ignoring us now that we seemed to be friends.

"Oh, *Anna!*" I felt tearful. I'd really thought she was
dead. She was playing her part in the trial with complete
calm, though, so I tried to keep my voice from shaking, too.
"What are you doing here, Anna?"

"I'm a witness. You know what I did at Ravensbrück. I'm a *good* witness because I've been on both sides of the fence. But I guess they won't get to me till after Christmas now—it would spoil the show after those other girls."

She held out a packet of cigarettes to offer me one—Lucky Strike. *Definitely* she'd been making friends with the American soldiers.

"How long are you here?" she asked casually.

"Just this week. I go home on Sunday."

"To Pennsylvania?"

"No, I live in Scotland. I'm in my second year at the University of Edinburgh."

"Studying what?"

"Medicine."

Anna smiled and sighed. "Well, good for you, Rose," she said. "Except for these trials, I'm not really going anywhere with my life. I guess you noticed the guards." She nodded at the attendant. "I'm a witness here in Nuremberg, but at the Ravensbrück trial in Hamburg, I'll be one of the accused. The Americans are just borrowing me here. When they're done with me, I get handed into the custody of the English."

"*Anna!*" I exclaimed. "What are you accused of?"

"Angel of Sleep, remember? Anesthetizing those kids before their terrible operations? And I knew what I was doing, too. I *knew*. I didn't have to do it. I made a lot of choices—good, bad, bad, good."

She struck a match and held it out to me. I leaned in to light my cigarette, then stood up straight and took a deep breath.

"What will happen to you?" I asked.

She let out a puff of smoke before she answered. Finally, she said slowly, "I'm not a murderer, but . . . you never know. This new 'crimes against humanity' covers a lot of ground.

And the British are running the Ravensbrück trial. Four of their special agents were murdered at Ravensbrück—you know, the spies everybody called the parachutists. Some of the British prosecution team is here now, interviewing the Ravensbrück defendants." She gave me a curious look. "Aren't you involved in the Ravensbrück trial, too?"

I shook my head.

Anna shrugged. "Well, I'm expecting about ten years in prison. It'll be interesting to see what Oberheuser gets. She was a witness at the International Military Tribunal before being put on trial here, so I feel like we have a lot in common."

"I guess it'd be good for you if she got acquitted."

Anna laughed bitterly. "I damn well hope she doesn't get acquitted! Evil bitch." She took a long drag on her cigarette. "Nice to share with you, Rose. Seems a little strange."

Words cannot describe how strange it seemed. I just said, "I know. I have the same feeling eating dinner with Róża."

"She's one of the Rabbits? Which one?"

"The one who looks like a little china doll. The one who didn't testify."

"You were pretty lucky to have the Rabbits taking care of you at Ravensbrück, you know."

"I know it," I said with my teeth clenched together, because I was in danger of bursting into tears if I tried to talk normally. "My whole transport was gassed. The Rabbits hid me."

"Oh—" Anna closed her eyes. "What, all the French girls on our work crew?" She was silent for a moment. "God. Those poor kids."

When she opened her eyes again I tried to shrug offhand-edly, the way she had about going to prison, and couldn't do it. I looked away, blinking. The attendant was knitting peacefully, oblivious to the intense conversation we were having—I suddenly realized that of course we were speaking English, so she probably couldn't understand us anyway.

"How'd you get out, Anna?" I asked.

"I swapped my number for a dead woman's—a Jehovah's Witness. Lavender triangle, nobody ever pesters them. And I just kept moving from block to block. No one tries to count you when they think you're dead! I was still there when the Russians turned up. I walked back to Berlin." Anna let out a long, smoke-filled breath. I don't think I'll ever be able to picture her *anywhere* but leaning against a porcelain washbasin and smoking.

"Must be nice to be back in school," she went on. "I spent a year struggling to feed my miserable mother and my grandmother in one room, with no heat, and then the Yanks arrested me. It was kind of a relief. Mama's having to pull her own weight now, and it's about time, too. Poor Mama." Another long drag. "Everybody got raped when the Soviets took Germany. *Everybody.* I turned up in Berlin not long after they got there, and Mama had stopped going out. She was letting her mother forage for both of them—this seventy-three-year-old woman out on the streets in the rubble, selling herself to Russian soldiers in exchange for bread. *Gott im Himmel.*" Anna took a deep, shaking breath. "Makes Ravensbrück look civilized. I put a stop to that. Found work for Mama, too, a good office job, work *I* should have taken, keeping accounts for a small building company that's been taken over by the Soviets. I guess she's all right now because she sends me packages."

"My gosh, Anna."

"I wonder what those American judges *think*," Anna said fiercely. "What are they *thinking* when those girls get up and tell them about what happened to them? The soldier boys are okay. They've seen things. They have some idea. But sometimes I really feel like everything is so *fucking* unfair. What gives those old men the right to guess what I've seen—what I've had to do? The right to judge me?"

She stubbed out her cigarette in the sink. The attendant sighed, tutted, and put down her knitting. She heaved herself to her feet again and pushed the ashtray that was sitting on the little dressing table right next to Anna a little closer to her, then turned on the tap and swooshed out the sink. Anna lit another cigarette.

"How'd you make your mother go to work, when she was too scared to leave the house?" I asked.

"Forced her," Anna said. "I mean, I really forced her. Pulled her out the door, pushed her down the stairs. I'm a *Kolonka*—green triangle, red armband. I know how to bully people, remember?" She laughed bitterly. "Every morning for a month, till she started coming along without a fight. I fought her and fought *for* her, too. I wouldn't let anyone touch her. She's better now—she made friends with the woman who runs the canteen where she works, and they visit each other—you know, play cards, darn socks, gossip about their terrible daughters. She gets up and eats every day. And you *have* to, you know? You can't just sit in a corner weeping or you'll *die*."

She looked over at me suddenly. "You *know*, Rose. You've seen people do it. You've seen what happens."

I have seen it.

"I don't know. . . ." Anna shook her head. "Maybe I did the wrong thing. Maybe I was too hard on her. But I had to do something. I had to get her going."

"Anna—is there anything I can send you? Anything I can *do* for you?"

"Well . . ." Her face hardened in its cynical frown. "Bah.

Bribe the judges?" Then she smiled a little, hesitantly, like it was something she wasn't used to doing. "Look, if I ever get out of prison, and we're ever in the same place at the same time again, I wish you'd take me flying."

I stubbed out my own cigarette in the ashtray and held out my hand. She took it.

"Deal," I said forcefully. "Scout's honor. I will take you flying."

"I am looking forward to it already," Anna said warmly.

4. THRUST

There's got to be power somewhere. The engine has to turn the propeller, and something has to start the engine. Someone has to lift the kite, maybe run with it. A bird has to beat its wings. Things don't magically take off and fly just because it's a little windy.

I spent twenty minutes on the telephone at the reception desk in the hotel, driving everybody crazy because I had to make someone translate for me whenever an operator came on. But I finally got through to the Operations hut at the temporary European Air Transport airfield where I'd landed nearly a week ago. I knew they were doing supply runs all the time, keeping Nuremberg stocked for the lawyers and soldiers and newspapermen.

"Yes, I know they're not supposed to take me back to Paris till Monday, but is anyone going anywhere tomorrow? *Anywhere?* Taking reconnaissance pictures or something? I just wanted to come along for the flight. We don't need to land—"

"Let me put you on the line with a pilot, honey," the disembodied gum-cracking American voice said kindly. "You're Roger Justice's niece, right? Yeah, we heard all about you. How's the trial going?" She laughed. Fortunately she didn't give me time to try to answer—I think she was just being polite and didn't really want to know. "I got somebody here you can talk to—"

"Hello?"

She'd handed the phone over. The voice was gruff.

"Can't get enough of joyriding in the C-47s, huh?"

It was Chuck Brewster, who'd flown the plane from Paris. I'd told him my story about buzzing the Eiffel Tower on VE Day and I'm not sure he believed me—I'm *sure* he didn't believe I'd been flying longer than he had, which is also true. He was a serious guy—neither one of us suggested he let me take over the controls for the fun of it—but we got along all right.

"Well, you're in luck, Miss Justice, because I'm doing a run down to Ronchi dei Legionari in Italy tomorrow morning to pick up Christmas dinner for this outfit."

I laughed. *"Christmas dinner?"*

"Yep, a couple hundred frozen turkeys straight from a farm in Connecticut, plus—would you believe it?—a dozen Christmas trees and all the trimmings, waiting at the docks at Monfalcone for the GIs camping out here over the holidays. You can come along if you want—it's about an hour and a half down, another hour and a half back. Plus a few hours there while they load her up. You can go to the beach!"

"You're kidding."

"Nah, I'm serious! We'll get someone to run you to the beach while we pack up. Right on the Adriatic Sea."

For a moment I couldn't talk—I could hardly breathe.

In my head I heard the voice of my murdered friend Karolina, whispering an impossible fantasy in my ear as we lay clutching each other for warmth on the filthy wooden bunks of Ravensbrück: *Let's go to the beach on the beautiful Adriatic Sea.*

"Hello? Hello?" came Chuck's voice. "You still there, Miss Justice? Bet you weren't expecting to spend the first day of winter on the Adriatic, were you?"

I let out my breath in a gasp. I didn't cry.

Instead, I asked brazenly, "Can I bring a friend?"

I shamed Róża into coming with me to the airfield.

"You know the story I used to tell about how my boyfriend

Nick was going to come and rescue us in a little plane—he'd land in the middle of the *Lagerstrasse* and we'd all fly away to the beach? You and I are going to fly to the beach today."

"It's December!"

"Okay, no red bathing suits this time. That'll have to wait till I can take you to the Conewago Grove Lake. Anyway, it doesn't matter. We have to do it for *Karolina*."

I was brutal. I didn't hit Róża. I didn't touch her. But I was brutal.

"Karolina was gassed instead of me—she took my place, she took my number, but she didn't do it for me, Różyczka, and you know it. She did it for *you*. She did it so I could get you out of Ravensbrück and you could tell the world what they did to you—what they did to *Karolina*. She wasn't as permanently damaged as you, but she still got a paper cone full of bacteria sewn into her leg and ended up so swollen with infection she couldn't walk for eight months—"

Róża was clenching her fists.

"I *know* what they did to Karolina," I went on mercilessly. "I know exactly what they did to every single one of the Rabbits. It's all been recorded by the people you work for, and maybe you haven't read the specific reports, but I have, because they're all part of Dr. Alexander's evidence. Karolina could have told the world herself. She'd be making newsreels about it—people would be using her work as evidence, too! She could have left me to be gassed with the rest of my transport, and she'd have stood up there in front of that tribunal and *showed* everybody what happened. But *you didn't*. And I'm not blaming you for that, but you are darned well flying to the beach with me. Because Karolina was going to and she's dead and you're coming along in her place."

By the time I'd finished, Róża was crouched in a heap

on the floor of our room, bent over her knees with her face in her hands. All I could see of her were her round shoulders in their sensible gray wool and the short, fluffy waves of caramel-gold perm. But she wasn't crying; her shoulders weren't shaking. She was thinking.

After a few seconds, when she was pretty sure I'd finished, she sat up and looked me in the eye.

"The Ravensbrück trial in Hamburg's not over yet," she said. "Tell the world yourself, Rose Justice! I know, you've got all these poems published and you're doing a story for your magazine, big damn deal. You sit in your room all alone at your typewriter, with no one watching if it makes you cry, and you take it to the post office and no one even knows what you're sending. How hard is that to do? *I* could do that. I've *done* that. My written testimony is part of the Lund files, too, you know. *NO.* If you want me to go flying with you for *Karolina*, you will damn well *go to Hamburg* for Karolina."

It was my turn to feel like I'd been punched in the stomach, and she saw it in my face. Róża let out one of her familiar, maniacal cackles. "You won't even have to take your clothes off!"

"I've already said no," I said faintly.

"Bah. Bribe the judges."

Which is exactly what Anna had said.

And suddenly it became like so many decisions I'd made during the war; *I didn't have a choice.* I had to do it whether or not I wanted to. Not just for Karolina, who was dead, but also for Anna, who was still alive and had no one to defend her.

You only fly straight and level in *balance.*

Anna and Róża are the opposing forces that perfectly balance each other to keep me in the air.

It was harder to get the words out this time than the easy promise I'd made to Anna in the washroom in the Palace of Justice.

"You've got a deal," I gasped.

Róża and I got up at the crack of dawn and shared a car with a couple of BBC reporters who were heading out that day with a lot of equipment. They wouldn't let us help them carry anything, and one of them actually went out of his way to take Róża's arm and help her across the churned slush to the makeshift Operations building at the airfield, which meant he had to do two trips—but sometimes you have to just give up being independent and graciously accept the kindness that's offered you. And anyway, this was without a doubt the sorriest excuse for an airfield I have ever seen, even counting the one they knocked up at Camp LA right after Reims was liberated. I guess that is our own fault for bombing Nuremberg's real airfield to smithereens.

I'm painting a scene of gloom, but in fact it was a glorious, *glorious* day—crystal clear and breezy. There had been another inch or so of snow overnight, so folks were frantically clearing a very narrow path up the runway. Chuck produced flight suits for us, which for some reason made Róża laugh her head off—her real laugh, which I'd hardly ever heard in all the time I'd known her, bubbly as champagne. "Are we going to go skiing?" she asked.

"Why skiing?"

"My mother used to put me in this awful snowsuit—baggy legs just like this, four sizes too big for me, and it was *purple*. She'd roll up the legs and hold them in place with rubber bands."

I'd never heard her talk about her mother, either.

There weren't any passenger seats in the plane—just benches along one side and plenty of room for cargo. Róża clutched my hand as we approached the plane. Dakotas are *big*.

"Don't worry!" I told her. "It's like getting in a bus. You've never flown in daylight, but it really is beautiful in the air. If you close your eyes while we're taking off—" I stopped abruptly, remembering Polly's reaction to the same words.

"I'm not a *baby*," Róża snapped, holding her head up, her china-doll cheeks rosy with the brisk December wind. "I said I'd do it and I'm doing it with my eyes open. Are you going to close your eyes in Hamburg?"

"You really are the world's worst pain in the neck," I complained. But my heart *ached* for her bravery.

I hadn't actually thought about our route when I'd set up the trip. I'd thought we'd see a lot of bomb-damaged cities—I'd seen *so much* bomb damage from the air. I'd wondered, briefly, when I first got the idea of taking Róża flying, if I could find someone who'd fly us over Ravensbrück. After I'd hung up talking to Chuck the night before, I'd had to go hide in the ladies' powder room and sob for a while. Oh, *Karolina*.

But I hadn't actually realized that this flight was going to give both me and Róża our first sight of the Alps.

The first part of the trip was mostly just snowy field and forest, gleaming swaths of white and increasingly huge tracts of black-green pine. Then, as we made our way farther south, the landscape grew rockier and steeper and we could see the crags of the Austrian Alps climbing ahead of us. They don't pressurize the C-47s, and they didn't have oxygen hooked up in the back, so the highest we flew was about 10,000 feet. That meant that there were moments when we were flying *between* mountain peaks. Grossglockner, Austria's highest mountain, was blinding in the midwinter's day sunlight, glittering white and gold and rising two thousand feet higher than we were flying. It was like flying over another planet—over another world, Oz or Wonderland or the moon.

Honestly—there were moments, many of them, when we were between peaks, with snowbound crags and rock all around us, when Róża really *was* so enchanted that she forgot to be scared. We were surrounded, as far as we could see, by our world's sheer unspoiled *majesty*. It was unspeakably, indescribably beautiful. It wasn't even barren. We could see glimpses of valleys and farms; there far below a touch of green where it hadn't snowed yet; there a river; there a fairy-tale village.

We were both pressed to the windows on opposite sides of the empty cargo plane.

"Did you *know?*" Róża gasped. "Did you *know* it would look like this?"

"I didn't even think about it! We just got lucky!"

"Even without the beach it is worth it. I won't mind so much getting work sewing on laundry tags if I remind myself about *this*."

I wasn't sure how to respond to that driblet of self-pity.

I asked cautiously, "Róża, what are you doing for Christmas?"

"There's a party at the Institute. It was fun last year—Poles and Swedes all mixed up. I don't know how much fun it'll be this year, though, since the funding is finished and nobody has work in 1947."

"Do you actually have a real possibility of spending the next few years sewing on laundry tags?"

"No. I haven't looked for that job yet."

"For the love of Pete."

No wonder she seemed so beaten.

"What are you doing for Christmas, Rose?" she asked. "Are you going to Pennsylvania?"

"How could I? It takes a week. I'd be on the boat on Christmas Day!"

Róża gave one of her raucous hoots of laughter. "*Fly.* Did you go last year?"

"No, I had an *awful* Christmas with my aunt Edie and Uncle Roger in England. I did nothing but cry all Christmas Day. It was worse than the year before. All of you were *gone.* And the next day, the twenty-sixth, they have this big annual party and there were about a hundred people in the house, and I just felt like a freak. So this year—"

Throughout this entire conversation we'd had our backs turned to each other, standing on opposite sides of the bowels of the plane, glued to the small windows. There was frost on the rivets and the gray ribs of the plane's interior walls. But outside, it was fairyland.

I said, "Róża, come back to Scotland with me on Monday. I'm going to stay with my friend Maddie for a week with her husband's family. Maddie *told* me to bring my friends. I know I promised you the Hotel Hershey, but I swear that Craig Castle will be *just as nice.*"

"Oh, how could I?"

"Easy! The place is always full of orphans and soldiers with missing arms—they won't notice you. I mean—"

She giggled evilly. "The soldiers will, I bet."

"Yes, they definitely *will,* but I meant that one more—"

"One more crippled orphan."

"Oh, STOP. You know what I mean." I drew a shaking breath. "And anyway, we are in the same family. That won't change."

Ahead of us, as the mountains dropped away, the black-green forest gave way to duller and brighter green ahead. The

Italian fields were tiny and patchwork—you could *tell* you were in another country. Far, far away on the horizon was an astonishing stripe of sapphire that we knew, but couldn't quite believe, must be the Adriatic Sea.

"There is a medical school at the University of Edinburgh that they teach entirely in Polish," I said. "They started it in the middle of the war. I could take you to meet my tutor and we could ask about it. You could do your high school exams in Edinburgh and maybe try the university course next fall—"

"We could share an apartment?"

"Of course! And Róża—" I choked a little, because it felt like we were making up another rescue fantasy. It felt like we couldn't *possibly* be planning something that would really happen. "Róża, we can *write our book*."

And honestly, why not?

Why not? We were free and independent. We were *grown-ups*. Even if she wasn't working to begin with, little Różyczka wouldn't be very expensive to feed. We might need more space than my bed-sitting-room offered. But not much. We wouldn't need much. We'd shared a lot less.

Now she didn't even say anything. She just came over to share my window with me and took my hand and squeezed it hard. And I knew it wasn't just another Nick Story, another impossible rescue fantasy. We were really going to do it. She'd come with me to Scotland on Monday.

She'd probably come with me to Hamburg in January.

We could see the coast as we landed, green flat fields arching lazily toward Yugoslavia, the docks of Monfalcone crowded with US Navy ships, the narrow strip of sand at the edge of the marsh across the bay. That was where we were going. It wasn't a resort—it wasn't Lido. But it was a beach on the Adriatic. It really was.

Róża let go of my hand as we landed. She watched out

the window, unflinching, the whole way down. She'd made up her mind she wasn't scared. I could believe she'd delivered plastic explosive for the Polish Resistance on her bicycle when she was in ninth grade. I could believe she'd told the SS Camp Commander she'd rather be executed than be experimented on again.

She climbed out of the plane without letting anybody help her.

Ronchi dei Legionari wasn't exactly tropical. That part of the Adriatic Sea is actually the most northern coast of anything connected to the Mediterranean. You can still see the Alps, blue in the near distance. The sun was shining, but the stiff breeze was chilly. It smelled like the ocean. It felt like spring.

I caught my breath in panic all of a sudden. If only we had something to *do*, I thought. I don't want to stand on a strange beach feeling blue about Karolina. We need sand pails and shovels to distract us. Something to collect shells in. Fishing nets—

Róża turned to me and said, "Remember Irina's paper planes? Remember the *glider*? My sister and I used to make kites out of newspaper. You think they'd let us have some paper and string?"

They did better than that. They gave us silk maps. The airfield had been a matériel supply depot since Italy's surrender to the Allies in 1943, and among other things they still had a big box of unused aircrew escape maps of all of southern Europe sitting in a corner of their radio room. Everybody on the airfield got involved—actually, I think everyone fell a little in love with Róża, swamped in her enormous flight suit with its rolled-up cuffs, with her fluffy caramel hair shining in the dusty sunlight streaming through windows still crossed with peeling tape so they wouldn't shatter in an air raid. Someone found a reel of fishing line and balsam strips to make a frame with. Another gum-cracking receptionist cut us a strip of the silver tinsel Christmas garland she'd draped around the door for us to use as a tail. She made us pose with her for a snapshot.

"You gals are nuts," she said approvingly. "Gosh, I wish I could come with you. It's mighty boring sitting here waiting for phone calls and watching the planes come and go. I don't speak Italian, so I'm too scared to go out by myself when I'm done—gotta wait for one of the boys to come along and escort me! Have fun!"

Sitting in the back of an American military jeep next to Róża, as one of the mechanics drove us along a muddy track through a pine swamp and we struggled to keep our silk kite from taking off on its own before we got anywhere, I felt very smug and lucky.

It is nice to feel that way.

"What does *nuts* mean?"

"She meant we're crazy."

"We are."

We'd walked right up to the water's edge, knee-high rippling waves that were a color I'd never imagined—an opaque, pale green, like mint sugar wafers. You could see the big steamers and Navy ships across the bay, the way you could from the little village of Hamble, just outside Southampton, where I'd been stationed when I was an ATA pilot. The sky was a pure, piercing blue, utterly without any cloud in it anywhere.

"Remember the sky at Ravensbrück?" Róża said.

"Yes, *always* beautiful, even when it was snowing."

"Remember the sunset the night you and Karolina spilled half a drum of soup on the kitchen steps?"

"Oh, I wrote a poem about that—clouds like flaming rubies and fireworks, and all of us sobbing over the horrible soup. The *irony!* What about the shooting stars that night in November, in the early morning roll call!"

"The Leonids!" Róża remembered. "And what about the *rainbow?* The full double rainbow? Lisette started to cry!"

"I *longed* to be in the sky," I said. "When it was windy like this, I just watched the clouds or leaves or birds racing overhead and I *longed* to be up there with them. It *hurt.*"

"Here we are," she answered softly. "Free in the wind!"

Suddenly she launched into my kite poem.

> "Hope has no feathers.
> Hope takes flight
> Tethered with twine
> like a tattered kite,
> slave to the wind's
> capricious drift,
> eager to soar
> but needing lift."

I stared at the brilliant sky, listening to Róża softly chanting my own words.

> "Hope waits stubbornly,
> watching the sky
> for turmoil, feeding on
> things that fly:
> crows, ashes, newspapers,

dry leaves in flight
all suggest wind
that could lift a kite."

She paused. The first thing I'd ever said to her was to recite a poem, so after a moment I finished this one for her, softly.

"Hope sails and plunges,
firmly caught
at the end of her string—
fallen slack, pulling taut,
ragged and featherless.
Hope never flies
but doggedly watches
for windy skies."

She was quiet then. The last verse isn't really very hopeful. Poor ragged kite, always waiting for a wind that never comes.

Finally Róża took a deep breath.

"It's windy now," she said.

She put down her walking stick to take the spool of fishing line. She played out about six feet and let go. The wind was fierce and steady, and the kite lifted like a bird. We both stared up at it, and it was like looking at a landscape from the air, the silk map bright with green and yellow and brown and blue. The tinsel tail snapped and flashed blindingly. After a second our beautiful improvised kite did exactly what the one does in the poem and plunged earthward—I grabbed it by the fragile frame before it nose-dived into the sand.

"It needs thrust," I said. "You have to run with it. Can you run?"

She gave me a dirty look. Then she broke into the bubbly champagne laugh. She turned and ran, limping but steady. She laughed over her shoulder, letting out line as I held the kite above my head.

"Run with me, Rose," she cried.

—by Rose Justice
Craig Castle, Castle Craig
December 31, 1946

AFTERWORD

DECLARATION OF CAUSES

Primo Levi, the author of possibly the most moving descriptions of Auschwitz in print, felt that the true witnesses to the atrocities of the concentration camps were the dead. Survivors like himself, he felt, could give only partial testimony. Memories become fixed or simplified or distorted as they are told over and over, making living testimony inaccurate. This was one of the themes we discussed at length at the Eighth European Summer School at Ravensbrück in August 2012—how memory itself is a construction, particularly as it becomes more and more distanced in time from actual events.

Rose's testimony is even further removed because I made it up. In Rose's story, I have constructed an imitation of a survivor's account. It has become a false memory of my own—Rose's dream of the icy wind in the empty bunks is *my* dream, the single vivid nightmare I had while sleeping in the former SS barracks at Ravensbrück during the week I spent at the summer school. My book is fiction, but it is based on the real memories of other people. In the end, like Rose, I am doing what I can to carry out the last instruction of the true witnesses—those who went to their death crying out: *Tell the world.*

What I'd really like to pound into the reader's head, if there's any lesson to be learned here, is that I didn't make up *Ravensbrück*. I didn't make up *anything* about Ravensbrück. Often, I have had to fill in the blanks—when the toilets stopped working, how thick the mattresses were, how you might improvise a sanitary pad. The *little* things. The terrible and the unbelievable, the gas chambers and the medical experiments and the twenty-five lashes, propping up the dead to make the roll call count come out right, the filth and the dog bites and the curl hunts and the administration and politics of bowls, *I did not make up*. It was real. *It really happened to 150,000 women*. And that is just one camp.

I did simplify some things in order to keep the pace going. I kept the Rabbits in Block 32 for the whole story, when technically they got moved into different blocks a couple of times during the winter of 1945. I left out the fact that between being selected and being gassed, prisoners got taken to another camp, about a mile away, where they were locked in unheated barracks without food or blankets and left to starve or freeze to death to make it easier on the limited capacity of Ravensbrück's makeshift gas chamber. I didn't explain that the female "SS guards" were technically auxiliary to the SS, which was all male. I didn't translate every one of Rose's conversations into three different languages before she could understand it.

In the preface to his book on Ravensbrück, Jack Morrison points out that it would have been impossible for a single prisoner to have as broad a view of the camp as the researcher who tries to look at all aspects of its six-year operational history. Rose's experience is limited from September 1944 to March 1945, which means that within the confines of *my* book, it's impossible to describe much of what went on before or after these dates. Also, Rose's experience is limited to an extremely closed circle of prisoners and their restricted movements—she never gets inside the textile factories or the kitchens, or is sent on coal-picking duty or unloads barges by the lake. She doesn't interact with children or Gypsies or Jehovah's Witnesses or the men's camp, all of which have their own moving stories of oppression and rebellion. Rose doesn't work in the prisoner-organized maternity ward, a story of miracle and heartbreak. After June 1943 and until the Auschwitz evacuees turned up in late 1944, there were very few Jewish women at Ravensbrück, and they were confined to a single block; their stories are also different. There is a lot more out there than the limited window on Ravensbrück that Rose's experience provides . . . just so you know.

Each of my main characters is inspired in part by real people, but they are original characters. There's no Róża Czajkowska or Karolina Salska on the actual list of Rabbits' names. However, Dr. Leo Alexander, Marie Claude Vaillant-Couturier, and the four Polish women who gave evidence at the Doctors' Trial—Maria Broel-Plater, Jadwiga Dzido, Władysława Karolewska, and Maria Kuśmierczuk—were all real. The doctors Fritz Fischer, Karl Gebhardt, and Herta Oberheuser were real, and so was Ravensbrück's commander in 1945, Fritz Suhren. (Rose only ever refers to him as "the stinking Commander.") Most of Ravensbrück's copious documentation was purposefully destroyed before the Soviet Army freed the camp, so the bulk of research on Ravensbrück comes from witness and survivor accounts.

Rose's mnemonic counting-out rhyme includes all the given names of the seventy-four Polish women experimented on in Ravensbrück. (The spelling of their names has been simplified for English-speaking readers.) Some of the women had similar first names or shared a name—in the poem each name is listed only once. The real names of these seventy-four women experimented on are printed in the background of the opening pages of this book.

Writing out Rose's handwriting sample made me cry. It was the first time I had ever really *thought* about the Declaration of Independence and what it means to say that life, liberty, and the pursuit of happiness are unalienable rights. *Tell the world.* I have tried.

ACKNOWLEDGMENTS

The editorial teams behind *Rose Under Fire* were much more actively involved in its creation than in any of my previous books. I am deeply and eternally grateful for their focus and enthusiasm. Thank you, Stella Paskins of Egmont UK, Catherine Onder of Disney • Hyperion, and Janice Weaver of Doubleday Canada—and thank you to my agent, Ginger Clark, who was involved in every single editorial discussion.

Obviously it wasn't just Ravensbrück that I researched for this book, and if you check my website at www.elizabeth wein.com you'll be able to find discussion of a range of details from aircraft interception to women pilots. I owe thanks to Steve Venus for information on V-1 fuses and prisoner accounts of forced labor in German factories; his website and collection can be viewed at www.bombfuzecollectorsnet.com. Katja Kasri was my German language consultant; her training as a history teacher means that whenever I ask her a question about, say, how to address someone using her prisoner number, she spends a couple of hours trawling newsreel footage and witness testimony to confirm the accuracy of the answer. Tori Tyrrell, Miriam Roberts, and Amanda Banks all read the manuscript at *least* three times and provided me with invaluable reader criticism and encouragement. Katherine Nehring also got tagged at the last minute as a "fresh eye" and provided much-needed annotations on a very tight deadline.

Last but hardly least, I am indebted to the generous sponsors and organizers of the European Summer School at Ravensbrück and to the Ravensbrück Memorial and International Youth Meeting Center for both their tremendous welcome and the wealth of critical thinking and resources they opened to me.

RAVENSBRÜCK CAMP VOCABULARY

(German unless otherwise noted)

Appelplatz: main roll call square
Aufstehen: stand up, get up
Blockova: (Polish) block leader
Bunker: secure cell block
Fünfundzwanzig: literally "twenty-five." In the context of
  Ravensbrück, a standard punishment of twenty-five
  lashes across the back of the thighs or buttocks.
Häftling: prisoner
Kaninchen: rabbits
Kolonka: (term unique to Ravensbrück) shortened form of
  Kolonkova, forewoman
Králici: (Czech) rabbits
Król: (Polish) a word that means both "rabbit" and "king"
Króliki: (Polish) rabbits
Lagermutter: Camp Mother
Lagerstrasse: main street in Camp
Revier: infirmary
Schmootzich: Rose's Pennsylvania Dutch interpretation of the
  German word *Schmuckstücke*, literally "piece of jewelry,"
  used sarcastically as a noun in the Camp hierarchy to
  mean a prisoner who's been reduced to little more than
  a malnourished and mindless beggar

Schnell: quickly, fast (in the context: "Get moving!")
Screamer: English translation of a widely used term for roll call siren
SS: abbreviation for *Schutzstaffel*, defense guard
Strafstehen: punishment standing
Verfügbar: a prisoner available for unassigned work detail
Zählappell: roll call

GENERAL BIBLIOGRAPHY

Longmate, Norman. *The Doodlebugs: The Story of the Flying-Bombs.* London: Hutchinson & Co. Ltd., 1981.

Lussier, Betty. *Intrepid Woman: Betty Lussier's Secret War, 1942–1945.* Annapolis, MD: Naval Institute Press, 2010.

Morrison, Jack G. *Ravensbrück: Everyday Life in a Women's Concentration Camp 1939–45.* Princeton, NJ: Markus-Wiener Publishers, 2000.

Quinlivan, J. T. "The Taran: Ramming in the Soviet Air Force," Rand Paper Series No. 7192. Santa Monica, CA: The Rand Corporation, 1986. www.rand.org/content/dam/rand/pubs/papers/2008/P7192.pdf.

Schmidt, Ulf. *Justice at Nuremberg: Leo Alexander and the Nazi Doctors' Trial.* Basingstoke, Hampshire: Palgrave Macmillan, 2006 (2004).

Timofeyeva-Yegorova, Anna. *Red Sky, Black Death: A Soviet Woman Pilot's Memoir of the Eastern Front.* Edited by Kim Green. Translated by Margarita Ponomaryova and Kim Green. Bloomington, IN: Slavica Publishers, 2009.

Whittell, Giles. *Spitfire Women of World War II.* London: HarperPress, 2007.

SURVIVOR ACCOUNTS
OF RAVENSBRÜCK

Geneviève de Gaulle Anthonioz, *God Remained Outside: An Echo of Ravensbrück*. Translated by Margaret Crosland. London: Souvenir Press, 1999 (1998).

Corrie ten Boom, with John & Elizabeth Sherrill. *The Hiding Place*. Bungay, Suffolk: Hodder and Stoughton and Christian Literature Crusade, 1976 (1971).

Margarete Buber-Neumann, *Déportée à Ravensbrück (Deported to Ravensbrück)*. Translated to French from German by Alain Brossat. Paris: Éditions du Seuil, 1988 (1985).

Countess Karolina Lanckorońska, *Michelangelo in Ravensbrück: One Woman's War Against the Nazis*. Translated by Noel Clark. Cambridge, MA: Da Capo Press 2007 (2001).

Micheline Maurel, *Ravensbrück*. Translated by Margaret S. Summers. London: Anthony Blond, 1959 (1958).

Wanda Półtawska, *And I Am Afraid of My Dreams*. Introduced and translated by Mary Craig. London: Hodder & Stoughton, 1987 (1964).

Germaine Tillion, *Ravensbrück*. Paris: Éditions de Seuil, 1988 (1973).

I have also drawn on accounts from survivors interviewed by Loretta Walz in her documentary film *Die Frauen von Ravensbrück (Women of Ravensbrück)*, 2005.

INTERNET SOURCES

"Voices from Ravensbrück" is part of the digital archives of Lund University in Sweden, and includes transcriptions, some in English, of many of the five hundred survivor interviews collected from 1945 to 1946 by the Polish Research Institute (www.ub.lu.se/collections /digital-collections/voices-from-ravensbr-ck).

The Visual History Archive of the USC Shoah Foundation, to which I was pointed by women's studies scholar and writer Dr. Andrea Petö of the Central European University in Hungary, provides over a thousand English-language testimonies of Holocaust survivors, including thirty-eight who were imprisoned at Ravensbrück. The site requires user registration and log-in, but it is free (vhaonline.usc.edu).

The Stephen Spielberg Film and Video Archive available on the United States Holocaust Memorial Museum website contains public-domain footage of Maria Kuśmierczuk and Jadwiga Dzido appearing as witnesses in the Doctors' Trial in Nuremberg on December 20, 1946, while Dr. Leo Alexander explains, in English, the damage to their legs (resources.ushmm.org/film/display/detail.php?file _num=1961&tape_id=b272053b-eb79-440e-8780-e8b0b 6c6364e&clip_id=&media_type=flv).

The Ravensbrück Memorial website (part of the Brandenburg Memorials Foundation) can be visited at www.ravensbrueck.de/mgr/index.html.

There is an excellent teacher's guide on Ravensbrück produced by the Kennesaw State University Museum of History and Holocaust Education in Georgia, available for download here: www.kennesaw.edu/historymuseum/pdf /tg-ravensbruck.pdf.

These web links were found to be working at the time of this book's publication.